HOW I
BECAME
THE HERO'S
ASSISTANT

Thomas Karl

NEWMAN SPRINGS PUBLISHING
320 Broad Street
Red Bank, NJ 07701

First originally published by Newman Springs Publishing 2020

ISBN 978-1-64801-693-6 (Paperback)
ISBN 978-1-64801-694-3 (Digital)

Printed in the United States of America

1

A New World!

"Hey, Mom, Dad," I started before taking a deep breath. "If you're hearing this, then… well, I'm sorry. I love you guys, but I think it's time I actually do this. It just feels like nothing matters anymore. Not that anything felt like it mattered in the first place. I've only waited this long to go through with this because of you guys. But I'm going to be selfish just this once and go ahead and do what I want. Be sure to fill Sparky's bowl once a day, no matter how much he begs for more food. If you give in, he's just going to get fat, so don't listen to his fake cries," I said as I thought about the sly orange and black calico cat that had been a part of my life for several years.

"Oh, and for the love of God, don't bother holding a funeral. No one would come, and it would just be a waste of money, so don't go to all that trouble, okay? Lastly, don't blame yourselves, please. It's not your fault at all. I'm sorry," I finished as I hit the stop recording button.

With a heavy heart, I scrawled a note, telling them to play the recording. I grabbed my ID, which stated "Name: Grayson Byrne. Sex: M. Hgt: 5'11" (180 cm). Wgt: 158 pounds (71.6 kg). Eyes: Brn. Age: 19."

I passed by a mirror and caught a glimpse of my shaggy jet-black hair as I threw on a sweatshirt and my glasses. I opened the door to my room and snuck my way down the stairs. I was about to open the front door when Sparky started rubbing up against my leg.

3

I leaned down and rubbed his cheek before softly petting his head. "Sorry, buddy, that's not gonna work this time."

"Mrow?" he let out as I stopped petting him and opened the door. I had to suppress tears as I said, "Don't worry, Mom and Dad will take care of you…I hope." I quietly closed the door, and the chill of night overtook me. I walked down the street toward a bridge that connected the suburbs where I lived to town. As I walked, all I could wonder was if I was making the right choice. I wouldn't back down like I had so many times before.

Everything was supposed to be different after high school, but nothing's changed. Everyone still avoids me, unless it's to make fun of me. I lied about Mom and Dad too. If they actually gave a damn, then maybe they'd actually come home once in a while. The only thing that's been keeping me going is my hobby. But does working to support my hobby really justify all the abuse I go through for it? Maybe I'm just looking at the downside of everything…maybe I shou—NO! I've done this too many times. No more thinking, no more trying to talk myself out of it.

I steeled myself and continued down the road. When I reached the bridge, however, there were tons of police cars and a bunch of cops on foot with flashlights near the river. *God, why couldn't I have had an original idea? Maybe I'll freeze to death on my way back home,* I thought dejectedly as I turned the other way.

In front of me was a truck quickly making its way toward the bridge. With a heavy heart and a grin, I whispered, "Lucky me. Please forgive me for this." As I jumped in front of it, there was no time for the driver to react, and all I could see was the blinding headlights. Soon after, I was taken by a cold darkness that felt like a blanket over my entire body.

*****

Suddenly, I awoke in a white room. I took a deep breath and felt as though I had been underwater for way longer than anyone should. As I looked around, I said out loud, "There's no way that I survived that, right? This doesn't look like a hospital room either. Where the hell am I?"

"Ahh, you're awake! To answer your question, I believe that this is what you people tend to refer to as heaven," said a deep voice from somewhere behind me.

Picking myself up off the floor, I turned around to find a man that didn't look anything special. In fact, he looked really plain. His face was very even, the only things that stood out were his green eyes and his forehead that was uncovered by his dark hair—he basically looked like if you took Paul Rudd and just slapped him in a silver suit.

"Wait a minute... If this is heaven, and you were standing there, waiting for me to wake up, then...are you God?" I asked the Paul Rudd imposter in front of me.

"Well, that's not my name, but yes, you could call me God, I suppose. Of course, if you want to call me something like High Overlord Supreme or something along those lines, I wouldn't be opposed to hearing that," the High Overlord Supreme said as he chuckled.

As he chuckled, I blurted out, "I committed suicide. Doesn't that mean that I go to hell?"

"My boy, that's just something the church says so that people are more terrified of killing themselves. You have nothing to fear. Besides, I've been keeping an eye on you for one of my projects. There's no way I could send you to hell!" God responded.

"Wait, wait, wa-wait, wait," I stammered, "this is really sudden! I mean, why have you been keeping an eye on me? Why not someone else? No, wait, before that, does that mean you've seen..." I looked at God in front of me with a huge grin-like frown and just simply balled my hand into a fist and moved it forward and back.

"What the... No! Wow, okay, that is not how I thought you were going to take that. That's disgusting, why wou—" God started retching. "Just gimme a moment."

As I waited for God Lord Supreme to continue on with what he was going to say, I started looking around at the room we were in. As expected of heaven, it was very regal. Though it wasn't the whole pearly gates-having cloudscape that I had imagined in my head, instead it was more of what I'd expect if I had stayed in a five-star hotel that had an Ancient Greece theme to it. It also managed to look plain at the same time, which shouldn't be possible. *How can you have something look regal with detailed etchings into walls but then also have it be plain? Then again, I suppose this is heaven, right? So I guess I can just chalk it up to that,* I thought to myself.

"Hey, High Lord Supreme, you good yet? You're starting to make me gag over here, I'm a sympathetic puker, you know," I called out in a somewhat sing-song voice so that he knew I was joking. *Would a deity be able to pick up on that thought?* I wondered.

"Yeah, okay, I'm good. Also, you don't have to do the singing thing. I'm God, remember? Omnipotent and all-knowing? I know more about you than you know about yourself!" God said almost condescendingly, then shifted his gaze away slowly after I gave him a look that showed he had confirmed my suspicions.

"All right. Back to business. As I said, I've been keeping an eye on you for a project. With that comes the knowledge that you're not cut out for a modernized world. With the amount of fantasy media that you've consumed and the amount of thought that you've put in on how you'd actually live if you were in one is…well, it's honestly kind of disturbing. Mainly because you worried more about how you would make it in another world instead of worrying about how you could live in the world that you currently resided in. But I'm not here to lecture you about that. What would be the point? With you completing the prerequisite of dying via truck, I'm able to reincarnate you in another world with all of the memories and abilities you have right now as a nineteen-year-old man," God said.

So the death by truck-kun thing in Isekai is a real thing? I wondered as I recalled many anime where the main character would die from being hit by a truck before they would be reincarnated into another world. *Wait, how would they even know that that's how you get reincarnated? Did God just like the trope so much that he decided to steal it for his own use? That's basically plagiarism!* I shouted out in my mind as I came to the realization.

All the while, I stared at God in utter disbelief of what he was saying. I'd be able to go live in a fantasy world? If it weren't for the fact that I died, I would just assume that this was some sort of practical joke!

"Are you being serious right now, God? Like, we're talking a fantasy world with elves, dragons, adventurers, magic—stuff like that, right?" I asked the deity excitedly.

"Yes, of course. Although it also comes with its fair share of risks. No one in their right mind would want to be reincarnated into a place like this unless they were a nutcase like you. Nowadays, there are a lot more thanks to your MMOs and RPG games. Speaking of RPG games, the world actually works a lot like one. By thinking certain commands, you can pull up information that would be akin to a character sheet. There'll be a mini-map in your vision at all times, plus there's a whole experience leveling system as well as parties and trading! It really was what I felt to be one of my greatest works. Of course, everyone else just had to ruin it. This is precisely why I want to send you there. You'll be able to learn the system faster than anyone! You played more than your fair share of fantasy RPGs before you went into the workforce and got stuck in that dead-end job. Of course, I want to send you with some special abilities too. That way, you'll be able to make a difference and hopefully change it back to something akin to how it was in the past!" God declared.

All of this was making my head spin. A world that was like a role-playing game? I wasn't entirely surprised since the thought had occurred to me a lot. I mean, God even said himself that I had thought about how I would survive in a fantasy world. Granted, I never really thought that I'd actually get the chance to do that. The only real thing that was confusing about all of this was how exactly those commands worked. *Wait a minute. Did he say that he wants to give me special abilities too? This literally is just an Isekai! My li...err death is literally just something that I've seen countless times in anime and manga!*

"Umm, what exactly did you have in mind, ability-wise, God? I mean, I'd like to sort of know what I'm about to get myself into before I commit to this."

As I said this, God looked at me with a grin on his face. "Well, I was thinking maybe I could give you some amazing magical ability or maybe make you into a super-strong physical damage dealer. Ooooh, or make you almost invincible! There's so much we could do. Just think about it!" God yelled out with visible excitement on his face. While he was revealing his ideas, I just sort of looked at him with a horrified expression, which he didn't notice until he looked right at me after telling me to think about it. "Too much?" he asked with a frown.

I nodded at him, making his frown grow to the point that it basically looked like I was getting a sticker of a frowny face. That's when I gave him my idea. "It wasn't entirely bad. It's just that I'll be having to live with this for my whole next life. Maybe we could just do something like a small gradual change? Like when I level up in this system of yours, maybe I get a little bit more of a boost than other people get to stats? That way, my growth would appear to be natural-ish and wouldn't draw a lot of attention? Or maybe give me some sort of magic that only I can use but something that isn't done in front of people."

"So you mean like a passive magic effect?"

"Yes! Exactly like that. That way, no one will be suspicious of my magic ability either. I'll appear to be normal and like them, just a little bit more useful. That way, people could just chalk it up to the margins of how I grew up or something, right?"

"Hmmm," answered God, "yeah, I guess that works. Well, with that being said…I'm assuming that you're accepting my offer then?"

As he posed that question, there was no doubt in my mind or delay in my response. "Of course, I'm going to go!" I spouted out.

It was then that God gave me a sort of smile that made me question if I should have answered so haphazardly. "Well, my boy," God said as he began to do a sort of motion that I could only assume was him starting to use some sort of power. "With this parting message, I send you to the lands of Zynka. I'm sure you know but the first thing you should do once you get down there is make your way to the Fighters Guild and join them! Tell the person who signs you up, 'Shtick zem vun schliay!' It'll summon me, and I'll explain a lot more then. Consider this your trial."

"What does that even mean?" I asked, and then not even a second later, my whole body started to feel like it was being ripped apart into tiny little chunks. Surprisingly, though, it didn't hurt at all. It just felt like pieces of me were becoming lighter and drifting off into the wind. Eventually, my vision left me, and all I could see was black. I couldn't even breathe, smell, nor feel! It felt like it did when I was dead.

*****

I woke up to the sound of birds chirping and the sweet smell of the air. Instantly, I started touching everywhere on my body to make sure everything was there and where it should be.

"Sooo," I said as I looked around, "where exactly am I?" I had appeared on a cliff of a large hill. All I could see were trees below me and what looked like a large wall and gate in the far distance. With a look of disdain, I said, "Did he really need to put me so far from my destination? Like, seriously, what did he gain by putting me here?" A little upset at my misfortune, I stood up and looked over the cliff's edge. The trees below looked like large decorated skewers. "Guess I'm not gonna be going down this way." I turned around and was about to start walking when I remembered that God had said. There was some sort of menu system in this world.

Sure enough, in the top right of my vision, there was a mini-map, like you'd see in most RPGs. Naturally, I tried to get a better look at it, but all that really happened was I was changing where I was looking with the map staying stationary in the top right of my vision. "He seriously made it so that the map is just there? It's basically like seeing one of those floaty eye things that move when you try to look at them! That's literally one of the most annoying ways to design that. Like, come on, dude, ALL I WANT TO DO IS LOOK AT THE DAMN MAP!" I shouted out in frustration.

As if it was listening to me, the map instantly enlarged, taking up most of my view. I jumped back in surprise before letting out a sigh of relief. If I hadn't been able to figure that out, not only would I have been annoyed for probably the rest of my life, I probably wouldn't have lasted long in this world. Taking a look at the map, it would seem that I was surrounded by a vast forest and that the wall I had spotted was only around five miles away.

"That wall must be huge then, right? Maybe I'm just really high up? Gah, whatever, there's no point in figuring that out, really. Five miles shouldn't really take me too long to get there, especially since most of it is downhill." I glanced around the map quickly to see if there was a clock of some sort.

Since there's a distance calculator, it's not too crazy to think that there may be some sort of clock, right? Worst case, I just tell the time by where the sun is in the sky, I thought to myself. Unfortunately, there was no clock, which was a mild inconvenience but an inconvenience nonetheless. Looking up at the sky, the sun was smack dab in the middle of it. *Well, I guess it's around noonish then. Assuming that it takes me a couple of hours or so to get to that wall, I'd get there around three. Hell, since I have so much time, I should get acquainted with the system before I go to the Fighters Guild,* I decided. My mind was set on figuring out how to use the system and everything that it contained. Usually, there's a "Help" command, so I tried that first.

"Help," I said, hoping that would be enough to work. Unfortunately, it wasn't which, to be fair, wasn't really a surprise since if someone was in danger and yelled for help at the top of their lungs, they probably wouldn't want a bunch of information to be thrown at them.

"Slash help?" I then tried, doubting that anything would come from a simple word addition. To my surprise, as soon as I finished, my vision became crowded with text coming from the bottom and moving up with each new line. It was similar to an opening from Star Wars, but it moved a lot faster. There were too many commands to count, so I only focused on the ones that sounded important. Among these were Stats, Status, Abilities, and Party. Getting accustomed to these would make it a lot easier to get information on myself and probably on my party members. *Of course, that's assuming I'll join a group,* I thought.

Stats was as anyone would expect. It had stat names and the amount of points you had in them. The stats were Strength (S),

Agility (A), Fortitude (F), Intelligence (I), Perception (P), and Luck (L)—in that order. There were also stats for my equipped "gear." The glasses I wore gave me +1 Perception, while the short-sleeved shirt, hoodie, and jeans I wore only served to give me +1 physical defense each. My shoes, however, not only gave me +1 physical defense but also +1 Agility!

So my stats at the moment were S: 10, A: 10 (+1), F: 10, I: 10, P: 10 (+1), and L: 10. My defense stats were put into their own sub-category, but the only one with a value was physical defense. There was a magical defense stat, but that had a big zero next to it.

"So stats are pretty standard. It's also nice that it adds on the bonus 'gear' stats. This part of the system's getting an A-grade from me. Good job, God," I muttered to myself, adding in a small golf clap afterwards. As I was about to close the window, I noticed out of the corner of my eye that my level was in the top left of the sheet. "Level 1," it clearly stated. For some reason, I felt disappointed see-ing that. Something about it just made me really want to have it say "Level 2." One just felt so…disheartening.

Shrugging off the feeling, I closed the stats window and sum-moned up the status window. Though when I thought status, no charts or anything popped up. A red bar accompanied by a grey bar underneath it appeared in the middle of my vision before shrinking down and taking a spot in the top left corner.

"Oh, my vision just works as an HUD, I guess? The red bar is my health, obviously, but what's that grey bar supposed to signify?" I said irritably. Brushing it aside, since I was sure that I would find out sooner or later, I decided to move on and look at the "Abilities" window.

In the "Abilities" tab, there were two sections—one for physical abilities and one for magic abilities. Underneath the physical abilities tab, there was nothing, but underneath the magic abilities, there was a subsection simply called "Sensory Magic." There was only one skill I could see in the sensory magic list, and that was an ability called "Track."

Track (P) (Level 1 required)—Allows one to
track any living thing, can be used for specified

creatures or a wide variety. MP requirement: 0.
MP usage: 0 MP per second.

"A passive magic effect, just like we discussed, huh? I guess this answers my question about the grey bar. I probably should've realized that was for mana, huh?" I grinned as I scratched the back of my head after realizing just how much of an idiot I was. "Well, let's take this baby out for a test drive, yeah?"

I realized right after stating my intention to test it out how lucky I would have to be to have something lurking nearby. If that were the case, though, would I really be lucky? Also, what if it wasn't obvious about how it showed the location of the creature? Disappointed, I let out a sigh before thinking to myself, *I'm in a forest, right? Technically, trees are living things, right? If this actually works, I'll be able to use something like saplings for the specified variety too!*

Coming to this realization, I simply thought about tracking trees. Almost immediately, it was very obvious the skill was in effect, not just because it was very easy to tell how the trees had changed from a normal green-leafed brown-barked tree to a shimmering crimson color, but also because on the mini-map, all around the area were little yellow circles indicating where each target of the track ability was. When I enlarged the map for what seemed to miles, all that could be seen was just a bunch of yellow dots. Occasionally, there were little blotches of green for grass and brown for areas with nothing besides dirt, but all of the yellow made them very hard to spot.

I wanted to test the ability more, though. *Now it's time to test this on an actual specified creature,* I thought. Of course, the creature was just tree saplings since there was bound to at least be a few in such a wide forest. Sure enough, once I changed my thinking to track only saplings, most of the trees changed back to their original color. The only ones that didn't, of course, were the saplings being used for the experiment. Taking another look at the map showed that there were only a few yellow dots nearby, and there were probably a few dozen in the rest of the forest.

"All right, cool, this is actually going to really come in handy. The fact that it only works for my eyes is great for not sticking out either! Though…there's gotta be some draw back to it, right?" I said as I looked to the sky almost as if I was expecting an answer from something up above. That was when I realized that the sun was beginning to set.

Wait, what the heck? I could've sworn it was just around noon not that long ago? Was I really that absorbed in the menus? Or does time go faster in this world? I thought to myself in a panic. "Okay, calm down and think. If we need to, we could probably track edible herbs and we could track fresh wa—Wait, no it has to be something that's alive! GAH!" I yelled out in exasperation before taking in a deep breath and then releasing it slowly.

"Okay, it's fine, I'm fine. I don't even need to prepare for a survival situation. All I need to do is start making my way to those gates and maybe eat some herbs along the way as well as avoid animals and probably people." With my new state of mind, I pulled up the map and found a clear path that was luckily nearby.

Beginning the trek to the wall, I walked downhill through the forest from the cliff I started at. Once I had made it deep into the forest, I switched my magic to search for bandits. *Bandits will probably be the worst thing to come across,* I assumed. I was confident I could probably outsmart any animals I came across. Humans were another story. If they harbored ill-intent, I probably wouldn't be able to come out of that unscathed, especially since I had no weapons nor a penny to my name in this new world.

I got to the wall sometime around midnight, mostly due to the weaving path I had to take to avoid any threats. I couldn't get close to the wall since there was a moat of sorts. It wasn't really a moat as much as it was a large hole in the ground with spiked traps coating nearly every inch of the ground.

I guess that makes it more of a trench, then? I thought to myself. From where I was, though, I was able to see just how tall the wall was. It was easily larger than a two or even a three-story house. If I had to guess, it was probably something like seventy feet (twenty-one meters) high, it wasn't as big as a skyscraper, but it was very large. Scattered among the wall were window frames that had light trickling out from the inside, illuminating some parts of the wall. The gate that I had spotted from the hill wasn't anywhere to be seen now as a drawbridge was covering the large hole in the wall.

Great. I have no way of getting in tonight, huh? I thought with my heart sinking, realizing that the stressful trek here had been all for naught. Then I thought of something. *Were there any guards on the road? It's a gamble, but if there were, then there should be someone stationed to lower the bridge in case one of them has something to report, right?*

Immediately, I shifted my tracking magic to search for "Bridge-lowering guard," and sure enough, two yellow dots showed up almost directly in front of me on the map. Although the tracking magic was quite useful, it unfortunately didn't work on a three-dimensional plane since it used the map to mark targets. So even though it shows the two guards in front of me, they could really be on any level of the wall.

Though the hindrance of not knowing what level they were on doesn't matter as long as there are guards to lower the bridge, I just hope they're near one of the windows so that they'll be able to hear me shout, I thought.

In the loudest voice I could muster, I said, "HOOOOOI, COULD SOMEONE PLEASE LOWER THE BRIDGE?" Once I let out my yell, a message, saying "Unlocked ability: Taunt," appeared in my vision.

> Taunt (F) (Annoying voice required)—
> Forces an enemy to shift its attention to you for
> five seconds. MP requirement: 0. MP usage: 0.

Did I just get roasted by a skill unlock? Well, it's not that bad. I still got a new skill. Though, does that mean that what I did just now was aggressive? I wondered.

While I was in thought, I heard a voice call down from above me. "DEPENDS ON 'HO THE 'ELLS ASKIN'! STATE YER BUSINESS HERE!"

The voice sounded a lot like how dwarves are portrayed in games and movies; it was really gruff. If I had to guess where he was just off of his voice alone, I would have called him a dwarf of Khaz

Modan from World of Warcraft! Just thinking about that made me let out a small chuckle.

"OI, WHAT'RE YA GIGGLIN' ABOUT DOWN THA'? I'LL SAY IT AGAIN, STATE YER BUSINESS, YA BASTARD!" he yelled back down fiercely.

Hearing it again and thinking about it, I actually didn't technically have business here. I mean, I just sort of appeared near here and figured this would be a good spot to go. The best I could do was just answer him somewhat honestly, right? "I'M A WANDERER WHO'S SEEKING SHELTER!" I yelled back up to the dwarf-sounding man, hoping that explanation would be enough. Before the guard could answer, I heard a snarl behind me.

When I turned around, I was met with the gaze of two large black wolves. My eyes widened, taking in as much light as I could from the dimly lit surroundings. The wolves were roughly twice the size of me, if I had to venture a guess. Their coats were sleek and smooth-looking. If I wasn't convinced that the wolves probably wanted to eat me, I would love to go and just pet them. Their eyes were yellowish orange in the light, and their claws were as big as my fingers. Not to mention their fangs that were just as long and thick.

I refused to look away from the two figures that strategically placed themselves so I couldn't escape. One was to my left with the other covering the right. They were just close enough that if I ran forward, they could both pounce on me. It was like a triangle of death with each one of us being one of the points.

I didn't see them because I swapped my tracking to the guards; just my damn luck. *Is it just these two or are there others in the area?* When my tracking magic swapped to search for animals in the area, only the two wolves in front of me were in the immediate vicinity.

Seeing that, I let out a sigh of relief, and for a split second, a few small icons caught my eye on the side my mini-map. One looked like a fist, one was a heart, and the last one looked like...a boot? In that split second, though, both wolves lunged, assuming that I had let my guard down. As if on instinct, I rolled forward. I didn't go very far, but I went far enough that the wolves missed me and were carried into each other by their momentum.

"OH, CRAWP! HOL' ON, LAD, HELP'S ON THA WAY!" the guard yelled down to me in a panic.

I had no time to respond as I recovered from the dizziness I gained from rolling. *God, I wish I was in shape. I haven't done a somersault in years!*

Behind me, I heard a *ka-shuck* accompanied by a high-pitched yelp, and a message in my vision that simply said, "+828 XP." However, I didn't pay a lot of attention to it. Instead, I turned around and sprinted at the remaining wolf before it could recover from the blow it took from jumping onto its friend.

The wolf didn't stand a chance. As soon as it stood up and took notice of me running toward it, I was already an arm's length away. It must have realized there was no chance it could get away and picked fight instead of flight. It lifted its giant paw and swiped across my chest in desperation with its claws, but it was too late. I bit back the pain and barreled directly into the wolf, sending him flying into the pit. I turned around and again heard a *ka-shuck*. This time, it could be heard three different times, and there was no yelp or any sound from the wolf after that.

I breathed in and out heavily. Sweat ran down my forehead, drenching my shirt. It was now that I noticed the burning pain in my chest from where the wolf had slashed me. Three large wounds spanning my entire chest were slowly oozing blood. Luckily, they weren't as deep as I thought they would be, but it was still deep enough to where I would for sure need to be stitched back up. I took my hoodie off and wrapped it as tight as I could around my chest, trying to stop the bleeding at least a little bit. *I just hope I'm sweating from exerting myself and this isn't infected,* I prayed.

Immediately after tightening my sweatshirt, I plopped down, still trying to catch my breath. It was then that a message popped up into my vision, saying, "+832 XP," and then another saying, "Level up! Level 2!" Noticing that, I hoped it was like some games where I would be instantly healed on level up. I looked at my health, and not only had it not gone up, but I was missing around 65 percent of my health.

"I would've died in two hits!" I uttered aloud in pure disbelief. If I hadn't rolled when the wolves had initially lunged at me, I would've died, there's no question about it. But who's ever heard about almost being one-shot by starting zone monsters? I got up and walked closer to the pit to look at the two wolves. The first one was only impaled in one spot, and a large organ of some sort was sitting atop the wooden spike. The other wolf, however, was closer to the wall of the town and was impaled in three spots, once in the throat and twice near its tail end.

"I guess that explains why I didn't hear anything from it and why I got the experience so late. I guess it died a slow death." After I uttered that, I thought, *Shouldn't I be more shocked by this? This is the first time I've ever been directly involved in the death of something. Even if it's just a wolf, I should still feel something. All I feel, though, is... relief? Sure, it was a fight for my life, but even then, shouldn't I feel some sort of sympathy?*

I also realized that this was the first time I truly felt alive and that my life wasn't worth giving up on. If it was, I wouldn't have even attempted to fight the wolves. I was already a completely different person than I was on Earth.

Soon, after the fight ended, the drawbridge finally crashed down. Running over the bridge were two men in white robes along with a woman who donned a scale mail vest. She also wore leather boots, pants, and gloves. As the three made their way across the bridge toward me, a feeling of unease took over me. It felt as if I had done something wrong and I was about to be reprimanded for it.

"Well, well," said the woman as she approached me. "You handled yourself pretty well for a human. What level are you around? No, wait, let me guess! Judging by how you moved and the fact that you're confident enough to not have a weapon, you're probably around Level 20 or so, right? Of course, we Magic Elves could have taken on those wolves at Level 12 with one hand tied behind our backs!" she spouted at me confidently with a deeper but still fairly feminine voice. It was pretty obvious that the two men behind her clearly didn't agree with what she had stated, judging by the looks of bewilderment they shot at her as well as the apologetic glances they threw at me.

"Actually, I'm—" I said before holding myself back for a second. What I wanted to say was that I was Level 2, but no one believe that. Even if they did, it would probably pose a lot of questions, and who knows what would happen to me? "I'm only Level 18," I finished with a grin.

"Hah! Well, you did good. Though it looks like you took a pretty big wound. Come on, let's get you inside so we can close that up along with this gate," she said, grabbing my hand, pulling me up with seemingly next to no effort. It seemed like if I resisted her at all, my arm easily could have been ripped off. When she let go of my hand, I almost immediately began to fall toward the ground. Luckily, the two priest-like men caught me before I made it too far down.

"Thank you," I uttered to them both as we walked.

They both just simply smiled and nodded their heads.

Then I posed a question to the party of Elves. "So just out of curiosity, are there no archers defending the gate? Or were you all hoping I was going to get killed?" With a slightly raised eyebrow, I looked to the two supporting me who looked away from my gaze.

Ahead of us, the woman stopped in her tracks and turned her head toward us, just enough so that I could spot one eye that was glaring at me. "Maybe you humans think it's okay to leech EXP off of each other, but we Magic Elves are a proud race. If you died in that battle, then you didn't deserve to live," she said with a fury that even a lion would cower from. We started moving forward again as if nothing had happened. Taking that as my cue to shut up, I took in the spectacle of a city I was now walking through.

It was a lot more than I had expected after seeing the crude trench of wooden spikes. There was a main road that was paved with stone. It wasn't like concrete or anything; it was more like the stones had been embedded into the ground, which made it firm and surprisingly even. Along the road were light posts that were plants instead of being made of metal! The plant grew straight until it formed a sphere-like dome of twigs that protected a flower, which attracted bugs akin to fireflies. Whatever these bugs were, though, the light that they emitted was far greater than that of a simple firefly. The whole city was seemingly illuminated by these plant-based light posts.

Lining the sides of the road were wooden buildings that seemed almost as if they had been made out of living trees. As we neared what seemed to be the middle of the town, there was a large fountain that also seemed to serve as a memorial site. A large black stone obelisk sat in the middle of the fountain with names etched into the black stone.

"We'll stop here for now. I'm sure you need some rest," the women said, looking out toward the stone. "After the priests heal you up a little bit, we'll take you to an inn, and then you'll no longer be my problem," she said, clearly happier as soon as she thought about not having to deal with me anymore.

"I'm sorry about my rudeness before. I've never really been around Elves bef—"

Before I could finish what I was about to say, one of the priests covered my mouth and whispered in my ear. He sounded more like a butler than a priest. "Say Magic Elves. If you just say Elves, the Madam General will most likely kill you. She already despises humans, so don't set her over the edge, please!"

As soon as the priest finished, I quickly added, "I mean, Magic Elves, so I didn't know about your customs. I swear I didn't mean to offend."

As I said that, the woman turned around and looked at me before just simply rolling her eyes and letting out a very irritated sigh. "It doesn't even come down to not knowing our customs. The first thing you did was lie to me, the second you insulted my race, and then you had the audacity to not even mention how amazing our city is! The insult I'm able to look past as your reasoning is believable, but whenever someone enters the capital of the Magic Elves. they are always amazed. Yet, you haven't even let out a single gasp or even have so much of a twinkle in your eye! Needless to say, I dislike you, even more so as well due to you being a useless human!"

As she shouted out that last insult, one of the priests who had laid me down during her spiel and began healing my wounds turned to her and politely said, "Madam General, with all due respect, I believe this man may just be in shock. Regarding the greatness that is our city, I believe the mood that was set before we officially entered probably made our guest think against speaking rashly. This, of course, is an addition to his near-death experience. His wounds are closing quickly, which means his fortitude is extraordinarily low."

As the priest talked, I felt more and more at ease. It wasn't as if all of the Elv—I mean, the Magic-Elves were all the same. It felt like at least someone understood that I didn't mean any offense. It was nice to actually have someone on my side, even if it was a priest who seemed more like an escort to a great leader.

The female general looked at the priest, and after a while, just stated, "You're right, I'm letting the past take ahold of me again. Sometimes I forget we aren't in wartime anymore." She then looked back at me, and in the glow of the fireflies, I could fully see her face. Her auburn hair and her amber eyes were the first things to catch my attention, but then as I looked at her face more, I realized that she literally looked like she could be a redheaded girl on Earth. The only exception to that was the fact that she had points at the end of her ears that were longer than mine, yet shorter than the priests accompanying her. She wouldn't look that out of place at a convention. If I saw her at one, I would just assume that she was a cosplayer. After a few seconds, she smiled and said, "Exactly! That shine in your eye is exactly what I wanted to see!"

As soon as she said that, I blushed and looked away, shyly saying, "Sorry, I just, uh…I hadn't really gotten to see your face before, and the fireflies made it really well illuminated…and somewhat cute?" As soon as I said that out loud, I felt like I was going to die of embarrassment. *Why did I say that? It's true, but I would never just say that on Earth! I just made this situation so bad. Please just kill me. It'll be more suitable than having to live with myself after saying that!* I screamed in my mind. When I looked back toward her, it seemed that our roles had reversed as she was the one blushing now.

Almost as if there was some sort of cue, both of the priests stood up at the same time, and the one who had taken my side said, "You should be sufficiently healed now. Do take care to not reopen your wounds. We performed first-aid healing magic, but it's not a miracle cure all." Looking back toward the female general who was still blushing, he stated, "The wolves must have also gotten to his pack. I doubt he even has the money required to stay at an inn. I suggest we pay for his stay at the inn tonight as well as a meal?"

Almost immediately, the general agreed. "Of course, it's the least we could do for not having helped him out of that mess!" she said while giggling like a schoolgirl.

I leaned over to the helpful priest and asked, "What's up with her? Why's she done a complete 180 all of a sudden?"

"It could be because she rarely receives compliments, especially on her looks. You see, Lady Sylia is a crossbreed between a human and an elf. Her father was a human who was a noble ambassador who took a little too kindly to an elvish wench who was involved in escortation. When she was born, it was quite obvious who the father was since no other humans came to the kingdom of Elsaria at the time, even to the small towns on the border. Since her father was such an important figure, however, he denied any accusations and refused to accept her. Her mother, however, was the exact opposite. She cherished Lady Sylia for the first few years until she was murdered. Lady Sylia was put into an orphanage, and due to her lineage, she was discriminated against all her life. She rose up in the Elven Army, besides all of that. Mostly due to her skill in magic from being part human and her agility from being part elf, she is truly the embodiment of someone going from zero to hero! This was all many years ago, though. Most men are terrified or jealous of her due to her achievements, so she rarely even gets to talk to them, much less receive compliments." Luckily, Sylia had somehow not heard the priests long explanation of her past.

"Shall we get going, Madam General? And...I don't believe I caught your name, sir?" the priest said, looking right at me with a quizzical look.

I gave him a blank stare, and without thinking, I just let out the beginning of my real name, "Gray—" *Oh no. I can't use my past name! God, what works with Gray! Grayle? No, maybe Grayham? No that would just sound weird if I just said "ham" at this point. It needs to be something that Gray could just be a nickname for!*

21

After a second of thought, I finished what I was saying and just simply said, "Grayson!" I didn't want to use my real name, but I ended up doing it anyway. My clothes already made me seem like I wasn't from here, but especially now that I used my real name, I was terrified that they'd find out that I was from another world. I didn't understand why I was so terrified about people finding out, but I was.

The priest just looked at me and said with his normal tone, "Shall we get going, Madam General and Sir Grayson?" The four of us walked in silence through the streets until eventually, we came to what seemed to be a trade district of sorts. The surroundings hadn't changed much, besides the fact that there were more merchant stalls as well as larger buildings akin to the living treehouses that we had seen before. The buildings also had large signs hanging off of branches by what seemed to be vines being used as a makeshift chain.

"Well, here we are!" Sylia boomed, looking way too proud for only having escorted someone to a place in the city. If the priest hadn't told me anything about her, my only opinion of her would be that of a glorified tour guide. A few seconds after having made the declaration, Sylia turned around, grabbed my wrist, and began pulling me into the small inn.

When Sylia opened the door, a small bell ring could be heard around what seemed to be a hollowed-out tree. The walls, floor, ceiling, and even the stairs all were the same sanded down type of wood. It was obvious that paint or something had been applied to the walls and part of the ceiling, giving it more of a dark brown as opposed to the sandy tan.

Directly ahead of the door was a man facing us. He was sitting in what seemed to be a stool behind a long lectern. To the left of us were stairs leading up, and to the right was a dining area with a large counter and many tables and chairs, none of which were occupied. In fact, the whole area was dark, and the only illuminated place was the lectern the man was seated at.

As I looked at the man, I noticed that he was barely looking over the lectern. For a moment, I thought he was dead before he began speaking in a very tired voice.

"So, you're the stray." He then let out a sigh and said, "A room for the night will be two copper."

Before I could even open my mouth to say anything, Sylia began to take charge. "We'll take three rooms!" she said. Then when I looked at her with a raised eyebrow, she explained, "It's late, and we don't want you getting into any more trouble than you already have. So we'll keep you company for the night, and you BETTER appreciate it." She took six copper coins out of a small sack that was fastened to her belt and was handed three keys.

"Ya know the drill, Gens, so explain it to the newcomer. There aren't other guests, but I'm going to sleep, so keep it down," the innkeeper said before he blew out the candle that was providing all of the light.

I could hear the shuffling of everyone but me walking toward the stairs. Someone stopped at what must have been the start of the stairs and said, "Ah, right, here, grab onto my hand. It completely slipped our minds that you can't see in the dark." Judging by the voice, it sounded like it was the priest that had been helping me since we met.

"You guys are able to see in the dark?" I asked the voice while we walked in pitch darkness.

"Yes, our natural abilities play a part in it, but otherwise, we use magic to enhance our vision further. Mostly anyone who can use magic can do it. However, I don't sense any magicules coming from you," the butler-sounding priest explained. I wanted to ask him more about how the magic of this world worked, but before I could, I heard a door in front of me open. I heard a snap, and suddenly, light poured out through the doorway with the priest saying, "This is where you'll be tonight. If you need any of us, Madam General will be across the hall, and us priests will be just down the hall on this side. Please have a pleasant night, sir. We'll talk more in the morning."

I said goodnight to the priest and decided that I would wait until tomorrow to ask him about magic. As I shut the door, I let out a sigh of relief and leaned up against the door. There wasn't much in the room. There was a bed with a window directly behind it, a desk with a lit candle on top, and a chair in front of the desk.

I guess that explains why it was only two copper. It's just the essentials. I walked forward and sat down on the bed before lying down across it. It didn't feel firm like a mattress, but it also didn't feel soft like it was just straw. It's hard to explain, but it just felt…right. Especially after the long first day that I had. I unbound the sweatshirt that I had put around me earlier after the wolf attack and found that the only evidence that the battle even happened was the large tear marks in my shirt. The wounds I sustained were completely healed without a trace. It's one thing to see it in shows and stories, but to actually experience it firsthand is something completely different! I got up and slung my sweatshirt around the chair next to the desk and decided that it was time for me to sleep. Luckily, the room was small, so after I blew out the candle, there was no chance of not finding the bed. As I climbed into the bed and got under the sheets, I looked up at the ceiling, and a large smile overtook my face. Somehow, my first day in another world was complete.

2

The Journey to Heirshield!

The next morning, I awoke to an ear bursting *BANG, BANG, BANG* on my door. I jolted up and instantly ran to the door. When I opened it, Sylia was in front of me with her fist clenched and an irritated look on her face.

"Do you KNOW what time it is, Grayson? Were you planning on sleeping all day? You're lucky you aren't a part of my squad. Otherwise, you'd be ripped apart. Come on, we need to talk, and we might as well do it over a meal."

By the time I processed everything that Sylia said, she'd already pulled me out of the room. This time, I could actually see the hallway thanks to the light creeping out from the rooms. It was long enough to contain three rooms on each side and had a small table in between each room with various vase-like objects on each of them. *Thank God I didn't bump into any of those last night. Otherwise, that would've been a mess.*

Sylia dragged me all the way to the dining area and sat me down at a table with the two priests from last night. To my surprise, those two looked just as tired as I felt. As the three of us exchanged glances and small nods of acknowledgment, the man from last night appeared with four mugs of what smelled like coffee. What surprised me most wasn't the fact that they had coffee in this world, but rather, the appearance of the man from last night. I thought that he had been an elf like the priests or at the very least a half-elf like Sylia. But no, the man standing before me was shorter than I was while sitting down. He was a dwarf! *I suppose I couldn't tell last night thanks to how dark it was and the fact that he had blown out the candle before hopping off of his stool,* I thought.

As I stared at the dwarf in amazement, he just grinned and said, "Guess ya didn't expect me to be like this, eh?" He still sounded as tired as he did last night. "I'm sure ya don't want to pose the question, but aye, I'm a dwarf. I take it the general didn't do as I asked last night, did she?" he said as he shot a glare up at Sylia who let out a chuckle and slyly looked away.

"Of course I did, you know me. I would never not do something if you asked me to."

I rolled my eyes and whispered to the dwarvish innkeeper, "You two seem close. Any chance you can tell me how in hell she became a general? From what I've seen of her, she's very scatterbrained and acts like a little girl who wants attention."

As soon as I said that, it was like the roles had been reversed. It was now the innkeeper's turn to laugh and Sylia's turn to glare, though instead of glaring at the innkeeper, she glared at me.

"Wanna know something funny, Grayson? One of the great things about being a Magic Elf is that our hearing is enhanced just like our eyesight." Sylia said.

I slowly turned and looked at her in horror as I realized she heard everything I just said.

"Could a little girl do this?" she asked as she picked up a fruit that resembled an apple and completely crushed it in her hand.

I quickly shook my head.

"Say something like that again, and that will be your head instead, understand?"

Knowing that this freakishly strong girl could probably keep her promise, I shook my head again and let out a resounding, "Yes, ma'am!"

After the innkeeper angrily cleaned up the juice from the fruit and started preparing food, Sylia began talking in a much more laid-back fashion.

"So, Grayson, what exactly brought you to this city?" she asked while taking a sip of her coffee-like drink, awaiting my response.

"Umm, a friend of mine told me I could join the Fighters Guild if I came here," I nervously said. I figured that lying would only make matters worse, and technically, what I said was true. After I said that, Sylia just looked at me with a blank expression, which morphed into one of confusion.

"Was that meant to be a joke?" she said, sounding concerned but having a very irritated look on her face as she drank her coffee.

"Um...no? Why would it be?" I asked, causing her to perform quite an impressive spit-take and begin coughing uncontrollably. I couldn't help, so all I did was nervously look around. The priests were obviously just as surprised as Sylia, if not more so.

"Sir Grayson, please excuse me for what I am about to say, but...are you a fool? The only way that a human could appear in this city is if they were escorted or if they were part of the Fighters Guild. Since you appeared alone and aren't a member of the guild...the only possible way that you're strong enough is if you've been poaching in someone's monster farm," the butler-sounding priest stated while giving me a stern look. It was almost as if he already decided that I was guilty.

"Poaching? I would never do that, I swear! Besides, how strong would someone really have to be to get here?" I asked trying to lead the subject away from being accused of a crime I didn't commit.

"Sir, I believe you told us you were Level 18 when we met, which was more or less confirmed by the fact that you were able to fight off monsters in this Level 20 area. If you're telling us that this isn't the case, allow me to join your party so I may check your status," the priest said.

It was as if this was their plan all along, and I fell directly into their trap. Not only did I take the bait, but I then took the hook and stabbed it through my cheek and was getting reeled in at an alarming pace.

Is there really nothing that I can do? Is protecting my secret worth it? What even happens if they find out that I'm from another world? The worst case would be I get tortured for information about Earth, and they try to invade it or something like that, right? I think my only play is to tell them the truth. To have to play my secret so early though is disappointing.

"All right," I eventually said to the priest. That was when I realized that I completely forgot to learn how to add party members when I was looking at the help menu. Luckily, a prompt appeared in my vision, stating, "Fiyore has invited you to a party. Would you like to accept or decline?" As soon as I thought the word *accept,* I saw two more sets of health bars appear below mine, each with a name and a number next to the name. The first said Fiyore (25), while the second one said Hjorn (22). My health bar also transformed to include my name and level.

When I stopped focusing on the health bars, I looked back toward the butler-like priest or now that I knew his name, Fiyore. What I saw staring back at me were the two priests in utter disbelief with their mouths wide open. With her breathing back under control and noticing that something had happened based on the other two elves' reaction, Sylia excitedly asked, "Well, what's going on? Did he actually slip up and is someone that we should take into custody?"

In response, Fiyore turned toward her before another name joined the group. The name was Sylia (42). At this point, all three of them were looking at me with their mouths open and their eyes wide.

"So, uhh…yeah, I guess the cat's out of the bag, huh?" I said with a nervous chuckle.

Without a word, Sylia got up from her chair, walked over to me, and stabbed my cheek with her finger. "Fiyore was right, you really are a fool! It would be amazing enough just surviving in this territory without seeing combat. Of course, you somehow managed to do more than that. You killed two Alpha Black Wolves." Sylia took a moment to breathe out a deep sigh and then continued on, "Listen, you're going to need to tell us everything about who you are. Otherwise, we're going to have to do some messed up things to find out. Trust me, I really don't want to have to do anything like that to you."

With how serious Sylia was now, it was like she was a different person entirely, instead of being the hotheaded, semi-racist, bipolar person I had seen up until this point. I instantly caved and decided to tell them everything about how I was from another world and mostly everything that had happened up until I met them. I decided to not tell them about my track ability, mainly because if these guys ended up becoming my enemy somehow; I didn't want them to know all of my secrets.

Surprisingly, they didn't say anything the whole time I was telling my story nor did they even have a hint of suspicion in their eyes. Once I had finished, Sylia said, "Well, that actually explains everything. I guess now I kind of have to forgive you for being completely ignorant about our race's customs."

"Wait, you're seriously going to believe me just like that? I mean, I've been lying to you almost this whole time! How are you all just accepting this?" I asked the group. I was completely unable to accept the fact that they would just believe what I said now after I had been deceiving them ever since we had first met.

"Well, Sir Grayson, it's a lot more believable than you think. After seeing your level and your clothes, it's not all that far-fetched. I'm sure you had your reasons about hiding your identity. Although one part of your story still doesn't make sense to me. How on Zynka were you able to defeat two Level 20 monsters?" Fiyore asked.

Really, I had absolutely no idea myself. I actually couldn't answer him. Thinking about it logically, there was no way in hell that I should have been able to defeat one of those wolves, much less two of them.

Taking my silence as a response, Fiyore added, "I suppose it doesn't matter. What does matter, however, is the fact that you are an other-worlder. We can realistically only provide you two options right now. The first is to stay here in service of the Lady General so that you can be kept under strict surveillance. The second would be to send you by carriage to the city of Heirshield. It's the human capital that just so happens to be the main home of the Fighters Guild. Of course, we would also like reports of your progress, so we would have to send someone along with you. This would also ensure that you don't meet an untimely demise. We won't do anything without your consent. However, I hope that you will indulge us in one of our requests."

Thinking about what Fiyore said, I really didn't have much of a choice. To live the life of an adventurer, I needed to be a part of the Fighters Guild. *Plus, being one of Sylia's underlings doesn't exactly sound like something I want to do,* I thought to myself.

"Well, if the Fighters Guild is in Heirshield, then I suppose that's where I'm headed," I stated. As soon as I finished, the three of them rose to their feet in complete synchronization as if they had practiced for hours the night before.

"All right then, Grayson. We have to report this to the elf king and arrange for your transport. Please remain here until we get back. Surely, you can do that correctly, right?" Sylia asked, to which I just gave a simple nod. "Great, then we're off. With any luck, we'll see you tomorrow. Oh, and Grayson? Sorry for giving you such a hard time before," she said without any hesitation in her voice. I didn't really take her as the type to apologize for something she'd done. But then again, Sylia seemed to completely ride her mood.

"Don't worry about it, Sylia, you were just cranky 'cause it was late right?" I joked as she and the priests walked toward the door to the inn.

She turned around to roll her eyes at me and replied, while smiling, "Sure, let's say that it was that and not the fact that you're a huge pain in the ass."

After they closed the door, the dwarf I was with let out a large groan. "They left before eating their damned meal! I'm going to have to run today, aren't I?" he complained as he packed the food into small containers before putting them into bags. With three bags in hand, he ran after the group, yelling something along the line of, "Yer not escapin' my cookin' tha' easily!"

*****

It took almost a day for the party to get back to the inn. They left in the morning and got back around midnight. In that time, I learned a few things from the menu. I learned how to add someone to a party and how to trade with people. Apparently, going through the trade menu is preferred so that you don't get scammed. If you used the menu to trade something, then the person you were trading with couldn't take the item back unless it went through the trade menu again. It also made it so that both sides had to accept the terms of the deal and both sides could see exactly what was being traded. That way, someone couldn't give less money or items than was agreed upon.

Other than these few things, there wasn't much other useful information in the menu. It seemed like I'd either need to be taught or learn it myself on my adventures.

Once Sylia and the priests returned, the dwarvish innkeeper who had been watching over me retrieved me from my room.

"Oi, Gray, looks like they got back earlier than expected. I'd hoped to get some more money out of ya, but what can ya do?" the innkeeper said with a hearty laugh. He wasn't able to hide the disappointment in his voice. He seemed more sad at the fact that he'd be alone again instead of his comment about money.

Even though it was only for the day, I ended up learning a lot about the dwarf. His family had owned the inn for generations. At some point, when his late father owned it, a fire broke out and almost destroyed the inn completely. Repair costs were higher than they had expected thanks to the war. Long story short, they ended up working out a deal with the elven king.

Basically, the inn was for people who had come to the kingdom for the first time, and the innkeeper had to send reports on the people that stayed to ensure they weren't a threat. The only other people who got to stay at the inn were people in government jobs. Usually, people in militaristic positions took advantage of this, which explained why Sylia and he knew each other so well. He was basically a government spy. When you think about it, it's kinda cool. With that being said, he rarely got close to anyone as a result of his work.

When we reached the bottom of the steps, Sylia was leaned up against a wall next to the door with her arms crossed. Almost immediately, after we came into view, she started speaking like she was giving a report. "Turns out the king already knew about you, so our job was made a bit easier. He actually had a shadow guard following you ever since you appeared. I can't disclose how they knew about you, so don't ask. Turns out that guard is the one that made it so you could beat those wolves."

"Wow, right to business, huh? Not even a hello? Thanks, Sylia, it's good to see you too," I said, a little disappointed at the lack of friendliness. *I may have only met her yesterday, but she feels like a childhood friend that I can poke fun at. Aside from that, what did she mean about that…shadow guard? How could they have helped me?* I thought.

Sylia looked at me with clear exhaustion written on her face. Whether it was from a lack of sleep from working or she was getting stressed, I couldn't tell. "Gray, I'm not in the mood. So please let us talk right now. If I want to be annoyed, I'll let you know."

"Promise?" I asked her, trying my best to lighten the mood up a little bit. *Of course, this could just make her want to kill me, but screw it, I'll take the gamble,* I thought.

Unfortunately, her expression didn't change at all, and the whole room got very uncomfortable to be in. The air felt like it was heavy. It was almost like it had finally rained after a long drought, and we had forgotten what humidity felt like. Eventually, she broke the awkward silence by cracking a half-smile and letting out a sigh.

"Sure, I promise. Can I continue now?" she asked me after conceding. Amazed that my gamble paid off, I cracked a smile and nodded. "Thanks. First thing: Those icons you said you saw were buffs. The guard that was trailing you happened to be a strong support-type enhancer. He made it so you moved faster, had more health, and were way stronger than you actually are. Second: We'll be leaving for Heirshield tomorrow morning. That way, a messenger can get there to warn the king of our arrival. Monsters will be less active during the day too, so it's less likely that our wagon will be attacked. That's basically all I can say for now. Any questions?" she finished.

Usually, "Any questions?" is just a way to conclude a discussion, but for once, I actually did have a question. "Umm, you said a lot of words like *we'll* and *our*. You're just using those as grouping terms, right? You don't literally mean that you're the one that's being sent with me, right?" I asked with a shaky voice and a nervous chuckle. *As much as I like Sylia's company, she makes me really uneasy. I mean, she is one of the two main reasons why I decided against the other choice I was given,* I thought.

Unfortunately for me, Sylia's smile turned from one of defeat to one that was much more sinister. "You're a lot sharper than I thought, especially for someone who must've died to get reincarnated here. To answer your question. Yes, I will be the one accompanying you. Personally, I think the king saw this as a chance to get rid of me, but he'll still be paying me, so I'm not getting the chance to call him out on it," she said as she balled her fist in the air as if she was cursing someone in the heavens.

I couldn't believe what I had just heard. It was starting to seem more and more like I was going to be stuck with this crazy woman, no matter what I did. Shortly after that, we concluded our "meeting" and attempted to get some rest before our journey to Heirshield the next day. I went to sleep that night having nightmares of the many ways that I'd be tortured by my first companion in my new life.

*****

The next day, we woke up early and gathered up all of our belongings, which was surprisingly little. It wasn't surprising for me to not have much. Sylia, on the other hand, was decked out in her usual armor with her weapon at her side and a medium-sized leather backpack that could realistically only carry essentials.

There's no way that she's carrying everything in that tiny thing. Maybe it's something like a bag of holding? This is a fantasy world, so that's not entirely an unrealistic possibility. I wondered to myself. Either way, it didn't matter to me what she brought with her, so I didn't bother to ask.

By the time the sun crept over the horizon, we were already loading ourselves onto a wagon. Apparently, we were important enough that the elven king gave us a message that basically gave us a free ride to the kingdom of Heirshield on a merchant's wagon. Luckily, that meant that we wouldn't have to ride with anyone besides the driver. Of course, that was also a double-edged sword, since the only one to talk to would be Sylia.

"You two must be mighty important if the king's paying me this much to get you to the kingdom! Now I won'tcha worry 'bout that, and rest assured, I'll get you there safe and sound!" the wagon driver assured us, sounding a lot like how anyone would imagine an old prospector to sound like. *He looks like a middle-aged man, even though he's an elf. I can only imagine how old he actually is if he's showing signs of aging as an elf,* I thought in amazement.

After offering her thanks, Sylia untied two small cords to let down some curtains. She quietly muttered something under her breath that I couldn't make out before a blue circle appeared on them.

When she caught me looking at her in confusion, she offered an explanation. "It's a guarding spell, though this one is only strong enough to guard against words. That way, we can talk to each other without him or anyone else overhearing. The king may trust him, but you can never be too sure. Merchants would sell their own children if it meant they'd get a few gold, much less a couple of strangers."

"Are merchants actually that greedy? Or are you just exaggerating?" I asked, mildly concerned. It's not as if I hadn't heard the saying before, but I always thought it was a joke.

"Well, it depends on the merchant and their children. Usually, if they have a daughter, they try to marry them off to a richer family of merchants to leech some of their status. If they have sons, however, usually the firstborn is taught how to be a merchant. Any others are either sold off or left on their own to learn other trades," Sylia explained with a look of disgust on her face. *With how she's talking about merchants, I'm kind of glad now that she used her word-guarding spell,* I thought, thankful that the merchant couldn't hear anything.

"That's actually really horrible. I mean, I didn't expect the world to be all peaches and roses, but…just wow. I have no words."

"Gray? What are peaches and roses? Obviously, it's something from your world, so don't even think about giving me a vague answer!" Sylia said, looking genuinely curious as to what they were.

"Well, peaches are a fruit, and roses are a deep-red flower. I'm pretty sure the saying just means that everything's not perfect. Though, I don't really get why it's a peach. Maybe I'm just remembering the saying wrong," I said, rubbing the back of my head and letting out a nervous chuckle. *Either way, the meaning of the saying is still there, so I guess it's fine,* I reasoned to myself.

Sylia looked intently at me as if she was studying me. Before I could make any sort of flustered reaction, the wagon suddenly stopped. Without a moment of hesitation, Sylia opened the cover's end while her other hand lay on her sword.

"Why are we stopping?" she said as she opened it.

If that curtain wasn't opened yet, and it still had the magic, would he even be able to hear her question? I wondered. Luckily, the driver didn't need to answer after we could see outside the wagon. There were a large number of men who must've been bandits on the road. I couldn't see past Sylia very well, so I thought to myself, *Track bandits.* This way, I could easily count how many there were and see if more were lying in hiding nearby. Thankfully, all of them were situated in front of the wagon. Not so thankfully, they had around fifteen of them.

I looked to Sylia and said in a hushed voice, "It's bandits. What's the plan? From what I can tell, there's fifteen of them, and they're all on the road."

Sylia kept looking forward toward the bandits with a huge grin. "I'm not sure how you figured that out, but at least it proves you aren't useless. Let's see what they want first. If they're smart, they'll let us pass by. If not, then they all die."

"Wha?" I said in reaction to her comment. "Why would they just let us pass? Isn't that the exact opposite of what they'd want to do as bandits?"

"Their highest level looks like a 14, but their strongest is a 12 that wastefully put all of their points into strength. Hell, you could even take some of them on since they're so weak. However, if a fight breaks out, then you're going to hide in here with the driver. Got it?" she asked, looking ahead but still having enough of an impact to where I felt as though I would follow any order she gave; not out of fear, but out of a desire to help.

Maybe this commanding presence is what made it so that she was able to become a general? I wondered. It was then that I noticed a little icon like when I fought with the wolves. This one looked like a flag;

however, instead of the boot, fist, or heart that I saw before... *Oh, it's an actual skill of hers, I guess. Useful,* I thought.

I gave her a slight nod and said, "Got it."

The weight of the situation was becoming clear. As soon as I did, Sylia pulled the driver into the back and jumped out in front of the wagon.

I looked down at the driver who had landed on the floor, narrowly avoiding hitting his head on the cargo. The old elf looked terrified and had tears welling in his eyes. At first, the thought that he had purposefully led us into this ambush crossed my mind. Seeing him now, though, there was no way. Unless he had missed his calling as an actor, he was just as much a victim as us.

I crouched down to the floor and put my hand on his shoulder. "Don't worry, she'll take care of everything. It's gonna be fine, all right?" I said with a soft smile. I don't know if I'm charismatic or if he was panicking, but the driver pulled me into a hug and started fully crying as he offered his thanks.

I could hear loud laughs from outside as if they were laughing at the man. That was when I heard Sylia's distinct voice say, "So you have no intention of letting us pass?" It was definitely Sylia, but something about it was much more sinister. After she asked that, everyone went silent; even the elf next to me stopped his cries. Sensing something was about to happen, the old driver let go of me, and we both moved toward the front of the wagon to see what it was.

A man who was slender but muscular took two steps forward while saying in a voice that was as smooth as butter, "Of course we aren't. Are ya scared, elf? Don't worry, we only want the cargo. I doubt you can even use that sword, so feel lucky that we aren't taking anything else," he finished as he looked Sylia up and down as if he was appraising her. "Wait a minute. You're a half-breed! Ahaha, now there's definitely no reason to take you. No one would want to buy you!"

It was at this point that I knew...he fucked up. Sylia drew her weapon in one swift motion and got into a battle stance. The only words she said were, "Pretty soon, I won't be the only half-breed here." If it wasn't for her cheesy one-liner, I would've thought that she was actually kinda cool.

The next moments made me realize just how underpowered I was in this world. The last thing I could easily see was Sylia digging her back foot into the ground before kicking off. Everything after that was a blur, and the worst part is that I was the only one who couldn't tell what happened.

Around a second after she kicked off, two men fell to the ground. One had a large slash down his chest, while the other was cut clean in two from his waist. *I guess the one-liner makes sense now, but did she really have to kill him like that?* I thought as I turned my eyes away from the corpses.

The driver beside me shouted out, "DON'T KILL 'EM! JUST KNOCK 'EM OUT, AND WE'LL TURN 'EM IN FOR A REWARD!" As he greedily rubbed his hands together, it became evident that Sylia was right—merchants in this world really did only care about money.

After he shouted that, a bunch of the bandits dropped to the ground without even being able to put up a fight. Soon there was only around four left as well as the man who was taunting Sylia before the fight started.

At this point, the fight slowed down enough to where I could actually see. Both sides were breathing heavily, and the four underlings had Sylia surrounded. The men had all sorts of weapons. A man-beast, who looked as feral as the wolves I had fought, had a large mace. Another was dual-wielding one-handed swords; a hunched back one was using daggers; and a man who was larger than the beast-man had a large woodcutter's axe.

Even though she was outnumbered, Sylia looked the most calm. It was a battle of who would strike first. If someone went for a hit and missed, then they were doomed. Failing to connect in a situation like this makes it so you get used as a shield, get counterattacked, or hit your allies. In this position, Sylia held the most power but also had no margin for error. In theory, Sylia should just be able to win based on numbers alone. Realistically, though, everyone had potential to do damage to her. If she was wearing full plate, then it could be a different story, but in her scale mail, there were tons of weak points for the blade users to exploit.

The brute with the large mace decided to swing first. Fortunately, he swung it like a baseball bat instead of using it like a crusher, which would've been the logical choice in the situation. Sylia quickly ducked beneath the mace, allowing her to spring forward to get beside him. Before he could complete his swing, she struck him in the back head with the butt of her sword, sending him down into the dirt and leaving his mace flying out of his hands into the hunchbacked man.

Seeing this, the remaining fighters had one of two responses. The swordsman took a step back as if in terror from two of their allies getting taken out from the result of one blow. The axe wielder had a different response. He charged forward, letting out a battle cry that even shook me and the old elf. At the end of his charge, he slammed down his axe like he was chopping a log. Sylia's response was to swiftly move her whole body to the left, narrowly avoiding the axe. The axe got plunged so deep into the ground that only half of the handle was visible. With the axe buried so deep, the man wasn't able to pull it free, no matter how hard he tried. Sylia didn't even use the sword to finish him; she gave him one swift chop to the neck, and he was taken out of commission.

At this point, the last one in the group was very hesitant for obvious reasons. His will had been entirely broken after seeing all of his allies fall. He decided to take the easy way out and threw his weapons away. The swordsman knelt down, accepting his fate.

With everyone defeated, the man that was taunting Sylia earlier started slowly applauding. "You were able to defeat my men. Not bad. You've earned the right to face me in combat! If you wish to run away now and cower in fear, that's too bad! It would be dishonorable for me to abandon the men that I owe so mu—"

Before he drew his weapon, before he even got to finish his monologue, Sylia used the blunt edge of her sword to hit him with so much power that he was sent into the ground like a meteor. When she sheathed her weapon and started walking back toward the wagon, the unexpected happened. He pushed himself out of the indentation he left in the ground and pointed at Sylia, yelling, "WHAT THE

HELL!" He ran fast enough to make it to the wagon before her and then faced her directly.

"Are you serious? I'm the big boss! You aren't supposed to just try to kill me while I'm talking! Where the hell is your adventurer etiquette!" he said, sounding more like a whining child than the boss of a group of bandits.

Sylia didn't say anything. She just walked right past him, not even acknowledging his existence.

He turned around, he reached out to grab her shoulder, uttering out, "Come on, at least give me an ans—"

Before he could reach her shoulder, she grabbed his arm with both hands and flipped him into the air. At the peak of the move, he let out an audible, "Uh-oh" before being slammed directly into the ground on his back. His body bounced up once and then fell to the ground where he lay entirely knocked out.

Sylia knelt down next to his body. "This isn't some story. I'm not obligated to show any mercy to a bandit. Gray, be a dear and grab the coil of rope from the side of the wagon and start tying these guys up," she said surprisingly politely.

She seems more…mellow? Maybe she just needed to get a fight in to relieve some stress or something, I thought. I grabbed the rope from the side and started tying up groups of bandits. I made a knot around their hands and then would move on to the next guy, leaving some rope so that they wouldn't be forced to be too close together. That way, if anyone was closer than they should be, it was easily noticeable. Plus, it would make it easier for them to move without tripping over each other.

It took me longer than I wanted, but soon enough, we had two lines of six bandits tied to the back of the cart. The coils the old merchant kept were surprisingly long, so we were able to cut off some leftover rope to bind their leader, since he seemed like he'd pose the most threat. We threw him onto the floor of the wagon so that we'd be able to keep an eye on him.

Once we loaded the unconscious leader into the wagon, I swapped my tracking to "Captives attempting to escape." *It's really specific, but it should technically work since it follows the skills descrip-*

tion. This way, we don't even have to see them to know that they're trying to give us the slip, I thought, proud of my use of the skill.

When all the bandits were accounted for, Sylia came up to me and whispered to me, "That battle took more out of me than I expected. I hate having to leave this to you, but while we move, could you keep an eye on the prisoners?"

"Oh…I mean, I was planning on keeping an eye on them anyway. So don't worry, you can leave it to me! You get whatever rest you can. You did great out there," I said, giving her a smile and throwing a thumbs up her way.

We headed back to the cart and sat down on either side of the bandit leader. As soon as she sat down, Sylia went out like a light. Clearly, she was more exhausted than she had been letting on earlier.

Jeez, if she was this tired, then she should've slept on the way here instead of talking to me about merchants and all that jazz. Looking at her, I couldn't help but feel a pang of guilt for making her fight all of those guys alone while dead tired. She could've easily lost if her body had given out at the wrong time. Suddenly, her effort in avoiding an actual fight with the leader made a lot more sense.

When the merchant jumped up onto the driver's seat, I asked him with a raised eyebrow, "Hey, where've you been?"

"Where d'ya think, boy? The dead don't need coins or weapons!" he said with a wide grin and holding out his hands to reveal two gold coins and a shiny dagger.

"You robbed the dead!" I asked in utter disbelief. It was one thing if he had killed them, but he didn't. Sylia did. It's like if someone you knew was trying to get a rare drop in a video game for a long time, and then as soon as it appears, you take it for yourself and refuse to trade it to them. It's just dirty and pretty messed up.

"Listen 'ere, boy, if the owner's dead, then any property of theirs you find is rightfully yours!" he said angrily and then continued, "Now if you don't want those boys back there ta die, I suggest you wake them up. After you peruse what items they have that you may, want that is! They sure as hell aren't gonna need anything where they'll be goin'."

At this point, the elf was basically in my face. It's like with each point he had brought up, he got closer and closer. I just nodded and got out of the wagon. *I'm not going to argue with a crazy man,* I thought as I started sifting through their pockets.

The bandits in the first line didn't have much. The only things of note were a few silver coins and some sort of book. One of the bandits in the second line, however, had an Enchanted Iron Dagger! At first, the dagger didn't seem like much. It seemed like it was just another of the bandits' normal weapons. Once I picked it up, though, it started to glow red. On further inspection, the hilt wasn't a normal leather strip-covered hilt either. The hilt was embroidered with what looked like gold and had some sort of green gemstone in the bottom.

At first, I thought the merchant was a complete scumbag for taking the loot off of those bandits. Now, though, I understood just how exhilarating it was getting loot! *Maybe it's due to the fact that this is the first time that I've gotten loot, but who knows?* I thought. The only way I could contain my excitement was thinking about how I had to wake up a bunch of bandits who would probably want to kill us as soon as I did.

Now that I think about it, how should I even wake them up? I thought to myself. *The ropes aren't loose enough for them to grab me, but I doubt that it'll stop those morons from trying to do something. I'll have to wake them up from a distance...* That's when I remembered something. It was like a little lightbulb went off in my head.

I ran to the front of the wagon, dropped my loot off inside, and said to the driver, "I'm about to wake them up, so get ready to go. Oh, you might want to cover your ears for this too."

Before he could respond, I moved to the other end of the wagon and thought, *Activate Taunt.* As soon as I did, a message popped up, indicating that the skill taunt was active. With the preparation complete, I took a deep breath and let out in a loud, much deeper than normal voice, "IF YOU DON'T WANT TO DIE, THEN WAKE UP NOW!"

Near instantly, all of the bandits jumped up out of terror. One of them was so scared he even pissed himself. A few woke up just from the surprise of it all and instinctively tried to reach for their weapons. Obviously, they didn't find their weapons, especially since they could barely reach out in front of them. The only ones that didn't react were the bandit leader and Sylia.

Either they're so high of a level that my taunt doesn't even affect them or the guarding spell Sylia put down is making it so they can't hear it. Though, would it affect both sides of the wagon? I wondered.

With all the bandits now on their feet, I thought, *Deactivate Taunt.* Sure enough, the message indicating that taunt was active disappeared from sight. I moved back up to the driver and tapped him on the shoulder.

"Alrighty, they're all awake, so let's head on out!" I said. Nothing could prepare me for what I was about to see. When the old elf turned to me, he looked just like he did when the bandits attacked. I instantly felt guilty and kept assuring him that I wasn't going to do anything to him.

After a little while, he calmed down, and from there on, the ride was pretty calm. I had to move some of his cargo forward so I could sit near the back. From there, whenever the track ability went off, I would yell at whoever was attempting to escape. Usually, it came down to three people who I called Two, Five, and Eight.

When it came to be around midday, boredom overtook me. There weren't many attempts of escape because it just got hotter and hotter as we left the forest. The forest turned to a wide open plain filled with flowers, rivers, and the occasional tree. With the increased humidity and less shade, the bandits were just focusing on moving without collapsing from the heat. It was awkward enough for them to move at a pace they aren't used to, but now they were getting sweaty, thanks to the humidity.

We had to let the horses take a break, which served as a much-needed rest for the bandits. I filled a waterskin with some water from the pails for the horses and went around, offering it to the bandits. Some would offer their thanks and accept, others would grudgingly accept, and a couple just flat-out refused or wouldn't even acknowledge the question. *At least I gave them the option. If they collapse now, it's no skin off my back,* I thought.

Eventually, we started moving again, and in my boredom, I inspected the items I took from the bandits. The book that I had found ended up catching my eye the most. The title of the book was *Magic Made So Easy, Even Slimes Could Learn It*. Based on the title, I assumed that slimes must be pretty stupid. *That kinda sucks. In my old world, there was a story about a slime who ended up leading a nation of monsters. Well, I guess that's one thing that's not going to be happening here!*

When I opened the book, the first page was entirely blank. *That's…weird. Maybe it has that blank page and then the next is the table of contents,* I thought, trying to come up with a reason why the book seemed to have no words. I turned to the next page, which was also blank. The third page was blank too! But the fourth page was something no one would ever expect…it was blank. I quickly flipped through the book, and sure enough, all of the pages were blank.

Flipping back to the first page, I blankly stared forward, not sure what to do. *Was someone writing a book? Was it a grimoire or something that only the person it was made for could use? Or was it something that if it was read, then it would lose all of its magic and instantly teach the person a spell?* At this point, my head was full of questions.

I let out a frustrated sigh and was about to close the book when something caught my eye. Random letters were appearing out of thin air on the page. The letters didn't look like normal ink, though they had a fiery glow as if they were being burned onto the page.

At this point, my brain was fried. First, I was disappointed, then I was theory-crafting about why the book was blank; now letters were just appearing out of thin air! *Obviously, it's some kind of magic, but trying to understand it is making me feel sick. At this point, maybe I should just give up and ask the previous owner what the hell's going on with this book,* I thought.

"Hey, Number 3, what's up with this book you had? Why are all the pages blank and then have random letters appear?" I asked, staring at the second bandit in the first line. He was sweating so much that his whole shirt had been drenched in sweat. Luckily, he was one of the ones that accepted water, so he was more inclined to offer an explanation.

He looked at me and said, "What the hell are you talking about? It's a book, why the hell would the pages be blank?"

Instead of giving him a response like I normally would, I figured it would be better to show him what I was talking about. I opened the book and held it up so that he would be able to see it from where he was.

"What are you smoking, kid? It's just like I said, the only way that you couldn't read that is if you were blind or...wait." he said as if he had just had an epiphany. He looked to me and said in an astonished tone, "Do you...do you not have magic? You see your health? Below that should be a blue bar, do you have that?"

Unfortunately for me, my suspicions that I had earlier had come true. If what this bandit wizard was saying was true, then I truly didn't have any magic. Naturally, I didn't want to believe it. *I honestly thought this was a possibility when I saw the grey bar earlier, but I didn't actually think that God would forget to make it so I could use magic!* I finally replied to Number 3, "No...the bar under my health bar is grey..." I looked down, feeling dejected. *I get sent to a fantasy world and I can't even use magic. I might as well have just been reincarnated on Earth during the Middle Ages, because that's basically what this is. Except it's a lot more dangerous.*

At this point, a few of the bandits had their full attention on me. Surprisingly, none of the usual troublemakers used this as a chance to try to escape. It's even more surprising now that they now knew I basically had no way of stopping them unless I chased after them.

"I've never heard of someone not having magic before, but it's not like it's all that important. Look at me, I just swing a big mace around. If you can't use magic, then just get stronger!" boomed the beast of a man that was one of the final four to fight Sylia. He wasn't trying to shout. It just seemed like that was his natural voice. It was deep and gruff.

I didn't understand why he was trying to comfort me, but all I could do was let out a dry chuckle. "Yeah, maybe I'll just do that," I said as I turned away and closed the back curtains. I let out a sigh. *There's nothing I can do about not being able to use magic, so I shouldn't let it get to me. But I feel robbed. Magic is one of the coolest thing's, and*

I don't even get the chance to use it. It's like going to a store as a kid and seeing a toy you really want. But then your mom tells you that you can have any toy in the store, except that one. Sure, you can get any toy in the store, but you can't get the one that you really wanted to play with.

I know it's childish to complain about it. It just sucks. With any luck, though, I'll be able to talk to God again and find out why he didn't give me any magic, I thought as I sat in the nearly dark wagon. Only small streaks of light came through the canopy's cover.

Not long after my breakdown, the driver opened up the front curtain and said, "We're about to arrive in the kingdom. Make sure you got everything, 'cause I'm goin' to talk to the guards to receive my reward and then ship back out as soon as I can!" After he closed the curtain, I opened up the back curtains and retied them to either side of the frame. The sun was setting slowly but setting nonetheless. Against the grassy plains and the flowing streams we crossed over, it looked beautiful.

After making sure that all of our captives were accounted for, I went to wake up Sylia. When I approached her, her eyes shot open as if she was possessed. I jumped from being startled by her sudden awakening. Of course, it happened right as we went over a large bump. As the wagon kicked up, I received a little extra air on my jump. Slowly realizing what had happened, I started panicking right before I slammed right into the floor of the wagon. I heard a resounding crack come out from my body. At first, I was afraid that I had broken the wagon before I realized that I was missing some health. Fortunately, it didn't hurt at all, but I also didn't know what I had just damaged. *Maybe I just take health damage instead of having actual breaks or sprains?* I wondered, grasping at straws.

"You'll be fine," Sylia said with a yawn. When I looked back over toward her, she had already grabbed her pack and was putting all of the weapons and loot I had collected from the bandits into it. *Oh, right, I wanted to ask her about that bag. Especially after seeing this,* I thought.

"Soooo…is your backpack a bag of holding or something?" I asked curiously. *If it's a bag of holding, then that means that spatial magic exists in this world!* I thought excitedly. *Oh wait, I won't be able to use it even if it exists,* I quickly remembered, making depression overtake my excitement in an instant.

"Aren't all bags considered bags of holding?" she said groggily, even though she was clearly very aware. "This bag has an enchantment to link it to an infinite space that's free of time," she explained.

In other words, she literally has a bag of holding. She can store a seemingly infinite amount of items, and anything she puts in there won't age since it's a dimension displaced from a time plane, I thought as I stared at her.

"Right, so I guess that's why you didn't have much luggage, huh?" I asked.

Sylia nodded and went over to the bandit leader. "Has he been like this the whole time?" she asked, looking over at me.

"If you mean has he been sleeping the whole time right there, then yeah. You really did a number on him, eh?" I responded.

The wagon slowed down before coming to a halt. It wasn't as sudden as it did when the bandits appeared, which could only mean that we finally arrived at our destination.

As Sylia stared down at the bandit chief, I peeked my head out the back of the wagon to see a familiar sight. There was a huge wall, though this time, there wasn't a trench filled with wooden spikes. We were in what looked to be a dirt circle where other wagons were along with the horses that pulled them tied to posts. It actually looked a lot like a medieval parking lot.

All of the bandits collapsed down to the ground, taking a much-needed break. After the driver tied his horses to the post, he came to the back of the wagon. "Well, it looks like y'all survived! Tell ya what, I'll go get the guards so that you two can go get settled in!" the old wagon driver said, still sounding like he should be digging for gold instead of driving a wagon across the country.

The one who responded to the driver wasn't me or Sylia but rather the big beast man who had tried to comfort me about not having magic. "Please, you just want them to leave so that you can collect the reward for yourself. Don't think they'll fall for your tricks, old man," he said in a deep voice that was much less friendly than when he was talking about me not using magic. His voice was just as booming as before, but the intent in his voice felt...darker. It set my instincts into a fight or flight response, and I wasn't even the one that he was directing anything to.

The beast-man's comment drew attention, but not enough for people to stop what they were doing. The driver was clearly terrified. All he said before he left was, "O-of course. I'll go get the guards, stay here!" before running off toward the gate. It was around that time that Sylia silently appeared beside me and pulled me further into the wagon. She pulled the back curtain closed and did the same guarding spell that she had done on the other side.

"What all did you take from this man here?" she asked sternly with a nod toward the bandit chief.

I looked at her, confused, slightly tilting my head to the side. "What are you talking about? I didn't take anything from him. Hell, I don't even think I took his weapons. Why? Did he have something important?" I asked. I had doubts that anything that this man was carrying was going to really be all that important, but Sylia must've had a reason to ask.

"I think he had a ring," she said as she leaned close and started to whisper. "This is going to sound crazy, but I think I know him. When I was asleep, I had a dream, but it felt more like a memory. If he's who I think he is, then he always wears his ring. If I'm right, and I'm pretty sure that I am, that ring would prove everything."

Immediately, I tried to switch my tracking magic over to "Ring," which only brought me to receiving a message that stated, "Tracking failed—Those without life do not leave footprints."

That's an odd wording, but it's technically true, I guess.

"It's not crazy. But I promise I didn't take anything, much less a ring! Who do you think he is?" I asked, trying not to pry too much.

"I-it doesn't matter. If you say he didn't have a ring, then I guess I'm mistaken. Besides, if that person somehow became a bandit leader, I'd have a heart attack," Sylia said, crossing her arms and letting out a sigh that seemed like it was out of worry.

Before I could try to sate my curiosity any further, the sound of many footsteps could be heard outside. I moved toward the back curtain and ripped both sides open at the same time. Ahead of us was the driver and a handful of guards who were replacing the bandits' makeshift binds with wooden shackles.

Some of the guards were wielding spears and wore dark leather armor, while others were in full plate, using a sword and a shield. Behind all of them was a short man who had long silver hair draping from beneath a crown. His body was obviously very built at one point but had lost most of its form with age. He had four guards accompanying him, each looking like they could probably take over a town if they decided to.

Their gear looked top-notch. Two guards wore what looked like some sort of lizard-scaled armor, while the other two wore metal armor that was pitch black. The two heavy armored men had greatswords that were as black as night. For lack of a better term, they seemed to be black knights. The ones in scaled armor had bows slung on their backs and wielded some sort of staff made of pure white wood.

Anyone could glance at the old man and automatically realize who he was, even without the regal clothes that he was wearing. This man before us could be none other than the king of Heirshield. When he spoke, all tension in the air seemed to disappear. If you could weigh tension in an atmosphere, a feather would be heavier. "I presume that you two are the guests from Elsaria?" he said, clearly to the two of us in the wagon. "I see you've brought gifts as well! Gather your things and follow. We should discuss things more privately!" he said.

I jumped out of the wagon, and soon after, Sylia came out with the still body of the bandit chief. "What are you doing? Shouldn't we just leave him here for the guards to take care of?" I asked Sylia nervously. My heart felt like it was going to burst out of my chest in the presence of the king.

Sylia didn't even care to respond. I shifted my attention from her to the king, and it seemed like he was staring at her with a wide smile on his face. *Hold on, my eye's must be playing tricks on me,* I thought as I rubbed my eyes. When I looked back, he was staring at the man Sylia had in her arms as if in horror. His face was pale. It was as if he had seen a ghost. "I was told there would only be two of you. Who would this man in your arms happen to be?" he asked, trying to maintain his composure.

"Oh, uhh, that's the chief of the bandits, your majesty. We wanted to keep him separate from the others, plus he couldn't walk since he was knocked out. So that's how he ended up in the wagon with us, sir," I replied quickly, offering a very poor explanation. *I shouldn't be this terrified of him. He's just a king. I should be able to at least talk like a normal person!* I thought, annoyed with myself.

"I see," the king said, looking somewhat relieved. He was still pale but didn't seem as terrified as he was before my explanation. "Bring him with us, and you"—he pointed to a guard that was with the driver—"I'm allowing you to decide how to deal with the rest of these ruffians in the captain's absence. Guests from Elsaria come with me. You two knights, make yourselves useful and help transport this brute." He pointed to the two black knights.

The knights nodded as they sheathed their weapons. They each grabbed an arm and supported him as they began following the king.

After giving his orders, the king turned and started walking toward the gate with his gang of guards. Sylia started to follow before glancing back at me. "Come on, we have a lot to discuss, and the day's nearly over," she said, snapping me to my senses.

As I ran up and started walking beside her, I wondered, *Why does it feel like something fishy is going on here?*

3

Heirshield Royalty!

As soon as we went beyond the gates, it felt like I was in a town in a fantasy game. Most buildings had stone foundations but were primarily made of wood, while more modern buildings were made of primarily stone and a marble-like mineral. The roads were actually paved with what seemed to be stone bricks. There were even bridges crossing over streams! I fell in love with the city the moment I saw it. By the look on Sylia's face, she was evidently not very ecstatic about being in the city.

When we got to the castle, there was a large map of the city on a message board of sorts. The city was a large circle with four districts that had roads to connect to the castle in the very middle of the city. The districts themselves weren't anything special. There was a housing district, a military district, a trade district, and the old town. Each district had a road that followed the inner perimeter and would connect to the other district's roads as well as to a gate on each cardinal direction. The roads all intersected at the castle in the exact middle of the city.

As we walked into the castle, two of the guards that were escorting us broke away and went to what looked to be...well, a guard house. When we got inside, my feelings of love started to form into something more like astonishment. The castle from the outside looked large enough, but the actual inside was ginormous!

To either side of the room, there were two large windows that had purple banners hanging between them. The banners had a golden emblem of a shield with a crown above it. To the front, there were stairs that went to a semicircle platform, which had stairs going to the second floor on either side. As if to point out that they're royalty, they even had a violet carpet lined with golden stitching leading from the door to the stairs. The interior made it seem more like a mansion than a castle.

When we ascended the stairs, we came to a set of double doors that looked like thin planks bound together with iron. The king didn't even stop walking as he pushed them open with ease. He opened them with such force that they flung all the way into the wall and bounced off. *Either he's way stronger than I thought or he's using some enhancement magic. Whatever that case, I'm thankful those doors are durable. Otherwise, he'd have to replace them every time he came into this room!* I thought as I imagined the door's splintering whenever he opened them.

The room was very obviously a throne room. It looked a lot like the other rooms, only it was a lot more regal and had a large chair at the other end of the room. Like many of the modern buildings in town, the castle was made of stone and marble, and even though the throne room also used these materials, it had a much more intricate design.

The room was a large rectangle with a massive chandelier coming down in the middle. A long carpet much like the one in the entrance was on the floor. Many guards with weapons in hand stood off to either side of the room against the walls. Behind the throne was a large window that came to a peak near the top as if it was pointing to the engravings made in the marble in between it and the ceiling.

As soon as the king entered the room, all of the guards turned and knelt down. When the king walked toward his throne, the guards would turn themselves with his every step to always face toward him. It almost looked like they were trying to turn while stuck in a crouching animation in a game. When he reached his seat, he didn't sit down like you'd expect. He turned to face the lot of us, and with a wave of his hand, he said to the guards, "Leave us. Oh, but leave the boy."

Naturally, a few of the guards looked around in confusion. But when they saw the black knights drop the bandit chief and leave, they followed suit and slipped out the door without any questions. The king sat down and buried his head in his face.

"How've you been, Silly? The elves weren't too hard on you, right?" he asked, dropping his hands and looking at Sylia.

"Uncle, I'm here on official business, so I suggest we catch up later. Though since you asked, it could've been better. At least the dwarves and their ale made it bearable!" she responded as she and the king started laughing together.

Meanwhile, I just stood in shock at what I had heard. *Maybe I just misheard them,* I thought as I raised my hand to indicate I had a question.

The king turned from laughing ecstatically to hiding behind his throne, seemingly terrified. *Now I have two questions,* I thought.

After a few moments, Sylia composed herself and said, "Yes, Gray?" still smiling, but creating a new serious air around her.

"First question, UNCLE!" I shouted out. "Second question, why's Uncle King freaking out?" I asked as I lowered my hand. "Did he forget to take his pills this morning?" I joked.

"Ha ha, very funny," she responded coldly, making it very clear that it was not funny. "First answer, yes, he's my father's brother. At least he claims to be my uncle, even though..." She trailed off with a dejected look before stating, "Second answer, you're an other-worlder. Not only that, but all we know about is that you killed two creatures twenty times stronger than yourself."

"But...you said the only reason I was able to do that was because of that shadow guard or whatever! Why is this becoming an issue now?" I cried out in despair and confusion.

"Because now you aren't just dealing with me, and yes, you're right, the buffs the shadow guard gave definitely helped you out. Do you really think buffs alone would make it so you won? If you think that, then you're a complete moron!" she said before flicking me in the forehead.

With a loud *THUNK*, I was sent flying across the room. I landed right beside the king before I quietly said, "Freakin' hell, that hurt!" Somehow, my health bar didn't decrease at all, but my self-esteem certainly did.

Before I could attempt to get up, Sylia walked over and sternly said, "Listen, Gray. I know you aren't a real threat, but since you're an other-worlder, you aren't going to have the best reputation. I won't waste time with a history lesson, but most if not all great tragedies occur because of other-worlders."

I looked to the king beside me whose expression alone was enough to convince me that Sylia wasn't lying. I sat up and leaned against the wall.

"Why haven't I been killed or detained yet? Hell, why was I brought before a king? One who also sent his guards away, if I may add," I said, changing my gaze over to Sylia and then back to the king. Being this close, I actually got to see the king's facial features. His forehead was wrinkled and he had a scar that stretched from the outside of his green left eye to his ear. If I wasn't this close, I would have just assumed it was another wrinkle. His nose was larger than expected, since his large silver mustache made it look much more proportioned from afar. If someone just saw his face, it wouldn't be a stretch for someone to think that he was a dwarf.

"If Silly trusts you, then I believe I can trust you as well. I'm just a bit hesitant is all," the king said, staring into my eyes as if he was talking directly to my soul. His cowardice had entirely vanished, and he seemed like the man I saw when we first met. "I may be able to trust you as a person, but that doesn't amount to much. It wouldn't be a surprise if you were unaware of a power you had since you're a newly arrived other-worlder. That's how it happened for most of the others that caused tragedies in the pas—"

The king suddenly stopped talking when he glanced toward the center of the room. He started staring daggers at something before he angrily said, "Well, well, look who decided to join us in the land of the living. Care to explain everything that's happened so far, son?"

He walked toward the bandit chief who was barely sitting up and looking around in a daze, completely unaware of his situation.

"W-where am I? What happened?" he asked before the king stood right in front of him. "H-h-h-hey, Dad, you look...well," sputtered the bandit chief.

That was when I realized the king wasn't using the word *son* to play the noun game. He was literally talking to his son.

First Sylia is his niece, then I find out I'm a danger to society, and now the leader of the bandits is the guy's son? How many twists are there going to be in this place? I thought, silently freaking out and praying to God so that he would stop trying to make my brain explode.

While I was having my mini freak-out, Sylia crossed her arms and stared at the ban...the prince with a furrowed brow. "Uncle is that...is that actually Ichol?" she asked in complete surprise.

"Unfortunately. The last time you saw him, he was so small. It's not a surprise that you didn't recognize each other," the king responded without missing a beat. "Now that we're all here, it's time for the real meeting to begin. Come, and make sure he doesn't try anything, Sylia."

We all followed the king out of the throne room. After taking a right at the stairs, we ended up in a room with a large round table and a circular skylight above it that mirrored the table's size.

Either the founders of this city really enjoyed circles or someone from Earth told them the story of King Arthur, I thought to myself. There were twelve seats in total at the table, all at the positions of numbers on a clock. The king sat at twelve o'clock, while Sylia went to three o'clock after setting Ichol down at six o'clock. So I naturally went to nine o'clock so that we would all be an even space away from each other.

When I was seated, the king cleared his throat and said, "Now, we're all equals at this table. I expect each of you to treat each other with respect. The first topic I wish to bring to attention is Ichol's misdoings."

As soon as that was brought up, Ichol looked down in shame. His father then said, "Your fate will be decided by these two, and we will be the ones to decide the fate of those who joined your merry band."

Sylia and I both exchanged looks of confusion and then turned our attention back to the king. "Sir, what exactly do you mean we'll decide his fate?" I asked before Sylia could open her mouth to ask the same question.

"What do you think I mean? You and Silly will interrogate him right now and then decide on a just punishment," the king said with his arms crossed and his head tilted to the sky.

This is more how I imagined a King to be. Though I figured he would act like this to his servants, not to someone he had just been cowering before in fear.

Unsurprisingly, Sylia wasted no time in questioning her cousin and quickly found out that we were the first people the group came across. She also found out that most of the members were gutter rats and sons of poor merchants. They all were involved so they could get money, but Ichol was just in it for the infamy.

"What do you mean you were in it for the infamy?" I asked when he made his claim.

"Father's always busy with politics and such. I thought that if I led a feared group of bandits and then betrayed them and turned them all in that I would get some recognition and we would grow closer," he said with his silky voice of confidence instead of his cowardly voice he had used for his dad and Sylia. *I thought that we were all supposed to be equal at this table.* I couldn't help but think that he thought of me as lesser than them. He wouldn't be wrong, but it still annoyed me.

"So basically, you were going to disappear, ruin countless people's lives, and then betray your men so that you could get closer with your dad?" I asked in pure disbelief. *Wouldn't it be easier to have just taken out an actual group of bandits?* I wondered.

"From what he's saying, that seems to be the gist of it," the king said, replying for his son. "Luckily, you were the only ones that had been attacked. Otherwise, this would be a lot harder to rectify. Be that as it may, he and his... colleagues must still be punished. Now that we know the details, I'll leave you two to decide his fate. Meanwhile, we'll use that father-son chat he wanted to discuss what to do with his followers."

The king rose out of his seat, and Ichol obediently followed. Soon after, they disappeared through a door that I hadn't noticed the whole time we were in the room. Sylia and I were left alone. A few moments passed, and neither of us said anything; for some reason, the atmosphere felt really tense. Perhaps it was because we were just told to become judge and jury for her cousin?

I decided to break the silence and said, "So… Silly, huh? That's a cute nickname, albeit a bit…silly." I looked at Sylia who had no reaction. From what I'd seen the last few days, I figured she would've either gotten angry or blushed and tried to explain it away. But instead, she was just sitting there, staring off into space.

I got up and walked over to Sylia. "Hello? Earth to Sylia? Actually, I guess it's Zynka to Sylia, right?" I called as I waved my hand in front of her face. I poked her face, I kept tapping the top of her head, and I even tried tickling her, even though it definitely would've ended in my death! After getting no response from anything I did, I walked toward the door that the king and Ichol went into. *I already have an idea for Ichol's punishment, and if Sylia doesn't like my choice, then I'll just have to face the consequences later. It's her fault for not responding*, I thought.

Hesitantly, I knocked on the door, and a few moments later, I heard the king give permission to enter. When I opened the door and walked in, I had to turn around because it seemed as if I had just walked into the room I came from. The only difference between the two was the only door, the one I had just entered from.

"It's a spatial magic spell, don't look so amazed, boy," the king explained while looking pleased with himself. "I imagine you wouldn't be here unless you and Sylia have already come up with something?" he asked with an eyebrow raised.

"Well, Sylia's a bit…frozen? I don't know if we should be worried about that. But technically, I came up with something, if you're okay with that," I said nervously. I don't know why, but my heart was pounding. Something about this whole situation was scaring me.

"Don't worry about her, I'm sure she's just lost in thought. Ever since she was little, she'd always get so focused that no one could get through to her. That aside, let's hear what you've got then," the king said. I took a deep breath and prepared myself.

"I want Ichol to reform the goal of the members of his group to make it so that they become useful members of society. They aren't bad people. They were just dealt a shitty hand, and then someone came along, telling them he could help them. They obviously thought they had no other choice. It's not fair for them to have been pulled into this and then not given an actual chance!" I spouted out.

I wanted to be able to do something for them. After hearing the story of how they were all gutter rats or merchants down on their luck, something made me want to help them. *I don't know the full details of them joining. But I do know that only a few of them tried to escape and one of them even tried to comfort me about not having magic. They're not all bad, and if we can turn them onto a better path, then we should!* I thought.

The king and Ichol just looked at me in disbelief until the king eventually said, "Very well. If that's what you wish, then I see no reason to not allow that to be a punishment. However, this takes care of the issue of what to do with the prisoners, so Silly will have to decide another, more personal punishment then. To be honest, other-worlder, I didn't expect you to care about this world's people like that."

"That seems slightly…worldist? Whatever racism is but toward someone from another world. Either way, I'll still take the compliment," I said, laughing nervously afterwards. "Oh, right, speaking of racism, could I ask you a question about Sylia?" *What a way to begin a question,* I thought.

The king's brow furrowed, and with a slight frown, he asked, "I take it Silly said something about you being 'a disgusting human?'"

I grinned and nodded.

With a sigh, he explained, "I'm assuming you know that Sylia is half-elf and half-human. Elves generally have a…superiority complex, to say the least. Not all elves have it, but a majority of them do. Silly is special in the sense that she has racial personality lapses. She acts the same for the most part, but she heavily shows traits of whichever race she's been around. At least, that's how my top healers explained it. I hope that answered your question well enough."

"Err...yes, sir, thank you for the explanation," I said uncomfortably. *I expected at least a little bit of resistance from him.*

"Now then, boy, how about you answer a question of my own?" he said with a commanding air around him.

I gulped and nodded. *Well, this explains why he answered it so easily. If he doesn't have to give information about himself or the kingdom to get information he wants, it works out greatly in his favor,* I explained to myself.

The king clasped his hands together and put his thumbs underneath his chin. "What's your goal here in Heirshield? Is it to become a grand mage, perhaps to become a merchant? Or maybe it's to lay siege and claim it for yourself? What drives you to become a citizen of this kingdom?" he asked.

The way he asked made me feel like he was my future employer conducting an interview instead of my future king. He seemed genuinely interested in why I was here. *Well, of course he's interested! He probably wasn't joking when he asked about me trying to take over the kingdom. I should try to put his fears at ease,* I planned.

"Well, I'm planning on joining the Fighters Guild. Beyond that, though, I don't really know. I don't plan on becoming some amazing adventurer or anything, but it's not like I entirely hate the idea of that, y'know?" I said, grinning and scratching the back of my head.

"I can't say I'm surprised. When you go down that path, please don't learn any spells destructive enough to destroy the city. I've had to put too many off-worlders to the gallows thanks to that," the king said, looking down in shame.

"Oh, don't worry about that, I can't use magic," I said in an attempt to assure him while I closed my eyes and waved my hand as if I was pushing away his worries. When I opened my eyes, both the king and Ichol were staring at me with wide eyes. "Uhh...you two okay?" I asked nervously. After all this time, I wouldn't be that worried if it was just the king. With Ichol becoming suddenly interested, though, I was worried.

Ichol turned to his father and spouted, "Y-you don't think that he's the one, do you? There's no way that it could be someone like him!"

"What? Is there some sort of prophecy or something that some magicless other-worlder who is going to save or destroy the planet or something?" I asked as I let out a laugh at my joke. The other two, however, weren't laughing. "Oh God, please tell me you two are joking! Or at least that I'm wrong!" I shouted out. *I don't want to be part of a prophecy. I CAN'T be part of a prophecy! To have the weight of the world on my shoulders! That's too much, man! It's gotta be a joke, there's no way it's not!* I screamed out in my brain.

"My boy, how you knew of the legend, I'll never know. The general public isn't even supposed to know about the chance of the hero destroying the planet. If you are the person the prophecy foretold, however..." The king grimaced as he trailed off. I wasn't sure whether he was thinking about the hero being me or the situation that the world might soon be in. Either way, I was somewhat offended.

Before the king could resume his thoughts, Ichol spouted out, "Let's go see how cousin Silly is doing, eh!"

Instantly, the king's face lit up. "Ahh, yes! Young Sylia is a guest. We shouldn't leave her alone!" he spouted as he quickly left the room, shutting the door behind him. It was clear that the old king didn't enjoy thinking about the subject and was quite glad to have a reason to leave.

As I made my way toward the door to leave, Ichol took a stance in between it and me. He looked me dead in the eyes and said in a low hushed tone, "Listen here, cur, you will not mention the prophecy to anyone. Nor will you bring it up around my father. I can't have him croaking from stress just yet. The first phase of my plan was going perfectly until you came along, and I refuse to let you ruin it anymore. Do I make myself clear?"

When he talked, his voice struck fear into me. It was like when a man loses his temper and shouts, except he had that effect without raising his voice.

I couldn't muster the courage to respond verbally, so I just nodded my head.

"Good, it's quite the pleasure to see that you know your place. Oh, and don't go mentioning any of this to Sylia or my father. This should just be between us, wouldn't you say?" he said with a devilish smile forming. He walked out the door before I could even respond.

I stood there for a moment in shock of what just happened and realized that I hadn't been breathing. *Jesus Christ, that guy... How did this brat of a prince suddenly turn into such a Chad? Have I ever been so unnerved that I actually lost the ability to speak?* I wondered. After my heart calmed down and my breathing went back to normal, I went through the door to find Ichol, staring at Sylia with his mouth wide open and a panicked look on his face.

"Can you do that? Actually, does it matter? It's your 'punishment,' so you kind of have to, right?" Sylia asked the panicking Ichol.

"Maybe if you were asking for normal lodging, I could easily do it, but you're practically asking me to get you a damned fortress? There's no way I can do that!" Ichol shouted out, sounding like an entirely different person than the one I had just seen. It was as if the man that I'd just spoken with never existed in the first place.

"What's going on?" I asked as I walked into the room before the door behind me disappeared.

Sylia shot a glance toward me and said, "Since I was asked to produce a 'more personal punishment,' I figured that Ichol could pay for our living expenses."

"Umm... What exactly are you considering living expenses?" I asked with my eyes narrowing as I walked to her side.

"A house with six beds, a kitchen, a living area, a bathhouse that has separate sides for men and women, an alchemy room, a storage room, an armory, a shooting range, a training ground, and a treasury. It's pretty simple. I don't know why this is such a big deal," Sylia said without any hints of hesitation or shame. When her list finished, I just stood there, staring off into space, attempting to comprehend everything she just asked for.

"How does that all even fit on a property?" I spouted out. "Also, I'm pretty sure you mean household expenses because living expenses is just the cost of living whereas household expenses take into account lodging," I accidentally said out loud when I just meant to think to myself.

"Then he's paying for our household expenses," Sylia said matter-of-factly. *So fast! She just took what I said about the differences as fact! She didn't even try to fight me on it,* I thought in surprise.

"No, nope, nuh-uh. It's impossible!" Ichol said. "If you want me to pay for a normal house in the housing district, I can do that. But I can't do what you're demanding! There's not even a property with enough space!"

"Actually," the king said amidst all of his sons shouting, "there is one place. You wouldn't be within the walls, but you would be on kingdom lands."

As soon as that came out of his mouth, Ichol slowly turned toward him and gave him a look as if to say, "Keep your mouth shut!"

"Oh? Where exactly would that be, Uncle?" Sylia asked, staring at Ichol with a huge sly grin on her face.

"Just off the coast of Loch Crest is an outpost that became abandoned after a war with the Amphobians. The distance would be quite a hassle if you were to come to town every day, but it would be able to suit all of your requests and then some."

The word *Amphobian* caught me off guard. *Was there a war with frogs and lizards? Could they have been giant frogs and lizards? Or maybe they were lizard-humanoids like the Argonians from The Elder Scrolls games! I think I'm gonna need to do some research into the races of this world when we get time,* I thought, making a mental note.

With a deep sigh, Ichol caved and hopelessly muttered to himself, "How am I even supposed to get the deed for an old military outpost?" Even though he had some huge and potentially evil plan for the kingdom, I still felt sympathetic for the situation he was in. Meanwhile, the other two just laughed at his distressed comment.

After everything had been decided, Sylia insisted that we go find an inn that would take us until our housing situation was completed. The king protested with promises that we could just stay at the castle, but Sylia turned him down for whatever reason. After a few minutes of arguing, the two settled on us staying for dinner and going to an inn that the king recommended.

Dinner was uneventful, especially since the food was ready by time we got to the dining room, so we didn't have to make small talk while waiting. When I heard that we were going to be having Orc, I was wary, to say the least. However, the food was surprisingly delicious. Orc tasted just like bacon or ham from Earth. Apparently, it was a delicacy since the Orcs only swelled in numbers every fifteen or so years before stagnating until the next time they had a "baby boom."

Once we finished our meal, Sylia and I decided it was time to take our leave. Not before the king could stop Sylia and give her money for our stay, though. By time we left, night had completely fallen, and the town was taken over by the light of lanterns. Even though Sylia insisted she knew the way, we ended up getting lost around the city until she finally swallowed her pride and asked for directions at a tavern.

With help, we eventually found our way to the inn. On the outside, it wasn't anything special. In fact, it looked more like a weapon's shop or something like that from the outside. As soon as we went inside, though, everything changed. It was so impressive that it would put most hotels on Earth to shame.

The lobby alone had to have been as large as the castle's foyer if not bigger! The floors glowed a dim yellow as if they were reflecting light from an unknown location. The walls were made to look like they were stones on a cliffside. The reception desk was manned by a small green fairy who explained that the desk was a living tree that had been grown into the shape when she saw the confusion on my face.

After Sylia got us a room with two beds, the fairy handed her a small crystal, and we proceeded through the halls. As we passed, I was able to catch a glance into the dining hall. The walls were lined with server stations that had food pans on top. A long counter attached to the kitchen was on the left side of the room. The chairs were already set on their respective tables, and the staff was cleaning up the trays of food as they closed for the night. It seemed like a normal hotel's dining room from Earth, although the size of the room and the variety of the food was fit for a king and his court.

Just past the dining room was a large archway that led to a courtyard that by no means should have been able to exist. The atmosphere reminded me of how I always imagined a rainforest would feel. There was a waterfall, and even though it was humid, the courtyard felt cool enough to where it wasn't uncomfortable. The trees that shot up toward the sky were so tall that there was no way we wouldn't be able to see them from the castle.

"Is this spatial magic?" I muttered to myself.

Sylia looked back toward me and said, "Nope. Wait, where did you even learn about spatial magic?"

"The king told me about it back when I walked into that room he created while we were supposed to figure out Ichol's punishment. Speaking of that... Actually, before I get sidetracked, what do you mean by no? If this isn't spatial magic, then how can this place exist in the kingdom?" I asked, genuinely puzzled on how it was possible.

"Short answer, the arch before the courtyard was a ley gate. Long answer, the mana line or ley line in the kingdom and this place is the same. Some mages called ley-makers figured out that, somehow, they could harness mana at points along a line to make a gate for instant travel down it. That's about all I know, though. I'm not well-versed in line-tapping," she confessed.

I raised an eyebrow at the term *line-tapping* but figured that some other-worlder probably coined it. That or it was just a pure coincidence. *It's probably just a method of magic that focuses on literally tapping into the lines. Though, if that's the case, wouldn't it be pretty useless unless they could manipulate the line or use the mana for some sort of production means? In terms of combat, it's very situational too, right? I guess this is another thing to add onto my list of stuff to look into,* I thought as I grinned.

While I was lost in thought, Sylia held out the crystal she had been given at the lobby. The crystal's shine brought me back to reality, and that's when I realized that we were at our room. I don't know what I expected, but it seemed that the courtyard we had entered was lined at the perimeter with buildings that looked like they belonged at a motel. I can say, though, that I wouldn't have expected to see a motel in the rainforest, much less in a fantasy world's inn.

When Sylia touched the crystal to a small pad, the door swung open, revealing the inside. There were two beds up against the right wall with a nightstand in between them. The nightstand had an analogue clock above it and a lantern on it that somehow lit itself a few moments after the door had opened. Straight ahead of the door was a small bathroom.

We walked in, and the door slammed itself behind us, causing me to jump. Sylia, however, just walked to the far bed without a care and collapsed on top of it, letting out a groan. "I hate that place, it's always so suffocating," she said in a way that made her sound more whiny than Ichol somehow.

I let out a chuckle, and Sylia pulled her head off of the sheets "What are you laughing about, Mr. 'I want you to reform the bandits?'" she asked mockingly.

I just dully looked at her and said, "Like you wouldn't have done the same. If you didn't care what happened to them, you would've just killed all of them. Also, I was laughing about you, ya doofus, imagine complaining about being in a castle with a king who adores you. Couldn't be me," I said, rolling my eyes. "You complain about it being suffocating. Do you know how uncomfortable I felt that whole time? It felt like I was just a complete nuisance!" I exclaimed out at her.

"To be fair, you kind of are," Sylia said nonchalantly.

When she said that, my heart just sank. *It's not like I don't know that, but you don't just say it...* I thought to myself. I looked down, sat on the foot end of the bed nearest the door, and a frown took over my face.

"Why do you think I'm making Ichol get us a place where you and your future party can live in and train? I gotta make you as useful as possible and make you have some sort of relations so you don't decide to destroy the planet with your otherworldly powers," she said almost mockingly but with a hint of seriousness.

Needless to say, I was taken aback by her thoughtfulness. "Wh-what do you mean?" I asked in surprise.

"Gray, my job is to make it so that you don't cause some disaster like the other-worlders before you. My personal objective is to make you someone worthy of being called my apprentice. Logically, the easiest way to do that is to help make you someone of high rank in the Fighters Guild. Though, to do that, you're going to need to join or create a party. Having a place to safely rest and train will make it so that your group's chances of survival are a lot higher too. So really, it's a win-win situation. You get to live, and I get a bigger legacy!" Sylia explained as if she was some sort of villain monologuing about their master plan.

I looked at her, dumbfounded. I honestly wasn't surprised by her objective, but instead the lengths that she was going to. "Should you have told me all of that?" I asked, failing to understand what she gained from deciding to tell me all about her plan.

"What's the point in not? You already owe me for making it, so I basically lost my job. Now you just know how you're going to repay me," she replied slyly. "Now get some sleep. You're going to join the guild tomorrow, and you need to get there around eight to get signed up before quests go out. Of course, that's if you want to find any groups that are willing to take you out on your debut quest."

At that moment, something crossed my mind. "Is there a sign-up fee or something like that? All I have is a few silver," I said as I pulled out the three silver coins I had taken from the bandits.

Sylia groaned, "How did they only have three silver? Gah, I'll spot you the money fo—" she said abruptly, stopping before asking, "Gray...did we ever collect the reward for those bandits?"

I had to take a moment to think before answering because so much had happened today. "I, uhhh, I don't think that we did," I answered. When I looked at Sylia, it seemed that our roles from before had reversed.

This time, it was her turn to look down with complete despair being shown in her eyes. It was quiet, but I could barely make out her saying, "That sly old bastard. I'm going to have to go back there tomorrow."

"Silly, you good?" I asked.

Luckily, it was enough to snap her out of it. "Yeah. Like I said, I'll spot you the money, and then I guess I'm going to the castle tomorrow to collect our reward so we have some bonus money," she said with a sigh. "Will you be able to find your way there okay? I'd rather us split up instead of both going somewhere only one of us needs to go," she explained.

"Yeah, I'll be fine. Also, you don't need to explain everything. I'm not a toddler that doesn't understand simple stuff like efficiency," I said, shooting a glare her way.

She just giggled and said, "Yeah, sure you aren't." Before I could form a rebuttal, she quickly shut off the lantern on the nightstand and said something along the lines of, "G'nigh!"

I let out a sigh of defeat and surrendered myself to the bed. I hadn't realized it the whole time we had been in the room, but the bed was an actual bed. Unlike the straw bed in the other inn, this was literally a mattress. It really was like someone from Earth had made this place. I fell asleep quickly after my realization with comforting thoughts of Earth.

4

The Fighters Guild!

The next day, I awoke to Sylia shaking me like a doll with a panicked look in her eyes. Still a bit drowsy, I sleepily made a noise, "Hmmm?"

Which Sylia responded to with, "GRAY, WE OVERSLEPT! GET UP! WE'RE GONNA BE LATE!"

In an instant, I was completely awake. Not so much from Sylia shouting right in my face, but more because it gave me PTSD of when I was in school and would oversleep.

The two of us rushed out of the room and ran through the courtyard. When I didn't see anyone in the courtyard or in the hall past the courtyard, I started to panic even more than Sylia had been. *How late could we have possibly slept?* I wondered to myself. When we stopped to catch our breath by the dining room, I glanced in and noticed people putting out plates of food with what seemed to be waffles, eggs, and sausages.

That was when I thought to ask, "Silly, what time is it?"

By the time I finished my question, she had already managed to grab a plate of food and wolf down part of it. With a half full mouth and a large smile, she said, "Time for breakfast!" Rather, that's what she tried to say; the whole response was very unintelligible.

I just stared daggers at her, unable to come up with the words to express how frustrated I was. *I've never really been great at waking up early. Especially when someone makes me panic for something as simple as the kitchen starting to serve breakfast!* I felt like I was about to explode with anger, though Sylia ran in and grabbed a plate for me before I could. "Just try some, trust me, it'll all be worth it!" she coaxed.

I grabbed the plate out of her hands and breathed out a sigh of annoyance. Sylia sat on the floor and looked up at me in anticipation as I picked up a waffle to take a bite. As soon as I took the bite, I felt as if I had just drunk a whole pot of coffee. If I had a stamina bar, I'm sure it would've just gone from empty to full in that moment.

Before I knew it, my plate was completely cleaned, and I was still yearning for more. Unfortunately, there was a sign on the dining room door that stated "NO SECONDS! WE ARE SORRY FOR THE INCONVENIENCE!" *Why did they let her take a second plate then?* I wondered.

I turned to where Sylia had been sitting on the floor to find her completely knocked out and quietly snoring. *How did she go back to sleep after eating something like that! Not to mention, why didn't she just go back to the room?* I wondered to myself. Part of me wanted to leave her there as revenge for waking me up so early, but I wasn't able to let myself. I flicked her forehead softly until it became annoying enough to wake her up.

When she finally woke up, her forehead had a small red dot on it from where I had been flicking. *I'm just going to keep that detail to myself. I don't have a death wish*, I thought.

"Gray, if you ever wake me up like that again, I'll flick you back just as many times. I won't hold back either," she sleepily said. Immediately, I was reminded of when she sent me flying in the throne room. A look of terror must have formed on my face because Sylia had a large, sly grin. "Good, looks like that's all cleared up. Oh, right! Here's the money for the sign-up fee." She handed me two gold pieces which I immediately tucked away into the pocket of my jeans.

When I looked back up, she was already gone. *How did she…?* I thought to myself, letting my thoughts trail off. When I walked into the lobby, I noticed there was a pocket map of the city. Naturally, I picked one up. *Even if I don't use it, I'd rather have it than get lost again*, I thought, feeling like yesterday's situation justified taking one.

Thankfully, the map had places of interest marked on it. The Fighters Guild was located in between the trade district and the military district. Unfortunately, the inn was in the old town district on the direct opposite side of the city. I shot a glance at a small clock near the reception desk. *It's only 6:30? I guess that I could cut through the trade district then to kill some time,* I thought excitedly. Getting to go to a marketplace was a dream of mine. *I hope it has an outside market and isn't just a bunch of buildings for shopping!* I prayed as I headed out.

The old town looked entirely different than it did at night. The light posts were just wooden crosses with lanterns hanging from them. The buildings were constructed entirely of wood with thatch roofs instead of the stone foundation and shingle roofs that the newer buildings had.

Navigating through the old town was easy enough, and I was out and onto the main road in no time. To my left was an exit to the city while to my right was the castle. To get to the trade district, I had to cross a bridge that split the sections of the city apart.

As I crossed the bridge, I noticed that the trade district seemed a lot more lively than the old town. The canals below the bridge had fishermen with nets looking to catch whatever fish came into the city from the river it was built over. The road had small crowds of people and many horse-drawn carriages that brought goods in and out of the city. The light posts were more akin to Earth's than the old towns, the only difference being the lanterns atop the metal pole instead of lightbulbs working off of electricity.

This time, I looked both ways before crossing the street, sure I was in a bit of a rush, but I didn't want to die in the same way that I died before. Getting hit by a vehicle, horse-drawn or not, wasn't something I particularly wanted to do twice.

The trade district's structure was significantly more complex than the old town. The district was outlined with buildings that were various shops and guilds. The main attraction of the district was the market that was in between all the shops. It seemed like you could find anything there from clothes to potions to food or even books on crafting. There was a tent or stall for seemingly anything you could ever need.

The complexity of the district didn't come from the market but rather the alleyways that stem from the main road to the market. There were only a few wide roads, which were primarily for vehicles transporting merchants' goods. So the alleyways that provided back entrances to the shops became narrow streets that flooded with people.

I didn't buy anything since most shops were closed, and the market sellers were still laying out their wares for the day. Plus, I had such a small amount of money to my name that I didn't feel comfortable spending. So I ended up using the district a lot like a school's library. In other words, I used it to get from one side of the district to the other without having to take any convoluted paths.

I pulled out my pocket map to figure out where I was. *From what I can tell, I should be an alleyway or two away from the guild house. Man, it feels like I set out on this journey to become an adventurer so long ago, but it's only really been three or so days,* I fondly thought. Usually, when time feels longer than it actually is, it's a bad thing. But this journey didn't feel horrible; instead, it felt meaningful.

I entered into an alley and heard a man's voice come from behind me, "You know, it ain't polite to hold onto so much coin and not support your local businesses," he said, putting a lot of emphasis on the "S's" in businesses. I expected to turn around and see a snake man, but it was much, much worse. I turned around, and all I could see was a petite woman in a velvet dress. She struck me as much more elegant than a merchant would be.

My face tightened as I squinted before taking off my glasses and rubbing my eyes to make sure what I saw was real. When I put my glasses back on, I heard, "What? You never seen a lady before?" in the same manly tone coming from the woman. I was too taken aback to reply. In complete confusion, my fight or flight response kicked in, and I ran in the opposite direction of the woman before hearing, "Oh, we can't be having that. Tyrone get him!"

In an instant, my body was grinding against the stone walkway. As I moved, I could feel tiny rocks embedding themselves into my face, tearing their way through the skin on my cheek. When I stopped moving, I glanced up as best I could at the figure on top of me. Tyrone was a small man. Standing up, he was about as tall as I would be while sitting down and slouching. He was also very… plump. He reminded me of how I pictured the Roman god, Bacchus, except shorter.

"Good boy, Tyrone. Now look for his purse. It must be underneath that tight shawl," the manly woman commanded. In one fluid move, he jumped up, flipped me over, and landed directly on my chest, entirely knocking the wind out of me. After a minute of not being able to figure out how to unzip my sweatshirt, he gave up and reached his hand into the tail end of the sweatshirt. At this point, I had more or less recovered from him jumping on my chest and decided there was only one thing I could do.

"HELPPPPP!" I screamed out, accidentally activating my taunt ability. The ability ended up boosting the volume of my shout, which caused Tyrone to jump back in surprise. One of his ears was leaking a small amount of blood onto the side of his face. From above me, I heard someone say, "Yeah, yeah, I was working on it. You didn't need to shout, kid." The mysterious stranger appeared right in front of me. Instead of doing a cool landing, he completely belly flopped onto the stone.

When he got up, the stone where he had landed was completely cracked. As he casually brushed the dust off of his clothes, I noticed that he had no signs of taking any damage. His long wavy blonde hair made me think of a warrior, although his rough wool tunic and leggings made him look like a peasant. *Then again, though, he did just fall from the sky and come out unscathed, so maybe he actually is a warrior?* I wondered to myself.

As he faced Tyrone and the mystery lady, he asked, "Myrolda? You're the one behind all the robberies in this area? When will you give up this same old song and dance?"

The woman in front of him snapped her fingers and then crossed her arms. "Come on, Falkeen, is it really a surprise? You know how I can't resist taking a few coins when that freshly minted smell

71

rolls around," she said, sounding a lot more like a woman now. *Was she using a spell to mask her voice?* I wondered.

The man named Falkeen let out a chuckle. "I'm amazed that old habit of yours hasn't died. Enough small talk, though, are you gonna come quietly? Or is it going to be just like every other time?"

Myrolda just gave him a cackling laugh.

Falkeen let out a sigh and said, "That's what I was worried about. Hey, kid, this is the part where you run away before the big battle breaks out and get a guard."

He didn't need to tell me twice. I rose to my feet and instantly ran away. As I ran, I shouted behind me, "I'M SO SORRY, THANK YOU SO MUCH, SIR!" I ran out of the alley and stopped to catch my breath. *Wait, since when do I act like a helpless child? Oh right, basically the whole time I've been in this world. I wish I wasn't so useless,* I thought before I went to find a guard.

Eventually, I finally found a guard and quickly explained what was going on before bringing him to the alley. All traces of Falkeen had disappeared aside from the crater he left when he fell. Tyrone and Myrolda were both knocked out cold on the pavement with a piece of parchment over them.

"Where'd that blonde-haired guy go?" I wondered out loud as the guard picked up the parchment.

Instantly, the guard knew who I was talking about. "Oh, it was Mr. Falk? This is usually how he operates, so I've never gotten to meet him in person. You're so lucky! People say that he's so strong he could defeat three dragons by himself! Others say that he's the first hero that we've seen in a long time! I would give anything to meet a legend like him!" he explained to me ecstatically. It was like he was a fanboy talking about his favorite celebrity.

For me, the experience was like I had just played a game with a pro player that everyone idolized, but I didn't know who he was. Then by the time I found out who they were, it didn't matter anymore.

"I'm sorry, I kinda went off there. You're free to go. If Mr. Falk didn't lay you out, then you're probably not a criminal. Don't worry about testifying either, this letter should be enough," the guard said as he raised the parchment.

"Oh, okay. Thanks for your help!" I responded, relieved that my plans wouldn't be ruined. When I turned to walk away, I felt a tap on the shoulder.

"Wait, you're a tourist, right? Where do you wanna go? I'll point you in the right direction. It's really easy to get lost in these alleys," he offered.

"What gave you that impression? I mean, I'm going to be staying here for a while, but it is my first time in the city. How could you tell that I was new in town, though?" I asked.

"So you're not a tourist? I just assumed that you were because of that pocket map. There's no use for them since everyone can just use the menu, so hotel's usually have them for people to take as a memento of their time in the city," he explained.

"I...I completely forgot about the map in the menu," I said, utterly defeated by not being able to remember such an important thing.

"Well, it's just speculation, but maybe that's why you were targeted. Ah, well, just remember the key points of the system, and you'll be fine! If you're going to be staying here in the city, you should get used to the layout, so I'll let you explore for yourself. Stay out of trouble!" he said with a smile.

I thanked him again and exited the alley.

As I walked toward the Fighters Guild, my thoughts turned to what the guard said about Falkeen. *It seems I met someone really powerful. I'm lucky that it was him and not a random person that was as powerless as me,* I thought. A part of me wanted to meet Falkeen again under different circumstances. Though another part of me wanted to never see him again. *He's always going to remember me as the guy who got sat on.*

By the time I came to that revelation, I was standing in front of the door to the Fighters Guild. All of a sudden, I got butterflies in my stomach, and my heart began to dance. *Once I walk through this door, my second life will change forever,* I thought as I took a deep breath and mentally prepared myself.

The instant I opened the door, I thought I had entered the wrong place. The place was completely run down. Small trickles of light poured in from two large dusty windows illuminating the wide room while making the atmosphere dreary. The floor in the opening was made up of a light wood with large holes that allowed you to see the outline of the rats beneath that were creating a song with their footsteps.

To the left, the floor transformed into a step that led to a cobblestone-floored room with many tables that hosted benches filled with groups of people. Some seemed to be on the edge of their seats, while others were simply enjoying breakfast and conversing with one another.

Directly to the right was a wall with six different cork boards that had their borders lined in different materials. Directly ahead was a wide counter with a woman and a man.

The man was the spitting image of an old Viking. His hair and beard were silver and in long braids. His face was very tight and had many wrinkles that seemed to stem from his eyes. He donned a leather cuirass with a visible chain mail vest beneath. Beside him was some sort of weapon with a long handle that stuck up over the counter. He was reading something that looked like a medieval newspaper.

The woman was a bit harder to get a good look at because her face was flat against the desk. It didn't take a genius to tell that she was sleeping. She seemed to be some sort of witch, even wearing the iconic pointy hat and jet-black robes. Beside her, she had a wooden staff with the classic circular curl at the tip. Her hair was a deep-green, looking like moss inside of a dark forest.

When I approached the desk, I went to the old Viking first. Before I could say anything, the old man calmly said, without looking at me, "Apologies, lad, but we aren't accepting job requests until after the current requests are released. You're free to wait in our dining area, however."

"Oh, I'm not… I'm actually here to register with the guild," I replied sheepishly to the old man.

He looked up from his paper and looked me up and down before slapping the back of the witch's chair, startling her awake with a jump. "Looks like you're up, lassie!" he said to the woman.

Now that she was awake, I was able to get a good look at her. Her eyes were a deep yet moderate purple akin to that of the purple hyacinth. Besides that, none of her features really stuck out. She was clearly young, however. "Hello... What can I...do for you?" she asked in a wispy voice with long pauses between her words.

"I'm looking to register?" I said questionably.

"O...kay, please...follow me," she said as she rose and walked out from the counter. She led me to a staircase that was against the wall of the stone floored dining area. It was so dark at the staircase that I had to be right on the woman's heels to keep sight of her. When we reached the top, there was a hallway that luckily had a skylight that lit up the area. There was a door on the left side of the hall, one to the right, and one directly ahead. We proceeded through the door on the left. As soon as I stepped through, it was like we had gone into an entirely different building.

The wood of the floor looked polished, there were two blood-red couches, and a table which had a blindingly bright crystal upon it. The room also had lanterns that expelled any remaining darkness in the room. On a wall was a tapestry of six circles that contained different symbols on them surrounded by a larger circle that seemed to be the planet.

The woman took a seat on the far couch and motioned for me to do the same on the other couch. Once I was sitting, she asked, "What is...your name?"

"Grayson, with an A," I replied.

As soon as I did, she pulled out a quill from seemingly nowhere and began to write in a circle that appeared below the now dimming crystal. "How old...are you?" she asked.

Technically speaking, I'm not even a week old, I thought before answering. "Nineteen."

To which she nodded and said, "A year...younger...than me."

I found it a little hard to believe that she wasn't younger. *She has no reason to lie about something like that, though. So I guess she is older than me, huh?* I thought.

The next command she ushered out took me by surprise. "Take your shirt...off and turn...around, please," she said as she picked up the dim crystal.

I felt my face getting hot as I got flustered. "Wha…What did you say?" I stammered out nervously.

The woman blushed slightly and bashfully repeated, "Turn around…and take off…your shirt."

I knew what you actually said, you didn't have to repeat yourself! But you can't just randomly say something like that! I screamed out in my thoughts. I stood up and slowly turned around. When I took my sweatshirt and my shirt off, I noticed that I was a little more lean and muscular than I remembered.

Now that I think about it, I don't know if I've taken my shirt off since coming to this world. I took my sweatshirt off when the wolf slashed me… I really need to get these sewn up too, I thought, realizing that I'd been walking around with a shirt and sweatshirt with large claw marks in them. *No wonder why the king and Ichol were looking down on me so much.*

I threw my clothes onto the couch in front of me. Shortly after, I felt a sharp pain in my back that made me take a sharp inward breath out of shock. Quickly, the sharp pain was replaced with a burning. My shaking hands shot toward my back to try to remove the source of the pain. It was as if I had turned into an animal. Near the middle of my back, I felt a large growth that was as hard as a rock. As I grasped and scratched at it, it felt like it was getting smaller and smaller. I could feel my heart racing, and my breathing get heavier and heavier.

My hands latched onto the rock-like object cementing itself inside me and attempted to pull it out but to no avail. Suddenly, my hands got cold, freezing even. The cold quickly shifted from my hands to the burning spot on my back. "Don't…worry, it's almost over," I heard the women say as the two heats mixed together to nullify the pain. Slowly, my breathing returned to normal. The sweat rolling down my forehead was the only indicator that anything had happened at all. Soon after everything stopped, my back began to feel cold instead of the warmth that I felt when the two sensations mixed.

The coldness disappeared, and the woman behind me said as cheerfully as she could, "You did…well. Not many…don't scream.

Please don't…move yet." From what I could hear, she was scribbling things down into the circle. "How did you…allocate your…points like this…from one level?" she asked, clearly taken aback.

"What do you mean? I never put points into anything. Was I supposed to? Wait, how do you even know that I've leveled?" I replied. *I know it's rude to answer a question with a question, and I just tripled down, but how does she know?* I wondered.

"The crystal that's…now inside you…displays your stats and… skills on your back. You're sure you…never allocated your…points?" she asked suspiciously as if she refused to believe that I hadn't.

"Yes, I'm sure. I feel like I would've remembered something like that, y'know?" I replied, slightly annoyed at being treated like I was lying. "Stay…here, please," she said as she left the room.

As she ran down the hall, I grumbled to myself, "Why would I say I didn't if I did?" Out of spite, I decided that I was going to look at what she had written down in the circle. *Now that I look at it, it's more of a hexagon. I don't think it's just an etching in the table either. That looks a lot like a slate board,* I thought as I looked at the shape on the table. The hexagon stated, "Name: Grayson, Age: 19, Level: 2, Stats: For each level, there will be an extra two stat points. Be sure to check that for each level, there are two. If there are less, please allow the applicant to allocate points. If there are more, double check the numbers. REMEMBER, all stats start at a base of 10 and will not include increases from gear! S: 12, A: 12, F: 12, I: 12, P: 12, L: 12."

I had to re-read the note left for the stats section. I now under-stood why the witch was so confused. *Judging by this, I should be about Level 7 instead of only Level 2,* I thought as I pulled up the stat page. *Sure enough, it's correct, aside from a few +1's and +2's from my gear. But those won't show up, I guess.*

"What exactly does this mean then?" I asked myself out loud as the woman walked in with a man who looked around my age. He was taller than me and wore a suit that was rougher than a nor-mal business suit. However, it still seemed a lot more formal than what everyone else in this world wore. His black hair made him look like one of those know-it-all villains you would see in anime. As he pushed up his glasses, they became illuminated in the light.

"That's simple. It means that you have a hidden skill. I've been given the rundown by my employee here. Zini, you can go, I'll take it from here. Shut the door on your way out as well," he said assertively as he moved to sit down on the couch across from me. The witch lady bowed and left the room in a hurry, closing the door as the man had asked.

He shot a glance up at me as I stood, seemingly paralyzed. "I really should be on the other side, but I digress. It's good to meet a new other-worlder. How long have you been here?" he asked, sounding somewhat concerned.

"I've been here for around four days," I said, refusing to meet his gaze for some reason.

At my response, the man seemed to be taken aback.

"Four days, and you're already Level 2? You're either skilled, extremely lucky, or have a death wish. Have you had your second meeting with...him, yet?" he asked as his confidence from earlier started to fade.

"No, I haven't. I was supposed to say some words when I signed up here to get to him," I replied, assuming that he had been talking about God. *Why does he seem so afraid, though?* I wondered.

The man let out a sigh. "Well, give me a few seconds, and we'll get that squared away. I'm sure you've figured it out, but if you haven't, I'm one of his vessels. Thankfully, though, I get to just go about my life until one of you comes along," he explained as he pulled some sort of bead out of his pocket. He must have noticed my prying eyes because he instantly explained what it was. "It's an herbal concoction of sorts to help with the pain. You'd be surprised at how much it hurts when your body's soul makes room for a God." After he swallowed the pill, he said, "Go ahead and say the words whenever you're ready."

My eyes widened as I racked my brain for the words. *He's talking about the words that God said right before he sent me here? He didn't even give me time to learn them! I guess I'll just try my best. Worst case, I just don't talk to God again, right?*

"Stick...them on schliay?" I questionably said. *It was something like that, right? I think I got the last word right, but the pronunciation was so weird, and he said it out of the blue right before I left! How could*

I be expected to remember something like that! I exclaimed inwardly, cursing God for not preparing me well enough for this.

After the last word was uttered, the man began rising off of the couch, his arms slumping behind him, and a bright light began pouring from his eyes. Just as suddenly as it began it stopped, and the man crashed down onto the couch. "Not the exact words, but close enough!" he spouted in an entirely different tone, almost like he was greeting an old friend.

As I stared at him, not saying anything, he began to get less and less ecstatic. "What's wrong?"

He spouted, "It's me! Your overlord sup—"

"GOD-RUDD!" I shouted as I cut him off. I stood up, and a tightness took over my face as I stared down the god vessel. "You've got a lot of explaining to do," I said in as threatening a voice as I could.

"What explaining could I have to do? You should explain how it took you four days to get here!" he said with as much hostility as I had.

"One of those days doesn't count, you bastard! If you're going to count me having to sit in an inn with an old dwarf for a day because the elves were trying to figure out what to do with me, then you can go... Why are you looking at me like that?" I asked.

At the mention of the elves, the god vessel's face mimicked mine from when I was trying to remember the words to summon God.

"What do you mean the elves were trying to figure out what to do with you? How did you end up in elvish territory?" he asked.

I decided to tell him what had been going on so far since we last saw each other. As I explained my past few days, his jaw dropped lower and lower. When I finished, he started spouting out questions.

"You don't allocate your points and you gain two to every stat, correct?" he asked.

I nodded in response.

He put his hand over his face and muttered, "Looks like the prophecy's begun. Also, you said your mana bar is grey?"

I again nodded to confirm.

"That's never been a problem before. Hell, there shouldn't even be a way for a magicless person to exist. It's not unheard of, but I have absolutely no idea why it happens. If you give me some time, I can bring something into reality for you to help with that, okay?" he asked.

God himself basically just said to me that if I would give him time, he would give me something that would make it so I could use magic. An all-powerful omnipotent being just asked me to give him time in exchange for power. I could barely contain my excitement at the fact I would be able to use magic and let out an, "Of course! Take all the time you need!" As an afterthought, I added, "Would we still be able to talk while you did your thing?" I wanted to minimize the time God spent in the vessel's body. Mainly because of the strain it seemed to put on him, but also because I didn't want the pill he took to wear off.

"Yes, of course. Multitasking is child's play! Besides, we need to talk about your reward for completing your first task," he said in a new businesslike tone. "Now that you've proven yourself, you get access to change your information. However, it's just this once and it's permanent, so be sure about everything!"

With a snap of his fingers, a mirror appeared before me that showed me my reflection. Though at the same time, it wasn't my reflection. The thing staring back at me was something with no features. It looked like a white mannequin. To either side of it was menu text. To the left, it stated "Appearance," and to the right, it said "Class."

"What exactly is this?" I asked, unsure about how this was a reward.

"Think of it as a character creator. You get to make your ideal self! Your body will change overtime due to stat increases, more muscular as your strength goes up, beefier legs as your agility goes up, stuff like that. Aside from that, though, you can make it so you look how you want. Though, since people have been calling you by name, you won't be able to change your name in this world...Grayson," God explained, finishing with a smug smirk.

Shrugging off his insult about my lack of creativity, I decided to take a look at the appearance tab first. When I opened it, I was greeted by many tabs, the first being gender. *Well, from what I know, I'm a guy, and I'd kinda prefer to keep it that way. Imagining the look on Sylia's face if I came back as a woman is tempting, though!* I chuckled at the thought as I selected "Male."

At my choice, the mirror before me shifted the appearance from the white mannequin to something that looked more like a man.

The next tab was "Body" with height and weight sub-tabs. For familiarity's sake, I decided to leave it at 5'11" (180 cm) and 158 pounds (71.6 kg). *When I had a growth spurt as a teen, walking felt so weird. I'm not going to mess with my brain by changing my height,* I reasoned. The mannequin shrunk in width but grew in height. *Why would this thing not have my height as the default? It's supposed to be a mirror, right?* I wondered to myself.

The next part, called "Structure," had sliders for muscle, thinness, and thickness. A part of me wanted to crank the muscle slider and give myself a completely ripped body, but then I remembered what God had said about my body changing through stat increases. *If I did that and then gained a load of strength, I would eventually just look like a walking bag of meat.* In fear, I decided to leave the sliders at default so that I would have some muscle as well as some fat so that I wasn't a complete stick. Lastly, there was skin tone. I felt no reason to change from my current shade, so I just selected a light peach tone.

After that, I moved onto the next tab which had to do with my hair. Before looking at it, I knew that I wanted something that was short and not hard to keep up with. The first few pages were longer hairstyles of varying thickness and length. Once I got past those, there were even more that seemed to include accessories. *How does... Are you allowed to take the bandana off?* I wondered to myself, unsure if the accessories would be part of your hairstyle forever. Eventually, I got to short hairstyles that didn't have a lot to them.

After sifting through pages of disappointing hairstyles, I settled on a thin, short, layered, overgrown look. When I selected it, I could feel my hair morph from thick to thin, making me feel like I lost a ton of head weight. My hair now went over my forehead somewhat, not enough for me to see it but enough to give me a bit of a rugged look.

The next thing to pick was my hair color. It looked fine in my normal jet-black state, but I wondered how it would look in different colors. After selecting all of the unnatural colors, I let out a sigh of defeat and decided to choose dark brown. *I kind of wanted some anime protagonist hair, but it's always so spiky. I hope I can get away with a nice style if I just color it weird, but I suppose that's not going to work. At least the dark brown is natural and looks far better!* I thought to myself, disappointed but trying to look on the bright side.

Next up was the eye tab. There were sliders for eye angle, height, width, and positioning. *You're not gonna get me with this one, God, I've played enough RPGs to know that the eyeball makes the character look normal or completely stupid, AND I know how easy it is to botch it!* I thought as I refused to move any of the sliders. I was dead set on having normal eyes…until I found the eye color section.

There were more than just colors for the iris. If you wanted to, you could have eyes that were completely black. You could even give your iris a misty look if you were so inclined. *It looks cool, but doesn't that imply that you're blind?* I thought, wondering if it would have an effect on my vision. I ended up making my eyes a light silver. I thought against it at first and was going to pick something more common, but then I realized that if anyone was curious about my foreign name, I could say that I was named due to my eyes! It was a stroke of genius!

Once I was done with the eyes, I finally came to the last tab, which had to do with my face in general. There was only one thing I could change, and it only came with a handful of options—the shape of my head. I ended up changing my pear-shaped head out for one that was more of a normal oval head. Once I had finished everything, a pop-up appeared in front of the mirror that asked, "Changes complete. Would you like to accept?"

Naturally, I hit "Yes."

At my confirmation, I lost my vision and heard the sound of glass shattering. An aching pain flared up all over my body, my hair felt like it was getting ripped out, my right eye felt how I imagined getting it scooped out would be. Even though the crystal implant hurt to the point where I felt like I was going mad, this was somehow much worse. I tried to let out a scream but to no avail. I couldn't hear anything. I couldn't feel anything besides pain. *Am I even making a noise right now?* I thought as I panicked at the loss of my senses.

Slowly, the pain began to dissipate. First, the aching stopped; the hair ripping stopped shortly after. My eye pain stopped for mere moments before it started up again, this time in my left eye. After my left eye's pain died, my eyes felt as though someone was pushing into them with all their might. Eventually, the pressure stopped, and my vision slowly returned, starting from the inside. Once I could see entirely, I noticed that everything looked darker.

Instead of looking at my surroundings, I found that I couldn't rip myself away from the broken mirror in front of me. Instead of seeing the mannequin that had been built up from my choices, I saw myself. Rather, I saw the old version of myself.

"Oho, so that's what you decided, eh? I thought I gave you a lot of options you'd have liked. I'm surprised you went with something so…plain," God said somewhere behind the mirror. "Don't let me distract you just yet, though, you still need to pick your class," he added.

Still breathing heavily from the shock of everything that just happened, I reluctantly shifted my focus over to the "Class" section. Instantly, I was greeted by a bunch of class names. They were split up into categories that were marked by a shield, a sword, and a plus sign.

The shields probably for taking damage, sword for doing damage, and the plus sign is more than likely just a medical symbol to imply healing, I thought to myself, instantly writing off tanking. *Taking damage isn't like in a video game here. It hurts. I haven't even been hurt by any spells or anything! Sure, I'll have points in fortitude to increase my health, but health is good in any class, right?* I reasoned, feeling as if I needed to give an excuse to not get hurt.

I also had to turn down any thoughts of healing, mainly due to the fact that when I attempted to select the section, nothing would pop up, and a loud buzzer-like sound would ring. *So all of the healing classes probably have to do with magic. Well, it's not like healing is my first choice anyway,* I thought with a shrug. I was more curious on how many different classes there could be for healing.

That left only the damage category, which opened up without an issue. There were four classes: Warrior, Rogue, Ranger, and Mage. Keeping in mind that I couldn't use magic, I figured I couldn't choose Mage.

So I only really have three choices, huh? Realistically, the warrior would probably be a good fit. Though, if I was a Warrior, I'd more than likely be close-up in fights and have to wear heavy gear, right? So if anything had some sort of cleave ability, I'd be getting hurt, and if we needed to retreat, I'd probably be the slowest. Really, the Rogue might have the exact same problem, aside from running away. Though if I was a Rogue, I'd usually be behind my targets, right? I analyzed, feeling like the Rogue was a safe pick.

Before I could select it, a vision of some sort popped into my head. In the vision, I was in a large cavern and was stabbing a large humanoid creature from behind. The creature was a giant. It was at least two times as large as myself. The outline of its body made me think of the Minotaur from Greek mythology. I couldn't make out any of its features, though; the monster was so dark that it was like I was looking at a night sky with no stars.

The people around me seemed to be the same way, although their outlines were filled with stars. Luckily, they seemed to be my allies and were holding the beast's attention. As I stabbed at the creature's leg, all was going well until one of my daggers sunk deep inside its thigh. With an ear-bursting roar, the creature kicked me back with the leg I didn't stab and sent me flying into one of the cavern's walls. As I crashed into the wall, a large stalactite came loose from the ceiling and impaled my stomach.

As soon as I was impaled, the vision ended, and a sharp pain took over my head. I put my palm up to my forehead and gripped my head. "What was that?" I muttered to myself, unsure of what I had just witnessed.

Without a second of thought or hesitation, I selected the Ranger class. *Is that what they call an ill omen? Would I have died if I picked the Rogue? Maybe I just have an overactive imagination,* I thought as the pain dissipated and the mirror disappeared to reveal God standing in front of me.

"The Ranger, huh?" God asked questionably. "Perfect choice for a man of your abilities. Looks like you're smarter than you seem, my boy!" he added excitedly. "You're going to use bows, right? You could use a gun, but since you'll have the added strength with your agility and perception, a bow could be fired with the force of a cannon! Although you'd have to find a bow that could take that sort of force, but that's not impossible at all in this world!"

He continued on, acting like a kid in a candy shop. In surprise, I cut him off and asked, "Wait, go back a minute. There are guns in this world?" Not once had I seen a gun throughout the last few days nor heard any talk of them.

"Well, they're not technically the guns you're thinking of. They're more like wands, but they use bullets! Instead of using a bullet with a primer and a casing filled with gunpowder, they use the tip of normal bullets and a fire crystal attuned for explosive magic to propel the bullet out of the barrel! The dwarves first tried to reverse engineer a gun from someone I reincarnated in the past. After they failed, the ley-makers took a crack and ended up improving the design to use less materials. Those mages are truly cut from a different cloth!" he explained, seeming almost as excited as when he was talking about how a bow would complement my skills.

"You know what I just realized, God? If you know all of this stuff and are supposed to be all-knowing, then why did I have to tell you about what's happened to me?" I asked suspiciously. Before I knew it, God had changed from acting like an excitable kid to being an awkward high schooler.

"Well... I mean... You know," he said as he looked down to avoid my gaze. When I asked, I was just curious, but now I felt like I needed to know the reason why.

"No, I don't know why. That's why I'm asking you, I sternly said.

As God kept his gaze on the floor, he said, "It's embarrassing..." Eventually, he cracked underneath my gaze. After a few moments, he let out a sigh and went on, "I'll do my best to put it in a way you understand. Think of all worlds like computers, okay? Us gods are the technicians. Most worlds generally only have one god or one set of gods. The Greek, Roman, Egyptian, Norse—all those gods are real. Earth is special in the sense that it was an experiment to see what would happen if we all worked on something together. At different points in time, one group—or in cases like mine, one god—would do most of the work at the time. This way, the other gods would be able to work on their own worlds. Unfortunately, Christianity became really popular and never really died, so I have to spend a lot of time on Earth. At one point in the past, I got stressed out about dealing with everything myself and asked some of the other gods to help me with this world. Somehow, someone made it so I ended up losing most of my 'administrator privileges.' That's why I didn't know about anything relating to you. I'm not able to do anything here on Zynka, even though I created the planet and gave it life." By the end of the story, God's voice was cracking, and it seemed like he was about to cry.

Maybe I shouldn't have forced him... Who knew that gods had issues like this? "Basically, your access is being denied, so you can't see what's going on here, and that's why I had to tell you everything? How are you here right now, though? Hell, how did you even reincarnate me here?" I asked. *If he doesn't have permissions, then something like creating new life shouldn't be possible, right?*

"Well, that's easy. Since you had existed on Earth, I just transferred your files. Certain 'soul files' already have permissions put on them to allow something like this. You have to remember, I've been watching your soul for a very long time. Every other time I offered you to be reborn here, you turned me down," he said in his new depressed state.

"That's what you meant when you said you were watching me for a long time when we met! I thought you were talking about just my lifetime!" I cried out in response.

God let out a groan. "I think our time is coming to an end, my boy. The pills are starting to wear off. Before I swap out, take this!" he said as he threw a pair of leather gauntlets to me. They looked normal aside from the two metal circles on either palm.

"This is supposed to help me use magic, right?" I asked with visible confusion on my face.

"Press the left button to suck in one of the six base magic elements' magicules from a spell or object, then press the right button to discharge it. If you press the left again after you've already sucked in an element, it will automatically disperse any magicules you've collected and take in new ones. If you don't understand what I'm talking about yet, ask Sylia to explain," he replied. Quickly, he added, "Oh, talk to me after you're Level 15 and are a bronze level adventurer! I can explain a lot more then. Ciao!"

I think he's the first person I've met that actually says 'Ciao,' I thought as the man in front of me shook for a few moments before falling to the ground. The man lay crumpled on the floor and said through heavy breathing, "Give me a moment…"

Complying with his wishes, I took a seat and put the gauntlets on. Unsurprisingly, they fit like a glove! They were tight, but not tight enough to restrict my movement at all. In fact the gloves felt like an extension of my own body. Remembering what God had said, I reached my ring finger down to the left circle on my right hand. Though nothing seemed to happen, the only difference was that the glove on my right hand turned to a mint green color.

"If you wish to test out your new artifact, follow me," said God's vessel as he pushed himself off of the ground. He grabbed the hexagonal slate off of the table and began to walk out the door. I figured that was my cue to follow him. *He isn't really giving me a choice when it comes to using this thing, huh?* I thought. I threw my ripped shirt and sweatshirt back on and chased after him. As we walked down the stairs to the first floor, I noticed that the only people still there were the young witch, Zini, the old Viking, and a girl with a wolf sitting at one of the tables.

"Where is everyone?" I asked the man leading me through the dining area.

"They're out doing quests. They generally won't be back until the evening, so we're free to talk about your…condition," he said as he shot a glance around the room. "When we are not in private, I ask that you refer to me as Guildmaster. Not many know that I am one of the…well, you know what I mean. I only hope that you can keep my secret better than you kept yours," he added in a whisper, leaving me blushing out of embarrassment.

Beyond a door in the back of the building was a training ground surrounded by the other buildings in the area. The left side of the field had a bunch of training dummies. Along the walls were racks with wooden swords and dull iron swords. The right side had multiple firing ranges. Half of them had bows with a few arrows, and the others had staves along with signs stating that explosive magic was prohibited.

"Well, what are you waiting for? Step up to the line and use your artifact. I'm curious about it myself. Be careful, though, I don't want anyone to die because of your inexperience." the Guildmaster said.

Nervously, I heeded his words and moved over to a part of the range for magic users. As I moved up to the firing line, my heart rate quickly increased. I glanced back toward the Guildmaster to see him staring back. To my surprise, he had a soft smile and gave me a thumb's up instead of looking incredibly serious like I had imagined.

I wouldn't say that I was relieved, but I would say that I was less tense after seeing that the Guildmaster wasn't a completely all-business type of guy. I lifted my right hand up and grabbed my forearm to steady my aim. I moved my index finger down toward the right button only to find it put a large amount of strain on my wrist. *This hurts way too much for my finger to not even go down far enough to press the button,* I thought.

I started testing out each of my fingers to see what would be the best way to hit the button. The only two that were capable of pressing the button without causing pain was my ring finger and my thumb. *If I use my ring finger, it messes up my aim because of how I fold my hand,* I thought, deciding to use my thumb for firing.

As soon as I touched the button with my thumb, the color of the glove melted away toward my palm. Then there was nothing. "Umm… Do you think I did something wrong?" I shouted back toward the Guildmaster. Before he could respond, I heard multiple ear-bursting thuds from in front of me. It sounded like an explosion went off. When I turned toward the sound, I found that the target I shot at was cut into six large pieces and had fallen to the ground.

Amazed by the result, I looked down at the glove. *Did that really just come from this?* I thought in astonishment.

"Try another element! Do world magic!" shouted the Guildmaster behind me.

World magic? I'm assuming that's just Earth magic? I guess it would be weird to call something Earth magic when they've never been to Earth, but don't people just call dirt earth *sometimes?* I wondered. I shrugged and put my hand down to the ground with a small gap so I could press the left button. Sure enough, my glove ended up changing to a dirt-brown color.

I moved down the line to another target and retook my stance. When I pressed the right button, a large boulder flew out of my palm. Surprisingly, there was no pushback, even though the boulder shot out at such a high speed. Then the boulder vanished into thin air, and the Guildmaster stood where it had been flying. "Maybe you should only use that artifact in dire situations. If I didn't dispel your earth magic, I fear we very well could have had another other-worlder doomsday scare," he said nonchalantly.

"On the plus side, we now know how powerful that thing is. But I want to see how powerful you are as someone with the Ranger class. Take a bow and fire at will when ready. As a ranger, you shouldn't have to worry about aiming since your arrow will fly to the target you want, but the better your aim, the less traveling it will have to do. Come on, hop to it!" he commanded.

I've only held a bow a handful of times in my past life. Is it really going to be that simple to hit the target? I wondered to myself.

When I picked up a bow at one of the ranges, my hand gripped it familiarly as if it was something I had done hundreds of times before. Before I knew it, I had already pulled an arrow from the quiver that stood upright in front of me and nocked it. *What's going on with my body? Is this another perk of the Ranger class?*

As I took aim, I closed my left eye and pulled the string back to the point that my hand was resting on my cheek. Everything felt perfect, my senses felt heightened, and I felt aware of everything around me. I could hear the bustling sounds of the market I had walked through, the flapping of a bird's wings in the sky above—even the calm movement of the rivers could faintly be heard in this elevated state.

It wasn't just my hearing that was better either. My sense of touch was elevated too. I could feel how much stress I was putting on the bow with my pullback. Even the feel of the wind was different, and it made it easier to tell the direction it was going. As a result, my body was automatically compensating for the wind's speed and how it would affect where the arrow would land.

I aimed at the top right of the blue circle on the target. All I had to do was let the arrow fly, and it would for sure be a bull's-eye. As I was about to let the string go, the door to the courtyard suddenly opened and slammed into the wall with a loud *CRASH!*

"WHAT WAS THAT EXPLOSION? DID YOU GUYS HEAR THAT? IS EVERYONE OKAY?" yelled the girl that was in the dining area.

In my heightened state, her voice sounded as loud as the explosion that she was referring to. Out of utter surprise, I flinched at the sound, and even though my arrow hit the target, it hit the four-point black circle on the other side of the target.

My mouth opened slightly in shock. *Everything had felt perfect, though. It was like being in an artificial flow state,* I thought as I turned my attention toward the Guildmaster and the girl who startled me. Now that I was actually paying attention to the girl, I noticed that she had some…extra features, to say the least. Among her light brunette hair, she had two large, fuzzy, black cat ears. Besides that and her tail that faded from grey to white, she stood out to me as a poor adventurer. She sported a set of burlap clothing with small bits of metal over it along with a battered wooden shield and what looked to be a chipped hatchet of some sort. *I feel like I'd be more protected in combat with this sweatshirt and jeans than she is,* I thought.

"Ah… If I recall, you're Kuhani correct?" the Guildmaster asked as he slightly turned toward the cat girl.

"Yeeeesss, sir, and my brother here is Kuhano!" she replied as the wolf beside her bowed his head down before the Guildmaster.

"Pleased to meet you two. You're the first beast-people that have shown interest in joining the guild. I hope that you two will do great things!" the Guildmaster said, unusually enthusiastically to the pair of siblings.

"Ahh…yes. I hope we will too!" said the seemingly cheerful Kuhani. "I know we're a lil' late because Kuhano kept trying to convince me to not get involved, but is everyone all right?" she added, showing concern.

"Yes, yes, everyone is fine. I'm just testing our new recruit, and we got a little carried away," the Guildmaster said, not technically lying but still bending the truth nonetheless.

Kuhani tilted her head to the side and put her finger on her chin. "But he's using a bow? How did he…" She trailed off before suddenly shouting to me, "HEEEEEY, ARE YOU LOOKING FOR A QUESTING PARTY?"

I looked to either side of me and then pointed to myself. *Does she actually mean me? She doesn't even know me!* I thought as the cat girl ran toward me.

"Of course I mean you, silly! Do you need a party? We just need a healer and another damage dealer to be able to go on actual combat quests!" she said, getting right up in my face. Her marble-like lemon yellow eyes really sold the fact that she was a cat girl.

"I mean, I'm not even officially signed up yet. Besides, shouldn't you choose someone you either know or can at least trust when it comes to combat ability?" I replied to her. Even though I was flattered, I wasn't too sure about just joining up with anyone who asked me.

"Come ooooonnnnn! If you're that worried about it, I'll watch your assessment tests and see if I should ask you to join based on that, okay?" she said, sporting a pair of puppy dog eyes, even though she was a cat.

"Is that even allowed?" I asked out loud with hopes that it wasn't.

"I'll allow it," the Guildmaster said, making his way toward us. "You never know, it might be good for you, Grayson. Plus, it'd help them out so give it a chance," he said.

"Really, Guildmaster? Thank you, thank you, thank you!" Kuhani cheered. "What are we waiting for? Let's go and get on with the test!" she exclaimed as she began running back toward her brother, Kuhano.

The Guildmaster leaned down and whispered in my ear, "Don't let her act fool you. Her time in this city has been horrible. How her will is strong enough to bear the endless torment, I'll never know. Even if you don't join her group, at least try to be her friend."

Before I could even ask what he meant, he turned to join the two siblings. As he walked, he said over his shoulder, "Oh, and don't even think about purposely doing bad. I won't count that first shot thanks to our interruption. Remember that you don't have to aim so much either. Just think of where you want the arrow to hit. Go retrieve your arrow and then wait for my call to fire."

I couldn't help but feel bad. Not so much at the fact that I got scolded, but more that I got scolded for something that was in the back of my mind. As I retrieved my arrow and waited, I thought to myself, *Why am I so afraid of joining a party? Is it because they seem a little weird? Or would I be that way for any group that wanted me to join them?* A part of me hoped that I'd be able to just quest by myself. *Maybe I'm just scared that no one will accept me, like on Earth.*

"Step to the line, draw, then proceed to fire at will," the Guildmaster called. Like before, I walked up to the line, and once I nocked my arrow, I went back into that heightened state. Unlike before, I thought about where I wanted the arrow to hit. *Right into the middle of the target.* I let the first arrow fly, and within a moment, it was lodged right into the bull's-eye. Within a blink, I already had another arrow nocked. Even though she was trying to be quiet, I could hear Kuhani's gasps of astonishment.

Do I pull a Robin Hood and split the arrow? Or should I just have it land next to it? I wondered to myself, confident in the abilities of the ranger to let me split the arrow and wanting to show off a bit. I decided to split the first arrow; that way, if the worst case happened where I had to pay for a replacement, it would only be one instead of four.

After I let the arrow fly, I could hear the cracking of the first arrow as the head of the second decimated it. Surprisingly, I heard no reactionary sounds after that. My last three arrows were all about the same as the first arrow had been. Grab an arrow, nock it, think about where I wanted it to land, have it hit near the second arrow. Once I ran out of arrows, I set the bow down on the holder and looked toward the three onlookers.

"So...that was good, right?" I asked aloud, unsure by the lack of reaction. Even after I had asked my question, I didn't receive a response. Eventually, I ended up walking toward them. "Hey, are you guys okay?" I asked as soon as I got there.

"Is something wrong? Why aren't you firing? Better question, how did you get over here?" the Guildmaster asked in response.

I looked at him in confusion. "What do you mean? I walked over here after I shot all five arrows. Was there another arrow and I just missed it?" I asked.

The Guildmaster looked away from me and shifted his gaze to the target that I had fired at. A look of confusion and astonishment overtook his face.

"How did you... When did you....? Kuhani, did you see anything after his first shot?" the Guildmaster asked, turning his attention to the cat girl.

"Nya-ha-ha, even with my enhanced vision, I couldn't see a thing," she said confidently with a shrug.

"Why did you say it like that? I thought that you actually saw it. There's nothing for you to be proud of if you didn't!" I shouted out, to which she just made a blank cat face as if she was the embodiment of the colon three text emote. With a sigh, I asked, "What exactly does this mean then? How could none of you see me shooting? I know that I was picking them up pretty fast, but even then, you should've been able to see that."

"Hmm..." the Guildmaster let out as a form of audible thinking. Before I knew it, he was behind me and lifting up my sweatshirt and shirt. "Amazing... You've already acquired a new skill," he let out in surprise. Quickly, he scribbled the new addition to my arsenal down on the hexagonal slate. The skill that I had received was called "Focus" according to what he wrote down. When I entered a focused state, my perception and agility stats would either double, triple, or quadruple based on my luck stat and how lucky I was that day (once used, the user must wait twenty-four hours before their stats may be rerolled).

"You must've hit the jackpot then and quadrupled your agility stat. That would give you 48 agility, so it's certainly possible I just couldn't perceive your speed. My perception is only 25, even with my glasses giving me a bonus. Perception is the direct counter to the Agility stat. My 25 allows me to comprehend an agility stat one and a half times greater. If your agility had only been tripled, it would have been 36 and would have been within my comprehension range," the Guildmaster said, providing the explanation as to why no one could see me firing.

"That was a lot of numbers, man. Basically, what you're saying is I had luck on my side, so I moved so fast that no one could even see me?" I asked, trying to wrap my head around the new skill.

"In a sense, yes. However, it would require you to be completely focused both physically and mentally. If you don't have a focus point to maintain, then your stat buffs will disappear, like they have now. Focus isn't a new skill either, so you could do research into it to help understand how to use it better and perhaps even find easier ways to activate it." he replied. Then under his breath, he wondered out loud, "Did it manifest when he picked his class or when he took my advice on thinking about the target?"

"Sir, what's a class?" Kuhani asked as she tilted her head to the side.

My eyes shot wide open, and I slowly turned toward the Guildmaster. Without missing a beat, he said, "Classes are specific jobs that people fall into from birth or if they meet certain specifications. Once they meet them, then they get the choice to become a certain class and will gain skills to do better at their certain job. Much like how you must have a lot of fortitude to be in the role of damage taker, damage dealers must put points in numerous skills. Then once they get the right points and go through the right ordeals, they'll go through an awakening of sorts and receive a class."

The way the Guildmaster explained everything made me question what I knew. *There's no way he's lying, but he definitely made some thing's way too obscure,* I thought, thinking about how I actually received my class. The way he explained it made me realize that he actually was lying. *If it was that easy to get a class, wouldn't nearly everyone have one? Slap some points into this skill until you have this amount in it, and then do these things. There's no way that knowledge wouldn't be passed down for future generations.*

"Wow, so Grayson's trained really hard, huh?" she asked cheerfully as Kuhano nodded to her.

I didn't know what was more embarrassing—the fact that the wolf agreed or the fact that a cat girl thought I was special. Little did I know that this would be my downfall. In my weakened flustered state, there were no defenses up when Kuhani said, "Now I have absolutely no problem with letting you on the team! Welcome to the group, Grayson!" When the message popped up in my vision to dissolve my group and join another's, I didn't even think of what it said and reflexively hit the accept button.

Shortly afterward, the Guildmaster brought us upstairs to his office. "I'm afraid you two will have to wait here while I talk to Grayson," he said toward my two new party mates.

"Aww, come oooon! You let us watch his combat test, why not let us stay?" Kuhani cried out.

"I only allowed you to attend his combat test so that you could gauge his abilities yourself. As this has no effect on your group, I have no reason to allow you to stay," the Guildmaster coldly said as if he had been talking to one of his subordinates.

With a very large exaggerated groan, Kuhani replied, "Fine, but when you two are done, you better find us!" She shifted her focus over to me as if I had any say in the matter.

I slightly rolled my eyes and said, "Don't worry, I will."

With my response, Kuhani let out a squeal of delight and swiftly ran down the hall. Her brother, Kuhano, lightly bowed and moved down the hall at a much more relaxed pace.

As we entered the Guildmaster's office, he shut the door behind us and said with a chuckle, "Those two really are something. I can't say I'm not fond of them, however."

"I know what you mean, but doesn't it bug you that their personalities are exact opposites of how their animal types usually are?" I asked.

"What does that matter? Beast-people are just normal people with traits of animals. It shouldn't affect personality at all according to studies," he replied, instantly killing my now flat-landed joke.

"Moving on, I brought you here to officially welcome you into the guild. Granted, I can't really deny you due to your other-worlder status, even without that. However, I would have accepted you. You're very strong and were reliable enough to find your way here from Elsaria. I thoroughly believe that you'll grow in many ways from joining as well," he said as he sat down at his desk and pulled something out of a drawer. After some quick words and a blast of magic, he threw the item to me. It seemed to be a necklace with a small wooden block on it that had my name etched into it.

"If I could give you a higher rank, then I would, but we have rules for a reason, so I'm sure you understand. That membership tag depicts that you are a new adventurer that has been recognized by the guild and granted the rank of wood. If you fall in combat, it will serve to identify who you are, no matter how mangled your corpse is," he said grimly. "No doubt, you saw the notice boards near the front desk as you entered the building. The material that the board is lined with is the ranking of the mission. As of now, you can only accept wood-ranked missions. Later on, you'll be able to accept iron, bronze, perhaps even gold-level missions if you live that long. Of course, I—"

So basically, the necklace is a dog tag? I thought to myself as I inspected the chunk of wood and zoned out of the Guildmaster's explanation.

"Grayson, are you paying attention!" the Guildmaster suddenly said in a much sterner voice.

"O-o-of course I am! You were talking about ranks!" I said, startled after being unexpectedly caught.

The Guildmaster's face was taken over by a surprised look. "My apologies, I suspected you to be the type to get easily distracted. It seems I was wrong. Now where was I? A-ha, ranking up, of course!

To reach the iron rank, you must complete three or more wood-level jobs as well as reach Level 5. Even though you have the stats of someone beyond Level 5, you should still achieve it. That way, you can gain more field experience. As I stated before, I believe that you're reliable, so I trust that you'll do your best to not let the guild nor your group down. This concludes my rant to you about joining. Congratulations!" he said with a light bow of his head as if he was taking notes from Kuhano.

Out of respect, I returned the gesture and enthusiastically said, "You can count on me! I won't let anyone down!" If it was left at that, I think I wouldn't have been embarrassed by the fact I just sounded like a knock-off brand Naruto. Unfortunately for me, the Guildmaster said as he pushed up his glasses that again became illuminated in the light, "Some people can make that sound cool. For you, it just sounds like you're trying too hard."

The words stung more than I expected, especially because that was one of the things I always wanted to say because it'd be cool. *What is with me being so self-conscious lately? First the thing about me joining the group, then Kuhani thinking I'm special, then this? I'm supposed to be the somewhat likeable, level-headed cool guy like the protagonists in manga! So why have I not been any of those?*

Amidst my mental breakdown, I was reminded of something, and before I could shut my mouth, I asked, "What about the sign-up fee?"

The Guildmaster raised an eyebrow. "I'm surprised you actually know about it. You're an other-worlder. God literally sends you here. The guild waives the sign-up fee. Three gold is an outrageous amount for a block of wood and a progression crystal anyway."

"Ha ha, yeah, that is a little pricey!" I said nervously as I reached into my jeans pocket and realized that I wouldn't have had enough to pay the fee.

"Well, if you have nothing else to bring up, you're dismissed. You can begin accepting noncombative quests tomorrow. Once you find a healer for your group that restriction will be waived. Also, you may want to get new clothes and a bow of your own since we don't lend out either," he said before I walked out of the room.

As I shut the door behind me I had to stop and take a breather. The headrush I had from the realization that I wasn't given enough money slowly faded. *I really must be lucky, huh?* I thought to myself.

Once the mini-adrenaline rush faded, I headed downstairs to find Kuhani and Kuhano waiting at one of the tables. Kuhani was leaning her head onto her hand as she traced something on the table with her other. When I walked over to the table and gave a slight wave, her face lit up, and her tail started swishing back and forth behind her.

"You're accepted, right?" she asked eagerly.

After I gave her a slight nod, she nearly shouted, "I knew it! I told you there was no way he'd be declined!" Then in a much more sullen tone, she said, "Sorry that we can't celebrate, though. Kuhano and I have to go now. I promise we'll do something tomorrow while we look for a healer, okay?"

Something about the way she was acting made me feel like what the Guildmaster said might've been true. I gave her a smile, nodded, and gave her a thumb's up. Thankfully, her face lit up again, and a large smile took over her face. With a wave, she and Kuhano left, and everything felt a lot emptier in the building.

I let out a sigh of relief and let out a few heavy breaths after I realized I hadn't been breathing. "I am not going to be able to survive with a cute cat girl in my party, am I?" After I chuckled to myself for a moment, I muttered, "I could barely say anything to her after the 'singing my praises' stunt she pulled."

As adventurers started to pour in from their quests, I decided that it was time for me to leave. As I made my way out and started heading toward the inn, I could have sworn I heard someone behind me say, "Thank god those filthy beasts aren't in here again!"

When I turned around, though, all I could find were people heading into the guild building. As I trudged my way back, only one thing was going on in my mind. *Are they... Could they have been talking about Kuhani and Kuhano?*

5

Acquiring Gear and a Healer!

When I woke up the next day, I was amazed. For once, I actually woke up before Sylia. *Oh yeah, Sylia must've gotten back after me. I was so tired yesterday that I just jumped into my bed as soon as I got here and pulled the covers over my head because it was freezing. I wonder how long everything took,* I thought as I lay there, procrastinating as I was getting out of bed.

I could hear birds chirping outside, so I figured it was morning. I lazily sat myself up and faced toward the window near the door as I rubbed the gunk out of my eyes. That was when I noticed the health bars of Kuhani (1) and Kuhano (1) in my vision and remembered I promised to meet them later. *If it weren't for the fact that I'm in a different part of the world, thanks to the ley line, I'd check where they are on the map and meet up with them earlier than we planned.*

A rustling sound behind me broke me out of being lost in thought. Out of glee that I woke up before her, I said, "G'morning, Sylia, you slept in, huh?" When I turned to look over my shoulder at her, I expected to just see her waking up over on her bed. What I did not expect was her looming over me with her sword inches away from my neck.

"S-s-silly? You uhh…you all right?" I said nervously as my heart started to pound. I couldn't even attempt to move my neck away because my body was completely frozen.

"Gray? Is that actually you?" she asked as she lowered her sword. Before I knew it, she was hugging me.

"Yeah, it's me. Who else would it be?" I asked while I sat, stunned.

"I thought you were dead! First you disappeared from the party, then when I asked around at the guild, they didn't know who I was talking about when I described what you looked like. Then I ran around everywhere and found out from a guard that you had been attacked by wanted thieves! I didn't get back until late in the night and didn't even think to check your bed because I just passed out as soon as I got in the room. Don't ever freak me out like that again! What even happened to your face!" she exclaimed as she tightened her grip on me.

This was the first time anyone ever worried about me like that. In fact, I didn't even know what to do, so I did the first thing that came to mind. I lightly put my hand on the back of her head, and in a sincere calming voice, I said, "I'm sorry I worried you. I should've thought about you. I completely forgot that we were even in a party together. I'm so sorry, Silly. God ended up changing my appearance. I didn't even think about it. Everything's all right, though, okay?"

Sylia refused to loosen herself from me, and I felt a drop of water on my hand. "Silly? Are you crying?" I asked out of concern.

"O-of course not, don't be ridiculous!" she answered as she buried herself deep into my sweatshirt and, without warning, blew her nose into it. I was going to voice a complaint, but I held my tongue. Normally, I would have said something, but if it weren't for me, she wouldn't be in this position now, so I just made a face and dealt with it.

"Why did you leave the party anyway?" asked her muffled voice.

"I signed up with the guild, and a group that needed a damage dealer asked me to join, so I accepted," I replied, giving her the *Cliff's Notes* and leaving out a large amount of detail.

Sylia detached from me and looked me dead in the eyes. "You already found a group?" she asked without any hints that she had been crying just moments before.

With a single nod, I was back to being hugged like a koala's tree. This time, though, the hug felt filled with a loving embrace as opposed to the one filled with fear of loss just a few moments ago. As she ruffled my hair, she said, "That's my Grayson!"

I felt just a bit flustered but significantly less so when compared to the Kuhani fiasco from the day before. It felt like when my mother would gloat about me to her friends. It was embarrassing, but at the same time, it felt nice to know that she felt I was worth bragging about. With Kuhani, it felt like when the girl I had a crush on talked to me of her own volition. It felt absolutely surreal, almost like I was dreaming. They were two entirely different experiences.

When she detached, she gave me a pat on the back and said, "Come on, let's go get breakfast. We can take our time and talk too. I want to hear everything that happened to you yesterday."

After we arrived at the dining area, we got our meals and sat down at a table for two people. *Why did we eat out in the hall yesterday?* I thought to myself. We were still early enough to where no one was there. Occasionally, someone would come in and grab a plate, but then they'd leave the dining room. Luckily, that meant that we were able to talk about whatever we pleased.

I explained to Sylia my run-in with the two thieves, the whole process I had to go through to join the guild, and of my second encounter with God. "Even though you explained it earlier, I thought I was just delirious from being so tired," she muttered.

I let out a nervous laugh and continued on telling her about my tests and meeting Kuhani and Kuhano, which brought about some odd glances from her.

"You said your new friends are two beast-people, right?" she asked, seemingly out of concern.

"Yeah, is there something wrong with that? They seem fine, but I heard some...things when I left," I replied, thinking back to the people entering the guild as I was leaving.

"Beast-people are feral, disgusting, horrible mongrels who have the strength of dozens of men. Rather, they used to be back when the greater races were at war with each other. Most of them are pretty docile now, but they did some horrible things in the war. From what you've described, though, those two are from the generation after the war, so they're probably fine. Just don't expect people to treat them all that well though," she explained.

Something about her explanation got me thinking, and before I knew it, I asked, "Silly... How old are you actually?"

When I asked, she dropped her fork and let out a sigh. "I knew you were gonna ask this eventually. If you must know, I'm around eighty-four now. I know I'm still just a child, but please don't let my age affect how you think of me."

Still just a child! I suppose she's used to having to deal with elves, but what's with this prepared response? Wait, just how old does this make the king then? I thought. "Sylia you're old enough to be my great-grand-mother. Not that that's a bad thing, I mean, if you were just human, I'd have assumed you were around my age!" I said, chuckling nervously. After receiving a penetrating glare, I quickly asked, "There's nothing I can say to make this better, is there?"

To which she simply replied, "Nope."

I guess this is why the 'Never ask a woman her age' saying exists.

We ended up finishing the rest of our meal in silence. After we were done, we stayed at our table, and Sylia told me about how her day at the castle had gone. Apparently, the king kept trying to convince Sylia to just live at the castle all day and was being the usual doting uncle that he always was to her. That aside, we now officially had the deed to Loch Crest's outpost. If we chose to, we could move in as early as today!

"I thought that the deed was going to be difficult to get?" I wondered aloud.

"Please, Ichol just said that because he didn't want to have to do any work. The thing was abandoned decades ago, so it couldn't have been that difficult to get," Sylia said, clearly showing her disdain for her cousin.

"I suppose you're right. I'm more worried about how he's going about my whole punishment. I feel more like I punished the people I wanted to help, y'know?" I said, disheartened at the thought of how much of an ass Ichol was. I felt Sylia's hand touch mine. The cold of her touch sent shivers down my spine, and I quickly pulled away.

Even though she seemed upset at my reaction, she said, "Don't worry. No matter what he's doing, couldn't be worse than them dying for being set up."

I wasn't entirely convinced, but for morale's sake, I gave a fake smile and said, "Yeah, I guess you're right!" I then quickly changed the topic. "So what's the plan today? Should we go to the outpost or what?"

"Hmm, I suppose there's no harm in going. We should take your new friends too, though, and depending on how trusting they are, they might not feel safe coming. Oh, right! Speaking of, request an invite to your group for me!" she said ecstatically as if she had just come to a shocking realization that was going to blow my mind.

I raised an eyebrow as I said, "What do you mean? We'd have a full party and wouldn't be able to invite a healer, right?"

Sylia let out a laugh. "Just do it and see! You gotta start trusting me," she said.

I wasn't sure of what she was trying to do, but I reluctantly gave her a shot. Using the system's invite system, I requested her invitation to the group. Even though it was simple, my heart started pounding. It could have been because of the explaining I would have to do to Kuhani later or it could have been due to the chance that Sylia was pulling a prank on me.

As I was left waiting in suspense, my head felt heavy, and I heard Kuhani's voice. Except I didn't hear it. The easiest way to explain it is that I thought it. *"Grayson? This is Grayson, right? Who's this person you want me to invite?"*

My eyes widened as I looked around for the seemingly disembodied voice. When I couldn't find anyone, I reluctantly tried the only way I could think of talking back. *"Kuhani? Can you hear me?"* I thought.

To my surprise, I instantly heard, *"Yes, I can, Grayson! How are you today?"*

I was amazed. I didn't recall ever seeing something about party chat in the menu. I wondered if this could be some sort of magic.

"I'm doing fine. The person I came here with asked me to suggest an invite for her. I don't know entirely what she's up to, but she says that we'll be able to invite a healer, even with her in the party," I thought back to the cat girl invading my mind.

"Oh? You're with a girl, huh? Okay, I can invite her," she said.

The way she responded made me think that she thought we were a couple. With that realization in mind, I quickly replied, *"Thanks, Kuhani! Also don't get the wrong idea, she's just a friend!"* I sounded way more defensive than I had originally intended.

It was odd communicating this way. It was like you were still talking except you didn't have to make any noise. When my head lightened, I figured that my thoughts were my own for the time being. *There's no way that it was just a coincidence that my head felt different, right?* I thought to myself. When I received no response, I determined that I must have been correct.

When Sylia joined the party, it was like whenever anyone joined a party. That all changed when her name and bars shot to the top of the list and gained a green eyeball next to her name. "Hey, Silly? What did you just do?" I asked, curious about the change.

"I'm now an overseer of your group! I'm able to see where you all are on the map and your statuses. The best part is that I don't take up a member slot, so you're free to invite your healer!" she ecstatically replied, after which she got closer and sinisterly said, "Keep this on the down low, though. If you tell anyone about this, we'll probably all be hunted and killed. This is a technique that only the ESO knows about, so I'll say it again, keep quiet about it."

"ESO?" I asked.

"Elven Special Ops. I would go into more detail, but if I did, they'd have to kill you. I'm an ex-member, but let's be honest, you never truly leave the ops. Now do you understand why I want you to keep quiet about this?" she asked.

I could feel the terror on my face as I quickly nodded my head.

"Good," she said as she stood up. "Now let's go meet this group of yours."

*****

As we walked through the streets, all I could do was follow Sylia and worry about how the encounter was going to go. I wasn't worried about her elvish racist side coming out, but rather, I was worried about if she would approve of them. *These are people that I'm going to be spending a majority of my time with in the near future. I just hope that Sylia can look past them being beast-people,* I thought.

This could make or break our party, especially since Sylia had this grand dream of our group living together and training at the outpost. Sure, it would make things more convenient, but Sylia made it seem almost mandatory. *She must have something planned aside from the whole apprentice thing. It's just a matter of time before I find out what.*

With worried eyes, I looked toward the sky. It already felt like I had stressed out enough for one day, even though it must have only been somewhere around eight in the morning. The spring sun warming me while the light breeze brought the refreshing smell of the rivers helped to melt away my stress. Even in this stressed state, I couldn't resist the reinvigoration that this world was bestowing upon me.

When I looked back down toward Sylia, I found that we were already coming up on the two beast-people. They weren't difficult to notice, though if it wasn't for the people shooting distasteful looks and clearly avoiding them, it would have been harder. Kuhani's tail and gaze seemed almost glued to the ground as she walked aside Kuhano.

"Hey, guys!" I said as I ran ahead of Sylia toward the two. I was surprisingly happy to see them. *It's been so long since I've felt like this. Is this because I kinda, maybe, sort of think of them as friends?*

At the sound of my voice, Kuhani's ears twitched, and her tail perked up. When she turned around and saw me, she transformed back into the chipper girl I had met the day before.

"Grayson!" she cried out with a wave as I approached. When her eyes shifted to Sylia, she seemed to become more timid as she poked her two index fingers together to form an upside down V and looked down toward the ground. "Y-y-you must be Sylia… Nice to meet you," she said, unable to tear her gaze from the ground.

YOU CLEARLY DON'T THINK IT IS! I screamed out in my mind.

Sylia didn't say anything as she looked Kuhani up and down.

Sylia suddenly got a glittering look in her eyes. When she pulled me aside, my heart began beating hard. Was she about to forbid me to adventure with the closest thing I could call friends? As she leaned closer, she whispered into my ear, "Gray, you didn't tell me she was so cute! Can I pet her? Can I, can I, can I?"

I blinked in astonishment from what I was hearing. "First of all, that's her call. Second of all, what could you possibly have been picturing when I told you about her?" I asked.

"I expected a girl with the ferocity of a lion that was forcing you to be in her group with her might and determination," she stated without hesitation.

Thinking back at how I described her, I can totally see how there was a miscommunication, I thought to myself as I face-palmed. When I went to clear up her misconception, I realized that I was left alone.

When I looked behind me, I saw something that almost made me faint. Sylia was petting Kuhani's head. At first, I thought nothing of it until I saw how much Kuhani was squirming. "Miss Sylia... Please stooop!" she cried out in between spurts of loud purring.

As I looked away in fear of being labeled a pervert, I thought to myself, *I must be in a chapter of some hentai dōjin, right? That's the only explanation. Only then would someone do something as lewd as this with no mercy!*

Eventually, Sylia's petting attack ended, and Kuhani was left crouched down in the street, whimpering with her hands protecting her head from another assault. With Kuhano headbutting his sister's defeated body in an attempt to comfort her and Sylia looming over the two with a satisfied look on her face, it was hard to tell which one should be considered a monster.

With our group leader meeting Sylia and being able to endure one of her deadliest attacks, public harassment, she was deemed as a suitable leader. Not just by Sylia, but by me and her brother as well. *Only someone with a strong will would be able to survive such a brazen attack!* I thought in admiration.

The two girls struck up a conversation together, leaving me and Kuhano to talk to each other. As we stood near each other, I began to wonder, *Is this the first time I've ever seen him not by Kuhani's side? This is bound to happen on quests so... I wonder...* Since we were alone, I decided to put my new plan into motion. "So Kuhano... Not to be rude or anything, but are you able to talk? Err... I guess I mean communicate with more than just gestures?" I asked the wolf sitting next to me. Now that I looked at him, he really was majestic. He was shorter than me while he sat, but only by about a foot, and his grey coat was very thick and fluffy. If it wasn't for his cold eyes, he would have looked just like a big dog.

"I can't talk. The most I can do is this spell. Though it's not like I want to talk anyway," he thought to me. After your mind gets forcibly broken into twice in a day, you somehow get used to the difference of talking and thinking.

"Oh, are you the one that let Kuhani talk to me earlier? Or was that something different?"

"Grayson, you don't seem stupid. Refrain from asking stupid questions, please," Kuhano thought to me.

"Well... Okay, I guess." *It's really hard to talk to him when we're alone. Maybe he's just someone that you need to take it slow with?* I thought as I sat with him in silence until the other two finished their conversation and came over.

"What's the plan looking like, you two?" I asked the two girls as they approached.

Before Kuhani could open her mouth to respond, Sylia already started saying, "We decided that we'll head for the outpost today. We're going to stop by the market before we go, though."

At first, the mention of the market set off my suspicious meter. *Why would we go to the market before we know what supplies we need at the outpost?* I thought as I shot suspicious glares at the two.

Sylia paid me no mind.

Kuhani, on the other hand, looked away and kept glancing back.

"Why are we going to the market, Kuhani?" I asked as I stared holes into her.

"L-l-lady Sylia, could you please explain? I'm afraid I don't really understand it myself," Kuhani said.

Her response made my soul leave my body as I thought, *She just said Lady Sylia, didn't she?*

"Ah, yes, please do explain, LADY Sylia," I said.

Sylia crossed her arms and said, "We're going to get you three some gear, even if it's just hand-me-downs from some washed-up guard. Oh, and Gray? Call me Lady again, and I'll punch you."

I didn't even have to look toward Silly to know what she was doing. If I had to guess, she was holding her fist up near her face. The thought of her doing such a cliché move made me chuckle out loud. "You really need to find a less violent way to get your point across," I said. Shortly after, Silly started laughing with me.

"Alrighty then!" Kuhani said cheerfully as she clapped her hands together. "Would you like to lead the way, Lady Sylia?" she asked.

Before I knew it, my jaw was aching, and I was flying through the sky above the buildings.

"WHAT DID I DO!" I shouted before passing out mid-freefall from panic.

When I woke up, I was on top of Kuhano's back like a piece of luggage. With a grunt, I lifted my head up and found that we were in the market. "See, I told you he'd be okay," came Sylia's voice beside me. "We should still let him rest, though! I knew he was special, but to be able to survive that punch and fall? He must be more special than I thought!" came Kuhani's voice to my right.

As my face flushed, I instantly regretted waking up.

With a sigh, Sylia responded, "You don't even know the half of it. He actually survived an attack from di—"

At that point, I rolled off of Kuhano's mattress-like back and landed, looking right up at Sylia. "Direct consecutive hits from you, right?" I said sternly as I heard Kuhani's startled yelp from the other side of her brother.

Sylia gave a smirk. "In fact, he's so used to being knocked unconscious from those hits that he's become such great friends with the ground. So much so that he'd lie down on a street that goods are brought in from."

Why did she say that so smugly? That's not really a big blow or anything is it? I thought to myself.

"*Gray, you're lying right next to horse crap. Not that I care or anything, just thought you'd like to know.*"

With a turn of my head, my body suddenly jolted itself into the air. On the plus side, my misfortune seemed to have lightened the mood somewhat.

"Now that we're all in the land of the living, here's what's going on. First thing's first, you all need armor. Well, two of you need armor. I'm not so sure about you," Sylia said, pointing toward Kuhano. "Oh, you know communication magic. Oh, thank you! You know, I know some support magic myself," Sylia said.

Wow, is that what I sounded like earlier when the girls were talking to each other? I must've sounded crazy to anyone who was just walking by!

"Okay, so we should still get armor out of the way for you two then. The armor you two need isn't especially high tier, so I think I know just the guy!" she added. With her leading the way, we somehow made it to our destination without having to ask for directions. It could have been because Sylia knew the marketplace well or because any crowds we went near seemed to disperse, clearing the way for us in a matter of seconds.

The shop was tucked away in the corner of the market. If you weren't looking for it, you'd never notice it. Compared to all of the other shops that were bright and seemingly full of life, it looked abandoned. The gnarled wood and the vines growing on the front made the shop look like a haunted house.

When we entered the shop, it was very obviously a place that was more affordable than most. A semi-high-ranked adventurer could probably buy the whole place out if they felt the need to. The store had many sets of armor, all of which looked dreary. If you were an up and coming necromancer or black knight, then this was the place to get your gear. *I'm all for the creepy attention-grabbing gear. Though maybe it's not the best fit for a new adventurer or someone who wants to avoid harassment,* I thought. One look at Kuhani's face made me realize I wasn't alone in thinking that way. Before I could think of an excuse for us to leave, Sylia shouted out, "Horrad? Are you in?"

At the call of the name, two earth-rumbling vibrations could be felt. After a few more, a door in the back swung open, and a gigantic man appeared, ducking below the doorframe as he walked through. Even though he ducked, it didn't help much. He was too big, so when he walked through the doorframe, most of the surrounding wall crumbled. After that display, I was frozen in fear as the giant made his way to us. Kuhano had dashed away somewhere, and Kuhani was hiding behind a suit of armor. The only one who showed no sign of fear was Sylia.

With a loud crash as he set down his foot, the giant stood right in front of Sylia and I. *He's a pretty big guy. Heh, I know what that means. Means he's got some big guts!* I thought, hoping that a joke would calm myself down. I nervously looked around as the large man in front of us pulled a crude pair of glasses from his pocket. He breathed on the large lenses that were held in frame by wood that would look more natural as building blocks. He wiped them off on his large linen tunic and put them on. At the sight of Sylia, his face contorted. In a deep but dopey voice, he spouted, "What you doing here? Me tell you never come here unless life or death!"

"Horrad, how can I explain why I'm here if you yell at me as soon as you see me? How have you been, big guy?" she said as if scolding a child, yet also as if she were talking to an old friend.

The large man in front of us let out a deep sigh. "You know me no mean to yell. It been better, it been…better. Who this with big aura?" he said, staring at me with his lemon-sized green eyes.

"This is Grayson. He's a ranger that I'm buying armor for. Preferably something leather or medium weight class so he can still move around easily but can take a hit if he needs to."

"Oho! He has class? What level?" he asked.

"He's only Level 2 right now. We also have a Level 1 beast-woman here who needs to be able to take damage without ruining her agility," she said to the large man who was deep in thought.

"Level 2 ranger be unheard of… Analysis start. Leather boots, cloth pants with metal guards? Won't restrict movement, plus the protection will be great. Leather breastplate with leather pauldrons should be good for chest protection. Maybe add a short grey mantle cloak too? It'll compliment those gorgeous eyes you have. Also hardened leather bracers will be perfect. It's unlikely that your bowstring will slap your wrist, but we should be safe rather than sorry. Analysis complete," Horrad said as if he had calculated everything in stock that would provide the best protection and flexibility.

As he went to go and grab all of the pieces, I leaned over to Sylia. "Just who the hell is this guy?" I asked.

"He's Horrad. He's an ogre-human hybrid. Don't ask how it happened because I don't know and hopefully never will. He always wanted to be an adventurer. Unfortunately, his prime was when the guild wouldn't accept anything besides humans. Long story short, he opened this shop to help starting adventurers. He helped me out with the whole 'No one knows how I feel because I'm the only one of my kind' thing I suffered from for a bit, so that's how I know him. He's usually a big fool, but when he uses his analysis skill, he becomes a genius," she responded.

By the time she was done, Horrad was already back with all of the gear and was eagerly bouncing up and down, waiting for me to try it all on.

After I was brought to a small dressing room, I started changing. *Why do humans have babies with everything?* I thought as I put a long-sleeved linen shirt on before putting the dark leather breastplate over it. It fit snugly across my whole torso. When I slipped the hardened leather bracers on, it was like they melded with my gloves to create a gauntlet. The gauntlet covered my wrist and forearm and felt as hard as a door when I gave it a tap with my knuckles. The cloak he had given me made me feel like I was about to be recruited to hunt titans. Not only was it warm and nonrestrictive, but it was even lined in crimson thread to accent the basic silver of the cloak. *Very stylish. Maybe a little too stylish compared to the rest of this,* I thought as I looked at the dark pieces of leather gear.

My pauldrons were hidden beneath the cloak and almost felt nonexistent. My new beige cloth pants came with sewn on multipurpose pouches, and a black belt that ensured they wouldn't fall off. *The belt was pretty unnecessary. The waistline is pretty tight,* I thought. The bottoms of the pants fit well into the black and brown leather boots that easily went up to my thigh. A set of metal leg guards went over the pants to cover my knee and above.

When I walked out, my first thoughts went to how expensive this was going to be. The gear felt amazing, but comfort comes at a cost. If we couldn't get the gear now, it would give me a decent short-term goal to work toward. *Now that I think about it, what even is my long-term goal? I mean, I know that I'm supposed to rank up in the guild, but then what? Even if I achieve moving up in the guild, is that really MY goal? I think that I'd be content with just being a part of a well-known adventuring party...at least just to start.*

I was so lost in thought that I didn't even notice the gasp of awe from Sylia. I only snapped back to reality when Horrad asked in his booming voice, "Everything good fit?"

Even though I knew Horrad wasn't a threat, his voice still shot a tinge of fear through my body. "Everything fits perfectly, but uhh... How much exactly is this going to be?" I asked in fear of not having anywhere near enough gold. Money was still a difficult concept for me to grasp in this world. *Ten copper is one silver, ten silver is one gold, and ten gold is one platinum. If it was a one to one hundred conversion, I'd be able to calculate costs in a second. Why couldn't it work like that? I know only going to ten should be easier, but it's just...not,* I thought as I mulled over the world's money system.

"Gear not great, only eight silver all, friend!" Horrad proudly boomed.

I couldn't believe what I was hearing. This gear wasn't great? Moreover, it was only going to be eight silver! *I guess this place really is somewhere for the poor, huh?* I thought. As I came to my realization, Kuhani stepped out of the women's dressing room.

Her new gear was a mix of many different types of armor. Below the waist, our clothes were practically identical. Above, however, was a completely different story. She wore a long chain mail shirt that had been fastened at her hips with a belt. Where it met her neck was a small metal plate that covered any skin that might've been unprotected. It also served as an attacher for two small worn metal pauldrons. She had long leather gloves that went up to her elbow and met the sleeve of her chain mail shirt. If she had a chestplate over her chain mail shirt, she would've looked like a warrior straight out of the Middle Ages.

"Pretty, all fit good?" Horrad asked Kuhani.

She responded, "It all fits perfectly! But…how much do I owe you for this amazing set of gear?" she asked.

Wait a minute… That's almost exactly what I said, but it had her unique charm! I realized.

"No worry, Sylia paying for everyone new armor!" he said, sounding surprisingly sly.

I shot a glance at Sylia who seemed like she definitely didn't say anything about paying. *It may be cheap, but if Horrad somehow gets her to pay, I'm not gonna complain.*

I walked up next to Kuhani and quietly said, "Don't worry, mine's only eight silver. Together, our sets will be, like, two gold pieces maximum. Plus, she has money to spare." I chuckled dryly.

"How much could she possibly have? From what she told me, she doesn't really have a job. Plus, she's around our age, isn't she?" Kuhani asked, evidently not comfortable about having someone else pay for her gear.

"Doesn't have a job? Did she say that? Also, she's in her eighties," I said with no hesitation. *Is she trying to hide her job for my sake? Or does she just feel like she doesn't have a job? Either way, I should probably be grateful that I'm stuck with her,* I thought in response to her lie to Kuhani.

A few moments passed before Kuhani burst out laughing. "That's a good one, Grayson! As if she could be a day over thirty, much less eighty!" she said with a snort.

Heh, if only you knew. I'm still a bit surprised about it myself, I thought as a small blonde-haired girl equipped with a yew wood staff and dressed in long black robes that were way too big for her burst into the shop, crying.

"Araya! What wrong?" spouted Horrad at the sight of the girl.

"I got kicked out of another group!" she said back as she sniffled. "I healed the boss monster we were fighting because he was in so much pain! Then everyone needed to use their healing potions to survive because I ran out of mana! After the fight, they all yelled at me and kicked me out!" she explained before releasing a new wave of tears.

I glanced at Kuhani who had the same shine to her eyes as Sylia had when they met. *Didn't she just say that she healed a monster and people would've died if they didn't use their healing potions?* I thought as I realized what Kuhani was about to do. I pulled her into the changing room we were next to and quickly said, "Don't you even think about it. Listen, I know how much you want a healer, but there is absolutely no way that we can take her!" trying to prevent Kuhani from inviting the lost cause of a healer in the other room.

"But Grayyyy! She's so sad, and we'll just be going on low-level quests. I'm sure she'll get better by the time we get to a higher level! Can't we just give her a chance?" she argued back, sounding like a child who was just told she couldn't adopt a stray animal. Before I could argue my point further, I saw Araya (3) along with her health and mana bar appear in the group section of my vision. I crumpled to my knees in defeat whereas Kuhani was squealing with glee.

I went after the wrong target. I thought that Kuhani was the only one who could invite people to the group. Maybe someone out there suggested her to the group, or maybe... I thought as potential scenarios swarmed my head.

As I was stuck in my trance, Kuhani started shaking me and saying things like, "We can go on combat quests now! Now we'll make money! Now we won't have to hunt for our food! Now we can contribute, and the other guild members won't hate us!"

That last one raised a red flag, but it snapped me out of my trance, so I sarcastically said, "Yay, let's go welcome her... Our new healer."

Kuhani either didn't catch my sarcasm or didn't care. She cheerfully pulled back the curtain, jumped out of the dressing room, and started talking up a storm to our new member who was still wiping away her tears. I slowly rose up and walked toward the pair of siblings with the new healer girl. *I need to talk to Sylia about this,* I thought as I scoured the room. She was at a counter next to the door Horrad had entered from. No doubt she was trying to pay. *Now's my chance while she has no real way to shrug me off.*

"This is my brother, Kuhano, and this is Grayson!" Kuhani introduced me as I walked up. I gave a small wave as I walked past them, making a beeline toward Sylia.

I know that she's somehow behind this. If she really is, did she not hear the part where that girl healed a monster? Does Sylia want us to fail and die? I furiously thought. It felt like I was the only one that was being the least bit sane about this.

When I got behind Sylia, I felt like I could be a demon. If I were in an anime, I would appear behind her as a looming dark figure with a glowing red eye and heavy breathing that could be felt all around. As I was about to open my mouth to voice my questions and complaints, I heard her say, "So, Horr, how did you find a girl with possibly the best healing class in the world?"

Intrigued, I held my tongue so that I could hear more.

"You 'member Lateran? She his daughter. He busy with Archbishop duty, so I watch little one while she grow as a Archpriest," Horrad said rather proudly.

"Wait, you're saying that geezer's still alive? Even if he is, I thought he wasn't allowed to marry because of his status as Archbishop?" Sylia questioned. I could almost hear her face getting tighter as she determined that the story didn't add up. When I noticed Horrad's nervous fidgeting, even I knew something was up. "He not… She bastard like you. Sixteen year ago, she born in secret and raised to awaken her class. Even though lived through horrible experience, she very loving girl! Not like you," he said bluntly with a grin.

Jeez, dude, you can't just say that! Some things shouldn't be said, no matter how true they are. That was a perfect example of one of those things.

Sylia went from an interested interrogator to a depressed damsel. Just by the way she held herself, you could tell the shift in her mood. "She feel that all life matter, even monster! Sometime she forget monster try kill her, though," Horrad added.

Hearing this is making me feel like a jerk. I mean, obviously, I'm right to care about my life. But something about her still having such a childish innocence is making me feel like a bad guy for getting all worked up. Besides, Sylia seems to genuinely think Araya will be useful because of her class. Maybe I just need to believe in her and stop worrying, I thought.

With a sigh, I walked back over to what would be our complete questing group. It was time that I actually introduced myself to Araya. When I was about to open my mouth, Kuhani's ears twitched, and she turned toward me. "Gray! Araya was telling us about classes, and guess what? She has one too! It's kind of sad that you two are stuck with a specific job for the rest of your lives. But at least you're strong and will always know your role in life, unlike me!" she spouted.

No one should be that cheerful when saying that. I can't tell if she is attempting to comfort me or make me feel bad.

Before I could respond, Araya walked up to me and just looked up at me. I didn't realize how short she was when she came into the shop earlier. Her head came up a little lower than my shoulders. When I stared back at her, I noticed that her eyes were yellow with a strong fire behind them that made them golden. Luckily, it was just her iris. Otherwise, I would've been worried about her health. If she was wearing bright gold and blue-plate armor, she would look like a holy knight on a crusade. Instead, she wore black robes with a purple trim that made her look more like a cultist.

"Are you the ranger?" she asked in a very light, yet commanding voice that made her sound as if she was an angel. At a loss for words, I simply nodded. "Pleased to meet you. I pray for your safety and apologize in advance for my shortcomings," she said as she bowed down.

A part of me was taken aback. *Does she know that I was completely against her joining the party?* Without even thinking, I patted her on the head and said, "Don't worry about it. We'll just have to work together to make up for each other's faults. After all, that's what party members do for each other."

It was something so surprisingly simple, but it seemed quite effective. Not only did Araya start to tear up, but Kuhani also started crying. Within moments, the two were latched onto me from either side and thanking me for "being so accepting." I wasn't so dense or modest as to not know what they meant or why they were doing this. *It doesn't feel like I did anything special to deserve being grappled by two cute girls, though. It's not bad. It just doesn't feel morally right,* I thought, somehow complaining about my good fortune.

"You aren't supposed to make your friends cry, Gray," Sylia grumbled from somewhere behind me with a deep breath akin to a growl. I couldn't put my finger on it, but something about her tone set me on edge. *It's almost as if I'm about to get—*

My thoughts were interrupted as I got punched in the back of the head, getting sent down toward the ground. Thankfully, the two girls had detached from me so they didn't fall with me.

I got into a stance as if I was in an elementary school tornado drill. As I crouched down, grasping the back of my head. I thought, *Yup, that's exactly what I thought was going to happen.*

"If you make them cry again, you'll get hit much harder than that! Got it?" she shouted at me.

While it was nice to see Sylia back to her normal self, I would have preferred if she were in a state where she didn't hit me.

"Minor heal," came Araya's voice.

A warm light enveloped me for a brief moment. The pain disappeared as quickly as it had appeared. *I thought that healing spells only restored health. I guess they're also able to quell pain.*

"Lady Sylia, why do you keep hurting Gray!" spouted Kuhani.

When Sylia turned toward Kuhani, she looked like the animated demon that I had described myself as earlier. All Sylia had to do was look at Kuhani to get her to shout out, "I'M SORRY, PLEASE KEEP HURTING HIM. I DON'T WANT TO GET PET AGAIN!"

I was really thrown under the bus just like that, huh? I thought.

"Oh, you don't, huh? Bad news for you. If we stay here any longer, I might just have to. You know, to clear the stress of us wasting valuable time," Sylia said in response.

At Sylia's threat, Kuhani ran out the door as she shouted her thanks to Horrad for his help. Kuhano bowed his head and chased after his sister.

"Looks like that actually worked. See you later, Horr, I'll write ya!" Sylia called as she walked out the door.

"I really rather you not," Horrad grumbled as he made his way to the door.

I let out a chuckle. "Thanks for all your help, man. When we need upgrades, we'll be sure to come back here," I promised while I leaned against the wall near the door, holding the door open while I waited for Araya to leave.

"And I find you best gear when come back," he responded to me. "If anything happen, you always welcome here. Be safe," he said as he pulled Araya into a hug. After a few moments, he let her go and said, "Go, Sylia scary when she in good mood."

Araya gave a small nod and walked out the door. A few moments passed before she stuck her head back in past the door frame. "Are you coming, Mr. Grayson?" she asked.

I looked to Horrad as if to say to him that he didn't have to worry about her safety. He gave me a large grin and gave me a nod like he understood. I pushed myself off the wall and gave him a wave as I walked through the doorway to the shop. The door slowly closed behind us.

I walked side by side with Araya in silence as we caught up to the others.

*****

It was around noon when we left the town to reach our new home at Loch Crest. After we left the shop, we went to a small weapon tent and bought a small wooden shield for Kuhani as well as a short sword. The shield was a bit bigger than a buckler, and the sword was a little over a foot long. We also bought me a short bow with a quiver full of iron arrows. I ended up paying for both Kuhani's equipment and my own. Luckily, it was only a gold and three silver, a little less than the armor we had just bought, which made sense since it was all low-level gear.

We split from the main road to a small dirt path that would barely be able to fit a cart. The road to the loch was a long one that seemed to never end. Not only was it made of dirt, but there were barely any trees to speak of in the plains. It was easy to tell that the days it snowed or rained were going to be the worst times to use the road. It also ran surprisingly close to a river, which meant that the path would be flooded if the river ever overflowed. *Whoever made this road is an idiot,* I thought.

Thankfully, on a day like today, the road was peaceful. The warm sun enveloped us and warmed us, countering the slight chill of the spring wind. The small animal-like monsters that walked near the road served as a reminder that I was in a fantasy world and not just in the Middle Ages. *Of course, one glance at anyone I'm travelling with has the same effect, but seeing a flying rabbit just made me remember.*

As to why a rabbit would need wings, I tried not to think about it, but the fact that it existed was enough for me. To my surprise, no one seemed to have their guard up. *To be fair, they've lived here their whole lives and know more about the creatures in the world. I don't know anything about this place, so it's kinda terrifying.*

I was able to secure a walking spot between Kuhano and Araya. Even though using a small girl and a large dog as shields could be seen as morally wrong, it didn't stop me. Thankfully, no one was any wiser to what I was doing.

"So, Sylia, how much farther exactly is this place?" I asked out of curiosity since we'd been walking for a while.

"We shouldn't be too far. We're about to come up on the water-fall the river from the loch feeds."

When she said that, we all stopped walking to try to hear the waterfall ourselves. *I can't hear anything.*

"Lady Sylia, your hearing must be amazing! I can't hear it at all, even with my bestial hearing!" Kuhani spouted in amazement.

Sylia slightly blushed and said, "Of course it's amazing. Why do you think I'm your group's overseer?"

"You're our overseer because you can hear well? I know what you meant, but think of how the things you say can be taken," I said sassily. I wasn't meaning to be a jerk, but with how much she physically abused me on top of the hour of walking, it just slipped out. Instead of a witty comeback or punching me, Sylia just scoffed and rolled her eyes.

After fifteen more minutes of walking, we finally came to a gradual slope that was accompanied by the sound of the crashing water. When we got to the top, the fort was in viewing distance. It was still quite a ways away, but we were able to see it. After a small break to look at the waterfall, we started walking again.

"Sir Grayson? How did you get your class, if you don't mind me asking? Were one of your parents a ranger?" Araya suddenly asked.

My mind went blank. *I knew this question was going to come up eventually. I didn't expect it to happen this soon!*

I took a deep breath and put on my most convincing voice, which just so happened to be my normal voice. "My class awakened shortly after my thirteenth birthday. My father was an exotic hunter who traveled around the world, fighting rare creatures with his trusty bow. Around a week after I turned thirteen, he took me on a small hunting trip and taught me how to use a bow. I leveled and put my points into what my dad told me to. After I woke up, I found out I somehow had a class and received a new skill. It just sort of happened. Why do you ask?"

Before Araya could respond, Kuhani's voice came from behind us. "I thought that you awakened your skill when you were taking your practical exam for the guild?"

I thought my lie had been pretty convincing, but I completely forgot about Kuhani. She doesn't seem like the brightest lightbulb, but of course, when it came to something like this, she noticed the discrepancy. Kuhano didn't really seem to care at the time, but his sister was way too friendly, so of course she'd pay attention and remember such a small detail.

"No, no, no, that was a different skill. That skill was called 'Focus.' The one I got for awakening was called 'Track.' It lets me see living creatures on my mini-map when I activate it," I quickly corrected. *I hate having to lie about stupid little things like this, but I'm worried they'll abandon me if I tell them about me being an other-worlder.*

"I didn't know you had a skill like that! Now I'm extra happy that I snagged you before anyone else could. You're the perfect scout!" Kuhani said gleefully.

I let out a sigh, thanking God that she believed me.

"If you got your class because of your father…then what did you inherit from Miss Sylia?" Araya asked out of the blue.

For once, I wasn't the only one who was taken aback.

"What do you mean what did he inherit from me?" Sylia asked in surprise.

"Well, usually, children receive attributes or traits from both of their parents, correct?" Araya asked back.

I figured this was what she was getting at. Now that it was spelled out, though, it was a lot easier to respond without the chance of having the wrong idea.

I shouted out, "Silly's not my mom! Why would I call her by her name then?"

Sylia also shouted out, "Gray's not my son! How could I possibly have such an idiot come out of me?"

The two of us looked at each other. I asked, "Would it kill you to not make fun of me for once?"

"You two aren't related? My apologies. You just seemed so close. I knew that Miss Sylia was an old friend of my father, so I based my conclusion off of that," Araya explained.

As we walked up to the fort's large open gate, I said, "Don't worry about it. I'm sure anyone could make the mistake." *I don't actually believe that, though. There's no way I could actually be related to her,* I thought.

Before anyone could add to the conversation, a loud screech came from the fort, and a large rat charged out at us. The rat was slightly bigger than Kuhano in length and much larger in width. It wouldn't be a stretch to say that it could be able to be ridden like a horse. The rat had large round ears like a mouse and eyes as big as gemstones with thick black fur around them. Its tail was like a large tentacle with a bone-white tip.

As quickly as it appeared, it had died, chopped into multiple chunks by Sylia. "No one told me about any giant rats," she muttered. "All right, you four, consider this your first quest! Clear the monsters out of their temporary home, and your reward will be getting to live here!" she yelled out at us like a commander.

So, it's just a coincidence that we got our combat gear before coming here? That seems unlikely, I thought. "Lady Sylia, wouldn't it be faster for you to clear them out yourself?" Kuhani asked in confusion.

"Of course it would, but if I do that, you won't gain experience, and I can't gauge how much I need to train you all. So go on and get to it. I'll be watching." Sylia argued before disappearing from sight.

"Why is that ability a thing?" I asked out loud. I let out a sigh and said, "No answer. All right, well, what's the plan leader?" I asked Kuhani who was standing in front of the fort's entrance with her weapons drawn. When she struggled to respond, I made a suggestion to try to push her along. "Do you want me to find out how many there are? Or maybe the terrain we're working with? Or anything?"

Thankfully, it seemed to help Kuhani. "That sounds great. Get in there, find out how many there are and what route will be the best for us to take out small groups!" she ordered.

With a nod, I used my tracking ability and swapped it to track "Hostile Giant Rats." *Hopefully there's nothing else in here,* I thought as my mini-map started updating. When it was over, I couldn't believe my eyes. There had to be a dozen of them just near the entrance alone. I took my bow off my back and walked along the wall until I found a small opening to slip through.

The inside of the fort was ginormous. A large watch tower stood in the center that watched over the camp. *If I'm able to make my way up there, I'll be able to see everything.* Slipping by all of the red dots was a breeze, mostly because all of the rats were inside of buildings. *Of course, that also means that when a door gets opened, a flood of rats will bear down on us like we're in a plague,* I pessimistically thought.

When I got to the tower, it was pretty easy to ascend the ladder. Part of me thought that the ladder's wood would've rotted, but it seemed luck was on my side. Once I got to the top, I could see the whole camp just like I planned. There were two bathhouses, a couple of firing ranges accompanied by a training dummy pit that held as many rats as it did dummies, a building that looked like a large house, a storehouse, and something that looked like an obstacle course that had a large hive-like structure made of large branches. *Either that thing's a nest or it's a really wacky piece of training equipment. If it is a nest, how are we supposed to destroy that?* I thought as I took in the rest of the surroundings. After seeing nothing else of value, I descended the ladder and went to report what I had seen.

Once I got back to the group, I quickly explained everything I had seen and then gave my opinion on what we should do. "The best way to do this is to take the fort one building at a time, I think. Then again, if we make enough noise, then the ones near the nest might come attack us from behind. What we do is up to you, Kuhani. We'll do whatever you decide," I said, ensuring her that she had my trust.

"All right. Gray, go back up to that tower and shoot from above. If you see anything coming from the nest, please take care of it! The rest of us will clear the small buildings one by one and thin them out. After that, we'll destroy the nest and then work our way through the biggest building," she ordered.

As we all nodded in agreement and began our assault, I thought, *I didn't expect Kuhani to actually be a decent leader or strategist. I still have a lot to learn about her.*

Acquiring Our New Home!

Everyone got into a fighting formation outside of the small storage building as I made my way up the tower's ladder. *I really need to either get a bow sling or craft a makeshift one for when we travel,* I thought as I climbed.

When I took my position, I noticed two things. The first was that most of the rats that were outside were grabbing sticks from the nest, dipping them into the loch, and then throwing them back onto the nest. The second thing I noticed was a humanoid shadow in a second-story window of the large building.

Either that's where Sylia is watching us from or I must be seeing things because I'm anxious, I thought, brushing off my observation. *The rat's wetting their nest is a bit concerning, though. Whatever, it's making it so there won't be as many to fend off if they try to flank us. At least…they probably wouldn't stop doing a job in progress, right?* I wondered. I brushed my worries aside and signaled the group to start the operation.

At my confirmation that I was in position, Kuhani moved quietly toward the storehouse door. *The storehouse is one of the places with the fewest rats. From what my tracking tells me, there should only be four rats inside,* I thought. Araya and Kuhano stayed back as Kuhani opened the door with her new shield defensively raised. The moment after she flung the door open, she pulled out her sword and planted herself firmly to the ground.

It was nearly impossible for me to see inside the building, so I couldn't tell what was happening until Kuhani suddenly got pushed back. In the new position, her feet were still planted in the ground. A deep line in the dirt was present where she had previously been, along with two rats that trapped the other two inside. *So on the plus side, they're so big that only two of them can get through the doorway at a time. On the down side, their size adds to their strength,* I thought as I raised my bow and began to focus.

The rats seemed to be stunned after their attack on Kuhani. I didn't see anyone cast anything or even attack the rats, though. *Maybe they've been living in darkness, and the sudden shift in light is disorienting them?* I wondered. With the rats being stunned, now was the perfect chance to take them out. I nocked an arrow and took aim at the rightmost rat. I swiftly aimed and thought about where I wanted the arrow to hit my target as I let it fly. In less than a second, the arrow flew straight into the rat's head, embedding itself into the skull with an audible *thunk!*

As the rat collapsed, a "+110 XP" message appeared to confirm my kill.

Before I could nock a second arrow, Kuhano leapt atop the rat closest to him, digging his claws deep into the rat's flesh. It was as if his claws were a hydraulic excavator's bucket digging into the earth. As the rat jerked in an attempt to shake off Kuhano, it doomed itself. The more it moved, the more Kuhano's claws tore at the rat. It wasn't long before the rat stuck in the building attempted to move forward and take a chunk of his own out of Kuhano. Luckily, I was still paying attention. *I might not be as fast as I was at the guild, but I'm still fast enough!* I thought as I let an arrow fly into the rat's front leg, causing it to stop and screech out in pain before I sent another arrow into its head. Another experience gain message appeared when the arrow hit the target.

The last rat slipped outside and had its attention on Kuhani. The two of them traded blows back and forth like they were in a turn-based combat game. Whenever the rat tried to bite Kuhani, she would bash it in the face with her shield and then counter by slashing at it with her sword. Large chunks of bloodied fur were filling the ground until the giant creature attempted to pin Kuhani under its massive body in a last-ditch effort. When it jumped in the air to attempt the desperate move, the battle was decided. Kuhani's superior cat-like agility let her move out of the way before the rat could land. It would've still had a small chance had it not twisted its body in an attempt to still hurt her. When it fell to the ground on its side, she was free to deliver the final blow. She swiftly stabbed the creature in the stomach and greeted us with a "+110 XP" message. *So the XP is shared between party members, huh?* I noticed.

With one more message popping up, it seemed that Kuhano had finished the rat he'd been toying with. After the battle, Kuhani kneeled down and let out heavy breaths. After making sure that there were no reinforcements coming, I set my bow against a half wall of the tower and slid down the ladder. When I reached her, the other two were already beside her. "You all right, Kuhani?" I asked, concerned. I hadn't seen her take a hit, and her health looked full, but I was still worried nonetheless.

"Yeah, I'm just a little winded. I've never had to deal with so much movement before. Real combat is completely different than training!" she said with a giggle.

If she's able to laugh, then she's all right, I thought, my worries shifting to the fact that this was her first taste of combat. "We still have around four hours until the sun sets completely. Even with breaks, we should be able to clear these smaller buildings and all of out here before then," I said, attempting to urge Kuhani to let the group take breaks. *I'd rather go slower too so that we ensure no one gets hurt. Even though we have a healer, things could still go horribly wrong,* I thought.

When Kuhani's breathing wasn't as heavy, I went and grabbed my arrows out of the rats we'd killed. The second and third arrow I shot survived, but the first one had snapped near the tip, rendering it completely useless. Our next target to clear out was the bathhouses. *Taking a bath right now sounds heavenly,* I thought longingly, grateful that we would soon have such a luxury in our grasp.

I went back up the tower, and the group proceeded much like how they had with the storehouse. The doors to the bath houses were sliding doors, yet they were significantly smaller than the storehouses doorway. *In theory, that should work to our advantage since it'll only let one rat out at a time,* I thought as I got set up with my bow. I noticed that the bathhouses were bigger than the storeroom, so there would be more rats.

In what world does a bathhouse need to be bigger than a storehouse? Either the army had way too many soldiers here or they had way too few supplies, I thought.

After I was set up, Kuhani swiftly slid the door open. In the next moment, she'd drawn her sword and stabbed into the building. Once again, I couldn't see the inside, so I was surprised when we gained experience, especially when I realized that the rat hadn't showed up on my mini-map. *That's…unsettling. Hopefully, that's the only one that didn't show up,* I thought. I decided to look on the bright side though. Not only was gaining experience a plus, but with one rat taken out, we only had to worry about five more in the bathhouse.

The rats that began emerging from the bathhouse were fatter and considerably more sluggish than the ones from the storehouse. When everyone noticed the difference, Kuhani and Kuhano took positions at either side of the doorway and would strike at any rat that dared to emerge. Once a rat lumbered out the door, Kuhani would stab at its leg with her blade, and Kuhano would slash its throat with his claws.

When three of the six rats had died, I hit Level 3! *Well, this is boring, I wonder what Araya's doing right now,* I thought as I looked toward her. She was sitting on a large rock that was up against a tree next to the wall of the bathhouse. She kept her eyes on the two siblings, but it was clear that her head was in a different place.

In the small window of time that I lost focus, disaster struck. From the bathhouse beside the one we were clearing, the rats were launching a counterattack. With a loud snap of the wood and a thud from the door hitting the ground, a swarm sprinted out.

In a matter of moments, the swarm was bearing down on the group. Araya had climbed up onto the rock she had been sitting on but was too short to reach any of the tree's branches. Three rats stood between her and any potential escape route she had. Kuhano had reacted fast enough to get away from the wall to not be cornered but was being circled by two rats that refused to give him an opening to attack. Unlike the other two, Kuhani was in the heat of battle. Even though she made no noise, the tearing of her pants could be heard. The rat that had broken the door somehow managed to remove Kuhani's leg guards and was sinking its large teeth into her leg. Her health wasn't draining quickly, but there was no way for her to kill the rat. Whenever she tried to turn her body, the rat would bite down harder. If she tried to slash at the creature, her sword would hit the wall. When she tried to stab it, he would detach and dodge her strike before lunging and reattaching itself in a different spot. As all of this was happening, the larger rats were still coming out of the first bathhouse.

There's seven rats on the field and two more on their way. The fastest I could shoot with the focus roll I got would take fourteen-ish seconds to kill the current amount and eighteen-ish if they all came out. I could try to go for collaterals to decrease the clear time, but if I do that, I run the risk of shooting one of my friends. If I shoot a rat near Araya, she'll be torn apart in an instant since the other two would no doubt jump on her. I could shoot the rat on Kuhani, but there's a good chance I'd hit her too. Our best chance is for me to take out the one behind Kuhano so he can attack and try to kill the fat one at the same time. God, please let this be the right choice! I prayed.

I pulled back as hard as I could and waited for a rat circling Kuhano to line up with the fat rat lumbering slowly toward Araya. As soon as the fat rat was blocked from sight, I let an arrow loose with the thought of hitting the fat rat in the head. The arrow flew toward my target, quickly tearing its way through the flesh of the rat behind Kuhano and into the head of the fat rat. The fat rat looked as if it was wearing a gag arrow-in-the-head headband as it crashed to the ground.

At the sound of the rat hitting the ground, Kuhano realized he was free to attack. He pounced onto the rat in front of him and fiercely bit down on its throat, instantly snapping its neck. The rat that was biting Kuhani panicked at the sight and tried to finish his prey in a similar fashion. Thankfully, she was too tall for the rat to reach her neck. The rat dug its claws into her hip as it tried to scurry up her body. But his attempt was cut short when his claws got stuck in the tightly woven chain mail shirt she wore. The only ways he could free himself was if he used her blood as a lubricant to slip his claw out or break off the claw. Unfortunately for him, his claws were curved, which made it so he couldn't push his claw further forward to inflict fresh wounds. The blood she had lost had already soaked into her cloth pants and dyed them a deep crimson. The only way the rat could get free now was to break off his claw, which he refused to do.

The other three rats that were cornering Araya took notice of their fallen comrades. One of them looked up toward me as if it was gloating that it was about to settle the score while the other two got ready to finish off our healer. Araya wasn't inexperienced though, and with the class of archpriest, she had many skills at her disposal. When the gloating rat screeched, and they all lunged for the kill, she screamed out, "WALL OF LIGHT!" and created a barrier directly in front of her, causing them all to slam into a shimmering golden force field of light.

Now's my chance! I thought as I took a deep breath and swiftly shot arrows toward the rats. The first rat took two shots to kill, the first hitting near its liver, and the second piercing a lung. The second died of a clean shot to the heart. I saved the best for last, but before I could attack the previously gloating rat, it had recovered and turned its full attention to me. With how fast he sprinted toward the tower, it made me realize that I more than likely wouldn't have been able to prevent this from happening, even if I had been paying complete attention. The rat leapt onto one of the wooden legs of the tower and, within a second, was on a half wall that made up the canopy.

If we hadn't run into the bandits on our way to Heirshield, I would have been a goner. I unsheathed my Fiery Iron Dagger and prepared myself. The rat was perched on the ledge, snarling at me, waiting for me to let my guard down to strike. My heart was beating fast. When it came to range, I was cool and calculated. When it came to melee, though, I was significantly more worried as I remembered my run-in with the wolves. I made sure to make no sudden movements and to not let my guard down as I closed the gap between us.

When I was a full arm's length away, I steeled myself and attacked. The rat was ready, though, and swiped at me itself with its long claws. As I tore through its flesh with my dagger, I felt the weight of its large paws on my arm, and I instinctively jumped back. Thanks to my bracers, I came out mostly unscathed. The bracers had three deep claw marks and a large hole where its fourth claw attempted to hold on. *This is hardened leather! My arm would definitely be out of commission right now if I didn't have these bracers! Why can't I have a large pit of spikes behind me for it to fall into?* I whined, once again thinking back to my fight with the Alpha Black Wolves.

Amidst my panic, the rat I was fighting erupted into flames. The smell of burning fur filled my nose, and its screams of terror filled my ears. The rat fell off of the half wall and onto the floor of the platform as it writhed in pain. I screamed out as I stabbed it again and again until both of our cries ended. As I breathed heavily, I came to a realization. *Thank God my dagger's enchantment took effect when I stabbed it. Consider this the second time that magic has saved my life. Wait a second... If this is magic... I can use this fire to destroy the nest!*

With my eureka moment and the plan to destroy the nest now formulated, I hesitantly reached my hand toward the still burning corpse. The warmth from the fire could only be described as pleasant as I pressed the button on my glove to absorb the magic. With my gloves turning a bright orange as it sucked in the fire, I was ready. I lifted the corpse up and lifted it over the half wall so I wouldn't have to worry about it being in the tower later on. As I looked down at the rest of the group, it seemed that the fighting had ended with many corpses littering the blood-tinged ground.

Kuhani was sitting, propped up against a wall while Araya knelt down next to her, healing the rat-inflicted wounds. Kuhano was seemingly uninjured but was understandably concerned for his sister. Even from up in the tower, I could feel just how low our morale was after this fight. Kuhano glanced up toward me and thought sternly, *"You should probably get down here."*

With the tone he had, I was prepared to be kicked from the group. Anxiety filled me as I climbed down the ladder and made my way over to him. I stood next to him and crossed my arms. I took a deep breath as I looked away and said, "I know... It's my fault. If there's anything I can do to redeem myself, I will." I was trying to hold back tears. I couldn't help but think that I could have prevented everything.

What the hell are you going on about? None of us could've antici-pated an attack like that. You did everything you could. Hell, I'd say you did more than you should've been able to. Besides, we're adventurers now. If we're prepared to take lives, we should be prepared to lose ours. Putting your crisis aside, we have a bit of an issue. Follow me, he thought as he led me toward the bathhouse the fat rats had been coming out of.

The moment we walked through the doorway, a smell of rotting garbage assaulted my nose. I had to plug my nose just to be able to move in further. The room we were in was a changing room of sorts, fitted with benches and makeshift lockers. The wooden floor had a step down that led to a stone floor fit with a firepit and a vent above it. Ahead of us, a sliding door was in pieces and scattered on the floor.

The room ahead of the doorway was mostly a normal bath. The tiled floor spanned two levels and had drains in multiple spots. The first level was for washing one's hair and body before going into the bath to soak. A few steps up, the second level held a massive tub that looked like it was a commercialized hot spring. A thick bamboo water slide was below a large tank that had a glass jar attached to it. The jar held an aqua ball of light that slowly floated around. The floor of the tub was glass that had a large orange ball of light floating underneath it. There was a closed drain in the floor that was the size of a wall clock. Even though the drain was closed, there wasn't any water in the bath. Instead, there were three small nests. They were much smaller than the one outside, but they were definitely nests.

What should we do? I would suggest we burn them, but the build-ing might be destroyed as well," Kuhano thought. I let out a sigh, and when my body wouldn't let me breathe back in, I had us retreat out-side. After catching my breath, I finally replied, "Yeah, we definitely shouldn't use fire. Water honestly might be our best option since it would go down that massive drain, but God knows what's actually inside those things. We might just have to dismantle them ourselves."

"Whatcha guys talking about?" called Kuhani in her usual chipper voice. Even though she had just been a rat's chew toy, she was already back to her old self.

"There's um…a few nests in the bath, so we're uh…discussing how to deal with them," I explained as I looked away from her. "And…sorry for not doing my job," I added.

"What d'ya mean? There's no way someone around our level would be able to react to how fast those things came out! Besides, they weren't that tough!" Kuhani replied, making me furrow my brow.

"What do you mean they weren't that tough! You were literally getting eaten by one! Your pants are still coated in your blood!" I cried out at her, staring at her literal blood-red pants.

"That's not fair! Just because they apply a bleeding effect doesn't mean they're strong! Besides, it can wash out…I think," she whined as she puffed out her cheek.

"How did that rat even get your leg guards off?" I asked.

Kuhani instantly became red in the face. "I, uh…might've forgotten to close the latch on the side," she explained, clearly embarrassed. I let out a sigh and turned my attention back to our problem. "So any ideas on how to get rid of the nests without destroying the building? Worst case, we can just leave it for after we clear the rest of this place."

"HEY, WHAT ARE YOU GUYS DOING?" Araya shouted.

When we all looked at her, she instantly covered her mouth with her hands and looked away nervously. When I saw the three rats from the training grounds running toward us on the mini-map, I realized I didn't have time to chew her out and prepared for a fight. I ran in between her and our new opponents. Thankfully, the other two did as well.

"Take the two on the right," I said as I let an arrow fly, instantly killing the leftmost rat. *I guess Kuhani's right about them not being tough. We still shouldn't underestimate them, though,* I thought. From behind me, I heard Araya shout out, "God smite!" as a large guillotine-like blade of light appeared from the sky. Much like her "Wall of Light" spell, it shimmered and had a warm golden glow to it. As it slammed down into the ground, the last two rats were chopped in half, and slowly, we all turned to look toward Araya with wide eyes.

"I thought you were a healer!" I cried out in amazement.

Even though I was praising her, Araya looked like she was a child being scolded. "I-I'm sorry, you're right. I'll go back to just healing," she said disappointed.

"What? Dude, you literally just chopped those things in half while they were sprinting! Like, you're good, girl. If you have mana to spare, just go for it 'cause that DPS will always be POG," I said. *Why is my excitement bringing out my Internet lingo dialect?* I wondered.

"W-what does POG mean? Never mind, do you... Do you really mean it? I'm allowed to use my attack spells too?" Araya asked with her eyes shining in anticipation.

"Err... We should probably ask our leader, but your attack spells are part of your kit. If you're not utilizing your whole kit, then why even have those spells? It's like me with taunt. There's literally no point in me having it," I replied. We both turned to Kuhani in anticipation for her answer.

With a visible smile, she said, "You don't need my permission, just use your best judgment!"

At Kuhani's response, Araya's face lit up as she ran and hugged her. "No one's ever let me use my attack spells because they were all afraid I'd hurt them! Thank you, thank you, thank you!" she said as she smushed her cheek against Kuhani's chain mail protected chest. I was struck with a wave of worry after hearing Araya's words and wondered if I had made the best decision.

After the two had their moment, I piped up, "We have around two hours before sundown. We still have to clear out the nest and the rats by the actual loch, but otherwise, we're making pretty good time. Realistically, we could destroy the nests in the bath too before going into the big building."

"Wouldn't it be better to go into the building now, though? We won't be fighting in the dark if we do it now," Kuhani suggested.

"For some reason, I have a feeling that we won't be fighting in the dark no matter what time we go in. But we won't have light outside if we wait, so I vote to clear outside. It's also worth it to mention

I haven't seen any rats in the building from my skill," I replied. *If we go later, then my suspicions will be easier to confirm, so it's beneficial for me if we go later,* I thought.

"Hm… Okay. Sir Grayson, if you say so, I'll trust you. I vote to clear the outside as well," Araya said.

"Oh, uh, thanks? I trust you too. Also just call me Grayson. We're equals and groupmates right? No point in using formalities," I responded. *Something about this girl confuses me socially. I can't tell if I should have my guard up or let it down. Jesus, she's the one in this group that's going to be the first to find out I'm from Earth, isn't she?* I thought, using my unease of her as a type of foreshadowing for myself.

"Well, if we're all in the trusting Grayson boat, let's finish these rats and destroy some nests!" Kuhani cheered as she raised her sword to the sky. Our spirits were amazingly high for our first real mission that almost ended prematurely just minutes earlier. When we marched past the firing ranges and the training dummy pit, we came to the point where we could see the large nest and the many rats guarding it.

Compared to the amount that had come out of the bathhouse, it was a miniscule amount. The fact that we were in a wide-open area and could see all of our enemies didn't win them any points either. While each bathhouse had six rats pile out of them, the area in front of us only had five. Two of them seemed to actually be guarding the nest whereas the other three only appeared to be gatherers. It was like we were about to lay siege to a small town where less than half of the population was trained for combat.

Even with the comparison, though, we didn't stop our advance. Without any words, Kuhani and Kuhano rushed toward the two rat guards and met them head on. Once they were engaged, Araya used her "God Smite" to kill a rat that had been dipping wood from the nest into the water. At the same time, I let loose an arrow at a rat bringing the wet wood back to the nest.

Even with the distance between us, the arrow flew and easily inserted itself into one of the rat's hind legs. The rat squealed in pain but made a mad dash toward the nearby forest. Even though the initial shot didn't kill the rat, I knew the shot would be fatal. The whole time it was running, shrieks of pain could be heard until a light enveloped it as it disappeared into the forest.

"Araya!" I shouted out as I let loose an arrow that embedded itself into the last rat's eye, instantly killing it. "Why did you heal that rat?" I cried out.

"It was in so much pain! If you don't want me to heal it, then either kill it in one shot or don't make it suffer like that!" she angrily yelled back.

I let out a sigh. *That's fair, I guess. As long as it doesn't happen when we fight a really strong monster, it'll be fine,* I thought.

As Kuhani and Kuhano finished their targets, we all reconvened. "That was a cinch! But...how are we going to destroy this nest?" Kuhani said, looking up at the giant rat nest that was easily double her height.

I confidently smiled and said, "Leave it to me guys, I have a trick up my sleeve just for moments like this! Also, you may want to get behind me because I honestly have no idea how strong this is going to be."

Saying that made me feel a little less confident, but it was true. With a few glances to each other but no words of protest, everyone got behind me. I took a deep breath and raised my right hand in front of me like I had at the guild and steadied it with my left hand. As soon as I pressed the button, it was like I had a flamethrower. A large vortex of flames flew out with the glove as the focal point. Even with all of the wet wood, the nest in front of us disintegrated to ash in moments. The flames were so hot that it felt like I was going to melt. Once the fire stopped spewing from the gauntlet, I realized how thankful I was for telling everyone to get behind me.

The ground that the nest once stood was entirely blackened. Anything that was touched by the flames was charred and glowing red. "Well... Looks like this would be a bit overkill for the nests in the bathhouse, eh?" I asked as I chuckled nervously.

When I turned around, everyone had their mouth agape in astonishment. "How did...? Mr. Grayson, how did you cast such high-level magic? I thought you were a ranger!" Araya exclaimed, clearly the most surprised.

And she's back to thinking she needs to add the prefix in front of my name. Wasn't it 'Sir' before too? Did I just get an upgrade? I wondered as I decided that it would be easier to not lie. "Oh, I can't cast magic. These gloves are an artifact that can store magic natures and unleash them. It's stupidly powerful, though, so I was told to not use it if I didn't have to. It's also permanently bound to my soul, so I can't even think about selling it or anything," I said with a smile. Sure I didn't tell them how I got such an item, but technically, I wasn't lying about anything. *Now that I think about it, I lie a lot huh? I should really stop that,* I thought as I made a mental note.

"Kuhani, did you know that Mr. Grayson had something like this?" Araya asked as she swiftly turned toward our cat-girl leader. "Well... I mean... No," she said dejectedly.

All of a sudden, I felt bad for never mentioning it. *I can't stand to see Kuhani sad. I gotta do something to try to cheer her up,* I thought.

"Well, I guess the CAT'S out of the bag," I said, before adding, "Fur real, though, don't rely on it, okay? It's PAW-er is a last resort only," I said as I walked toward the lake and pressed the button to absorb the water nature.

"YOU CAN'T JUST NONCHALANTLY DO THAT WHILE YOU SPOUT CAT PUNS!" Kuhani yelled.

"Would it be better without the puns?" I asked.

"NO! I mean... Yes? I'm confused. The point is, don't just use that thing!" she answered.

"But why not?" I innocently asked. "It's not like I'm hurting anything by taking a little bit of water. Besides, this could save us at some point."

"Or it could cause us all to die of drowning!" Kuhani argued.

I shrugged "Yeah, okay, that's fair. But you're just going to have to trust me. I mean, we were all in just as much danger if not more before you all learned about it, right?" I said back.

With a loud groan, Kuhani said, "You just had to pull out the 'Trust me' card, didn't you? Fine, do what you want. Let's just finish clearing this place out already, and if you kill us, I swear I'm going to kill you," she said as she started stomping her way toward the bath-house with the nests.

I stood there in stunned silence. Araya looked at me and shrugged with apologetic eyes before running after Kuhani. *"Unlike my sister, I think your artifact could be really useful. Though, I'm surprised. She hasn't opened up like that to anyone in a while. She must like you more than I thought. She'll get over it soon. Maybe sleeping in a bed for once will cool her down,"* Kuhano thought to me as we started walking toward the bathhouses.

"You guys haven't been sleeping in beds?" I asked in confusion.

"No one in town would give us a room, even though we had the coin. So we've been camping out in stables or in the plains," he responded. *"You'd be surprised at how pillowy tall grass can be. Lots of bugs, though, bit of a damper,"* he added with a sound that automatically made me think he was disgusted, even though I'd never heard it before.

I just frowned, unable to respond. *What are you even supposed to say to that?* I wondered as I put my hand on his head.

"What do you think you're doing? I'm not my sister. Don't try to pet me or I'll gut you," he thought as he pulled away.

I let out a laugh. "That was a joke, right?" When he didn't respond, I asked again, "Kuhano? It was a joke, right?" My laughter slowly faded, and I took a few steps away from him.

The nests in the bathrooms were miniscule in comparison to the main nest that we'd already destroyed. "So...I'm not allowed to use the water I abso—"

"NO!" Kuhani shouted as she cut me off.

I let out a disappointed sigh. "Okay, you win. So... You guys wanna grab sticks from the nests and use that as a way to draw straws?" I asked since I doubted anyone wanted to be the one breaking down the nests.

"That sounds like fun! Let's do that!" Kuhani said as she went to grab a stick.

So don't bring up the magic gauntlet thing, and she won't be angry. Got it, I thought as I picked out a stick.

I should've focused more on what stick I grabbed because when we came back together, I, of course, had the smallest one. When I was destroying the first nest, I found out what was causing such a rancid smell. It turns out that the rats used their feces as a type of adhesive.

"I can't wait to wash my hands after this," I grumbled as I pulled sticks out of the bath. As I dismantled the first nest, I found out they were quite spacious inside. So much so that there was room for a dozen baby giant rats. They were small, around the size of newborn kittens, and had little to no hair on them. A sense of dread overtook me as I realized. *Holy crap, those fat sluggish rats were mothers!* I didn't want us to kill literal babies, but on the other hand, if we didn't, they'd grow into the monsters that we had to face off against.

"Hey, guys? Can you come in here real quick?" I shouted to the group.

In a few moments, they were all here except for our healer. "Where's Araya at?" I asked Kuhani who had been outside with her.

"She insisted on taking a bundle of sticks to the forest. What's wrong? Did you get hurt?" she asked out of concern.

"No, I'm fine. Hell, it's probably better she's not here honestly," I said as I motioned for the two of them to get closer. When they did, they saw the baby rats in the remnants of the nest.

"Oh no," Kuhani quietly said, "what should we do? They're going to die from starvation, right?" she asked as she turned to me.

I looked down toward the ground and whispered, "It'd probably be best for us to mercy kill them...right?"

With a sound akin to that of a groan, Kuhano said, *You two go, I'll deal with this.*

"What do you mean you'll deal with this?" I asked.

He looked at me and rolled his eyes. *Gray, you're a decent guy, but let's be honest here. I'm just a wolf that can use magic. I might be a beast-person, but I'm significantly more beast than man. All I see is here is a free meal,* he said back simply.

The thought of Kuhano eating the baby rats almost made me vomit. Killing them was bad enough, eating them was a whole other story. I felt a slight tug on my arm and turned to see Kuhani with her face completely drained of color. I simply said, "Okay," and nodded to Kuhano as I followed her out of the building.

As the sky grew darker, so did our expressions. Since there weren't many other sounds, we could hear the tearing of flesh and the snapping of bones that would be accompanied by a "+5 XP!" message.

"When he does things like this it makes me think that people are right. We really are monsters," Kuhani said softly, breaking the silence.

I didn't even know how to respond or even if I should. "What do you think about us, Gray? Why would you join our group knowing what we are?" she asked.

"I dunno. I guess I just think of you two as anyone else. I mean, you two are the homies, so...I dunno. I guess I like you guys. Even though Kuhano acts like a jerk, I'm pretty sure he's a *tsundere*, but I don't think either of you are monsters. You two were also the first people to make the initial effort to be my friend. I guess that's why I joined the group. So yeah, I think that answers both questions," I nervously answered. Finding the words was difficult, to say the least. It was even more embarrassing to say, and I ended up saying more than I wanted because I was so flustered. Usually, I would've said what I thought the person would want to hear, but for once, I actually gave my opinion.

"Thanks, Gray. I won't say everything's better, but it makes me really happy to hear you say that," Kuhani said with a small smile. "Though...what's a *tsundere*?" she asked.

"Eh? How do I put this simply? A *tsundere* is someone who's rude and unfriendly in the beginning but becomes friendlier over time. I dunno, I just think that's Kuhano, though maybe he's just a butt," I explained.

"Oh! Yeah, Kuhano's definitely a *tsundere* then!" Kuhani said.

It felt like we should've laughed, but in this situation, neither of us could bring ourselves to. When Araya joined us, I explained what was going on, and we all sat around in an awkward silence that no one knew how to fill.

When the sky was lit up with stars, Kuhano came out as if nothing had happened and thought to us, *It's done. I took care of the other nests too. Let's clear out the big building now. We can clean up the remains tomorrow.*

Part of me was trying to trick myself into thinking he meant the remains of the nests, but I knew what he meant. With a nod of agreement from Kuhani, we all made our way toward what would be our final encounter of the night.

When we opened the door to the building, we were greeted by a fully lit house. Ceiling lanterns were hung perfectly to make it so that the whole interior was fully illuminated. "What could have lit all of these lanterns?" Araya asked aloud as we all funneled in.

"Whatever it was, it wasn't a rat," Kuhani responded, sounding far more serious than she usually did. Directly ahead of us was a staircase that led up to a second level. Normally, you would go toward the first point of interest, but we were well aware by now that we needed to be careful. We moved directly to our left into a hallway that had a window at the end. Besides a few paintings with large tears in them, there wasn't anything of interest in the hallway itself. However, where it led was a different story.

Through a door in the hallway was a room with absolutely no windows. There was a large table in the middle of the room, and the walls were plastered with maps. *What is this? Some sort of war room?* I wondered. At the opposite side from the door was a built-in fireplace with a map of the surrounding area above it. I stared at it a few moments before saying out loud, "Oh, it's a play on words. Because normally, you'd put a family crest or a kingdoms crest above the mantle, but we're at Loch Crest. So the map itself is a crest. That's kinda funny. I mean, I wouldn't burst out laughing or anything, but it's amusing, I can admit that much."

Everyone just stared at me blankly. *We're in what could possibly be the most dangerous part of this "quest," and you're wasting time on that? Miss Sylia was right,* Kuhano projected as he rolled his eyes.

"Wha—Come on. Why do you have to say it like that?" I cried out.

"Apologies, Grayson, but I'm afraid I must agree with Mr. Kuhano," Araya added, Shooting me down even more. When I turned to Kuhani, she looked like a deer in headlights before slowly turning away and whistling.

I walked out the door and dejectedly mumbled, "I hate you all."

"Grayson, we shouldn't split up!" Kuhani cried from the war room.

Before I could respond, I heard Araya say, "He'll be fine, Miss Kuhani, he may be a bit silly, but he's dependable. If there are any rats here, he'd be the first to know. Aside from this safety, though, anyone can tell that he's been holding onto a lot of stress from earlier. We should let him have some time to himself."

I let out a sigh. *Leave it to the healer to notice something like that. Was I really wearing my emotions on my sleeve that much, though?* I thought as I wandered around aimlessly. *I know it's probably nothing, but I should use this to kill my suspicions,* I thought as I walked up the stairs.

The second story had two doors that I could see as well as a window at the end of the hall. Out of curiosity, I walked to the window and looked outside. Sure enough, I could see the guard tower in the middle of the outpost, but something didn't seem right. *If I'm correct, there should be a window in the room to my right. And if I wasn't imagining things… there's a good chance of someone being in there.*

When I found myself at the door, I could feel my hands getting clammy and my heart beating harder as I reached toward the handle. When I grasped it, I just held it as if it was somebody's hand. I took a deep breath and pulled the door open.

To my surprise, I was in what must have been the sleeping quarters for some of the soldiers. The room felt cramped with the amount of space the furniture took up. The wall ahead of me had three bunk beds, each with a dresser against the wall across aside from the one to my left, which had its dresser below the window.

With a sigh of relief, I walked into the room and made my way toward the window. When I got into position and stared out the window, I mentally confirmed that this was exactly where the shadow I saw was. "This is too awkward. There's no way they wouldn't just use the window in the hall. I guess I was just seeing things," I concluded as I closed my eyes and scoffed at myself. When I turned around to leave and opened my eyes, I saw a large rat in a torn lab coat on two feet, wearing large circle glasses with small cracks in them, staring back at me.

"What were ya spyin'?" he asked innocently.

Instinctively, I jumped back and slammed right into the wall.

"My lord, fella, are you all right? I didn't mean to scare ya. It's just been a while since I've gotten to talk to people."

To my surprise, he had a slight Southern accent to his voice.

I leaned over the top of the dresser and held my back. "Yeah, yeah, I'm good, man, don't worry about it." I looked up at the rat who was staring down at me from the second bunk of the nearest bed. He had dark-brown eyes and light-brown unkempt hair that went everywhere.

"You sure you're all right? I can whip you up a healing potion that'll make you right as rain!"

"It's all right, really. I didn't take any health damage or anything like that. Thanks, though. I'm Grayson, how about you?" I asked. I had other questions I wanted to ask like "What are you doing here?" and "Why do you sound like you're from Texas?" but I held my tongue.

"Oh, right, my name is Dr. Crice, but you can just call me Crice, my friend," he said as he jumped off of the bunk and held out his paw. He had a major hunchback, so he was slightly shorter than me, even though he was an absolute unit of a creature. I grasped his paw and gave it a firm shake. "So are you a physician then? I thought that healers were basically doctors?" I asked.

"Ha ha, no, I just studied at college for a long time," he said as he waved his hand.

"College?" I asked. *I don't remember anyone saying anything about college, much less any sort of schooling,* I thought to myself.

Crice looked like a cornered animal. After a few moments, he let out a sigh and asked, "Okay, can I be straight with you?"

With a nod from me, he continued, "I'm from another world. I know how crazy that sounds, especially with how I am, but I swear I am. It's one of the two reasons that I live here instead of in the city or a town."

"Yeah… That's not that surprising. You're really bad at hiding it. Are you from Earth or a different planet?" I asked without skipping a beat.

Crice blinked as if in a daze. "I'm from Earth… How do you know about Earth?" he asked.

Is this guy serious? I thought before saying, "You're joking, right? I'm also from Earth. I thought that was kind of obvious. On a separate note, though, what was the other reason that you don't live in actual civilization?"

As I talked, Crice went through many emotions. At first, he seemed ecstatic to the point of tears, which then shifted to sadness, and then became very serious when I asked about his other reason.

"You… You have to be kidding, yeah? I thought being a giant rat would've made it obvious. I'm sure you know about werewolves. Whenever the moon is full, those that suffer from lycanthropy transform into a man wolf hybrid and lose control of themselves, yadda, yadda, yadda. Basically, I have a form of lycanthropy that turns me into…well, this. I don't lose control of myself, but I'm sure you've heard about the prejudices of beast-people. People seem to think I'm one of them and treat me like I'm some kind of wild animal. Adding that onto the unfair treatment we get as other-worlders made me realize the best choice was to just leave. I followed the river out of the western gate and found this place. To my surprise, the giant rats welcomed me with open arms. I tried to get them to not attack people, but most of them were brutes. I'm happy they're gone now. So no hard feelings about that," he finished with a worn smile.

"Damn, I expected you to be a murderer or crazy. No offense, I just didn't think it was going to be something that tame. I'm sorry you were treated like that," I said with a heavy heart. I didn't expect to feel this much emotion for someone I barely know, but we have a bond that next to no one else in this world can understand. I didn't realize just how much I missed being able to talk about anything I wanted without the worry about my identity being found out.

"You don't need to apologize, friend. I'm sure that you face hardships just the same. If you don't mind me asking, though, did the guild finally send out a request to kill me?" he asked in a tone that wasn't hostile but rather accepting.

"Why would the guild send a group to kill you? We're just the new owners of this place and were going to move in."

"Wait, so you aren't going to kill me?" Crice asked with narrowed eyes.

"I mean, if you try to kill us, then maybe, but otherwise, not that I'm aware of," I said with a shrug.

"You said that you're the new owners, right? What does that mean for me?" he asked.

I didn't even think about that. We'd basically be kicking him out of his home, I realized.

"I'll think of something, but ultimately, it's going to be the whole group that has to decide. They're pretty accepting, but maybe if we show them that you have some use, they'd be more willing to let you stay here. What did you go to school for?" I asked as I racked my brain.

"I was a chemist," he said as he stood taller, showing how proud he was.

"Okay, we can actually work with that. You're an alchemist now, right? Obviously, we'll tell them about the wererat thing, but let's keep the other-worlder part under wraps, okay?"

With a nod from him, I took the lead and led the rat man downstairs to talk with the group.

When the two of us walked down the stairs, we were greeted by Araya who was leaning her head against the wall while supporting herself with her staff. "Araya? Are you all right?" I asked as I raised my bow, preparing for an attack.

At the sound of my voice, Araya slightly moved her head and drowsily said with a yawn, "Hi, Gray. I'm just sleepy."

I relaxed my guard and let out an irritated sigh. "I thought that we were under attack. There're beds upstairs. It should be safe, but make sure it is before you go to sleep."

Araya lazily opened her eyes and started slowly walking up the stairs, not even noticing Crice. When she reached the intermediate landing, she looked down and said, "Miss Kuhani is in the room to your left. Goodnight." She gave a bow before walking up the next set of stairs.

"So…that was our healer. She's a pretty young archpriest who's a bit hard to get a read on. We only met her today, but she already fits in, so that's a good sign," I said over my shoulder to Crice as we walked down the foyer toward the door. *Come to think of it, I've only known Kuhani and Kuhano for probably thirty hours. It feels like we've been together forever, though,* I realized.

When I opened the door, we came into a dining area that was connected to a rather large kitchen. The dining room had a small rectangular table in the middle of the room with a few surrounding chairs that were broken and had cobwebs on them. Compared to the rest of the house, this actually looked abandoned. The kitchen had an island in the middle with a countertop and a crude stone oven tucked beside a doorway where Kuhano was lying, but otherwise, it was very bare.

Kuhani was leaning on the island as she wiped off the dust. "I sent Araya to get some sleep," I said, announcing my presence.

"Oh, okay. Where did you end up disappearing to?" she asked as she looked up. At the sight of Crice and I, she completely froze.

"I, uh…went upstairs and found something that I need to talk to you about," I answered.

Snapping to reality, she slowly began reaching for her sword.

Crice must have noticed because he closed the distance between him and I so he could hide behind me. "Calm down, Kuhani, he's mostly harmless," I said in an attempt to deescalate the situation.

"Mostly?" asked Crice with a raised eyebrow as Kuhani stopped reaching for her sword.

"What? Do you want me to gloss over the fact that you're a wer-erat? If you want others to trust you, then you need to be open with them like you were with me," I answered as if on impulse, letting his not-so-secret secret out instantly.

Kuhani just stood there, watching us bicker until Crice asked, "Then why did you not want to tell them that I'm an other-worlder like you? If we don't want to be talkin' with our tongues out of our shoes, shouldn't we be completely transparent?"

I blinked in pure disbelief at what I just heard him say (the other-worlder part, not the tongues out of our shoes thing.)

"Gray? What does he mean he's an other-worlder like you?" Kuhani asked as she slowly started walking toward us.

I took a moment before saying, "Well, um… It's like he said… I'm an other-worlder. But I'm still the Grayson you know!"

I took a step forward suddenly, which made Kuhani stop her steady approach and take a step back. I stopped moving when Kuhani sorrowfully asked, "Does Lady Sylia know?"

Before I had a chance to respond, Sylia's voice echoed around the room. "Yes, I've known him since he first came here." Then she came out of the shadows. "Has he done anything to make him untrustworthy so far, though?"

"No! I wasn't thinking that he was untrustworthy, I swear! I was thinking that he thought he couldn't trust me," Kuhani quietly replied, looking down, ashamed, her tail drooping entirely onto the floor. She mustered her voice and said, "I'll get over this. You're reliable, and I consider you a friend, so I'm going to do my best to make you feel the same way!" she shouted to me with tears streaming down her face.

"Wait, Kuhani, I already told you that I think of you as a friend! How are you not mad at me or scared of me? I thought that everyone was afraid of other-worlders?" I asked.

"Of course I'm afraid! But you're you! Sure, you're odd, but you don't seem like someone that would try to kill everyone and take over the world. I trust you," she said, sniffling.

"But… But I thought that other-worlders were feared because all the world's tragedies have been linked to them in some way?" I stammered.

"*Yeah, but you're an idiot,*" Kuhano thought.

"Exactly! Oh… Uhh, I swear that's not what I meant, Gray!" Kuhani added.

Sylia burst out laughing while I was just in stunned silence. "Glad to see that you all agree with me now! With that out of the way, I'm making the executive decision to allow the rat man to stay.

I honestly expected him to be hostile and thought you'd have to kill him. Good job getting him onto our side, Gray."

"Wait, you knew about him?" I asked as I pointed to Crice who looked hopelessly confused by everything.

"Of course I knew about him, why do you think we got you all geared before coming here? I told you, this was just a way for me to see how you all need to improve. Some of you were better than I expected, and some were worse than I thought," she said as she looked around.

"I don't even know how I'm supposed to react to this. I'm not surprised because it's you, but I can't believe you'd send us into this," I said straightly.

"Calm down, Gray. They were Level 1's, they were so squishy that you all should've been able to one-shot-kill them if you chose where to hit them correctly. That being said, we'll have a lot to talk about tomorrow. For now, all of you should get some rest."

I was going to argue, but I suddenly became aware of how tired I was. "After all of this, I could use a rest." Kuhani quietly said before leaving the room.

"Well, I guess that settles it. Come on, guys," I said as I started to leave with Crice and Kuhano behind me.

"Hold on, rat man. You and I need to have a talk," Sylia said before we left.

Crice and I looked at each other before he shrugged and said, "Go on ahead, it ain't the first time a pretty girl asked me to be alone with her. The girls should use the room on the left while we use the room on the right, unless y'all don't care about that."

"Alrighty, I'll let them all know. Good luck," I said to him as we left the room and proceeded upstairs.

"*Is Grayson even your real name?*" Kuhano asked as we were walking.

I let out a small chuckle. "Unfortunately, I froze up when I was asked about my name and ended up using my real name," I replied, recalling when I told Sylia and the elven priests my name.

"*Idiot,*" he thought back.

I lightly tapped on the door to the girls' room. No response. I knocked harder. No response. I lowered my head and breathed out a heavy sigh. "Pardon the intrusion," I said as I opened the door. Immediately, I was greeted by the sight of Kuhani in a white lace nightgown. "Wow, you look…amazing?" I cringed as the words fell out of my mouth.

Instead of getting punched like I'd come to expect, Kuhani just smiled with sad eyes. "You won't tell me you're from another world, but you'll give me a compliment?" she asked, making my heart skip a beat. "Teasing," she added as she stuck her tongue out.

"Right," I said as my heart pounded. "Anyway, do you want us all to sleep in the same room or separate us gender-wise?" I asked as I closed my eyes in an attempt to calm myself down. *Stop it, Gray! You broke her heart. You are not allowed to have flirty thoughts or any of that crap until you make things right!* I thought as I awaited her response.

"Hmm… We should probably get used to sleeping together since we'll have to camp out together on quests. Let's use this room then!" she said without a hint of embarrassment in her voice.

"O-okay. I guess I'll sleep over here then," I said as I walked over to the bed nearest the window.

"Could you two be any more awkward? I hope you two make up soon," Kuhano thought as Kuhani put out the lanterns and the moon's glow began to illuminate the room. She jumped into the bed across from mine while Kuhano claimed the floor near the door.

The bed was harder than I would've liked. Kuhani, however, seemed like she was in love with her bed as she rubbed herself all over it, seemingly marking her territory much like a normal cat would. *As long as she doesn't spray, I'm completely fine with this. Wait, do girl cats even spray?* I thought as I lay there.

"Gray? Out of curiosity, why didn't you tell us?" Kuhani asked softly.

I turned my body toward her and said, "It's not that I didn't trust you guys. I was scared. At first, I lied out of habit, but then I realized that if I didn't keep lying, then the truth would come out. From what I was told, I kinda figured that anyone'd abandon me if they found out my secret, and I didn't want to ruin my chances of being in this group."

Kuhani turned on her side and looked toward me. "Gray, my brother and I are hated by mostly everyone because we're not human. Don't you think that we would be the most willing to accept you?"

"Well, I can't say the thought didn't cross my mind, but I didn't want to take the chance," I said, ashamed.

"Lady Sylia and my brother are right. You really are an idiot, Gray," she said with a smile. "Maybe if you come clean about everything, I won't feel so bad about you lying to us."

Oh, she's manipulating me. I didn't expect that from her. Though is it really manipulation if I was just going to tell her anyway? I wondered. I let out a sigh, "I don't think there was a whole lot. I lied about how I got my class, and…actually, is that all? Now that I think about it, I don't even know."

"Are you sure you aren't hiding anything?" She eyed me suspiciously.

"Why would I lie again when I'm trying to prove I trust you as well as regain your trust? That would just do the opposite," I said with hostility. "I'm going to sleep. I'll answer more stuff tomorrow when we're all together," I added in annoyance.

"Are you serious?" Kuhani asked excitedly.

I started making overexaggerated snoring sounds to get the point across.

With a small cheer, she added, "All right. I'm gonna make a huge list of things to ask you about!"

Yeah, whatever, just don't question the validity of my answers then, I thought as I drifted off to sleep.

7

Answers and Preparation!

"**S**ir Falkeen, there are too many of them! We have to retreat!" I heard someone yell.

Where am I? I wondered as I looked around at the hellish landscape around me. I was in some sort of cave where the stone was charred and glowing red with steam rising up from small holes. The steam that filled the stagnant air smelled like metal and had a red tinge to it. The heat in the cave was so unbearable that I felt like I was going to melt.

Two people were ahead of me. The first was a large beast of a woman who wore a full suit of purple plate armor and wielded a large tower shield in one hand with a war hammer in the other. Even in all of the armor, it was clear she was a woman; however, it wasn't clear if she was even human. *I can't even imagine how strong someone'd have to be to wear all of that, much less one hand a war hammer!* I thought in astonishment.

The other was a more familiar sight. It was the man who had saved me when I was being chased on my way to the guild. His gear was entirely different than when I met him. He was decked out in armor that made him look like a paladin in a fantasy game! His armor was silver and had small accents of gold. To my surprise, he wore no helmet, allowing his golden hair to add to his paladin-like image. His primary weapon was a large blade of golden light that incinerated a pack of skeletal burning dogs that were attacking him and his party.

"We're almost done cleansing this damn tomb! We can't retreat now! We have to push on!" he shouted in response to the first voice I had heard.

"R-right! It was foolish of me to think we could give up now!" the voice said back.

I looked toward the sound of the voice and saw a small man with pointy ears sticking out of his green-colored bowl-cut hair. The white robes he wore were drenched with sweat, and he had no weapon in hand aside from a book. After muttering some words, a bright green glow enveloped us all. Suddenly, the heat felt like a mere inconvenience. I could only imagine the relief that the two people wearing full plate felt.

The two ahead of me continued to carve their way through the hordes of infernal dogs approaching. The woman moved gracefully through her enemy's lines, even though she should've been weighed down by her gear. Anything that attempted to damage her would have their attacks blocked before getting bashed by her shield or pummeled by her war hammer. Falkeen was casually walking and would swiftly slash with his sword whenever an enemy came near. Nothing attempted to attack me or the green-haired elf as we followed the two through the hellscape.

The group approached a double door made of some sort of mineral I had never seen before. The door was so large that it reached the top of the cave. On various points on the door were carvings that depicted a mountain and some sort of large creature.

"Leave this to me, my lord," came a soft, elegant voice from the purple-plated woman. She holstered her weapons as she took a few steps forward before punching the door with all her might, shattering it into pieces.

"You just destroyed a magically reinforced azunalite door that was the only thing keeping that damn thing in there. The worst part about it all is that I'm pretty sure we could've just pushed it open!" the green-haired elf seethed.

"Oh... My apologies, I suppose we could've. You must admit, though, it was kinda cool."

If you say that it was cool, that just instantly makes it uncool, I thought in response to the woman.

"What's done is done, Violet. Besides, those damned things seem to be afraid of this thing. You two ready for this boss?" Falkeen asked as he walked over the mound of crushed door.

"One moment, I'll buff us really quick," the elf said.

"Thanks, Salad Bowl! We can always count on you," Falkeen said with a large smile.

The elf let out an annoyed sigh. "How many times must I say that my name is Klaus and not Salad Bowl!"

"Come on, you know I'm just joking. Really should give that nest some styling, though," he muttered. "Thanks for the buffs! OH! Top my health off too, and let's go!" Falkeen requested like an excitable kid as he jumped down the mound into a large circular chamber.

"Then don't run out of my range, you idiot! I know you're excited to use that new sword of mastery thing, but come on!" Klaus yelled at Falkeen.

Sword of mastery? What is this? The Legend of Zelda? I guess it could be argued that this is a temple of fire too, huh? Whatever happened here must've turned this tomb into the cavern it is now, I thought.

As if sensing Falkeen's presence, the room went from a pitch black to emitting a red glow like the rest of the cavern as soon as he touched the ground. The glow didn't come from fire like the rest of the tomb but instead from large stones in the middle of the room. At first, they looked like normal stones until they started rolling and stacking on top of each other.

Within moments, a giant made of solid molten rock stood in the middle of the room. I had to tilt my head all the way back just to see its face. Instead of looking like a pile of rocks, it now looked like a third-grader had broken something and hastily tried to glue it back together; only the broken object was a bunch of rocks, and the glue was magma.

"A magma giant? So that's why monsters were awakening and driving the apostles of flame out of the temple. I can't believe that a powerful flame spirit came here and transformed into a magma giant!" Falkeen said with a laugh. "This is gonna be fun!" he shouted as he pulled out a longsword with a blue glow that released a beam of blue light as he swung.

Wow, it really is just like in Leg—I thought, getting cut off by a disembodied sound that startled me awake.

As I slowly came to, I realized I was being woken from someone's loud shouts.

"Wake up, you lot, Sylia wants everyone to meet in the war room!" I heard Crice say.

I lazily opened my eyes and turned my head toward the window to see that it was barely daybreak. I slowly sat up and looked around the room to see everyone else doing the same.

That was all a dream, huh? How active is my imagination that I came up with such a ridiculous scenario as that? I wondered as I recalled my dream. Without uttering any words, the four of us moved like zombies down the stairs toward the first room that we had explored the night before. *It's way too early for this. I can't believe Crice was okay with waking us up for Sylia.*

When we entered the room, Sylia was looking at the map above the mantle. "Oh, it's a play on words," she muttered to herself before noticing we were all in the room. She cleared her throat and said, "I've spent the last few hours gathering my thoughts about how to train you all. Now that you're all here, I'm going to go over your performances and explain what you'll be doing for the next few months," she explained as she turned around. "You four are going to need to do something big if you want your band of misfits to be recognized. Lucky for you all, I think I have just the thing to do that!" she added as she threw a poster onto the table. It was for some sort of group arena event the guild was hosting.

"Lady Sylia, you can't possibly mean you want us to compete, right? There's no way that we could fight in the Battle of the Groups, much less win!" Araya said with wide eyes.

"Of course you're all going to compete. You don't have to win, but under my guidance, you'll be able to get third place in the overall bracket no problem! You'll definitely win in the Wood Rank bracket, especially since you all seem to have some form of teamwork already. Even if it is very crude."

"Uhh… What exactly is this Battle of the Groups thing?" I meekly asked.

"Right, I forgot that you wouldn't know. Basically, it's an event that the guild holds near the end of the year's third season to raise the people's morale before the fourth season comes. There are brackets for each rank along with an overall winner's bracket where the top teams of each rank will go against each other. Usually, the Woods get knocked out pretty early in the final bracket, but I have a feeling that you four can change that!" Sylia explained.

"But wouldn't people in even Iron have a significant advantage over us due to levels alone?" I asked.

"Normally, yes. But two of you have actual classes, and one of you is lucky enough to have an outrageous amount of stat points," she said, looking toward Araya and I. "You other two will have to make up for the lack in power. But I'm sure you've faced much greater hardships, so I believe the two of you can do it," she added as she shifted her gaze toward Kuhani and Kuhano. "Speaking of stats, you four went up a few levels, so you should have some stat points, yeah? Kuhani, put two points into Agility and two into Fortitude for now. Kuhano, I recommend one Perception, two Strength, and one Agility. Araya, do either two Intelligence, or one Intelligence and one Luck. Either one is viable, but if you don't want to have to rely on crit heals, then sink your points into intelligence."

Sylia seemed to be unfittingly serious. Instead of goofing around when it came to the other three, she was actually attempting to make them better fighters. *Something's fishy here,* I thought as I looked back at the poster she had thrown over at us. That was when I noticed the rewards.

First place in any bracket would receive four platinum coins. Then for being a finalist in the overall bracket, both groups would receive an immediate rank up. For winning the overall, the group would receive rare magical items for each person in the group.

Not gonna lie, these rewards are pretty insane, but they seem totally out of reach. Each rank requires you to be a certain level and have a certain amount of experience in quests of that level. In Wood bracket, we'd be well enough off. Beyond that, though…. It seems impossible.

"Gray, I can already tell what you're thinking, and trust me, it's not impossible for you four to become finalists or even win the overall, especially after you've trained with me for the next six months!" Sylia said, sensing my uneasiness. "Now all of you, listen up. I'm going to give you pointers on what you can improve upon right now!"

As silly as I thought our goal was, I definitely wanted to improve my combat abilities. *If we fight in the tournament, we're almost guaranteed to get through the Wood battles off of power alone. If we lose, then we lose basically nothing. It's a low risk for a high reward any way you look at it! Plus, four platinum is a lot of money. If we needed to stay at an inn again, if it's six copper a night with three meals a day, then we could stay there for over a year and a half! This amount of money could no doubt get us some insane gear if we won!*

"Gray! Are you paying attention!" Sylia shouted at me.

I looked around with a nervous grin and admitted, "I, uhh…I definitely was not."

Sylia let out a large groan and started again. "All right, I'll only explain this one more time so that Gray knows what everyone else will be working on. Kuhani, you're to focus on attracting the enemy's attention and dodging their attacks. You don't have as much health as other protectors, but your speed makes it so you'll be able to dodge more attacks. Kuhano, you need to work on executing your target instead of letting them die slowly. The faster you take out one target, the faster you can move onto another, and the less damage your opponents can output. Araya, as a healer, you're nearly perfect, so I want you to help Grayson perfect attacks with his artifact. You can use the time to raise your proficiency with your attack spells too. That way, Grayson won't be holding you down. Remember, the more proficient you are with a spell, the less mana it'll take and the more damage it will do! The fact that it takes 25 percent of your mana is ridiculous."

Araya and I looked at each other. While I had a surprised look on my face, Araya wore a warm smile. It put me at ease. I couldn't tell, though, if she was smiling at me or smiling because of Sylia's compliment about her being a perfect healer. "A quarter of your mana! I know your damage is amazing, but that for sure has to get lower! Wait…if we're getting your atta—Sylia? What exactly are you proposing we do?" I asked, completely confused and a bit concerned.

"Simple, I want you to use your artifact to absorb her light magic and figure out how to use it without unleashing a damn apocalypse. This works as a good transition to talking about you, Grayson. You're surprisingly versatile, but you seem to not realize your worth. The fact that you even thought to go for a collateral shot for a multi-kill so soon after becoming a ranger is impressive. Plus, you made the right call at the ambush. Most low-levels would've gone for the single rat hindering your protector. That or they would have attempted to save the 'defenseless healer.' You need to be more confident in yourself. The less time you waste arguing with yourself, the more time you'll have to fix the situation. Hesitating for a second can mean the death of your whole group later. Even if one of you makes a wrong call, if you all back each other up, it'll be more effective than just one person making the right call. All of you would do well to take that to heart."

"I see… Is there anything else I should work on?" I asked. Part of me was happy about how I was praised, but my heart felt uncomfortably heavy. *It was constructive criticism, but self-confidence has always been hard for me to control. Plus, now people could actually die because of me! I see her point, but I don't know a good way to make it so I'm more sure of myself.*

"These six months will be good to build up trust with each other too. You may be trusting each other with your lives, but I'd say you all have a long way to go when it comes to normal trust," Sylia added.

"W-well, I trust him just as much as before! We talked for a little bit last night. I understand that he had his reasons and that it wasn't that he didn't trust us!" Kuhani shouted out.

"Oh? I thought you were the one who was the most worried about him not trusting you all?" Sylia rebutted with a raised eyebrow.

"I might've overreacted at the time," Kuhani confessed as she tried to hide behind her hands. "I was worn out and not thinking properly at the time. I'm still disappointed that he felt he had to lie to us, but I can't fault his reasons! If I was able to hide that I was a beast-person, then I would. But I can't, and now that the metaphorical cat is out of the bag, I want nothing but the truth between us all! Okay?" Kuhani asked somberly.

The range of emotions I felt was a roller coaster. I was confused, relieved, ecstatic, and then remorseful. I felt so bad for making Kuhani feel like this that I thought I was going to cry. I gave her a small smile and nodded when I felt the warmth of my tears falling down my face. It wasn't normal crying where my throat got hoarse, though. The tears were just slipping out of my eyes. *I guess I'm happy that Kuhani isn't as hurt as I thought.* I let out a chuckle at the absurd thought and said, "Man, this is embarrassing. I guess this is where I make due on my promise to answer any questions you guys have, eh?"

We all took seats around the table with me taking the seat near the hearth. I couldn't tell if it was because they wanted me to be at the head of the table or if they just wanted to make it so I couldn't escape. Either way, it didn't matter to me. To my surprise, Araya was the one to ask the first question.

"Did something happen last night?" she asked in utter confusion. That was when it hit me that Araya had absolutely no idea that I was an other-worlder. *Right, she was asleep last night when everyone found out!* I realized. "Well, I'm an other-worlder. Specifically, I'm from the planet Earth. I don't know if that's important. Same with Crice who's just kinda hiding there in the corner." *I can't believe he hasn't reverted back to his human form yet,* I thought.

Araya stared at me with her usual smile, and then her mouth opened and her brow furrowed. She then began frantically looking around at everyone who in turn stared back at her to see her reaction. "He isn't joking!" she shouted out. Everyone gave her a small shrug. "Why am I the last one finding out about this?" she cried out.

"Well, you went to bed earlier than everyone else last night," I responded straightly.

Araya crossed her arms as she let out an annoyed sigh and began pouting. "It's not a huge surprise, but you should've told me first or at the very least not dead last!"

"Wait, you're not scared of me? Instead, you're mad that I didn't tell you first? And since when did you start calling me just Grayson?" I cried out in response.

Araya shrugged. "It was obvious something was weird about you. You were always the most odd, especially when you made up a story to explain how you received your class. Everyone who has one knows about the treacherous ritual one goes through to receive a class. I assumed that you were lying to protect Miss Kuhani and Mr. Kuhano's dreams of awakening one. You seem like a nice person, and I'd like to think I'm friendly enough to know people's secrets, so yes, I'm not scared and I'm a bit upset. To answer your last question, I began calling you Grayson when I realized you were prone to events that made me embarrassed to look up to you."

"Hey, you just slipped in something really hurtful there," I said.

Araya just shrugged and went back to her normal innocently smiling self.

"Well, now that we're all caught up, anyone else have anything they want to ask?" I threw out.

"How did you come to this world? Did you use teleport magic? Did you invade in a carriage from the sky?" Kuhani asked with a glimmer in her eye.

I almost felt the need to lie so that I wouldn't disappoint her. *That would just have the opposite effect, though,* I thought.

"I died," I said nonchalantly. I closed my eyes and crossed my arms. "Specifically. I committed suicide. My old life was miserable. I was stuck in a dead-end job where it felt like everyone hated my guts. On top of that, I had no friends, and my parents were almost never around, so I couldn't talk to anyone really. Plus, I was an otaku who just played video games and watched anime in my free time! I thought if I worked for my hobby, I could deal with life, but that evidently didn't work. That's basically how I got here. Magic doesn't exist on Earth, and I wasn't rich enough to take a rocket ship here or anything. Hell, the people on Earth aren't even aware of life on another planet. It was always just a theory." When I finished, I opened my eyes and looked out, noticing that everyone had different reactions. Kuhani looked somewhere between mortified and nervous. Araya had her hands together as if she was deep in prayer. Kuhano was licking himself. Lastly, Sylia was looking at me with an apologetic look on her face.

"I'm sorry, Gray, I didn't mean to bring up bad memories," Kuhani said, putting words to Sylia's look.

I looked her in the eyes and smiled. "Don't worry about it. It's all in the past now. Part of me is glad that it happened because without it, I would've never met you guys."

"Let's move on before this gets too sappy. Did adventurers exist in your old world?" Kuhano thought to the group.

"No...well, in the past, I suppose, yeah. But by the time I was alive, the world really didn't need adventurers. Anything that could be considered a monster was already able to be defeated by anyone. A majority of the world was already explored, and even things outside of our world were being explored."

"But you seem like you were born to be an adventurer, except for how you sometimes complain about how you need a break. Maybe you're more of a tactician than an adventurer."

"Hey, I never complain audibly! I'm never going to figure out how your whole thought projection thing works. Anyway, I used to play a lot of video games. Specifically, role-playing games where you are an adventurer. So I'm not physically used to the role, but I more or less understand tactics and basic concepts," I said, hoping that it answered his nonexistent question.

Next, it was Sylia's turn to ask a question. "What were your parents like?" she asked shyly.

I was completely taken aback. I didn't expect this from Sylia at all. *Not only did she ask such a personal question, but I didn't expect her to seem shy. She's usually very "I'm the boss, do what I say, answer what I ask when I ask it, I know the best course of action!" If this was my first impression of her, I would forever think that she was the type who was very cute but too shy to show her true self most of the time.*

"Well, like I said, my parents weren't around a whole lot. It wasn't their fault, though, they both traveled a lot for work. Not that we really needed the money, though. My mom became a stewardess who would fly to all sorts of countries when I started middle school.

She'd always bring back some sort of souvenir for me from the countries she flew to. Usually, she'd work three-day or even four-day trips and then have a few days off. She was kind, but she was a huge airhead. She couldn't even do housework without making a bigger mess, so it usually fell to me to clean or make dinner for us when she was home. Well, that or we'd eat a frozen meal," I said with a laugh.

As my thoughts drifted to my father, I slowly stopped laughing and let out a sigh. "My dad wasn't around at all, really. Even when he was home, he'd just go out drinking. I don't even know what he actually did for work. All I know is that he was gone a lot and made tons of money. For some reason, I think that he was probably hurt the most when I died, though. When I was sixteen, I was grabbing his wallet for him before he went out one day, and there were a bunch of pictures of him, Mom, and me in it. Before that, I thought that he was just a work-absorbed jerk that didn't care about his family at all. It was just nice knowing that he cared about us in some weird way. So I can't really say what my dad was like. Either way, they both tried their best in their own way. They always had my interests in mind and supported me whenever they could," I finished.

I felt like I had said something bad about them, but that's how our family was. Nothing I said was wrong or slanderous, but saying it out loud felt...wrong, almost. I loved them, but thinking back on it, I much preferred the odd family that I had now.

"So does anyone have anything else to ask?" I asked, bouncing into a tone that mirrored Kuhani's usual "chipperness." When I looked around, everyone was looking at me with pitiful expressions. "You guys good? Is something wrong?"

"Gray, you don't have to answer anymore today. We didn't realize that your past was so...disappointing? That isn't right, it just seems kind of sad. How about we all get something to eat and start training? You can take a day if you need it, though, Gray. I know how painful talking about old memories can be," Sylia said as she came around and put her hand on my shoulder.

I looked at her with a raised eyebrow. "I'm fine, really. Are you all sure you're okay?"

Instead of answering, though, everyone walked up and crushed me in some sort of malformed group hug. "What the he—URH!" I let out as we all fell when I pulled away out of surprise. Even though I was being crushed, it wasn't bad being in a group like this. Slowly, everyone rose up and, one by one, apologized for pressing so hard, and every time, I had to tell them that there was nothing to apologize for. For some reason, even Crice apologized, which made no sense to me. After his apology, he offered to cook for everyone. For obvious reasons, they were hesitant but followed him out of the room.

Eventually, just Sylia and I were left. "You know, they all probably sympathize with you in their own ways. I know that I wouldn't like people to dig up my past and interrogate me," she said to me.

"I don't want them to feel bad for me, though," I said as I looked down. "They're my friends, y'know? Wasn't it you who said that I'm not supposed to make my friends cry? They weren't crying, but they might as well have been with how depressing this got."

Sylia looked at me and rolled her eyes. "You know that's not what I meant. Besides, they're not just friends anymore. You've finally all taken the first step. They're family now, whether you like it or not," she said as she started making her way for the door. "I'm gonna be helping Kuhani and Kuhano today, so don't hold Araya back if you decide to train. Have her use different spells on you and see what you can do with them. I don't know how your gauntlet works, but it seems like it magnifies power somehow. Either control the amount it puts out or figure out how to transform it into specific spells. Crice is going to be cleaning up those remains in the bathhouses, so don't train over there, okay? Don't want to get the water and fire spirits riled up."

"Sounds like a plan. Though, what do you mean by water and fire spirits?" I asked.

With a groan, she said, "Quick answer, magic elements exist because of spirits. The baths use water spirits to create water and fire spirits to keep the water warm. If another magical element were to come into contact with them, it would cause them to have a... less than ideal reaction. Luckily, they're contained, but if the glass were to break, then this whole outpost would be wiped out if they came into contact with each other or a different element's magic." If she didn't look dead serious, I almost would have thought that she was exaggerating.

That's terrifying! Although... it could be useful in certain situations. Then again, they're spirits, though, right? Were they alive and are now dead? Or are they a being made up of mana that's alive? Are they even alive! I'm going to have to read up on this at some point, I thought, somewhat ashamed of the fact that I thought about using the spirits as some sort of weapon, especially since I had such an overpowered magical weapon anyway.

"Okay, so no magic in or around the bathhouses. Got it!" I said as I gave a thumbs up to Sylia. *I hope I didn't just trigger the tempting fate trope and we're going to blow up the outpost somehow. That would just make everything we did yesterday pointless!* I quietly prayed to myself.

After we ate, we split up into groups and went outside. "Are you sure you're up for this, Grayson? I know I can heal wounds, but I can't heal emotional wounds, at least not well," Araya asked me, clearly plagued with concern as we made our way toward the forest's edge near the charred remains of the rat's nest.

"Of course I'm sure! Besides, if I take a day off, then I pull you down with me."

"If you say so, Grayson," Araya said with a sigh of defeat.

I let out a wry chuckle. "Thank you."

"Yeah, yeah. Since I'm not forcing you to take a break, how about you tell me how you actually got your class? Of course, you don't have to tell me if you don't want to, but I'm really interested!" she politely bargained. After contemplating whether or not I should tell her, I came to the conclusion that there was no point in keeping it a secret.

"Just don't think that I'm crazy, okay? When I signed up with the guild, I got to talk to God for a second time. He let me change my appearance and pick between the three combat roles and then a class in one of those roles. Since I can't use magic and I didn't want to feel pain, I picked a damage class. I had four choices, but one was a mage, so I really had three. I ended up picking Ranger on a whim.

That's basically how I got mine, though. What about you? You said that you had to go through some sort of ritual right?"

When I asked about the ritual, Araya stopped walking and went into a sort of thousand-yard stare state. After a few moments passed, she came back to her senses but looked noticeably weary. "I'll tell you about it some other time. It happened less than a revolution ago, and it was…terrible. I'm thankful that you didn't have to go through such a process. The only reason I survived and can survive was because I was raised entirely for it."

I sat there in stunned silence. As much as I wanted to pry, I knew that it wouldn't lead anywhere I wanted. *What did she mean that she was raised for it? Does everyone with a class have such a horrible experience? By revolution, did she mean social revolution or a planetary revolution, like a year?* I had tons of questions but none that I could ask. Instead, I just patted her on the back and said, "Well, when you're ready, I'll be here to listen."

"Thank you," she said as she raised her hands in prayer and bowed. "Let's start training now! I won't use any damage spells today since I won't be able to use the baths to regain my mana. With that being said, we should be able to go at least until noon before I need a break!"

So mana can be regenerated by taking a bath? I imagine sleeping and eating certain foods would work too. I wonder if it's spiritual and meditation could work? I wondered.

With a thumbs up from me, I recommended, "Maybe we should work on precision absorption first? I've only really absorbed magic from still targets. I imagine trying to absorb a moving spell would be way more difficult. Plus, I don't want to get chopped in half when you use your damage spells later on."

"Sound's good, Gray! I didn't even realize that was something you'd have to be conscious of. I definitely don't want to accidentally kill you!" Araya said before we got started.

Generally, Araya would throw a healing spell on me, and I would try to absorb it with my gauntlet. Every time she did, I wouldn't absorb it. *Her spells are just flashes of light. I can't even rely on my eyes to figure out when to absorb it.*

"I see why we need to train now," I said while panting. "I honestly thought this was going to be way easier, but absorbing an actual spell is harder than I expected," I confessed. I more was just audibly complaining to myself about why it was so difficult.

"I can use 'Barrier of Light' if you think that would help? You haven't even been focusing that hard but you seem tired. Oh no, were we right? Were you just trying to act tough for my sake so that I could practice?" she asked without any hints of sarcasm. If it had come from Sylia, I, for sure, would have thought that she was just making fun of me, but Araya seemed genuinely concerned. As I mulled over her words, that's when I came to a realization.

"Focus! Of course, I should have been using my focus!"

Before Araya even had a chance to ask what I was talking about, I had raised my bow and was focusing hard on a tree knot. To my dismay, though, nothing changed.

"Grayson? What are you doing?" she asked.

"I'm trying to activate my skill to make my perception higher so that I'll have a longer window of time to react to your spells! For some reason, though, nothing seems to be changing," I quickly tried to explain as I was getting more and more frustrated.

Suddenly, I felt Araya lift up the back of my shirt. "It says here that you can only do it every twenty-four hours and that you still have a six-hour cooldown."

My face reflected how stupid I felt inside. *How could I forget about the cooldown?* I cried in my thoughts. *But even then, I just can't roll again. I should still be able to increase my stats by focusing on something. Am I not able to completely focus for some reason?* I wondered as I let out a nervous chuckle, "Right, I guess I forgot about that." It felt as though Araya was looking down on me; figuratively, of course.

"Like I said, I can just use Wall of Light so that you can get some con—"

"NO!" I shouted. "If I don't learn to work off of your normal spells, then it's just going to make things harder for us." Even though I had just tried to give myself a handicap, it felt like having a stationary wall would ruin the purpose of this training.

"Okay. But please remember to not overdo it. I have around 80 percent mana left, so even using it sparingly, we'll have to take a break in a couple hours."

"How exactly does mana regen actually work? Do you just have to not cast spells for a while?" I asked. *Usually, in games, you regenerate mana outside of combat. Well, or you'd have a certain amount of mana until you can rest.*

"No one ever told you!" she exclaimed. When I shook my head, she let out a sigh and started to explain. "There are five ways to regenerate mana. Certain races have passive regeneration, but humans aren't one of them. The four other ways include eating, bathing, meditation, and sleeping. That order is from shortest to longest time," she explained, looking quite happy with herself.

"So bathing and sleeping is kind of out of the question, huh? Wait a minute, is that why you were dead tired yesterday? Did you use a majority of your mana?" I asked after I came to the realization.

Araya blushed and started fidgeting. "No, I was just tired! You're thinking too much into it!" she protested.

Clearly, I was right, though. The more she tried to convince me otherwise, the more I believed that I was right. Eventually, I had to concede so that we'd actually be able to continue training.

Over the next hour, Araya would cast a healing spell, and I'd try to absorb it to almost no avail until...

"All right, get ready! Healing light!" she shouted out.

I closed my eyes and took a deep breath. Right as I began feeling the warmth of the light, I pressed the button on my gauntlet. Instantly, the warmth faded, and my gloves were shining with bright light. The radiating light was a symbol that proved that we had finally succeeded!

"You did it! What did you do differently this time?" Araya excitedly asked.

"I closed my eyes and waited longer than usual. Earlier, I was trying to absorb it when I saw it, but this time, I waited until I felt it's warm embrace."

"Well, now that you have it figured out, this should be easy as pie!" Araya said as she pumped her fist in the air.

I thought that she was more reserved. *But then again, I suppose she is still a kid,* I thought to myself at the sight of her.

"What are you waiting for, Grayson? Use a spell!" Araya shouted out in anticipation. It seemed like she was more excited about this than I was.

What can I even do with light spells? I thought. *I could obviously use a healing spell, but surely, there must be something else. What if...?* I wondered as I thought of a spell that paladins could use in World of Warcraft. With the thought of the spell in mind, I pressed the release button, making sure to point away from Araya and the fort.

In a moment, a translucent figure in the form of an angel crashed down before us. It was like he was made up of pure light. He had the look of a guardian clad in plate armor equipped with a steel bulwark shield that had a large white sun in the middle. His wings were a pure white with the feathers having silver stems. He turned to me and knelt down. His voice was light but was filled with power. "What is thy bidding, my king?"

I looked to Araya and then looked back at the guardian before me. Both of us were amazed at the summoned angel before us. *He's almost the spitting image of the 'Guardian of Ancient Kings' spell that I remember! I think that I added some things, though, I don't remember him being this detailed or having a shield,* I thought before I asked, "Umm... What exactly can you do?"

"I can be your guard, your blade, or even your closer of wounds, my king," he answered instantly.

I looked to Araya and whispered, "Did we just create a summon that can fulfill all roles?"

"I think you did, Grayson. That's...amazing to say the least. Something like this should theoretically be impossible," she whispered back.

"Your orders, my king?" it insisted.

"Right, um... Please rise. If you don't mind me asking, do you know how long you can exist in this realm?" I asked, trying to get as much information on the new summon I'd created.

"I will remain here until you order me gone or I sustain enough damage to break my ties to this world," he answered.

"You're telling me that you're basically permanent?" I shouted out in utter amazement.

The angel before us nodded.

"What would be a job befitting you, though?" I wondered out loud as I tried to come up with a job for him.

"Forgive me, my king, but after going through your memories, I believe that guarding this compound would be the best job for now. I deem this area to be unsafe for you and your allies. I would be much more at ease if you allowed me to defend against any threats."

"You're able to go through my memories? I'm not entirely happy about that, but you had my interests at heart, so it's fine. I see what you mean too, so I'll allow you to guard the fort. Before you do that, could you go and introduce yourself to everyone? I don't want them thinking that you're something dangerous. Oh! I forbid you from going near the bathhouses, though! If you've seen my memories, then I'm sure you understand why."

"My deepest thanks, my king. I will make introductions and then perform my duty around the outer wall," he said before walking away from us, leaving Araya and I to stand there stunned by what just happened.

"Grayson? If you could create that from a normal healing spell, then what can you do with stronger spells?" she asked.

"I...I don't know, and I'm honestly a little terrified to find out. But stuff like this might just give us enough of an edge to actually win. This is just the first spell too. If this glove's creations work by reading my thoughts like I think it does, I could come up with much stronger spells. Though, maybe we should just stick with small, not overpowered creations for now," I said, slightly terrified at the amount of power I now held.

*****

The next six months were just a taste of how insane this new world was. Every day felt meaningful as we pushed ourselves to the limit of our abilities. The spells that Araya and I created were all outlandish and thought to be impossible. Our spells ranged from making pure weapons of the elements to spells that did something as simple as make a floating lantern. We logged every new spell we made into a small book that would be given to the council of mages when Araya was able to cast all the spells that were contained.

On top of our spell creations, Araya attained new proficiency levels over her damaging spells and somehow over her healing spells. Of course, her damaging spells were lower since we waited a while before using them. Luckily, Araya quickly learned how to make her "God Smite" dull enough so that it wouldn't cut me in half if I mis-timed my absorption. Once we started our training with her damage spells, the timing became significantly more difficult to absorb. Sylia taught me that since I couldn't see the spell or feel it, I had to sense its energy. It took me around a week for me to finally understand what she meant. Eventually, absorbing Araya's spells was so easy that I could literally do it in my sleep.

Every few days, Sylia would bring us all back together to attack her with everything we learned. All the while, she would be teaching us how to cooperate better as a group as well as techniques that we could use to exploit our enemies' weaknesses.

It wasn't until around three months in that we could manage to even hit her. Technically, we never even beat her in a fight, but around four and a half months in, she insisted that there was nothing more that she could teach us. Unable to accept that, we forced her to continue training us in different styles.

I learned melee combat instead of my usual bow/magic style. Araya would use attack magic entirely instead of a mix of healing magic and attack magic. Kuhano ended up picking up world-based healing magic, which also held support spells that would buff things like our armor and regeneration. We were all aware that Kuhano knew magic, but none of us expected him to be able to heal so well. Kuhani continued to tank, but she swapped to dual-wielding daggers to enhance how quickly she could attack. Even when she had her shield, she would barely block due to her proficiency in avoiding, so it was nice to have more damage be put out without changing our group composition much.

Outside of the group, Crice ended up becoming a sort of caretaker for us. He handled all of the cooking, cleaning, and getting supplies. It may be because he was somewhat Southern, but his sweet tea and the chicken and dumplings he made were to die for. He never managed to get any fur in the food, though why he never transformed back into a human, I couldn't say.

On another note, when he was fixing up the storeroom, he found an intact alchemy set. With his vast knowledge of chemistry from Earth, he quickly learned how to make potions and even changed the recipes to make the potions more effective. Occasionally, he would ask me to use my tracking skill to find herbs that he needed, but otherwise, he was pretty self-sufficient. Needless to say, the time before the tournament flew by, and finally, the day for sign-up was here.

"Grayson, you aren't bringing your bag?" Crice called out as we were walking out of the gate.

"What bag? I don't have enough stuff to need a separate bag," I responded as I twirled around, showing all of my equipment on me. I had my quiver on my back, my armor equipped, a small sheath on my right hip with my dagger placed inside. My bow was in a makeshift bow sling that held the bow over my shoulder so that I didn't have to carry it. And on my left hip, I had a potion pouch that Crice made to store and protect three small vials of health potions.

"I suppose you've got a point there. Do your best, y'all. I'm rootin' for ya!" he called back.

I gave him a wave and then turned to the angel standing near the gate. "Keep the place safe. If anything happens and you're unable to deal with it, come to me, okay?"

The angel before me bowed and said, "As you wish, my king. May your enemies find regrets that they were on the wrong side of history. I pray for your safe return."

I grinned at his "wrong side of history" comment, but it wasn't unusual for him to say something like that. Little did he know that we truly needed to defeat our enemies, though.

Around the same time, Sylia started training our secondary skills. She confessed to me that we were basically out of money. As it turned out, fixing up an old military base and buying supplies for six people was quite costly. Sylia only had nine gold when we left Elsaria, and the elven king hadn't been paying for her reports of my progress. The only reason we'd been able to keep buying supplies was because Crice would sell a majority of the potions that he made. *As long as we get the four platinum for winning the bracket, we'll be fine,* I thought to myself as we started making our way toward Heirshield.

"I can't believe you didn't bring the bag Mr. Crice worked so hard to make. Do you know how long it took him to get the materials for that?" Araya whispered to me, clearly upset.

"I'm sure he understands. Besides, I don't have any reason to carry a big bag like that. If we were going on a quest, sure, but we're going into the city," I responded.

Araya rolled her eyes and said, "Fine, but you better make it up to him somehow."

When we got to the waterfall, Kuhani asked, "Lady Sylia, I've been wondering something for a while. Couldn't we have just fought monsters and leveled up? That way, we'd be getting combat experience and more skill points, plus we'd still be in the Wood bracket since we wouldn't have done enough quests!"

Honestly, I've been wondering the same thing. I mean, sure, we're stronger tactically now, but if we don't have the strength to back up our plans, then it's next to worthless, I thought in agreement.

"I never explained that? Being above the level cap for your rank makes you ineligible to compete. So if any of you went above Level 5, we'd be screwed, unless you did the quests to rank up into Iron which would make it so you'd be facing up to Level 15s. Plus, Wood level quests are very...not worth it experience-wise or financially. Basically, it would have been a lot of traveling and a lot of wasted time," Sylia explained. "I'm going to call this now. You four are going to destroy the Wood bracket. In fact, I want you to use your secondary skills. Save your mains for later on. Even though you're in the lowest rank, everyone from the higher ranks who have a brain will be paying attention to your combat abilities."

"Wasn't our training supposed to be a fallback, though? For if Araya fell in combat or Grayson managed to lose his bow?" Kuhano thought to us all.

"It was, but I believe you misunderstand what Miss Sylia is saying. If our opponents believe that Grayson is a melee attacker, then they won't expect him to launch a ranged attack. If they believe that you're our healer, they'll leave me free to heal. It's a simple deception," Araya contributed.

"Wait. Did I really just understand something before Kuhano did? Who's the idiot now? Idiot!" I taunted at him.

"Just the fact that you care about something so insignificant proves that you're still the idiot here. Moron."

"Urk!" I let out. I wasn't expecting an actual comeback. "That's...fair," I responded, feeling dejected.

"Well, at the very least, you've learned some humility after all this time," Sylia said with a laugh.

As we continued making our way toward Heirshield, we were having small conversations instead of walking in silence like we had six months prior. Every now and then, we'd stop to pick bundles of Enchrydian. Enchrydian is an herb that Crice uses in almost all of his healing potions. It's a lot like peppermint and is pretty common, but since Crice uses a ton of it, we gather it whenever I notice it.

When we reached the city, it was like a breath of fresh air. Even though the city was built over the river, the air was significantly less humid than we were used to. Granted, we lived by a lake, so anything would probably be less humid. Walking on the stone walkway was significantly more comfortable than walking on uneven dirt paths or rough patches of sand. The bustling city was a nice change of pace when compared to the quiet lakeside home we had.

Even though we had just arrived, Sylia gave us no time to catch our breath and forced us to go right to the guild hall. All was well until we came into sight of the building.

"Miss Sylia, do we all have to go in there?" Araya meekly asked as she looked to the ground. "Of course you all do. They need you and your membership tags to register you as a team. I'm assuming you're afraid of people making fun of you?" she asked Araya.

Without words, everyone but me nodded at the same time.

"You guys too? Sheesh, okay. If it helps put you at ease, Gray will go scout it out. There shouldn't be many if any people in there since it's only been a few hours since quests have gone out," Sylia said.

I gave her a cold stare and started walking toward the building. *Why couldn't she have done this? Why do I have to do the grunt work?* I annoyedly thought.

I walked into the building and thought I had been transported back to my first day in the guild. It looked just as run-down as it had that day. It was hard to believe that the owners of this place would be holding a tournament with such magnificent prizes.

"Mr. Gray...son?" I heard a familiar voice ask.

I looked toward the service counter and saw the moss green-haired witch looking at me sleepily. "Hey, you're...Zini? Right? I'm kinda surprised you recognized me," I said with a smile.

"Well... It's on your...membership...tag," she replied.

"Oh," I said, looking down at the necklace that I had completely forgotten about. "So where's the Viking?" I asked, looking at the empty seat next to her. *The old man made quite an impression when I first came here, even if we didn't talk all that much.*

"He...died," she said, looking down.

"WHAAAAT!" I shouted out in surprise. "I mean, yeah, he seemed old, but he was insanely fit! There's no way that man of men is dead unless a monster took him out!"

"You're...right. I was...joking!" she said with next to no change to her tone.

I looked at her with eyes that could only be compared to a dead fish. "Why would you joke about that? You almost gave me a heart attack," I scolded in a completely monotone voice.

"Sorry... He just has...the day off."

I let out a sigh of relief and looked around. There were a couple of regal-looking people talking with the Guildmaster at a table, but aside from them, there wasn't anyone else. *Looks like we're in luck then,* I thought as I turned around to leave. "I'll be back soon. We sign up for Battle of the Groups here, right?"

"Yes? Also...your group must...all be in...the same rank," she answered as I walked out the door.

*****

When I reached the group, Kuhani and Araya were sitting on the edge of the canal, looking down into the water. "All right guys, don't worry. Aside from the desk girl, there's only two other people, and they're talking with the Guildmaster," I reported to the group.

"Really?" Kuhani asked hesitantly but relieved.

"No, I'm lying. Of course, really," I said sarcastically.

With a nervous chuckle, Kuhani said, "Right, okay. Let's go, guys."

She took the lead, and everyone followed her, semi-confidently. When we all walked in, Zini was taken aback. "Where have...you all...been?" she asked. To my surprise, she ran around the counter and hugged the three other members of our group. Kuhano even let her hug him, even though he obviously was uncomfortable about it. "I thought...you all...left or died," she said as she held back tears.

"Um, what's going on exactly?" I confusedly asked.

Kuhani broke out of the hug and had a large smile on her face. "Zini was the one to help Kuhano and I sign up. She used to constantly be encouraging us. 'You two...will definitely...find a group!' is what she would say," Kuhani explained with a near perfect impression of Zini.

"She was one of the first humans to treat us like actual people. We owe her a lot because without her constant encouragement, we would've left the guild," Kuhano explained.

"I see. I'm assuming she did the same for you, Araya?" I asked.

"No! She just really likes me for some reason!" she said while attempting to escape from Zini's grasp but to no avail.

"For some...reason? It's because...you're so...small and cute!" Zini said with a twinkle in her eye as she continued to hug Araya with an iron grip.

I let out a small smile. *No denying that, I guess,* I thought.

Suddenly, Sylia let out a very overexaggerated cough that caught everyone's attention. "We're here to sign them up for the tournament," she stated with an annoyed look. Apparently, that was enough to get through to Zini because by the time I looked back over, she was already behind the desk getting some sort of machine ready.

"Of course! If you'll just…put your tags inside…this slot… please," she said to us all with a smile. She seemed a lot more at ease than when I had come in.

Maybe I was a bit hard on her about her joke, I reflected as we put our tags into the machine's slot.

When we put our tags in, it sucked them all in and made a loud thud. Soon after, it shot our tags out like a toaster with a small ring of a bell. "Oh good…you're all…set! Wood bracket…will fight in…two days. Weapons and armor…will be…provided so that…no teams have…unfair advantages," Zini said as she gave us a folder full of papers.

Sylia snatched up the folders and motioned for us all to leave. As we all waved our goodbyes to the witch at the desk, I noticed the Guildmaster shiftily looking at us. As soon as our eyes met, he tore his gaze back to the two in front of him. When we got toward the middle of the road, Sylia instantly said, "Of all the damn people to be in there. Of course, it's that woman and that son of a—"

"Whoa, whoa, keep it PG-13, Silly. What's wrong with her? She seems nice enough. What could you possibly have to hate her for?" I asked with a raised eyebrow and crossed arms.

"Don't tell me you can't guess!" she angrily shouted at me.

My raised eyebrow stayed stationary as I shrugged and said, "Nope, I really have no clue. Is it the long pauses she takes when she talks?"

"Her chest, Gray! There's no way you didn't notice!" Sylia exclaimed in a whisper, trying not to bring attention to herself.

I had to do a double take. "Wait, you're serious? Girls actually get jealous about that? I thought that was just a silly trope to promote fan service in stories. Sorry to disappoint, but I didn't notice. I try not to pay attention to that unless I'm romantically involved with the person, not that that's ever happened," I responded with another shrug.

Sylia put her hand in front of her mouth as if she was trying to conceal a laugh as she said, "What? Do you prefer men, Gray? Is that why you hang out with Crice so much?"

As soon as she said that, I transformed into the "Blinking White Guy" meme from Earth. "Didn't expect you to take it that way. But so what if I do? What would you do then, huh?" I challenged.

For once, Sylia didn't have a reply.

"Of course, I don't actually like guys. I just don't have great luck with relationships and find Crice's company enjoyable since we can talk about our old home. Anyone would like that!" I thought.

"Oh, thank God. You actually had me worried there for a second, Gray. If you were actually...y'know, and the church somehow found out. If you're lucky, you'd only be executed," Sylia said as she let out a breath of relief.

"That's a joke, right? The church wouldn't actually execute someone for that? Though, I guess it's not that surprising since this is a medieval world and all," I said before realizing, "Hold on, how did you—"

"Oh, you accidentally projected your thoughts to us again," Sylia answered before I even finished my question.

"What do you mean again?" I shouted out. *This is the first time I'm hearing about this. Since when do I accidentally project my thoughts? How is that even possible in the first place!* I cried out in my head, hoping that no one heard how pitiful I sounded.

"Kuhano's proficiency with communication magic went up, so he's able to just permanently keep it going. For the past few months, you've kinda been doing it. Disappointingly, nothing bad has come out of it, though," Sylia said with a half frown. "All we've heard is your concepts for spells and the techniques you'd be able to improve on."

"Why didn't any of you tell me?" I asked as I attempted to keep myself from thinking.

"Well... Uhh... It was Kuhano and Lady Sylia's idea!" Kuhani said as she instantly cracked. "Lady Sylia said that if we could hear what you thought during combat that we might learn something, and then Kuhano agreed and never disabled his spell that linked you to us all. But it's like Lady Sylia says! We'd only hear you when you were frustrated or excited and your thoughts had strong emotion behind them! I swear we didn't hear anything you wouldn't want us to hear!"

"If it's been going on for that long, then why ask me about liking Crice like that?" I asked Sylia, embarrassed at the thought of the question. "You know what? Just…never mind. I don't want to know why you'd think that's appropriate or funny or whatever. How about you tell me the other reason you were getting so angry in there?" I said disappointingly.

She looked at me with a frown. "Can we talk about that privately?" she asked.

Without any questions, the rest of the group went toward the canal. When they were out of earshot, Sylia said, "The king of the elves is in there talking with the current Guildmaster."

"Wait, you mean the guy that hasn't paid you at all since giving you this job to watch over me? Even though you've been going through all the work of writing up reports and sending them to a far-off kingdom!" I asked angrily.

Sylia looked down in shame. "Y-yes, that bastard exactly."

At her response I instantly forgot about how angry I had been with her and shifted my anger toward the elven king. "I'm going in there to talk to that jackass," I stated.

At my words, Sylia's eyes grew, and she grabbed my arm firmly. "No, you aren't, Gray. I know you want to help, but anything you do to him will just make things worse," she said.

"Sylia, he's made you super-stressed about money for way too long, just because he's gone radio silent randomly. If you're going to let him get away with that, then I'm not. It's that simple!" I argued, unable to comprehend why she wouldn't call him out.

"You're going to have to let him get away with it for a little bit longer then," she said as she raised her fist.

"*Uh-oh,*" I thought.

"Uh-oh, indeed, Grayson. Don't worry, you'll be fine in time for the tournament," she said, disappointed that she had to do this to stop me. Before I could react, she launched her fist toward me with all her might. If she was wearing any armor, my face would have been destroyed. I could feel her knuckles dig deeply into my cheek before I went flying toward the wall of the guild's building.

"Why does this have to be the trope that I got stuck with?" I wondered before I slammed into the wall and passed out.

The Tournament and Beginnings!

When I awoke, I was on a bed, and it felt as if my brain was clouded. My head felt like it was swaying, even though it was stationary on the pillow. Outside the window next to my bed, the sky was brightly lit from the light of the moon. At the realization that I was awake, I said aloud, "I feel horrible. Definitely never going to argue against Sylia ever again." I tore open the pouch on my hip and took out a healing potion. I popped the cork and gulped it down.

The potion was thick and cold with an overwhelming taste of mint. It was like having a mint-flavored honey stick, except there was no honey, and the stick was just a vial, and it came out like a normal liquid instead of slowly making its way out of the vial. *Maybe it's actually nothing like a mint honey stick now that I think about it.*

When I finished drinking the red liquid, my symptoms seemed to disappear entirely. "That's definitely a good plan. Totally not saying that because it would make you less of a pain in the ass," came Sylia's voice from the shadows before she came into view.

"What is with you and acting like you're some sort of assassin, always coming out of the shadows, saying something you just heard?" I asked her.

"Force of habit mostly. Plus, it's fun. How are you feeling?" she asked.

"Well, I think I had a concussion, but the potion seems to have gotten rid of that," I said. "So what excuse did you give to the group for punching me?" I asked, figuring that she had lied so that our money troubles didn't leak.

"I told them you made fun of how small my breasts were," she said nonchalantly.

"Oh okay, nothing to... YOU DID WHAT?" I shouted out.

"It's the only thing that made sense at the time! You can't blame me for your lack of self-control," she argued.

My frustration was so intense that I thought I was about to get another form of head pain. I let out an irritated sigh. "I'm assuming they all think I'm complete scum then?" I asked, more worried about what the group thought instead of Sylia's unstable foundation for her argument.

"Araya doesn't, but she clearly doesn't believe that you would do something like that. Kuhano just called you an idiot and said you deserved it. Kuhani was the most torn up about it. I think it's a mix of the stress of the city and then the fact that you did something that would put strain on the bonds in the group," Sylia explained.

"Except I didn't do that. You just said that I did." I let out a deep sigh. "Either way, I should probably find a way to apologize for my 'actions,' eh? If we're worrying about the relationship of the group, it'll get in the way of our teamwork during the tournament," I said.

"I...I didn't even think about it. I actually messed up for once. I haven't messed up since I took you into the city. I can't believe this, I'm sorry, Gray."

I was taken aback. "Since when do you apologize? Are you feeling all right?" I asked, almost convinced that this girl couldn't be Sylia. Her face turned red as she turned away.

"This is exactly why I don't. But this whole thing kind of is my fault. I'm sure Kuhani won't hold a grudge, but just think about what you'll say to her before your fight tomorrow."

"TOMORROW?" I shouted out suddenly. "I was passed out for a whole day?" When I realized what that meant, my eyes widened. "I need to go back to sleep before I accidentally focus on something," I muttered to myself.

"Right, I forgot that you do that morning focus routine to use your skills stat roll. Get some rest then because we're waking up early for you all to warm up before you have to go to the arena."

"Alrighty, will do. Oh, and Silly? Sorry about being a stubborn idiot yesterday. I was just angry that jerk has been taking advantage of you for half a year," I said, disappointed in myself for losing my temper.

"You don't need to apologize since it's my fault. Besides, if we didn't have some sort of issues, then life would be too easy and boring," she said with a wink.

After she left the room, I lay there in bed for a while, thinking about what I could possibly do.

"The best thing I can think of is to apologize. Everything else I can think of just feels like it'll dig me into a deeper hole or not help at all. At least Araya doesn't believe that I said that. I don't know if I'd call her my best friend, but we have spent a lot of time together these last six months. I guess that's why she was able to see through Sylia's lie. I'll have to thank her for that. But if it wasn't for Kuhani, I'd probably be group-hopping and not getting close to anyone in this world. I owe her a lot more than I think she realizes. Of course, I'm not going to let her know that, but I definitely need to figure out something to do for her to apologize for this whole thing. I don't need her to forgive me as long as we get to terms where we can communicate in combat. That'll be enough for me," I thought before I drifted back off to sleep.

*****

"Grayson! Come on, wake up!" I heard as my eyes shot open due to something suddenly pushing down on my stomach. In front of me was Araya looming on top of me. I peered out the window, and the sky was barely tinted orange. "Grayyyy," she whined as she started to shake me.

"I'm awake, give it a rest. No pun intended," I said with a yawn. *I've been out for over a day, and I'm still yawning? Hold on, who the hell is this fan service meant for!* I wondered as I realized Araya's position. "So...why are you on top of me?"

"W-w-well, you weren't responding, and I wasn't able to move you without getting a better grip," she said while looking side to side and blushing.

"Oh, sorry, I guess I was pretty conked out, eh?" I said as I sat up. "Um… Are you going to get up?" I asked.

She jumped a little after she realized what I was asking and clapped her hands together. "I'm so sorry!" she said before she removed herself from my bed.

"Don't worry about it, especially since I should be thanking you for not getting wrapped up in Sylia's lie," I said with a smile.

"I knew you couldn't have done that! Though you already thanked me last night, I just wanted to say that to your face. I'm sure Lady Sylia had her reasons for lying, but I can't believe she would come up with something that out of character for you," she said.

I thanked her last night? I don't remember this at all… GAH! I projected again, didn't I? I realized. *Oh, crap. That means that Kuhani must've heard my thoughts! Which means either she knows that Sylia lied and is going to confront her or she's going to play ignorance and might try to manipulate me like she did all that time ago!* I thought.

"Well, I was a bit of an idiot and gave her no other choice than to punch me. Given the context of the conversation you guys had heard, it makes sense that's what she went with," I said with a shrug. "How about we head to that warm-up thing Sylia had planned?" I suggested. I secretly hoped that Araya would take the lead since I didn't know where we even were.

"Oh no! I completely forgot about that! You're a lifesaver, Gray! Come on, let's go!" she spouted as she lifted her robes and started jogging out of the room. It took me a moment to realize that my guide was already leaving, but as soon as I did, I jumped out of bed and followed after her. *Why would they not take off my armor! I mean, at least I don't have to throw it on now and don't have to worry about who undressed me, but who in hell sleeps in their armor?* I thought when I realized I was in my full set of gear.

When I exited the room, there were two things that made me feel like luck was on my side. The first thing was that we were in the rainforest motel that Sylia and I stayed in our first few days in the kingdom. The second thing was that Araya was significantly slower since she had to be careful to not trip on her robe. When I caught up to her, I was actually able to walk at a comfortable pace. Even though

I was able to run longer and faster than I was able to six months ago, it was still nice to just be able to take it slow.

I was surprised when I found out we weren't meeting very far from our rooms. Within a few minutes, we met up with the group atop a bridge that stood over a small river that had to have been man-made. "Wow. Everyone's actually here on time, that's new," Sylia said as we approached.

"Do we have to do this neooooow?" Kuhani asked sleepily. "Can't we just do some stretches before we fight? We don't even have Crice's home cooking to energize us!" she added.

"Your first fight is in three hours, so you're going to loosen up your body NOW," Sylia stated, putting a large emphasis on now. Usually, no one contests her like this, so it caught all of us by surprise.

With a squeal, Kuhani said, "I'm so sorry, I didn't mean it like that!" Clearly, she was wide awake by now.

The "warm-up" wasn't all that bad, aside from the fact that we woke up so early. We mostly just did stretches to get the blood flowing and did a teamwork exercise. It was like I was back at my old job before I died. The only differences being that this time, I was not being left out, and instead of playing a game, we were watching each other's backs to defend each other from Sylia's attacks.

The goal was to not let a single hit in for five minutes, which shouldn't have been too hard. Somehow, though, it ended up taking us a full hour before we finally succeeded. Afterward, we got an earful about how we needed to trust each other and expect attacks from all angles. Thankfully, we got to have breakfast after that, which completely reenergized us after expelling so much energy in the teamwork exercise.

Wait… Why are we trying this hard? Isn't this just the wood bracket? We're at the upper end level wise, and we can fight for hours against a Level 42. Sure, we can't do it with the fighting styles we'll be using, but there's no way that we can lose this, right? I thought to myself as we ate. Something wasn't sitting right with me, but I decided that I must've just been overthinking everything.

When we finished eating, we had around an hour to make our way to the arena and sign in before they started the bracket. Since

Wood was the lowest bracket, it was also the longest, mainly due to the fact that just about anyone could sign up with the guild, find a group, and then join the tournament. Because of that, it started horribly early, which just so happened to also work as a way to trim groups out. Sylia made us head to the arena early to avoid us being trimmed fat.

As we made our way to the arena, I figured it was a good time to apologize to Kuhani. "Hey, Kuhani? I wanted to say sorry for saying such a messed up thing to Sylia. I know that you probably think I'm a huge jerk, and if ther—"

"Don't worry, Grayson! Lady Sylia explained everything to me last night. We'll win this, no matter what, and it'll be because we all worked together! I'm proud of you for almost going against Lady Sylia to stick it to that jerk of a king. If someone tried to stand up for me like that, I think I'd fall in love with them," Kuhani teased.

I gave a chuckle at her joke. "Looks like I'll have to find a way to do that for you then. I'm glad that this all worked out somehow," I said. *Wait, did I just flirt with her? That completely goes against my thoughts on dating people I work with! Now that I think about it, this is the first time I've ever flirted with someone. Maybe she didn't notice because I did it so naturally?* I thought as I glanced at her beet-red face. *SHE DEFINITELY NOTICED!* I screamed out in my thoughts.

Thankfully, we walked into the part of the arena for competing groups just moments later. "Oh, good… You all…made it!" Zini said as we walked up to the sign-in desk. "Miss Kuhani? Are you…feeling all right?" she asked, concerned.

"Naver batter!" Kuhani squeaked, completely butchering what she tried to say.

Zini gave her an odd look and said, "Okay… Here's the match-ing…list. You may wait…in your waiting room…after you clock in." After we used our membership tags to confirm we were there, she said, "Good luck! I'll be…rooting for you!"

After we said our thanks, we headed to our waiting room. When we walked in, the first thing we noticed was the rack of weapons against the back wall with a full body mirror beside it. In the middle of the room was a table with an orb on it and a card that explained that it was a "Spying orb" that would let us watch the battles from inside the waiting room. *So it's basically a TV?* I thought as I sat in one of the four leather chairs around the table. After I sat in the comfortable chair, I took a look at the list Zini gave us.

There are thirty-two slots for participating groups. Only around half of the slots are filled, though, I noticed. Shortly after my observation, our group filled one of the empty boxes. Our names appeared as if they were being burnt onto the list. It appeared as a bright orange before transforming into what looked to be normal black ink.

By the time sign-in finished, there were twenty-four groups competing. A full quarter were disqualified due to tardiness. Since we were one of the last ones to sign up, we would be fighting in five battles at the most. The first eight to sign up got to go ahead in bracket and would only have to fight four battles total if they managed to get to finals. We used the spying orb to try to get a read on our future competition. The only issue was that the fights were really boring to watch.

"Why didn't he block that?" Kuhani wondered out loud when a group's protector took a slash from a sword head on. Groups were encouraged to fight with everything they had and not worry about hurting the other groups. An anti-death field and a pain-nullification field had been put up around the arena so that nobody could die or feel an immense amount of pain. When your health points hit one, you were considered dead and would have to kneel down where you had been slain. If you didn't comply with that rule, then your whole group would be disqualified.

"Is this truly what we're going up against? I feel like we were better than this before Lady Sylia's training," Kuhani muttered in disappointment.

"You're definitely not wrong, but we should still watch. If we know the strategies that our enemy is going to use, it'll be way easier to beat them, y'know?" I said as I paid attention to the melee damage dealers who were just randomly swinging.

"I know that, I just didn't realize watching someone fight could be this…sad. I can't wait to watch the higher ranks fight!" she said as her anticipation started taking over.

Eventually, someone came to our room to lead us to the arena. *"I've made it so that we should all be able to talk with our thoughts. That way, we won't need to waste time talking,"* Kuhano thought to us all as we were walking down the hall to the gate.

"Good thinking, man. No pun intended," I said. *Why have I been making so many puns recently? Is it a nervous tick like Spider-Man's witty remarks when he fights?* I wondered as we walked out into the arena.

Walking out into the bright light, we were greeted by the cheers of hundreds of spectators. The arena itself was a large circle surrounded by rows upon rows of filled seats. There was a small platform where four people sat—the Guildmaster, the king, and the two other people I had seen the Guildmaster talking to days earlier. *So that's the elven king then?* I wondered as I stared daggers at a slender man who wore a green sweater vest-like tunic. His face was clear of any hair or blemishes, and his long silky hair that went below his shoulders could only be compared to a finely spun strand of spider silk. His hair seemed to naturally flow toward the back of his head, leaving his jade-green eyes free to see everything. He sat beside a large gong and the king of Heirshield.

The sky was free of any clouds, and the warmth of the sun felt like a nice change compared to the cool waiting rooms we had been in. The arena had a rough wooden floor that was covered in a thin layer of sand. When we walked out further, the gate behind us slammed down, trapping us in the arena.

"Hah! Beast-people? I refuse to let you savages move on to the next round. Prepare to meet your doom!" the man in front of us yelled out. He was muscular and had short hair that stayed still no matter how much he moved. If it wasn't for his plate armor, he would've looked the part of an American army general. He had a small wooden shield and a shortsword, both of which were provided by the guild.

The three people behind him looked almost as militant as him. They seemed to be very serious aside from their taunts. One of the three was an archer, while the other two seemed to be mages of some kind. Without seeing them before, it was impossible to tell which one was their healer.

"I'll keep their guardian busy. Gray, you go after those spell-casters, and Arie, take out the ranger! Keep buffs and heals on me and yourself, brother," Kuhani ordered, completely unaffected by their taunts. We all nodded and unsheathed our weapons. I had taken two iron daggers, which I was used to. The only difference from my normal setup was that I didn't have a flame enchant on one, and I had a backup dagger which would allow for a few extra moves.

A man handed the Guildmaster a small mallet. When he hit the gong next to him, the battle officially began. With the start of the battle, a projection of each of the team members and their health bars appeared in the sky, which made it significantly easier to tell who to target if it came down to taking out the lowest health target. I instantly charged forward along with Kuhani. The man who had uttered the initial taunt earlier brought his sword down directly between the two of us. Kuhani dodged to the right while I dodged to the left. Instantly, Kuhani recovered and leapt toward him with her daggers ready. He blocked Kuhani's attack with his shield, and the two became locked in battle.

With the guardian's attention being held, I was free to continue charging toward the spell-casters. Compared to Araya who already had casted her "Wall of Light" to protect herself from any arrows their archer sent her way, the mage's casting time was slow, and their aim was sloppy. One of them shot a small fireball that flew to my side, completely missing. *All he had to do was aim straight. Are these guys serious?* I thought as the fireball fizzled out before hitting the arena's wall.

Before he could cast another spell, I had already closed the distance and gotten behind him. Before I could attack him, Araya finished casting her "God Smite" and hit their archer, instantly dropping his health to one, taking him out of the fight. The mage flew into a panic at the sight of the guillotine of light, screaming things that I couldn't make out. I put my arm over his neck from behind and whispered, "Calm down, it'll all be over soon," before stabbing him in the chest, causing blood to splash onto my face. I left him sobbing hysterically after I lowered him down in the spot where he was "killed."

Instantly, I turned my attention to the healer who was only focused on his guardian friend. It was as if he didn't care about the fact that his two damage dealers had already been dealt with. I slowly crept up behind him and stabbed him in the neck as if I was a Rogue. If there was one thing that I hated about daggers, it was the ripping of the flesh that I could feel while I pushed it into my target. He didn't even have time to react before he was pronounced dead.

Within the next few moments, I was behind the guardian, and Araya was to his side, getting a spell ready. *"Gray, don't get close. This guy's style is weird. Arie, don't shoot spells either. I think he'll try to swap positions with me so I get hit,"* Kuhani quickly explained.

With no healer, he wasn't going to last long anyway, so we just watched the fight. Every slash he made was parried, every lunge he went for was sidestepped, and every bash he would go for would stop short since Kuhani made sure to move back after every attack. Whenever he missed his mark, Kuhani would retaliate with an unarmed attack of her own.

"Where are your daggers?" I asked, wondering why she was just punching him.

"They're stuck in this guy's arm and shoulder! I can't retrieve them!" she responded.

Sure enough, when I got good luck, I noticed a dagger in his shield arm and one in his sword shoulder. I circled around to Kuhani's side and thought to her, *"When you jump back after this next attack, take my daggers."*

After Kuhani's next dodge and counterattack, she jumped back and swiftly snatched the daggers out of my hands. *"Thanks, Gray! Who knows how long this would've taken without these!"* she thought as I ran back toward Kuhano and Araya.

The rest of the fight took half a minute. When the man swung his sword, he stumbled and fell to the ground on his stomach. He was clearly exhausted and dazed from Kuhani's punches that had left his face battered and bruised. Before he could attempt to get up, she jumped on his back and stabbed a dagger into the back of his head.

When his health hit one, the gong was sounded again to indicate the end of the battle. The crowd didn't make a sound. They were still in shock at how one-sided the fight as a whole was. Healers rushed out onto the field to heal both sides. One stopped to heal me but was surprised when I explained that the blood on my face was from the enemy. After they made sure we were all okay, they went to the other team. The man Kuhani beat up had to be carried away since he was still unconscious after his healing.

"I hope he'll be okay," Kuhani said with regret in her voice.

"I'm sure he'll be fine. He was tough enough to keep two daggers stuck in him while he fought. Besides, he was a jerk to you and Kuhano, so I can't say he doesn't deserve this," I said in an attempt to comfort her as we walked back to the waiting room.

"I guess. Hopefully, he makes a speedy recovery so he can apologize then!" she said with newfound happiness taking over.

I patted her on the back. "Hell yeah, who knows? Maybe you guys will be friends after this," I said with a chuckle. "It's a bit impressive that you silenced a crowd that big with your fight, honestly," I said in admiration.

"That...probably wasn't entirely because of Lady Kuhani," Araya said, staring at me.

"What d'ya mean? She was totally kicking butt out there. Anyone would go quiet getting to witness that!" I exclaimed.

"Gray? Maybe you should take a look in the mirror," she said.

"What? Because of the little bit of blood on my face?" I asked as we entered our waiting room. I went over to look at the mirror by the weapon rack and found that the left side of my face was caked in blood. It even made me cringe and get extremely squeamish at the sight.

"Okay, I look like a serial killer. I'm willing to go 50/50 on the crowd silence thing," I said as I washed my face off with a warm towel. "Do we even need to talk about the fight? I feel like it was way easier than I was expecting."

You think you had it easy? I didn't even have to do anything except for stay out of the way! Their archer gave me a new appreciation for you, Gray. I didn't realize someone could be so dumb that they would keep firing at a wall of light and not understand they can't break through it," Kuhano thought.

I couldn't tell if he was leading into an insult or trying to be genuinely nice. It was a surprise to hear that they wouldn't try to attack the healer, though, which meant that they didn't even understand basic targeting. *I don't even think they determined who would focus what target,* I thought.

"Their healer was also subpar," Araya criticized. "He wasn't even casting half the time. Plus, he was also only focusing on keeping their protector alive instead of giving defensive buffs to everyone. Honestly, the whole group felt like it was just cobbled together at the last minute," she added.

"What if they were? It would make complete sense! They signed in after us too! Oh my God, there's no way they weren't new! I can't believe I did that to someone who was new!" Kuhani cried out in distress.

"I'm sure they weren't new. Even if they were, I'm not going to feel bad for them for not preparing," I said coldly. Something about fighting other people and not having to worry about actually killing them triggered something in me. It made me feel like I could do anything. Part of me couldn't wait to fight actual difficult opponents.

"Gray? Are you okay? The way you said that was a little…scary," Kuhani said with her tail sticking straight up behind her.

"My bad. It just makes me angry, y'know? It's bad enough they were making fun of you guys, but then they weren't even ready to give it their all? It just makes me feel like they insulted you even more," I explained.

"As happy as I am that you care, don't worry about them. We're used to people making fun of us. You, Arie, Lady Sylia, the Guildmaster, and Zini are the only ones that haven't, so we're used to ignoring them. Thanks for being so sweet, though, it means a lot to me," Kuhani said with a charming smile.

Instantly, I felt myself going red. *This is her revenge for earlier, isn't it?* I thought as we sat down and started watching the next fight.

The fights we watched were just like all of the others: Boring. It wasn't even worth paying attention to the fights. I couldn't wait to get back in the ring. The only thing I was worried about was how the crowd would react to us.

Eventually, someone took us to fight again. This time, when we went out, the crowd was unusually silent aside from a certain woman's cheers. It was obvious what the crowd was thinking: Would this be another massacre? Or would it be an equal struggle like all the other fights?

The group that appeared before us looked very weak and on death's door. One of them even started hacking up a lung like they were about to keel over and die before the fight even started! All of the anticipation I had coming into this fight faded and transformed into confusion. *"Um… do we really have to fight these people? They look like they're already beaten,"* I thought.

"I have to agree, they do look quite sickly. Perhaps we should just try to make it quick?" Araya thought with a merciful look in her eye. Before anyone could respond, the gong rang.

To our surprise, the group before us sprang into action like we had in our last fight. They shed their disguises that had made them appear as if they were about to die. Their healer stayed in the backline, uttering spells that were giving buffs to her teammates. Meanwhile, the other three were running toward Araya, Kuhani, and me, each one aiming for a different target.

The one that was aiming for me was an elvish woman with two daggers in her hands. When they revealed they were disguised, my anticipation for the fight flared up. *"They were using disguises to lull us into a false sense of security! This is a prepared team!"* I thought excitedly. I couldn't wait to cross blades with the woman in front of me. I didn't move an inch until she began trying to unleash a flurry of attacks at me. Thanks to my focus rolling an X3 earlier and me devoting all of my attention to her, the attacks looked sluggish. I didn't even have to use the dagger in my left hand to deflect all of her swipes.

A part of me wanted to see if anyone needed help, but I couldn't tear my eyes off of the enemy before me. The elf had a large grin growing on her face with each slash. Either she had another plan in mind or she thought she was wearing me down with each attack.

Eventually, though, I started getting bored and started to study her face. She had unnatural blue hair that was in a ponytail. Her eyes were a dark brown with blonde eyebrows above them. Her lips were coated in a deep black lipstick. *Is she this world's equivalent to a goth girl?* I wondered.

As I was lost in my thought, I dodged one of her stabs instead of deflecting it, and she went flying straight through with it due to the power she had been putting behind each attack. I didn't even look back to acknowledge our mistakes. As she flew past me, I brought my left elbow down hard and knocked her into the ground. If it wasn't for the pain nullifier, I probably would have been in pain myself.

When she hit the ground, she bounced up and flopped down before I pulled out my back up dagger and plunged them both into her hands, making the impromptu decision to attach her to the wooden floor so she wouldn't be able to counterattack. I picked up her daggers and felt bad as she apologetic screamed to her teammates. I looked up to the sky and saw that she had half of her health remaining. When I looked down, I glanced toward Araya and saw that her opponent was already lying there, defeated, along with the guardian who had engaged Kuhani.

All that was left was the elf who had attacked me and their healer who was cowering in fear across the arena. Seeing that no one needed my help, I said, "Sorry, the whole daggers in the hand thing was pretty messed up of me." And I delivered the killing blow. As soon as she was pronounced dead, their healer surrendered, and the healers once again rushed the field. We had won again without any deaths or taking damage.

As we left, the crowd had a mix of cheers and boos. We figured the boos were for the healer's surrender, so we paid it no mind. When we got back to the room, I was ecstatic. "Did you guys see how many attacks she was throwing out? She clearly must be sinking all of her points into Agility!" I excitedly said as we walked into our waiting room.

"You're right, she was moving pretty fast. You're lucky that we could heal her hands. Otherwise, she'd never be able to grab a weapon again," the Guildmaster said from one of our chairs.

"G-G-G-Guildmaster!" Kuhani shouted out in surprise. "What are you doing here?"

"I need to speak to all of you," he said. "Come on in, don't be shy, and close the door behind you," he added.

As soon as we all entered and closed the door, the Guildmaster threw a spell on the door.

"Where the hell have you four been this last half a year!" he shouted. Before he gave us a chance to respond, he added, "I thought you all were dead. All of you were people of interest, and you managed to fall off my radar without a trace! You all just disappeared suddenly and then randomly come back and fight like seasoned veterans! How did you even learn to fight like this without gaining experience? Well? Go on and explain yourselves!" Kuhani whimpered as Sylia mustered the strength to reply.

"W-w-well... I mean... W—"

I steeled myself and took over in Kuhani's place. "We've been at our home, training with the ex-elvish general Sylia. It was my fault that we all disappeared. The day after I joined, we all met up to buy gear. That's when we met Araya and invited her to join our group. After that, we made the journey toward our home at Loch Crest where we've been staying for the last six months. If you need to blame someone and punish them, then pick me," I responded sternly as I placed myself in between him and the rest of the group.

The Guildmaster looked at me, speechless. He was clearly upset but had to take a couple minutes to find his words. "I'm not going to punish anyone. Even if I wanted to, there's nothing I could do without the limits of my power being brought into question. I'm glad you're all safe. I wanted to chew you all out the other day, but I was stuck talking to the beast king and the elf king. There's something important we need to talk about now that I know you're alive. I'll be hosting a meeting the day after the tournament ends. I invite you all to come. I can't stray here for too long, so I'll give you the details at a later date. I'm glad to see you all haven't changed," he explained before removing his magic and disappearing without a trace.

While the next fight went on, we talked about the conversation with the Guildmaster. "I can't believe you threw yourself to the

Guildmaster's mercy like that to save us! What's going on with you today?" Araya asked.

"What d'ya mean? It's my fault we kinda just vanished into thin air," I responded. "I thought he was going to kick us all out of the guild, so I had to do something to take responsibility."

"You need to rely on us more and understand that we're a group, Gray. If something happens to one of us, it affects the whole group. Even if he was going to kick us out, I'd rather us all be together than lose any one of you!" Araya cried out.

I begrudgingly said, "I see what you're saying, but—"

"No buts. You promise me right here, right now, that you won't try to sacrifice yourself to save all of us ever again," Araya sternly said as she held out her pinky.

I let out a sigh and said, "A pinky swear? I know you're young, but come on, this isn't third grade."

Araya's only response was to intensely stare at me and move her pinky closer to me. After a few moments of being under her piercing gaze, I cracked and let out a sigh of defeat. "Fine, I promise I won't sacrifice myself to save the group and will work with you all to get us out of any situation we find ourselves in. Happy?" I said as I wrapped my pinky around hers.

She unleashed a beaming smile. "Very."

"Are we going to go to that meeting that he mentioned?" Kuhani asked us all.

"Dunno. I say we play it by ear and decide what we do when he gives us more information. Sound good?" I asked. With a nod of agreement from everyone, the conversation ended, and no one had anything else to bring up. We ended up watching the next three fights in silence until it was our turn to fight again. When we went out into the arena, this time we were greeted by murmurs in the crowd. It was an upgrade from the silence from before, but it didn't feel anything like the cheers that greeted us at our debut.

The group we were up against this time had three girls and one guy. The guy didn't look like anything special. He had messy overgrown red hair and just looked really tired and detached from the world. The girls, on the other hand, looked crazy. One was dressed in black and had a gleaming gold and steel sword. Another one was clad in white and had a large ruby red scythe. Both of them had long bubblegum pink hair in ribbonlike twin tails. The last one had brown hair that was wrapped up in a bun and had bright amber eyes. Her eyes looked like they were made of light copper as opposed to the golden eyes of Araya or the lemon-yellow eyes of Kuhani. She seemed like a large sweater would fit her style more than the leather corset that sat over her snow-white blouse. Besides that, though, she seemed really plain. My instincts, on the other hand, screamed to me that she was anything but. *"Hey, guys? Something about this group is freaking me out. I think I'm gonna go full focus mode. Sound good?"* I thought to the group.

"So it's not just me? Definitely go for it then!" Kuhani thought back in response.

When I was studying her, our eyes connected. She smiled and waved at me with her free hand. In her other hand, she was holding a bow that looked like it was made of crystals. The only odd thing was that she didn't have a quiver on her back. I let out a sigh and waved back. *There's no reason for ill feelings to be outside the battlefield, right? No reason to not give her a wave back, eh?* I reasoned to myself.

When the gong sounded, I shifted all of my attention to the girl and started charging right for her. To my surprise, the girl shot an arrow of pure fire toward me. If I hadn't decided to give it my all, I probably would've been toast instantly. The arrow itself wasn't very fast, but with me charging directly toward it, the story was different. I threw the dagger in my right hand into my left and absorbed the spell, turning my gauntlet a fiery crimson. *Guess I'm going lefty for this,* I nervously thought.

"Gray, you've got incoming. Scythe girl looks like she's going to try to go for your legs," Kuhano thought to me.

Before I could reach the plain archer girl, my path got cut off by the girl with the scythe. As Kuhano called out, she swept her scythe low in the direction I was running. Thanks to his warning, I jumped over it in time. If he hadn't warned me, I probably would have been taken out right there.

"Oho? You managed to avoid that? You're an interesting one," she said with a psychotic laugh.

"Thanks for the heads up, Kuhano, that was the second time I was almost taken outta this fight," I quickly thought.

"Maybe if you used your tracking, I wouldn't have to call out for you, idiot," He rebutted.

I had no time to respond as I slid in the sand and changed my focus to the girl with the scythe. I threw the dagger in my left hand in her general direction, which she easily dodged. "Fufufu, was that supposed to hit me?" she asked as she looked toward the knife.

"No, but this one is," I said as I launched a fireball from my gauntlet. The fireball traveled like it had come out of a cannon and hit her directly in the stomach, burning a hole through her clothes and charring the inside edges. As she flew back into the wall, the plain-looking girl shot another arrow toward me, and I moved my right hand to my side to absorb it out of habit.

I heard a *schklew* and felt something hit my hand. Out of confusion, I brought my hand back into view and saw an arrow sticking straight through it. I looked toward the girl and shouted, "Usually, that goes a lot better in my head." She furrowed her brow and shouted back, "The arrow or the idea of catching it?"

"Both!" I yelled as I started closing the distance between us while she was caught off guard. I pulled my backup dagger out of its sheath with my left hand and started my assault. When I attacked, she raised her bow and blocked my attack. Instead of losing her cool like the mage from before, she actually fought back. She blocked my next two attacks before swinging her bow like it was a sword. Thankfully, I was able to bend back far enough so that it didn't hit me.

Since her bow was so big, she couldn't control her swing, and the momentum made her swing wide, causing an opening to reveal itself. I went to stab her shoulder blade, but before I could, she let go of her bow and kicked up with the momentum, knocking my dagger out of my hand. With no weapon, there wasn't much I could do when she raised her hand in an attempt to finish me off with a spell. Without thinking, I used all of the speed my agility would allow me to. In her eyes, I appeared right next to her in less than a second before I slammed the back of my hand against her spell-casting hand. The arrow that was going through my hand had also gone through the hand she was using to cast spells. *Was turning us into a shish kebab really my best plan?*

"Ehhhh!" she gasped out in surprise. "How did you—You were holding back this whole time?"

"Well, I wasn't trying to, and I was holding back significantly less than the last fights. But I guess you have me beat, so go ahead and cast a spell with your other hand and finish me," I disappointedly said as I accepted my fate.

"Umm… I, uhh… I can't," she responded, just as disappointed. "I have a catalyst crystal embedded in that…hand," she said as she looked toward her hand that was shish kebab-ed with mine. From what I could see of her, she was blushing.

"So you can only cast spells from that hand then? That puts us in a really awkward position then. I guess we'll just have to either surrender or wait for someone from one of our teams to finish the other person."

"Couldn't we just pull the arrow out?" she asked, bringing a third option into the mix.

"Nope. I don't know what this arrow is made out of, but it's going straight through both of our hands, which means there's a very small amount of blood working to get rid of the gut holding the arrow head in place. So unless you want to make yourself bleed a ton or have me pull the arrow back through our hands, that arrowhead will make that wound big enough to remove that crystal," I explained. *God, I hope this bluff pays off,* I prayed.

The girl made a noise of disapproval before turning her head to face away from mine. "Okay, yeah, let's not do that!" she shouted out. *I could've just snapped the arrow and made a break for my dagger, but that seems like a lot of effort when I can just stand here with someone who's given up,* I thought to myself.

"I can't really see anything besides your friend with the scythe. How's everyone else looking?" I asked the girl next to me.

"Huh? Oh, uhh… Maya's still fighting your guardian, and Noah is defending himself from your priest's attacks. We didn't think that anyone would be able to keep up with us after we got permission to use our weapons. This is a real bummer."

"Wait, you got to use the weapons you usually use?" I asked in surprise.

"Yes? We're in quarter finals. Everyone's allowed to use their normal weapons now. Are you telling me you didn't know that?" she asked.

"Absolutely no idea. That would've been nice to know, not that I have much of an upgrade, but still," I said with a sigh of annoyance.

"Don't be modest. I'm sure your weapons are miles ahead of what the guild provided. With how skillful you are, you must've had tons of opportunities to get amazing weapons!" she protested.

"Nope, all I have is an iron dagger with a fire enchantment and a normal short bow," I confessed without thinking.

"Eh! That's it! I...If you don't mind me asking, what's uhh... what's your name?" she asked timidly.

"Oh, right, my bad. My name's Grayson, how about you?" I said as I held out my hand out of habit. *She isn't even in front of you, you idiot!* I thought as I put my hand down. "Grayson? I don't think I've ever heard your name around the guild before. I'm Pauline!" she said as she held out her hand.

"Well, nice to know we both have the manners to offer a handshake after introducing ourselves. Nice to meet'cha, Pauline," I said, mentally face-palming at both of us for wanting to shake the other's hand in this situation.

"Do you, uhh... Are you staying in the city for the whole tournament?" she asked while blushing.

"Yeah, at least I'm pretty sure we are. Why do you ask?" I asked suspiciously. *She's not some crazy person and is going to try to find me and duel me again, is she?* I wondered to myself.

"W-w-w-well, you seem n-nice enough. S-so if you don't have anything to do, would you, uhh... Would you accompany me tomorrow?" she asked very quickly.

I raised an eyebrow and turned my head to look at her beet-red face.

"WOULD YOU JUST KILL EACH OTHER ALREADY!" a man in the crowd shouted out in front of me.

"DUDE, WE'RE TALKING! BESIDES, WHAT WEAPONS ARE WE SUPPOSED TO USE? OR DO YOU PROPOSE WE PUNCH EACH OTHER TO DEATH!" I shouted back at the man in the crowd who shrunk back at my response.

Pauline just started laughing hysterically, which hurt with how much her hand was moving. "Hey, I enjoy having the arrow hole get ripped open as much as the next guy, but can we like…not do that?" I asked.

"Oh, and I don't think that my group's doing anything, so sure? I don't really understand why you want me to do stuff with you, but I'm interested. Just find me after today's fights, and we can talk more about it," I added, accidentally agreeing to my first date. Not just my first date in this world but my first date ever.

"Really?" she shouted out in surprise.

After I gave a nod, her face lit up, almost to the point that it was glowing. *Wait, it actually is glowing?* I thought as Araya's "God Smite" came down upon Pauline, sending us both careening to the floor. When we fell, the arrow snapped in two, disconnecting our hands. When the healers rushed the field, I was the only one from our team that received any healing.

As we walked out of the arena, Pauline waved to me with an enthusiastic smile, and I waved back. "What was that all about?" Araya asked me while giving me a suspicious glare.

I nervously chuckled and said, "I think I ended up making a new friend somehow. That aside, though, did you guys know that we could be using our weapons from here on?" I said, trying to change the subject.

"WHAT!" Kuhani shouted out.

"Actually, wait, the only one that matters is Arie. You should go get your staff then!" she said to Araya who puffed out her cheek and reluctantly went to get her weapon while we went into the waiting room.

"Soooo," Kuhani said in a sing-song voice, "what happened between you and that girl?" she asked excitedly as we closed the door.

"What, you mean Pauline? She made me have to actually try and go after some crazy movement, we got stuck together, and had no way to beat each other, so we ended up talking. She wants me to 'accompany' her around town tomorrow. That's all," I answered.

Kuhani stared at me with a tilted head before saying, "You're going on a date with someone you just met?"

Needless to say, I was taken aback. "When you put it that way, that does sound a little crazy. But I don't think it's a date. Why would it be a date? It's not a date. That would be insane to go on a date with someone who doesn't know I'm an other-worlder," I said with a nervous chuckle. *If I think it's a date, then I'll get really nervous and awkward. Besides, it's not a date. Why is Kuhani implanting this in my mind. It's kinda WeirdChamp, kinda cringe, not gonna lie,* I thought, falling back into my Internet dialect as I started becoming really nervous.

"Well, either way, it's good that you're talking to someone other than us. I was afraid we were going to be stuck with you forever!" Kuhani said as she started laughing.

"I guess that's one way to put it," I said.

When I looked toward Kuhani, she looked dejectedly suddenly. "You aren't going to leave us for them, right?" she asked.

I walked over to her and lightly flicked her forehead. "Why would I join a group of random people? Besides, I already told you, she's just a new friend."

"Right...just a new friend," she said with a fake smile.

When Araya got back in the room, the atmosphere was noticeably awkward.

"Did something happen?" she asked as she came in. Everyone remained silent until Kuhano thought, *"I was just here. Those two are the ones being weird because Gray's going on a date with a girl he just tried to kill. Just wait until the next fight, I'm sure they'll be fine after that."*

"You're going on a date with that girl?" Araya shouted out.

"It isn't a date! Why would you tell her it's a date, Kuhano?" I asked him.

"You two are a woman and a man getting together at a certain time to go around town and spend time getting to know each other. That's a date," he explained.

"Well, okay, when you put it like that, it's a date. But it's not a date. We're just becoming better friends, that's all!" I exclaimed.

Araya gave a small laugh and smiled. "It's about time you got to meet someone. You shouldn't say it's not a date, though, that's rude to her," Araya scolded.

"Jeez, okay Mom, I'm going on a date, I guess," I said before getting bombarded with questions about things like what I was going to wear and what we were going to do until someone came to get us for our next fight.

Unfortunately, our next fight didn't even happen because the team that we were pitted against conceded before the match even began. They didn't even walk into the arena to do it. They just simply said they gave up and left the event altogether to their guide. Before we knew it, we were in the finals match against a team that had only gotten there via luck. While luck is a stat, I doubted they were foolish enough to go into that. I just simply meant that they were lucky to have gotten that far. If they had been pitted against Pauline and her group, they no doubt would have lost.

When they came onto the battlefield, it was obvious which team was going to win just by how they composed themselves. The group before us was full of what could only be described as common thugs. A man with a bald head and a scar over his right eye, a man with a skull tattoo that spanned his entire face, a woman who had no weapon but a smoking pipe, and a man wearing a…butler uniform?

"Um, I know I haven't been paying attention, but who are these people?" I thought to the group.

"You told me earlier that we should pay attention to the fights! Basically, the main one to worry about is the woman. But I want Arie to take her. Gray, I want you to take the butler. I should be able to take the other two!" Kuhani thought to us.

"Sounds like a plan. On a separate note, since when do you call Araya Arie? It's been bugging me all day," I thought back.

Before she could respond, the gong rang, and I was already in front of the butler. I wasn't even thinking before I had already put my dagger through his head, taking him out of the fight in an instant. The woman was staring at me with her eyes wide before she blew an insane amount of smoke out of her pipe.

I couldn't see anything, and it was hard to breathe. It was like I was stuck in a fire. I dropped to the floor and cut off a piece of my cloth shirt before going next to the butler. "Sorry about this, but I'm gonna need to borrow some blood," I said as I held the cloth piece next to his head wound. *I remember reading that using a wet cloth can help reduce smoke inhalation. I really hope that using blood instead of water works,* I prayed as I held the rag to my face and dropped to the ground before attempting to crawl out of the smoke.

"Guys? I'm trapped in some sort of smokescreen," I thought as I tried to use my tracking ability to find anyone but to no avail. *Not only is this smoke clouding my vision, but it's jamming my mini-map? How is that possible?* I wondered.

"Guys, are you all right? Don't tell me you're all dead," I thought out, imagining the worst-case scenario.

"Gray? I thought we lost you. It seems this smoke is making it so we can't transmit our thoughts to anyone outside of it. It's just the smoke lady out there, but she just trapped us all in here too!" Kuhani responded.

"Gray, are you able to hybrid magics?" Araya thought, her voice sounding drowsy. *"I dunno, I probably should be able to? Why? Are you saying this smoke is made up of two types of magic!"* I cried out in amazement at the spell we were trapped in.

Before Araya answered, I pressed the button on my glove, dyeing it a deep brown and clearing the arena of smoke.

Everyone besides me was incapacitated with an insane amount of coughing. *"How much of that smoke did you guys breathe in?"* I wondered as I rushed toward the woman and plunged my dagger into her chest. As her health quickly dropped, she took on a maniacal grin. "You're too late! With my smoke in your lungs, you'll slowly die while my allies heal from the smoke in theirs!" she uttered before she dropped to the floor in defeat.

Sure enough, the three that we had previously defeated rose from the ground with their health points rising quickly, whereas our team's health was drastically lowering. The only one not losing health was me. At the sight, I was plunged into a pit of hopelessness. *"Gray, remember your promise earlier? Well, forget that for now, we believe in you. Do whatever you can to beat them!"* Araya thought, replacing my despair with hope.

"Are we just going to gloss over the fact that they were considered dead but are being allowed to heal?" Kuhano thought.

"You can do it, Gray! We'll see you when you win!" Kuhani thought as they all collapsed down to the ground.

My heart was racing, mainly due to being nervous but also because of excitement I felt. Even though all three of my enemies had been fully healed, the only enemy fully ready to fight was the butler. Unlucky for him, I had no intention to actually fight fair. *I'm in a one versus three. It would be suicide to not use underhanded tactics. I don't want this to be too easy, though. I at least want the crowd to be entertained,* I thought as I looked back to what I had learned to envision the spell I wanted to create.

I really hope this works! I thought as I imagined a smoke screen that would cloud only my enemy's vision with grey smoke but not my own or anyone without hostile intent. To us, it would give a slight indication that the area was different, but to my enemies, they would be lucky to see their hands outstretched in front of them. I pressed the button on my gloves and let forth a large amount of smoke that made everything look blurry. It was as if the arena was a grill, expelling heat and causing refraction. The butler looked around himself in a surprised panic before he calmed himself and strengthened his guard.

"I'm amazed you survived Miss Mitzel's smoke. But your wits will only get you so far! If I can't see you, then I will merely listen for you!" he called out as he closed his eyes. It seemed he'd forgotten the display of my agility at the start of the fight. *How do I get smoke out of his lungs so that he doesn't heal?* I asked myself. There were only two ways that I could think of. The first way was to punch him really hard in the stomach so that he would expel anything he had from his lungs. The second way was to take my dagger and forcibly open his lungs for it to escape. *I kinda want to avoid that second one if it's possible,* I thought, picturing how gruesome it was.

With a half-baked plan in mind, I moved at my maximum speed and used the momentum I had to throw my fist square into his gut. To my surprise, it actually worked, and he coughed out large puffs of smoke. While he cleared his lungs, his other teammates were finally coming to their senses. I wasn't worried about them, though I hastily took note of where they were before I stabbed the butler through the heart. With no smoke to heal him, he was once again left to feign death.

"Have we already won?" the man with the scar above his eye gruffly shouted.

"The woman's smoke hasn't cleared, so I imagine no, sir. I find it hard to believe that someone could possibly survive her spell, though. It must be that damned beast. She clearly has the most health. I humbly plead that you allow me to finish her and drink her blood!" the skulled face man said with a snake-like voice.

Is this guy some kind of cultist? For real, who in their right mind would want to drink someone's blood? I wondered.

"Are you out of your mind? Imagine the diseases you would get from that filthy bitch!" the scar man responded with a hearty laugh.

My disgust at the cultist's comment turned to anger toward the scarred man. Without thinking, I pulled out my second dagger and rushed toward him from behind, plunging my daggers in between his ribs, instantly piercing his lungs. His laugh abruptly stopped, and he couldn't even cry out to his skull-faced friend due to his unavailing attempts to breathe. I stabbed him a few more times for good measure before he collapsed back onto the ground, still attempting to breathe. *"Sorry, Kuhani, I still can't forgive anyone that says crap like that,"* I apologized.

"I found you!" the skull faced maniac called in a sing-song voice from behind me before swinging his katana-like sword. It was like a cold finger was dragging itself over my back, except the finger was a sword, and it wasn't over my back—it *was* in my back! I leapt forward and took note of my now missing 35 percent health. *That much from such a small attack? If I get hit two more times, it's all over!* I exclaimed in my thoughts.

The man didn't even raise his defense after I backed away. Instead, he licked my blood off of his sword. "Mmmm, exquisite. I didn't think I'd find such a delectable dish here. I simply must have more!" he said as he collapsed to the ground. He grabbed large clumps of sand that had been soaked in my blood and greedily shoved them into his mouth. *Okay, the licking off the sword thing I could just write off as being a crazy badass. But this? I think I'm going to throw up,* I thought with an involuntary gag.

I shoved my disgust aside so I could try to deliver a killing blow from behind while he was distracted. When I was about to stab him from behind, he snapped his head toward me. I felt like I was in a horror movie, and the moment of hesitation I took cost me. In the lost moment, he dug his sword through my left shoulder. *It's over. All he has to do is rip it out and slash my neck,* I thought as my health dropped to a quarter remaining. I had entirely given up. There was nothing I could do.

At least, that's what I had thought. To my surprise, he didn't pull out his sword and finish me. Instead, he dug his face directly next to his sword and lapped at my fresh wound like he was a dog drinking out of a bowl. Part of me was disgusted, another was horrified, and the last part of me knew that this was my chance to take victory. While he was greedily consuming my blood, I clasped the dagger in my right hand and stabbed up into his jaw. When the blade couldn't be seen anymore, his wide-open eyes shot toward me, and I jerked the hilt to the right. The loud snap of his neck echoed around the arena, serving as a bell to declare that the battle was about to end. I let go of the dagger in his jaw and grabbed my back up from my left hand. When I punctured both of his lungs and his healing stopped, the battle was finally considered over.

The healers rushed the field, and I absorbed the smoke screen that I had created. For the first time in any of our battles, everyone on the field needed to be healed. After our treatment, we were told to stay in the arena. The other team left after they were healed. The woman was yelling about how useless everyone else on the team was.

The butler and the scar-faced man seemed to be taking her words to heart, but the skull-faced man was clearly paying no attention as he gave me a lustful look until they all went out of view.

"I never want to see that guy or think of him ever again," I mumbled to myself.

"I can't believe you actually did it, Gray!" Araya cheered when the healers concluded their healing and let her move.

"Weren't you the one who said that you all believed in me?" I asked, taking note of her discrepancy.

"Well, yeah, but then you got stabbed in the back, and when he stabbed you in the shoulder, it seemed like it was all over."

"I have to agree. I thought you were going to be slashed to bits!" Kuhani added.

"So we're all in agreement that I should have lost that?" I asked.

They all nodded their heads, and I fully agreed that I should have lost there. "Thank God that it was a deranged psychopath who loved the taste of my blood then, right? Either way, we won. I definitely didn't expect there to be another group that would make this so hard," I confessed.

"It should be difficult. I would be disappointed if the final match wasn't at least a little challenging," the Guildmaster said as he walked toward us. "I must admit, this result wasn't unexpected. But I'm still proud of you all nonetheless. Your quick thinking and your teamwork proved more than enough. Even against insanely overpowered magic, you were able to pull through. This is the type of thing you'd only hear of in stories. I'm glad I was able to witness such a feat."

When he reached us, he went in the middle of our group and spread his arms out wide before yelling, "Please congratulate this year's Wood bracket victors! They faced many hardships to be able to get this far, and I'm sure they'll overcome many more! We should all look forward to seeing them in the upcoming Winner's Tournament!"

After he finished, the crowd cheered louder than they had in any of our battles.

After his speech, we were allowed to leave. We stopped off in our waiting room to return the weapons we had taken from the weapon rack before going to claim our reward of a platinum coin each. While we collected our reward, our weapons that we usually used were returned as well. As we waited for the man at the desk to find Kuhani's weapons, she leaned over to me and said, "The inn we're staying at is called the Grinning King's inn. Okay? Tomorrow, we were going to watch the Irons fight, but we can just relay the information we gather to you, so don't worry about a thing, okay?"

"Um... Okay?" I said questionably. I didn't understand why she was telling me these things until Pauline and her group came around the corner. When our eyes met, she stopped dead in her tracks and she seemed to become really nervous. I ended up approaching her while her teammates walked past her toward the exit, paying no mind to her sudden state of immobility.

"Hey! It looks like I actually am free tomorrow. Where d'ya want to meet up?" I asked casually, hoping it wasn't obvious that my heart felt like it was about to burst out of my chest. *Why did they have to call it a date? Now that's all I'm going to think about!* I thought nervously.

"Really? Umm, I could meet you at yo—"

"Oho? If it isn't the man who not only beat me but managed to win the whole tournament. Did you come to rub it in?" the pink-haired girl with the scythe interrupted.

"Huh? Why would I do that? Also, uhh...sorry about your clothes," I said, looking down at her still charred shirt.

She rolled her eyes and scoffed. "I have tons just like it, so it's whatever. Out of curiosity, you are the Grayson that won, correct?" she asked me with a suspicious look in her eyes.

"Yes? Who else would I be? I don't think there's a lot, if any, people that look like me," I responded. Out of the corner of my eye, I watched Pauline who looked like a scared schoolgirl.

"You just...I can't find the words to explain it. You seem entirely different than the person I fought against. You really are interesting," she stated. "So what business do you have with me?" she asked assertively as if she was the only one that was worth talking to.

"Oh, Pauline and I just needed to talk about some stuff, so to my knowledge, I have nothing that concerns you. Speaking of, what were you trying to say before she interrupted us, Pauline?" I asked her. She nearly yelped when I said her name. "I think it was something along the lines of where we were going to meet?" I said in an attempt to jog her memory.

"Oh, umm... Where are you staying? I-I-I could just meet you there near midmorning," she answered timidly, shooting glances toward the girl with the large scythe.

"Oho? Do you not understand who I am, boy? You must not. Otherwise, you wouldn't be wasting your time with my underling. I am Mia Partino, daughter of Duke Augustus Partino!" she said proudly.

"Cool, thanks for finally introducing yourself," I said before turning back to Pauline. "We're staying at the Grinning King's Inn over in the old town district. I'll wait outside around nine-ish for ya!" I said with a smile to the horrified Pauline.

"Hold on a moment, boy! Are you telling me that even knowing of my lineage and that girl is a servant, you still intend to carry out your plans with her?" Mia cried out.

I turned briefly and glared at Mia. "Why wouldn't I? What's wrong with you?" I annoyedly asked. Mia was getting on my nerves. *Why is she acting like she's one of Cinderella's stepsisters? What's the point in trying to hurt this already awkward girl's social life?* I wondered.

Pauline was gazing at me in awe when I heard a voice behind me. "What's going on here?" the voice demanded.

"Sister! This man intends to accompany this girl when she goes into town tomorrow!" Mia whined after shooting a smug look at me. It was like she was trying to play the victim in all of this.

"Oh? How cute! Pollie, you didn't tell me you met someone! We have to make sure you look amazing tomorrow!" Mia's sister, Maya, said excitedly. Part of me felt like she was looking down on us, but I was just happy that she wasn't treating Pauline as bad as Mia was.

"You better clean yourself up too! And if anything happens to her, I swear I'll make you regret it!" Maya threatened as she pointed at me. Mia just stood there with her mouth open from the shock of her sister escalating the situation.

"I promise to do my best to look presentable and keep her safe!" I shouted out, suddenly standing at attention like I was a soldier.

"Great! Also, congratulations on your win. Our match definitely proved that you all deserved to win. If you lovebirds have nothing else to say, we'll be taking our leave. It's been a pleasure meeting you," Maya said before leaving with her sister in tow.

"W-well I guess I'll see you tomorrow," Pauline said, before offering a wave and running to catch up with the two sisters.

"That was…something. Eh, Gray?" Kuhani said, walking over to me.

"Definitely can't deny that. Let's never get involved with nobles if we can avoid it. Now that I think about it, why would a couple of nobles become adventurers anyway?" I wondered as we walked back over to the group.

"I dunno. Maybe they're rebelling against their parents. Ooh! Maybe they're family has fallen to ruin, and they have to take on odd jobs just to survive!" she brainstormed.

That is a complete 180 for reasons! I thought.

"You should ask Pauline tomorrow so that I don't die of curiosity! Besides, we need to find Lady Sylia, so we have no time to waste thinking!" Kuhani said cheerfully.

When we found our way outside, it was already dusk. The tournament had taken all day, as expected. Thankfully, the other brackets would be much shorter. We found Sylia waiting near the spectators' entrance to the arena. The first thing she said when we approached was, "You guys were amazing out there! You aren't still hurt, are you? I can't believe they actually let those psychos fight!"

"Why does it sound like you've heard of them before?" I asked.

"Well, I'm purely speculating. But I'm pretty sure that the guy who had the sleek sword is the new serial killer that leaves his victims drained of all their blood. That would make sense with what he was doing to you, right, Gray?" Sylia asked.

"I mean, it could be that or there could be a vampire on the loose, I guess," I replied jokingly. *Clearly, the guy had a couple of screws loose. But I dunno if I'd instantly jump to calling him a serial killer.*

Sylia let out a nervous laugh. "Let's hope it's not a vampire. The last time one was loose, dozens of people died before he was caught, and nearly a hundred died trying to execute him."

At Sylia's comment, I made a mental note. *That's terrifying. So vampires are real here and insanely strong. It's probably safe to assume that werewolves are too, but then again, I already figured they were when I found Crice and learned about lycanthropy existing.*

"Somehow you guys managed to beat them, though! I'm so proud of you, guys!" she said as she pulled us all into a large hug. "Now, I hate to be the person who cuts the celebration short, but I suggest that we pool half of the reward for living funds. Then you guys can use the other half for personal spending money while we're in the city!" Sylia added, clearly blissful that we wouldn't have to worry about money for a while.

I thought the plan was to use all of the winnings for living funds, though? I wondered.

"That sounds perfect! That way, we can pick up some souvenirs for Crice while we're here," Araya said as she stared directly at me, reminding me of her suggestion.

"Plus, Gray can use the money on his date tomorrow!" Kuhani spouted, before taking on a classic cat face and adding, "Oops!"

Sylia looked at me with a raised eyebrow before asking, "Date?"

I could feel myself turning red as I avoided her gaze.

"Yeah, I, uhh… Everyone kinda gave me the okay, so I'm going out with someone tomorrow," I confessed.

"Who would want to go on a date with you? Is it that girl you were holding hands with for a whole fight?" Sylia teased.

"We weren't holding hands! But yeah, you guessed right. Besides, it's not even a romantic date or anything. We're just gonna go around town together," I responded.

"I already told you, that's exactly what a date is, you moron," Kuhano thought.

"Honestly, I think it's good that you found someone. She's skilled too, so maybe you'll get to learn some things from her," Sylia added.

"Wait, so you're okay with me going out and skipping out on watching the bracket tomorrow?" I asked, completely taken aback. *I mean, I was hoping for this, but I expected to have to fight a little harder,* I thought.

"Of course I am! Information can be passed around, but a first date is a once in a lifetime experience! Well, maybe not for you since you got the whole bonus life thing. Just make sure that you look nice and be sure to compliment her. I'd hate to see you mess up your first relationship outside of the group," Sylia said, acting like a doting mother.

I let out a nervous chuckle. "Right, well, thanks for your permission, Silly. Now that's outta the bag, how about we give you the money?" I asked as I opened up the trade menu and offered five gold coins. When Sylia accepted the trade, the platinum coin transformed into ten gold pieces, and five of them flew into her hands. Everyone else did the same without any complaints.

"All right, that's everyone. Let's get back to the inn so that you four can get some rest. I'm sure you're all exhausted, right?" Sylia asked after she had received all of our coins. I hadn't even noticed how exhausted I was until she said that. I felt like my body was going to drop.

Did she really have to bring that up before we got back to the inn? I wondered, cursing my newfound exhaustion that I'd have to carry the whole way back. Apparently, everyone else felt the same way because we all ended up agreeing.

As we walked back to the inn, Sylia pestered me with questions like, "Where are you going to take her?" and 'What are you going to wear?" By the time we got back, I felt even more exhausted than I had when we left the arena. As soon as my head hit the pillow, I was out like a light.

9

How I Learned My True Purpose!

For the first time in a long while, I woke up feeling completely refreshed. Usually, we were woken up early and would be worked like dogs until we went to sleep. Needless to say, it was a nice change of pace. I lumbered out of bed and washed my face at the sink. Now that I knew how faucets worked in this world, I could only think of the little water spirit inside, spewing water out of its mouth.

After I washed my face, I took a glance at the wall clock. I learned earlier that the clock worked off of two small magic capsules. Basically, they're batteries that hold magic instead of electricity, which made the clocks more like modern clocks than the mechanical ones I had envisioned. It was half past eight, so I still had some time before I had to meet up with Pauline.

"I suppose I should clean myself up. Though, did she mean how I looked or my clothes?" I wondered out loud. I hoped that it was the first because I neglected to bring a change of clothes. If I was on Earth, not changing my clothes every day would bug me, but in this world, there wasn't any deodorant or body wash, so everyone just rocked their natural smell. Even when we washed our clothes, there was no soap to truly clean them. It was disgusting at first, but I got used to it after a while. *Maybe I could absorb some water and combine it with the Enchrydian's oils to make some sort of power wash spell? I wondered.*

I filled the sink with water while I grabbed a few leaves to soak in the water. When I absorbed the water nature, I imagined a bubble of water around me that would provide enough pressure to feel like I was being scrubbed. I held my breath and closed my eyes as I hit the button. Within seconds, the water that had been forming a cleaning coat over me dispersed, and I felt infinitely cleaner. Even my gear looked better aside from how wet it was. *It's not as good as soap, but it's way better than nothing,* I thought.

I grabbed a small wooden comb that the inn provided and combed my hair. Even though it was such a small task, it had big results. My hair usually would settle into the style that I had selected when I was changing how I looked, but if I purposely changed the style, it would stay how I wanted for the day.

After my hair was styled to the side, I placed my hand to the air and absorbed the wind nature. I thought of a spell that would work like a dryer for my entire body and clothes so that I could easily air dry them all. When I pressed the button, it was like I was in a wind funnel. As my clothes flapped in the wind, I could feel the water disappearing. "I can't believe this worked so well!" I said after it had finished, admiring how clean I was. "Even the baths don't get me this squeaky clean. I should've come up with this months ago!" I exclaimed.

I used the leftover leaf water in the sink as a makeshift mouth-wash to make my breath smell better. I grabbed one of the leaves before I spit the water back into the sink and let it all start draining. I chewed the minty leaf in an attempt to freshen my breath a little bit more.

With me looking miles better, smelling better, and my breath not smelling as horrible as usual, I decided that I was ready to go near the entrance. *I really hope she's not one of those types that show up a few hours early and then says that they just got there,* I thought with a grimace. I grabbed my bow sling and my bow as a precaution and headed out. As I walked through the inn, there was absolutely no one to be found. It was like it had been abandoned overnight. *It feels like I'm in an episode of The Twilight Zone. Where is everyone?* I wondered.

When I got outside at around 8:45, Pauline was already there waiting for me. She didn't look anything like she had the day before. The only way I was able to realize it was her were the bright amber eyes she sported. To my surprise, she was wearing a pink sweater and a grey skirt. *Useful for multiple seasons. Ready for all types of weather,* I joked to myself. Her dark-brown hair wasn't up in a bun today. Her bangs covered her forehead, and to either side of her head, she had chin-length curly hair.

I let out a laugh when I realized who I thought she looked like. A look of worry came across Pauline's face. "Do I really look that bad?" she asked sadly.

I instantly went on full damage control. "No! No, you look super cute! Especially your hair! The style just reminded me of a mix of two characters from a game I used to play, and it caught me off guard," I answered truthfully.

"Let me guess… Makoto and Haru from Persona 5 Royal?" she guessed confidently.

I couldn't believe what I was hearing; not because she got it mostly right, but because there was no way that she could have known that.

"Um… I mean, I never got to play Royal, but yeah. How did you—" I said to her, my amazement written all over my face.

"My friends used to say the exact same thing! It was so embarrassing because they kept trying to get me into cosplay! I even stopped wearing my hair like this because of them. Maya usually straightens it for me now since I can't use wind magic to style it, but she refused today because she thinks it looks better," she said with a large smile spanning her face as she recalled her past. Slowly, her smile faded as the two of us both realized what just happened.

"Wait! You're from Earth too!" We shouted out in surprise together.

I nodded at her. "I can't believe you're an other-worlder!" I said.

"Where are you from? And what year?" she quickly asked.

I gave her a concerned look before saying, "Uh, America, 2019. Does the year really matter, though?"

"Um... So you've been here for around eight years then? That would explain how you've become so skilled in combat," she said, the second half-sounding like she was thinking out loud.

"Hate to burst your bubble, but I've only been here for around six months. Where could you have gotten eight years from?" I asked with a raised eyebrow.

"What? You've only been here for six months? This isn't fair, why are you so much better at fighting than me?" she cried out.

"I got trained by the ex-general of the elven army. I'm actually a ranger too, so the whole dagger build is a little awkward for me," I said with a nervous laugh. I didn't mean to make it sound like I was bragging, but as soon as I said it, I was afraid that's how it came off as.

Pauline stared at me with her mouth agape. "I lost to you in your off-spec?" she muttered in complete disbelief.

"Err... Uhh... Yeah. But I'm sure you haven't been here that long, right? Plus, my skills are stupidly overpowered!" I said in an attempt to make her feel better about her loss.

"I've been here for two whole years. I became a part of the guild around fourth months ago, though, so I guess you're right," she said, hanging her head dejectedly. "I was taken in by the Partino family as a maid. When Lady Mia and Lady Maya decided to join the guild, I was sent along with them to ensure their safety. Them being nobles is why our equipment is so good," she added.

"You've been here for two years? Wait, then why did you think that I've been here for eight?" I asked, still confused.

"You said you're from 2019, right? I'm from 2025, so six years difference plus the two years I've been here would make it eight, right? I'm not being an idiot, right?" SHE explained.

"Oh, that actually makes a lot more sense... Wait, did you say you're from 2025? Hold up, if you've been here for two years, you've talked to God a few times then, yeah?" I asked.

Pauline suddenly shifted from being a somewhat shy girl to almost seeming like she could be a punk. "Ugh, don't talk to me about that jerk. I still can't believe he expects the seven of us to go to war against a god," she complained casually. When she noticed I was looking at her with a blank stare, she said, "Oh, jeez, he hasn't told you yet, has he?"

I shook my head.

"Err... Let's walk and talk. Not many people will be around today, so we should be fine to talk about it, plus my social anxiety should be...manageable," she said as she started walking away. I felt like my life was about to become significantly more interesting but also annoyingly complicated. "Has he even told you about how he lost control of this planet yet?" she asked.

"Yeah, but that's pretty much all I've been told," I responded.

"At least that idiot did that much," she muttered. "I'll try to put this in simple terms because I don't even fully understand it myself. Basically, he's reincarnated seven people who were worthless members of society obsessed with fantasy literature, games, etc. In this world, each one of us is the embodiment of one of the six stats in the world, and it's our job to stop Ares, the god who took control of this world, from plunging the world into endless war. The best part is that we don't know when he's going to strike, and we don't know who the other other-worlders are unless we slip up in front of each other like I just did with you. Plus, we can't really let other people know because they're terrified of us! I've met two of the others, excluding you, in the past two years. We generally keep in touch to try to get connected with the others, but we've run into a dry patch when it comes to finding the last four. Well, now three" she quickly explained like she was a businesswoman.

I guess that when it comes to our situation, her anxiety goes completely out the window, I thought. "I feel like this stuff should've been explained to me way earlier," I complained. "And hold up a sec, did you just say that we're going to have to kill a god?"

"Technically, I said stop a god. Now it makes more sense of how he lost control of this, world right?" she said. "I'm amazed he didn't tell you any of this, especially with how well you fight. You must have played a lot of VR games or you're just uber-talented," she added.

"You think I could afford a VR headset? Even if I got one, I'd probably only play Beat Saber," I responded, feeling embarrassed that she'd think I was the latter of her two options.

"Well, thankfully, you're on our side. I can't imagine the monster you're going to become later on. Sorry if I'm being really straightforward and impatient. I really hate this whole determined fate thing that we got forced into," she said apologetically.

"Don't worry about it. I like people who are direct," I said, brushing off her apology. "So do you know Crice? He's the other-worlder who's also a wererat," I explained.

"I actually don't. Looks like you're already being more useful than some of the others. Just two more to find then. I pray that we can find them before Ares begins his assault," she said back. "But whatever, we'll leave worrying about that to future us. If you have any questions about this world, I'm confident that I can answer next to anything!"

"I honestly think I have more questions about you than about this world," I said without thinking.

Pauline stopped walking and turned toward me, revealing her flushed face. "Uhh… Wh-what do you mean you have questions about me?"

"You're from my future basically. Isn't it natural to have questions about what changed?" I lied, thinking quickly to avoid embarrassment.

"Oh, that's what you meant," Pauline said, sounding relieved. "Tell you what, if you somehow manage to find one of the last two other-worlders, I'll answer any questions you have about the future and my personal life," she said.

I contemplated her demands for a moment. *It's super unlikely that I find another other-worlder though, right? Unless it's like how stand users attract other stand users in JoJo. But I don't lose anything really from failing, so I might as well just accept her side quest.*

"Fine, on one condition. I get to ask at least five questions of anything I want," I said as if I was a foreign diplomat negotiating for my country.

"Okay, deal," Pauline said as if it was no problem. "Good timing for finishing that up. We're here!" She added as we stood outside of a shop for weapon repairs.

"Why are we here? There's no way that your bow is trashed and needs repairing," I said, looking at the crystal bow that seemed to appear out of nowhere on her body. It was beautiful; up close, it seemed like it could be made of ice instead of crystals. "We're here because I refuse to let you use such a low-level weapon, especially now that I know you're an other-worlder. I can't let you die and I need you to become more powerful so that I have a higher chance of survival in the final fight!"

"Putting a bit of pressure on me here. I mean, I'll do my best to get beefy before then, but I don't think that I'll make that big of a difference," I said carefully. I didn't want to say that I would be useless, but I also didn't want to commit to being super useful either.

"Don't be modest. I've seen you fight already, remember? Now tell me what's up with your skills so I know what bow to get you," she demanded.

"We barely even know each other! It would be rude of me to accept a gift, much less a bow from you!" I protested.

"I'm going to get you a new bow whether you like it or not. If not for your sake, then for mine. At first, I thought today was just going to be a casual nice day with a guy th-th-that... Never mind! The point is that today changed as soon as I found out our futures depend on each other! So tell me your skills or I will find them out by any means necessary," she said, raising her fist.

Why did I have to be cursed with the abusive women trope? I thought to myself before I cracked and told her about my tracking and focus skills.

"Okay, so you'd basically be good with anything. What about that magic that you used? I've never heard of someone being able to counter a spell and then unleash it in a different form," she asked.

Without hesitation, I explained to her about the gloves I had and their overpowered use.

"God gave YOU that! You're telling me that he gave you a way to use any type of magic that you come across in any way that you want?" she screamed out.

"Err...yeah. I didn't have the ability to use magic, so when I met him again, I asked him about it, and this is what he did," I said, attempting to shift the blame over to him.

"I should've asked for something like that! Instead, the head maid at the estate implanted this fire crystal in my hand so I'd be able to start fires. Then again, that thing is stupid powerful: Luckily you aren't an idiot; otherwise, the whole kingdom would be in ruins by now. Anyway, that rules out any guns or bows that use your magic to enhance itself. I'll find something. Stay out here, and make sure no one else comes in," she ordered before she went into the shop.

As I stood by the door, I couldn't help but think about how different she seemed now that she could talk normally with me. Not only did we not have tons of people around, but we also didn't need to worry about each other finding out that we were other-worlders. *Even though she seemed a lot more confident, it seemed to fall apart when I said I had questions about her. I wonder why she's so nervous about that. Then again, she was nervous about discussing today's plans yesterday. Maybe I'm not the only one who was convinced by others that this is a date? Either way, her being nervous isn't the biggest mystery here. Who buys a bow from a repair shop?* I wondered as I looked out at the street, thinking of the possible hellscape the peaceful city would become if Ares took over.

A war with Ares, huh? Is that even going to be possible to win? Why would God try to hide the fact that I would have to fight against a deity anyway? I'm sure he has his reasons, but I could've been preparing this whole time. Now that I know, I have to pour everything into getting a higher level after the tournament, I thought, determined to do whatever I could to improve our chances against such a great threat.

After a while, I ran out of things to think about, and my mind began to wander. There weren't many people out since a majority of the city was at the arena, watching the tournament, so I didn't have to pay too much attention to my duty. After around a half an hour, Pauline came out with a bow that looked like it had come out of a video game.

At a glance, you could tell that it was a recurve bow, but it looked entirely tricked out. The limbs were made out of some type of ebony-colored metal with purple runes etched into them. The string itself looked as though it was made of glass and would break after a single shot. The grip was smooth and silvery, fading to black near the arrow rest which had a single pin sight above it. On Earth, a sight wouldn't be very exciting. But here on Zynka, sights are usually only made for guns and are very shoddy. This sight was so pristine that it looked like it had been brought from Earth.

"Wha-what is this?" I asked in astonishment. Before becoming a ranger, I wouldn't have been able to care less about a bow. But looking at this now, I was freaking out.

"It's your new bow," Pauline said as she opened up the trade window to transfer the ownership of the bow to me.

"There's no way I could accept something like this! It must have cost a fortune!" I exclaimed.

"You don't know the half of it," Pauline muttered, looking back toward the shop.

"What was that?" I cautiously asked as I struggled to make out her words.

"Nothing! It didn't cost that much." She laughed, waving off the cost. "Besides, I got it specifically for you, so you have to take it!" she demanded. "What would I do with a second bow anyway?" she asked.

It was clear how stubborn she was going to be when it came to me taking the bow, so I let out a sigh of defeat and reluctantly accepted it. Part of me was brimming with joy about getting the bow, but most of me felt horrible. *I definitely have to do something to make it up to her,* I thought as I accepted the trade and received the bow.

"Now that you've accepted it, how about you tell me what stat you're supposed to be?" Pauline said.

I furrowed my brow. *So this was her plan? Get me to accept something crazy and then use it as a way to get information out of me? If she just asked me like a normal person, I probably would've told her whatever she wanted to know,* I thought.

"I actually don't know. Is there a specific way to figure out what stat I embody?" I asked.

Pauline let out a sign of annoyance. "He really didn't tell you anything, huh? When you leveled, you should have had a stat go up a point before you put in your two points for leveling. That stat is supposed to be the one that you're the physical form of."

"Oh. Stupid question incoming, what stat would I be if when I level up, all of my stats go up by two?" I answered with my own question.

"Uhh… Are you being serious?" Pauline asked with both a look of surprise and distrust.

"Why would I lie after you gave me this thing?" I asked, holding up the bow she just gave me.

"Th-that's not what I meant. If your stats are doing that, then…I can't believe how lucky I am!" she spouted, barely able to contain her excitement as she started jumping up and down.

"What do you mean? How do my stats being like this make you lucky?" I asked. *Obviously, I'm aware that my stats make everything easier, but how would it benefit her? At least, how would it benefit her to make her act like this?* I wondered, not being able to make any sense of what was going on.

"If your stats are like that, you're already worth six people of your level. Imagine if you were Level 50. You'd basically be Level 300! You're the fabled God Killer we were told about! I can't believe that it'd be you, though. I thought that Falkeen was for sure lying about him being the other-worlder of luck," she explained.

"Wait, Falkeen? Blonde hair, kinda badass, but at the same time isn't, and very…what's the word?" I wondered as I tried to describe him to her.

"Ungraceful, stupid, always charging into battle without making sure everyone else is ready, yet somehow makes it so everything works out?" Pauline said.

"Yeah, that's actually spot on. So he's another other-worlder? I guess I'm not really surprised since he's considered to be the world's closest thing to a hero," I said.

"How do you even know Falkeen? Are you a fanboy or a stalker or something like that? He's not exactly the type of guy you just run into in the street," Pauline asked.

"That's funny because I literally met him in a street. I mean, he was in the street. I was on top of it," I said with a chuckle.

Pauline looked at me in confusion. "What does that even mean?" she shouted out.

"Long story short, I was in trouble, I called out for help, he came crashing into the street from the rooftops, and I thought that the other way would be a funnier way to explain it," I replied.

"Tch, that sounds just like him. I can't believe you've met three of the six others in just half a year," Pauline said. "I'm even happier I got you the bow now. I really hope you stick it to him in the Winners bracket. Be sure you put him in his place. You definitely won't win, but at least give him a scare for me. I'd love to see his face after taking damage from a Wood!" she exclaimed.

I let out a chuckle. "I'll have to get to fight him first, but if I get there, I'll do my best!" I promised. At my words, a rune on the bow started to glow, and a coat of energy lathered itself onto the bow. I was so startled by it that I dropped the bow out of fear that something was about to happen.

"Well, that was rude of you," Pauline said, putting her hands on her hips.

"Wha—Why did it start glowing? Why won't it stop?" I shouted out as I stared at the bow.

"Have you never heard of a living weapon before? It's obviously onboard with fighting against a strong opponent and wants to lend you its power."

I looked back and forth between Pauline and the bow. "You're telling me this thing's alive?" I said, nervously lifting it with two fingers.

"Living weapons are super powerful because they'll grow alongside you instead of being stuck at a certain power level. Though it takes twice as long for them to level up than a person. If you use the inspect feature, you can see the level of the item and its experience bar. As it levels, it'll unlock abilities that can help you. Each rune is a leveling milestone. Usually, it's around increments of ten to unlock them. It should be able to use a small amount of its magic right now, though, so it's not entirely useless," Pauline said.

"Are you a frickin' game guide or something? That was a lot to take in," I said as I inspected the bow. The menu stated, "Bow of Forgotten Darkness. Level 1, required XP—2,000."

What's with this edgy name? I thought.

Pauline blushed at my comment and said, "I've just been here long enough to learn things that should be common knowledge for adventurers. You don't have to flatter me!"

"Either you don't know what flatter means or you think that was a compliment," I muttered as I picked up the bow. "Well, I guess that we'll be working together from now on, Foda!"

"Foda? What kind of a name is that?" Pauline asked with a giggle. "Well, I'm not going to call it Bow of Forgotten Darkness all the time, and the name Darkness raises some red flags. It's like a four-teen-year-old who's a wannabe goth named The Thing. So I'm taking the beginning of forgotten and the beginning of darkness. Mix that together, and you get Foda!" I explained.

"That's...childishly simple," Pauline said as her giggles trans-formed into full-blown laughter. "Whatever floats your boat, though, if FODA isn't raising any objections, then I'm sure it's fine with it," she added, snorting after she shouted out my new bow's name.

"Foda's simple, tactical. I permit it. I trust you'll use me well," Came a dark voice that chilled me to the bone. I nervously looked toward the bow.

"Pfft, you should see your face! I'm assuming you just heard Foda's voice for the first time? I can't imagine how yours sounds since it's a dark bow and everything!" Pauline said.

"Terrifying," is all I uttered in response to Pauline. She just kept laughing and said, "Well, you better get used to it. Prelu talks to me all the time! Oh, man, gimme a second to calm down. I'm in that state where everything is funny for some reason. You're so great to be around!" she added as she continued to laugh. After a while, she finally started to calm down.

"So, Prelu?" I asked curiously.

"Oh, right, my bow is the Crystal bow of Preludes! We might've been saving her magic for the finals, but she's a light bow. The exact opposite of your dark bow!" she said as she held her bow up toward the sun in a victory pose.

Where does she even pull that out of! I thought after witness-ing the bow appear as if from out of nowhere for the second time. "You laughed for that long at the name Foda when you literally just removed three letters from the end of your bow's name?" I exasperatedly shouted out.

"We're both bad at naming things. I can't help that yours is funny. I never said I gave mine a good name. I just went with what I felt," she said. I couldn't argue with that. After all, that's basically all I did to name Foda. *Huh. If we end up in a relationship and have a kid at some point...who's going to name it?* I jokingly wondered.

"Hmm, they should be ready by this point. Now that we've gotten all of the unforeseen business taken care of, let's go do what I had planned! I-I mean if you're okay with that," she said as she started to blush.

"Definitely, if there was a specific thing you wanted to do, then we should've done that from the beginning," I said as I picked up my new bow. When we started walking, Foda's aura slithered over my body to my old short bow and disintegrated it, leaving the sling hanging off my shoulder. *"You don't require any bow other than me,"* it said creepily.

Something about the way it talked made me feel like it was going to try to corrupt my mind and have me do unthinkable things. *Hopefully, this feeling isn't foreshadowing,* I thought as I attached Foda to the now empty sling while I followed Pauline.

Walking through the market made me realize just how many people there actually were at the arena. The few experiences I'd had with the market made it seem like it was always full and bustling. The emptiness today could only be compared to a ghost town. The only people that were still around were old shopkeepers who waited patiently for the odd traveler to wander by.

With the large amount of money in my possession, I wanted to browse around and window shop at the stalls, but Pauline was on a mission. She made a beeline straight toward a shop on the outskirts of the square. It had a small bright pink awning with two sets of green metal tables and chairs beneath it. "A-a-all right. Follow my lead," she said before taking a deep breath. The way she said it made me prepare for a difficult challenge ahead. Hell, she even looked terrified!

What could we possibly be about to do? I exclaimed as I silently prayed that I wasn't about to become an accessory to a crime.

With a look of determination, she ripped the door open, and we stepped into the shop.

"Welcome! How can I help yo—Oh my! I didn't expect any young lovers to come in for the special today! Usually, you young folk all enjoy the tournament!" an old woman greeted from behind a counter.

As soon as we walked in, my nose was assaulted by the smell of fresh bread. After all of my worrying, we were just in a bakery owned by a sweet old lady. *Wait a minute, did she just say lovers?* I realized as Pauline grasped my left hand. My initial reaction was to pull away, but her iron grip refused to let me escape.

"Y-yes, but we heard that your l-l-lover's biscuits are to die for! S-so I insisted t-that we come g-get some!" Pauline stuttered.

I glanced at Pauline. I couldn't believe that she was serious. *Couldn't she have just come and gotten these without me? The name's just thematic, the cookies are probably heart-shaped,* I thought.

"You definitely heard correct! But how can I be so sure that you two are actually lovers? For all I know, you could have just dragged some poor sap in here," the old woman asked as she eyed us suspiciously.

That's basically spot on! I shouted out in my mind.

"Show her your bow, s-s-sweetie," Pauline said as she held out Prelu.

I shot her a glance of confusion but reluctantly held out Foda. "O-our bows act as a symbol of our l-love for each other. We exchanged them after our one-year a-anniversary so a part of us would always be with the o-other on their journeys," Pauline lied. If she hadn't just given me the bow on a whim, I would've been convinced that she had this planned!

"Hm… That sounds believable. But to prove my doubts wrong, how about the two of you kiss so I know for sure?" the old woman said with a sly grin.

With just a glance, I could tell that she wasn't buying our act and was trying to catch us in the lie. *Is this the end? It definitely is unless I do something right now. I wouldn't care about something as silly as this, but Pauline did just get me a sick bow. God, this better be enough to clear my debt to her,* I thought. I turned toward Pauline, but she was just standing there like a deer in headlights.

I poked her cheek to snap her out of it. "You forced me to miss the Iron groups fight for this and you freeze up? After going on about how much you want these things, you're just going to give up? We kiss all the time in private. Doing it in front of one person isn't a big deal, right?" I asked, trying to make our lie more convincing. There were two reasons why I chose this method instead of just kissing her. The first: It proved to the old bat that I wasn't just a random guy that didn't know her. The second: It told Pauline that if she was willing to do such a crazy thing for these cookies, I would be there to back her up.

Pauline looked me directly in the eyes. It was as if she was trying to talk to me without using any words. *"Prelu says that her master wishes to know if you're truly okay with this,"* Foda said.

I cracked a slight smile and gave her a small nod. *It's cute that she would've given up if I wasn't okay with it after coming up with such an outlandish lie. Don't tell Prelu I said that,* I thought as I slung Foda back over my shoulder and grabbed Pauline's hips. Slowly, our faces moved closer and closer together until I could feel her warm breath on my face. I started having second thoughts, but I was too deep to retreat now.

"All right... All right! I'm convinced. I'll allow you two the taste of my special biscuits!" the old lady shouted at us before we kissed. Part of me felt like it was a trick, so I pulled away slowly. It wasn't until my hands were off of her hips that I realized just how hard my heart was beating. Judging by how red Pauline's face was, her heart was probably beating just as hard. We didn't utter a word to each other before she went to the counter to buy the special biscuits. While she did that, I looked around at all of the different types of bread as I calmed my dancing heart. The one that sounded the most appetizing was the glazed cinnamon roll.

When Pauline had two bags of biscuits in tow, she motioned to me that it was time to go. As we exited the shop, the old lady called, "Have a nice day! May the coming years treat you both well!"

We sat at one of the tables directly outside, and both of us let out a sigh of relief. "T-thanks. I can't believe y-you'd go to such lengths to help me," Pauline said as she pushed a bag of biscuits toward me. "T-these are for you. It's an, uhh…an apology for tricking you into coming here with me."

"Don't worry about it. Good thinking with the bows, by the way. Both the lie and the silent communication thing," I responded as I looked into the bag. The cookies were heart-shaped as I had expected, but they were bite-sized and had a mini-heart of frosting atop them.

"T-thanks. I couldn't have done it without you, though. I'm amazed that you were willing to k-kiss me, though," she said, blushing.

"Well, I couldn't just ruin your chance at these things. Besides, it would've been less awkward to have my first kiss with a friend, right?" I asked with a chuckle.

"You haven't kissed anyone before? But you're so…never mind. Anyway, you pretty much have a harem in this world, so how have you never kissed anyone?" she asked as she threw a biscuit into her mouth.

"Different worlds, I guess, literally and figuratively. In my old life, I wasn't exactly the most likable guy. I was weird and an otaku. I imagine you know what that's like. In this world, I guess I haven't really been looking for a relationship like that. But then again, no one's approached me, looking for one either. So I guess I'm just unappealing?" I admitted with a nervous chuckle.

"That's r-ridiculous! I won't pry into your old life, but y-you're an insanely skilled f-fighter. You're h-handsome, and d-don't think I'm weird, but you're easily the best s-smelling person I've met. Y-you're even nice enough to help s-someone you just met by acting like you're their l-lover," Pauline stammered guiltily. "I-if I didn't feel bad about u-using you… No, I don't think I'd be able to handle d-d-dating you at all, actually," she added.

"Likewise, but that's an oof. Was that meme still relevant in your time?" I asked.

"Barely. P-people overused it so much it lost its meaning. T-that aside, this was all I wanted s-so you can go. B-but y-y-you don't have to if you don't want to, though," she stammered.

"I'm down to keep this 'date' with you going. I can't believe everyone tried to convince me that this was a date," I said.

With a blushing face, Pauline said, "Y-you weren't the only one people t-tried to convince."

I let out a laugh as I started nibbling on a cookie. "By the way, we can go somewhere else if you want to drop the nervous girlfriend act," I offered. *It's cute, but if she has to put effort into it, I'd rather her not force herself.*

"T-trust me, I d-don't think that would h-help," she said.

The rest of the day felt peaceful, perfect almost. We sat outside the bakery and talked about our past experiences in our new lives. I learned about a few of the other-worlders that Pauline had already met. When the old woman started closing the shop, we realized that we had been there all day. Before we left, the woman shoved her supply of lover's biscuits on us free of charge.

"I only sell them one day a season. Their limited availability is part of their selling point! They'd just be going to waste if you don't take them!" the woman explained. Naturally, I let Pauline take the leftovers before walking her back to her inn.

We made a quick stop at an outside market shop that was still open to buy a gift for Crice. I ended up getting him an herb pouch that was able to store an infinite amount of herbs and keep their freshness. *It's basically a bag of holding that you can only use for one type of item,* I thought as I handed over a measly gold for the item. When we reached the inn, Pauline stopped outside the door and turned toward me. "T-thanks Grayson. I...I had a really nice time today. Honestly, I can't r-remember the last t-time I've had th-this much fun," she said.

"I actually had a lot of fun too. We should do this again sometime. Though, let me know if I'm posing as your boyfriend next time," I jokingly said.

With a small laugh, she said, "No p-promises." She looked down and let out a nervous sigh. "C-close your eyes. A-and n-no peeking okay!" she suddenly said.

I furrowed my brow. "Um... Okay?" I questionably said as I closed my eyes.

A few moments passed when I heard her quietly say to someone, "What are you doing? Go away!" before throwing something toward them. "What wa—"

"No peeking!" she shouted at me, cutting me off before I could ask my question.

I rolled my eyes beneath my eyelids but still complied. I heard her take a deep breath before I felt her lips on my left cheek. I was completely frozen in that moment, even after she quickly squealed, "Good luck at the tournament!" before opening and slamming the door to the inn.

Wh-what just happened? I thought, slightly panicking.

"Prelu says that her owner doesn't understand what happened herself," Foda replied.

T-thank you Foda, that explained a-absolutely nothing. L-let's head to our inn, I thought, feeling like I had taken the role of a nervous boyfriend.

*****

The next few days consisted of us scouting out the competition for the finals. I didn't pay a whole lot of attention to most of the fights, mostly because my mind would be in a different place. *It was just a spur of the moment thing. She didn't mean anything by it. It was just a thanks for helping her out*, I would think, trying to come up with any reason to not think too much of it, but to no avail.

The only fights that I could focus on at all were the finals of each bracket. The winners of the bronze bracket would have their mage sacrifice the rest of the group to cast an instant kill spell that would win their fights in an instant. The silver and gold winners didn't do anything flashy, but they were powerhouses with amazing armor and weapons that made up for their many mistakes.

The palladium bracket was the scariest one by far. The teams were so powerful that they seemed like they could take on nations if they were so inclined. Needless to say, Falkeen's group ended up taking the win in the finals. The Battle of the Champions bracket was completed and released shortly after. Luckily, the only groups standing between us and the finals were the Iron and Bronze winners.

The next day, the tournament began. We were all using our normal weapons and our main specs from the get go. Even though we were the first fight of the day, we were sent to the waiting room that we had been in during the wood bracket. The previously opened weapon rack had a blue field that prevented access to the guild's weapons. The spying orb had a bird's-eye view of the arena where a lone man stood with a wand to his mouth. "Check! Check! All good? All right! Let's get this show on the road everybod-ay!" he shouted, causing the crowd to cheer. "Before we do, though, here's a word from our sponsors!" he said, which was met with a resounding groan from the crowd.

"Sponsors? An announcer? This is starting to look like an event from my world. Is he using magic to enhance the volume of his voice?" I asked.

"The wand he has is constantly expelling wind magic to carry his voice around the arena. So technically, no, he's not making himself louder," Kuhano thought to me. *"Can we talk about your new bow, though? I didn't want to be rude, but that thing is freaking me the hell out."*

"Since when do you worry about being rude?" I joked, which received a scowl from my wolf-like ally. "Well, you have instincts like an animal, don't you? Y'know, like the whole you can tell that an earthquake is going to happen before it does and stuff like that? It only makes sense that a living creature of darkness would set you on edge," I added.

"That thing's alive!" Kuhano exclaimed fearfully.

"Are you allowed to use that? Shouldn't it count as another member of our party then?" Araya raised.

"It wasn't a problem when Pauline used Prelu. x

"Prelu? Come to think of it, you never told us how your date went. So, come on! Spill it!" Kuhani pestered.

"I'll, uhh...I'll tell you later. How about you tell me what our opponents are using?" I asked in an attempt to change the subject.

"Fiiiiine. But you better actually tell us later!" Kuhani complained. "Their guardian uses nothing but a tower shield, their healer uses water magic to heal and restore mana to his allies, one of their damage dealers has a spear, and the last one has a magical sword of fire," Kuhani explained, brimming with pride about the fact she could remember them all. "Magical fire sword? Sounds like he should be my main target then," I mumbled to myself as I came up with a strategy.

"Araya, stay close to me then. I'll take out the spear guy from a distance, and if the fire sword guy comes close to us, I'll just absorb his blade," I commanded. When I revealed my strategy, Araya let out a small gasp. "That was quick! I'll be counting on you to protect me then, partner!" she answered.

"The shield guy is going to be a bit of an is—" I started saying when I was interrupted by someone barging into the room.

"It's time for your fight. Do your best! I'm rooting for you guys!" the young man in front of us spouted out. I had no idea who he was, but he seemed friendly enough as he escorted us to the gate.

When we walked through the gate onto the sandy arena, the announcer shouted, "Here's our Wood bracket winners! With multiple impressive performances, they left us yearning for more despite their backgrounds! They ripped a win out of the jaws of defeat in a match that amazed everyone! They may have not registered a group name, but their skill has made many of us wonder where they came from! Therefore, the good people at the guild have bestowed upon them the name of The Wondrous Woods! Let's give them a warm welcome!"

Around a third of the crowd actually cheered while the other two-thirds gave unenthusiastic claps. *There are a lot more people here today than there was at our bracket. The chances that people even saw our fights are slim to none,* I thought as I looked at the crowd.

"Now, here's our Iron bracket champions who took an amazing win that proved you don't have to stand out to win! They're probably the most normal group here in terms of power, but they've won the hearts of the people by standing up against any opponent and managing to come out on top. They're the Underdogs! Let's give 'em a cheer!"

Instantly, anyone could tell what group people were more excited for. The cheers from the crowd shook the arena. I almost felt bad about having to beat them to proceed in the tournament. Our enemy with the spear was a man wearing a kimono-like robe. Their healer was a feminine-looking guy with platinum blonde hair and a large blue ball-tipped scepter in his left hand. *Actually, is he a girl? He's beautiful, but something about him makes me really think that he's a guy,* I thought before coming to the conclusion that their gender didn't matter.

The man with the sword of fire had spiky bright orange hair and just radiated pyromaniac energy. It was something about his eyes that made him seem that way—lifeless but then full of joy whenever he glanced down at his sword. The man with the tower shield was huge. He looked like he could be the brother of Horrad. At first glance, there was only one way I could think of to beat him. If I was the MVP of our group, then he surely had to be the MVP of theirs.

"Show a little bit of impartialness, everybody, we're all here to have a good time! It wouldn't do for a group to be discouraged because they feel like the crowd isn't on their side!" the announcer said. Something about the way he said it made it feel like he was rubbing salt in the wound. Instead of discouraging me, it just made me want to beat these guys even more.

"Let's get this fight started! When I get to one, it'll be an all-out brawl to the death! Five, four, three, two, one! Fight!" he shouted out as he used wind magic to fly up to a viewing platform above the arena.

As soon as the fight started, I nocked an arrow that Foda then shrouded in darkness and fired it toward their spear-wielder who hadn't even taken a step. It looked like the arrow was about to hit him when he jumped up in the air and cut the arrow in half with his spear. *Damn, I guess it wouldn't be the champion's tourney if it was that easy,* I thought.

"Give it a second," Foda replied.

By the time I nocked another arrow, the spear had been consumed by the same darkness the previous arrow had been coated in. Out of fear or surprise, the man dropped the spear to the ground.

I let the nocked arrow loose and caught him right in the head as he was staring at his spear in shock, pinning him to the wall.

"Ouch! That's gonna leave a mark! That's not how you catch an arrow, Mr. Yari! You're supposed to use your hands, not your head! This mistake is gonna cost Yari's team big-time! The kill is credited to Mr. Grayson, the contender that led his team to victory in the Wood Division Finals! He still refuses to show any mercy to his enemies, even with a bow instead of his usual dagger!" the announcer called out, confirming the death of our enemy.

"Nice job, Grayson!" Araya called. Thankfully, she was right next to me because when I looked toward her, their fire-swordsman was about to lop off her head. *I only rolled a 3X stat increase today, but I should still have enough speed!* I thought as I threw Foda into my right hand and lunged forward.

"Hah! I can't believe Thorwine was right! You're a damage dealer, not a guardian. You should worry about keeping yourself alive, moron," he said as he changed the direction of his blade toward me.

"And you should worry more about your opponent's abilities!" I shouted back as I absorbed his blade. "Now, Araya!" I shouted. With no weapon and nowhere to run, he was defenseless against Araya's unarmed "Punch of the Gods" spell. Tip: Punch of the Gods is a spell that coats the user's hand in pure light magic! She punched him square in the gut with her light-enveloped fist. He keeled over on the ground, grasping his stomach in response to her hit.

"Yo-you c-c-c-can't think that's going to beat m—" He tried to sputter out.

Dude, you can barely even breathe right now, I thought as Araya interrupted him.

"You're right, I don't think just that will. But that's why I have this! God smite!" she shouted out as she called down her guillotine of light upon him.

"Yowch, clean up on aisle three! Down goes Dafrea! The kill is credited to the Archpriest Araya! Imagine losing to a healer, and in close quarters too! How embarrassing for him!" the announcer mocked. "It's a two versus four with only a healer and guardian up! Will the Underdogs be able to make a surprising come back? Or will their story end as soon as it began? Let's find out!"

I know he's just trying to hype up the crowd, but he's super distracting, I thought.

"Woah! In a sudden turn of events, Kuhani Andante falls to Thorwine the guardian! This could have been a clean sweep from the Wondrous Woods if only Thorwine didn't have a skill that increases all stats by 15 when he's in a dire situation!"

"Huah! There's no way you're allowed to just tell us his skills!" I shouted at the announcer.

"Sorry, kid, I'm just doing my job and explaining things for the audience! If you want to make it fair, I could tell them all one of your skills to make it even?" he taunted.

Who in their right mind would ever want that? I wondered before dropping it.

"That's what I thought! Too bad for you that it's a one versus three now! Healer Sanadel has fallen to Kuhano Andante while I was too busy arguing with a contestant!" he shouted out. *"Dude! Did you not just hear that he gets stronger in dire situations!"* I yelled at Kuhano.

"She died from bleeding, there was nothing I could do unless you wanted me to heal her!" he argued.

Wait, that was a girl? Actually, never mind that! What can we even do? There's no way my arrows will be able to get through his armor. Unless... I wondered, thinking of the arrow of fire that Pauline fired in our fight.

"We could do that, Master, but I only have enough power to coat two arrows until I need to recharge," Foda said.

After a moment of contemplation, I thought, *"Screw it, let's do it then. Kuhano, get ready to shred him."*

Without missing a beat, Thorwine began sprinting toward me with his shield raised. He was slow, but each step he took shook the very earth. I steeled myself as I took a deep breath and summoned forth an arrow of fire from the sword I had absorbed. When I nocked it, Foda coated it in darkness magic. *Thank God this isn't a spirit. Otherwise, we'd be getting blown to smithereens,* I thought.

"Fly, Straight Arrow of Flame's Darkness!" I shouted as I let loose the jet-black flaming arrow. As soon as it collided with Thorwine's shield, it instantly started to crack from the attack as he pushed against it. Even after the collision, the arrow continued to burn and attempt to force its way forward. The shield was able to block a majority of the cursed flames, but as it continued to decay, Thorwine's armor started to take damage. When the flames faded, Thorwine flew forward with nothing but his undergarments on.

He was able to force his way through that? The thing was propelling itself with so much power that it could've rivaled a damn rocket! I thought as he was closing in on me. I was at a complete loss for what to do. Before I could come up with a plan, the gap had been closed.

Thorwine grabbed me by the throat and lifted me off the ground. *It...hurts? Isn't there a pain nullification field, though? Just how strong is this guy?* I thought as I struggled to breathe.

Araya looked on in horror as I was getting choked out by this monster of a man.

"You're easy to read, kid. When something doesn't go your way, you panic. This loss wasn't your fault, though. You just didn't have all the information to create a sound enough plan," he said as my consciousness started fading.

Before I completely blacked out, I saw Kuhano leap onto Thorwine's back, digging his claws deep and sending us all careening to the ground. When I slammed into the ground and the two of them fell on top of me, I was assaulted with such intense pain that I instantly passed out.

*****

"Gray! Gray! Thank God, you're finally awake!" Araya called out as I slowly opened my eyes. I was on the arena floor, looking up toward the sky.

"We thought you found a way to die in the anti-death field!" Kuhani cried out with a sigh of relief.

I blocked the sun from my eyes and slowly got up. "What happened? Did we win?" *Honestly, I'm more interested in if we won than what happened,* I thought.

"Yeah, we won. Kuhano managed to beat Thorwine! Though he kinda, maybe, sorta did it by sacrificing you. After he threw off Thorwine's balance, you were crushed under their weight. But with your soft fleshy body in the way, Thorwine didn't have any even ground to push himself up, so Kuhano was free to unleash a bunch of attacks on him!" Kuhani explained very animatedly, doing moves for each thing she explained.

I looked toward Kuhano who was hanging his head in shame. "Good job, man. Though I have some moose-clays, guys, I'm not soft!" I exclaimed. He looked up toward me, his shame disappearing.

"I don't need you to tell me I did good. And it doesn't matter how muscular you are if you don't have the intact bones to keep your body supported. So, uh...sorry about breaking all of them, by the way," he thought, surprisingly being sincere.

In a panic, I moved all of my limbs to make sure they weren't still broken.

"Don't worry, sir, all of us are healers who are top of our class. I assure you, you're fine," a healer who was nearby said.

"Looks like everyone's made a healthy recovery! Our first winners of the day are the Wondrous Woods! It was a quick first match, but it sure was entertaining! Once everyone clears the field, we'll get the next match underway! If you aren't on the field, don't go anywhere because we're just getting started!" he said, indicating that it was time for us to leave as the crowd cheered.

When we got back to the waiting room, I took a seat and started thinking about what Thorwine said. *Usually, I have a plan, yeah, but I like to think I work well whenever something doesn't go as planned. I'll admit that having a big man running at me terrified me and made me freeze up, but come on! Anyone would be freaked out by that! Then again, maybe I should just go all out. If I didn't hold back, I would've easily been able to avoid him. With 3X to my 18 Agility, I'm sitting at 54, which means someone would need 36 Perception to even see me! I used too many hidden abilities that round too. I hate how much I'm rely-ing on these gloves now that I know how to control them better.*

"*Gray, come on, it's time for our second fight. Snap out of it!*" Kuhano thought as he softly sunk his teeth into my leg.

"GAH! WHY?" I shouted out until he let go of my leg. "How is it even already time for our next fight? We've barely been in here," I cried out as I looked at the bite marks in my leg.

"The Gold team just completely destroyed the Silver team! They were like *Kapow! Schling!* And the Silver team was like *Blagh!*" Kuhani explained with onomatopoeias.

"I haven't seen you this hyped in a while. You all right?" I asked as we were walking to the gate.

"I'm more than all right! We're fighting in the Champion Tournament! That might not mean a whole lot to you, but to us, it's crazy. Getting to this point is the dream of many adventurers!" she explained.

"I guess that makes sense. I guess I just didn't realize that you cared so much," I said hesitantly. *I mean, it's good that she's happy and everything, but is it really good for her to have reached a goal so easily?* I thought. Something about it felt off, but a happy Kuhani breeds happiness, so I digressed.

When we walked into the arena, the announcer gave the same spiel of who were and gave a brief summary of our last fight, which probably didn't need to be said. "And on the other side, we have The Pact! The Pact took the win in the Bronze bracket by sacrificing themselves! Kinda obsessive, don't ya think? But that just shows how much they want to win! Will they play by their own terms? Or will we see a fight that lasts longer than a spell? The only way to find out is to watch! Let's get this fight started. Fi-Fo-Th-Two-One, go!"

It took everyone a few moments to realize that the announcer actually just started the fight. Before I could even nock an arrow, their sorcerer had already created a circle in the sand and begun an incantation that he would use to sacrifice his teammates.

"Drugan, that guy with the bow can absorb magic! Why do you insist on this strategy when it's probably going to backfire on us!" one of them shouted at the sorcerer.

"Cut your yacking, moron. You're ruining my concentration. Be a good little sacrifice and accept your role. You want to win, don't you? This is the only way a worthless piece of trash like you will be useful," the sorcerer shouted at the young warrior. As he shouted, the hood of his cloak slipped off, revealing that he had no face. In fact, he didn't even have any skin. He was a skeletal mage.

"A skeleton? Isn't he a monster? I mean, a low-class monster, but still a monster nonetheless!" I thought to everyone in the group as I was taken aback.

"Low-class? Gray, we'll need to teach you about monsters when we get back home. Skeletons have the most affinity with the dark magics. I should be able to destroy him with my magic, but it might just purge him, which means even with the anti-death field, his soul would move on," Araya thought back in response.

"If there's a chance of actually killing him, then don't do it, Arie!" Kuhani shouted in her mind as she ran toward him.

"Kuhani? Wouldn't it make more sense to stay back near me so I can absorb the magic that would instantly kill us?" I thought to her when the sorcerer finished his ritual.

Instantly, his three allies fell to the ground, writhing in pain as a purple essence left their bodies and collected into floating balls. The three balls started to quickly hover toward Kuhani, Kuhano, and I. Each ball had a purple line linking them to one of us.

"They're quick, but do they seem slower than when we watched them a few days ago?" I asked out loud. I definitely wasn't seeing things and was sure that if I fully focused, they would be moving at a snail's pace. *"Here's the plan: Avoid these orbs and beat that skeleton down. If I need to absorb the orbs, then we'll have them come to a focal point, and I'll try to absorb all three of them at the same time,"* I thought out to everyone.

"Sound's good, Gray! Let's go!" Kuhani thought out as she started leading her orb away from the path she wanted to take toward the skeletal mage. I nocked an arrow and fired it at the skeleton's head. When it reached him, it hit some sort of invisible field and instantly disintegrated.

"Simplistic fool. Did you really think I wouldn't be protecting myself?" he shouted at me.

"He's shrouding himself in dark magic, like I do," Foda said.

"What do we do against that then?" I asked.

"The ritual should have expended most of his mana. If you keep attacking him, it should eventually drain his magic. But those orbs worry me. I feel like I've felt that energy before."

All right, so it's a battle of attrition then, huh?" I said, completely disregarding his worries. I began firing arrows like a machine gun as I made distance between myself and my orb. I started firing with twenty-nine arrows in my quiver. Within moments, I had to take note of the five arrows I had left as the shield finally broke with an explosion of darkness.

"You realized you could break through my shield? Even so, to do it so fast? I will enjoy crushing an opponent like you. You're the first that seems to possess an inkling of intelligence or skill! No matter, though, I will merely regenerate my mana!" the skeleton shouted as he started creating a large circle in the sand.

"Oh no, you won't!" I said as I fired one of my last arrows toward his head. For once, the shot actually connected, and his head went flying off.

"Phew! Thank God that's over, I was actually getting worried," I said with a laugh.

"Fool! You don't think me to be so easily defeated, do you?" the skeleton said as his skull jumped back over toward his body. I let out a sound of audible confusion.

"How is he still alive after that!" I exclaimed out in my thoughts.

"I was worried about this. It seems I may need to use magic against him after all," Araya thought out disappointedly. *"Grayson, you'll need to absorb these orbs so I don't accidentally hit them. If his barrier exploded, there's no telling what these orbs will do when attacked."*

I looked toward her and gave her a nod.

"But, Arie! If you do that, he'll die, won't he?" Kuhani cried out as she and Kuhano ran to my sides so that we could easily make the death orbs overlap.

"That's...a risk we're going to have to take," Araya answered hesitantly. Anyone could tell that Araya didn't want to do this, but she also didn't want us to lose. The orbs moved closer together as the skeleton's head hopped toward his body. "Undead Purification," Araya sadly uttered as she started to cast a long incantation.

If she's started it before I've absorbed the orbs, it must take a long time to cast, I thought as I moved toward the focal point of the orbs. As soon as the orbs looked like a Venn diagram, I held my hand out, ready to absorb them when they came together fully. If I didn't get the timing right, then I would be screwed. I'd either get only one or I'd be bombarded by three instant kills all at once. *Then again, that's a good fallback for if I mess up because it shouldn't actually kill me... right?* I thought.

I narrowed my focus, and sure enough, the orbs started moving as slow as molasses. It was as if I was watching a race that only sloths could find interesting. When they finally converged together, I clicked the button on my gloves and absorbed all three of the orbs. At the moment I did, the inside of my entire body felt like it was on fire. Even with the pain nullification field up, all I could do was scream from the immense amount of pain.

"Master, you're taking on too much dark magic. You have to release it or you'll die. As much as I enjoy death, I would hate to part with you so soon," Foda said.

Even through the immense pain, I understood what he was saying. As I reached toward the release, I could feel something invading my mind, twisting my thoughts. It sounded like Foda but more feminine and vastly more sinister, though there was something about it that intrigued me. *"Wouldn't it be easier to simply give in? Embrace me. I promise your pain will subside, and you'll have an infinite amount of power at your disposal,"* a voice coaxed me.

Part of me trusted the voice and was already willing to give in to it. The more sane part of me, however, knew that something was wrong.

"This mortal is mine, Yami. You're supposed to be roaming the plains of time for all eternity. You have no business being here, much less trying to grasp the mind of my master!" Foda said.

The voice let out a spine-chilling laugh. *"You claim ownership, yet, you call him master? My, how you've fallen, Lukial. I could barely even recognize you in this sad state! It won't be hard to take him from you if you're this pathetic now,"* it said to Foda.

Umm, if I can have a say? I'm never going to give into something like you. You're clearly evil! If characters like Naofumi and Ichigo couldn't get corrupted, then I refuse to get beaten out by fictional characters! I thought to Yami. I struggled to, but I pressed the button to release as fast as I could, not even thinking about what to turn the magic into.

"Poor boy, you already have. It's time you learned reality is much harsher than fiction!" Yami said as the dark magic inside the glove was expelled out as a fairy-like creature cloaked in darkness instantly flew toward the skeleton's head. After flying in front of him, as if to taunt him, it flew out of the arena.

"I really hope that's not going to come back to bite me in the ass later," I said as I lay on the ground, unable to move and covered in sweat. Kuhani and Kuhano stood over me, trying to make sure I was all right. *"I want to assure you guys that I'm fine. But honestly, I can't even speak right now,"* I thought, absolutely terrified.

"Tha-that's impossible! We have a soul contract! I summoned you and freed you of your eternal prison for this! You can't just use that boy as a way to release yourself after stealing my flesh and soul! You damn wretch!" the skeleton shouted after the dark spirit before collapsing to the ground. "I... Everything I've worked for. There's nothing left. It's all over. I can't even kill myself! I'm cursed to walk the planet like this forever!" he said with deep regret in his voice. He looked toward Araya and started scrambling toward her before kowtowing in front of her. "Please, Priestess. You're the only hope that I have left. I've sinned greatly, but please forgive me and send me on my way! I can't stand to stay in a world where I have absolutely nothing!" he pleaded.

To my surprise, it sounded like Araya stopped casting her spell. "What good would that do you?" she asked as if she was a mother yelling at her child. "You just said yourself that you have a soul contract. If I kill you, then your soul goes on and empowers whatever that thing was! You may have nothing left, but you have time. Time that can be used to repent for your sins and to build up a life again. Stop overreacting, forfeit, and get on with your undeath," she said.

Everyone was stunned into complete silence. Even the announcer had nothing to say about the situation.

The one that broke the silence was the skeletal sorcerer himself. "I dislike admitting this, but your words ring true, Priestess. I'm undead. I have all the time in the world to right my past deeds. I could even sleep in a crypt for a revolution if I wished or work to enact my revenge on the very being that made me this way. Thank you for opening my eyes. I surrender," he said.

"Well, that sure was interesting folks! Who would've expected the Wondrous Woods to claim another win? In fact, with this win, they move onto the finals! This is the first time in the history of this tournament that a team that's Wood rank has made it to the finals! Though it seems like we might have to take a short break to find out just what happened! Keep those seats warm and your expectations warmer! Stay tuned!" the announcer said as the medics once again rushed the field.

Aside from the sacrifices, I was deemed the one in most critical condition. Even after receiving healing from them, I was taken away on a stretcher. *"I swear, guys, I'm all right!"* I tried to assure everyone in the group, though from their reactions, as I was getting carried away, I just seemed to make things worse. I was brought to a room that had multiple uniform beds next to each other. If it wasn't for the vast amount of medical equipment, I wouldn't have thought that it was a hospital room. After I was lifted into a bed, I was forced to stare at the ceiling until someone came up to me.

"Hello, Grayson, right? Congratulations on your win. We don't exactly know what's going on, but we're going to have you get some rest while we run some tests, and hopefully, you'll be able to answer some questions after that. Just relax, you're safe here," he said before casting a sleeping spell on me, instantly knocking me out.

10

How I Became the Hero's Assistant

When I awoke, everyone was sitting around in the room. Not just Kuhani, Kuhano, and Araya, but also Sylia and the Guildmaster. How they were able to get permission to wait here was pretty obvious.

"You gave us quite the scare," Sylia said, alerting the others to the fact that I was awake. "Who would've thought that you'd have to compete against someone who made a deal with a sentient spirit of darkness? It's almost like the guild has been neglecting to do background checks," she said as she stared daggers at the Guildmaster.

"S-sorry," I said drowsily.

"Why are you apologizing? Do you even understand what happened to you?" Sylia asked.

"No, not really. I just remember absorbing a large amount of dark magic and then talking to something," I said as I tried to recall what happened before I was put to sleep.

She let out a sigh before explaining, "You remember how magical elements exist because of spirits? Those spirits produce so many magicules of their element that their bodies can't contain it, and it's released into the world. Those magicules are what we take in and distill into our own energy. This energy is more commonly known as mana. The issue with what happened is how many raw magicules you took in. Obviously, people who increase their intelligence stat can take in and convert a large amount, but no one's ever taken in enough to be on the same level as a spirit. That's basically what you did."

Before I could ask any questions, Pauline burst through the door. "You moron! What made you think that you should pull a stunt like that? If you didn't have that glove, you'd be dead! Do you have any clue how big of an impact your death would have on—" she shouted with tears in her eyes before noticing that there were other people in the room. "On all of u-us?" she meekly finished.

"Pauline? What do you mean if I didn't have my glove?" I asked out of confusion, dodging her question. *Hold that thought. Is she wearing her bangs down, a wavy ends hairstyle? I thought she didn't like it?* I wondered. Now that she had noticed that there were other people in the room, her social anxiety had kicked in, and she became significantly more shy.

"Uhmm… Your glove should have been overloaded from the a-amount of magic. Y-you can't use it anymore, r-right?" she asked.

Testing her theory, I looked at my glove, which was still dyed a pitch black from taking in the dark energy. When I pressed the release button, nothing happened. It was the same result when I pressed the absorb button. "Great. Amazing. I can't believe I broke an artifact from God," I let out. "I just made those last six months of spell-crafting and perfecting our teamwork with this thing nearly worthless. Sorry, guys, looks like I'm going to be a lot more worthless," I shamefully apologized.

"Gray, these last six months have helped us all improve. Sure, not having your magic abilities will make things harder. But the work we've all put into building our teamwork and fighting styles wasn't for nothing! So please don't say that you made the last six months worthless all because of your stupid glove!" Kuhani comforted.

"Grayson, you helped me better my magic. Even if what we learned from our sessions are now worthless for you, they helped me become a better adventurer! Even if you don't have your gauntlet, we all know how skilled you are with your bow. Plus, you even have Foda now to pick up any slack!" Araya said. Slowly, everyone shifted their focus over to Kuhano.

"What? I have to say something too?" he wondered. Kuhani gave me a stern look, and after a few moments, he let out a sound akin to a sigh. *"You didn't totally suck with the glove, but now that you've been taken down a peg, you're closer to us all. You won't be able to carry us anymore, but you're definitely still going to be useful. There, you all happy?"* he thought.

For anyone else, it would've seemed insincere, but we all knew that Kuhano was speaking from the heart. Everyone but Pauline and the Guildmaster nodded at him. *He really is just a big softie hiding behind a tough exterior, huh?* I thought.

"Now that you've all had your time, I'd like to ask Grayson some questions before you all have to fight. Privately," the Guildmaster said. Since it was the Guildmaster, no one could really refuse him, so everyone made their way toward the door and left. "Except you, Miss Pauline, you stay here as well," he said, causing Pauline to jump in surprise.

When the door closed and we were the only ones in the room, he began. "I'll get to the questions about your condition later. If Miss Pauline wasn't here, I wouldn't do this now, but I'm thankful that you both met each other so I can. A few months ago, I lost all contact with God."

"How does that work? I thought that you were supposed to be his vessel?" I asked.

"I don't know. He knew that something was going to happen, though, so he gave me some instructions before I could no longer talk to him. Pauline, how much have you explained to him already?"

"Just about everything that God should've handled as soon as he decided to reincarnate Grayson," she said with a scoff.

"Good, that makes all of this easier then. Around the same time that I lost contact, a tower was said to have sprouted out of the ground like a plant near a small town to the south. I've sent many scouts there, and it seems to have some sort of connection to Ares. That being said, it's highly likely that something in that tower is severing the ties that God has to this world," the Guildmaster explained.

"So basically, you want us to go there and find a way to destroy it or something? Is that what you're getting at?" I asked.

"Gods no. At least not until you're a higher level. If you both went at this point, you'd more than likely die, and we need to avoid that as much as possible, especially since someone seems to find himself in trouble more often than he's not," he said as he directed his gaze toward me.

"What's the point of telling us then?" Pauline asked. "If you don't want us to go, then why would you bother telling us all of this?"

With a sigh, the Guildmaster said, "Miss Pauline, I'm positive you aren't as dense as Mr. Grayson. For his sake, I'll explain, though."

"You do know I'm right here, right?" I asked in response to the blatant remarks he made.

"It's simple. If you know of the danger, you'll be less likely to pursue a rumor regarding that tower. Not that either of you have been taking requests and could hear rumors like that. I assume that will be rectified after the tournament. Hopefully, it will also give you two a sense of urgency when it comes to your growth," the Guildmaster explained after pushing up his glasses, which somehow illuminated from the light to the side of him.

"Did he ju—" Pauline began to ask before I cut her off.

"Yes. Yes, he did."

"In the middle of the first quarter of the next revolution, I intend to send out a raiding party to attempt to take the tower. The minimum Level requirement will be 30. Hopefully, you two will be able to join said raid."

"The middle of spring? That'd only give us around five months to gain twenty-five-ish levels! You can't seriously think that we'll be able to do that when over half of that is in winter!" Pauline exclaimed.

"I believe that it's possible if you put your mind to it. Besides, I merely am just letting you both know what's going on. With God MIA, leadership of the other-worlders is falling to me, and I intend to set you on what I believe is the best course of action. I encourage you two to bring your groups to the meeting tomorrow so that we may discuss our operation further," he said. "Miss Pauline, please tell the others to come back in while I ask questions about Grayson's condition," he asked.

Pauline reluctantly walked across the room as she spouted, "I'll do what you ask this once, but only because it's to help him!"

As everyone funneled back into the room, the Guildmaster asked, "When you were screaming in the arena, was it due to pain or something else? Can you even remember?"

"Definitely the pain. It was as if someone had given me a ton of paper cuts on the inside of my body and then plunged me into a bath of lemon juice," I responded.

"I see. Do you feel any of that pain now?" he asked.

I took a moment to try to focus on what I was feeling, if anything. "I wouldn't say I feel pain, but something is...different?" I questionably replied.

"Well, if you're not in pain, then that's all that matters! I'll stop wasting your time so you can prepare for your next fight. We'll start the fight in thirty minutes! Glad to hear that you're not in pain still so we can continue with the tournament!" he said as he left the room.

As soon as he left, Pauline said, "Is he serious? Does he really care this much about the tournament that he'd just wave off what you said about something feeling different? That's the biggest sign that something more happened because of that whole thing!"

"I mean, I can't ruin the event just because something feels off. Besides, I still gotta keep my promise to you," I said as I got out of the bed. Any attempts I made to seem cool were entirely ruined the second I tried to walk. I was bombarded by dizziness and stumbled like a drunk before Pauline caught me.

"Ehhh!" she exclaimed as she started turning beet-red.

Araya helped her move me back to the bed I had gotten up from. "Grayson, there's no way you're going to be able to fight. You can barely walk," Araya protested.

My head was spinning, but I wasn't going to let myself bring the team down. "I'll be fine. I'll just have to stay near a wall or something," I said as I fell backward on the bed.

"Master, you still have a vast amount of Yami's dark energy in your system. I can attempt to draw it out, but I can't guarantee it will help. You could have the...priestess purify you. It would be painful, but it will expel any energy and cleanse you of the harmful effects," Foda said.

"So my options are take a gamble or have a for sure result that will hurt. I guess I'll go with the guaranteed method since we have limited time," I said out loud in response to Foda. I could feel everyone but Pauline look at me like I was going crazy until I asked, "Araya? Foda says that I still have dark energy in my body. Could you purify it for me?" I asked as I sat up and glanced toward my bow that lay propped up against the wall.

"A-are you sure? Depending on how much is coursing through your body, it could kill you," Araya tried to protest.

"Don't worry, I'm prepared. So please help me so that I can be useful in our last fight of the tournament!"

With a disapproving look and a sigh, Araya conceded and starting drawing a magic circle with a stick of chalk.

"If you're doing this because of your promise to me... Please, just forget about it!" Pauline pleaded with me.

I turned toward her and shakily moved my hand up to her head, even though it sent waves of fatigue through me. "I'm doing this because I want to. Getting to keep my promise is just a bonus," I said. "Don't worry about me, all right? I'll be fine, I promise," I added as I gently patted her head.

She gave me a small smile. "All right. As long as you promise," she said as she sat down next to me and laid her head on my shoulder.

Jeez, first she says she wouldn't be able to handle dating me, and then she does stuff like this? If she keeps this up, I might start getting the wrong idea about our relationship, I thought.

After a few minutes Araya finished her circle and had Pauline and Kuhani lay me down in it. "Miss Pauline? Kuhani? Could you stay here and hold him down?"

Hold me down? I wondered. Suddenly I was becoming very nervous.

"No matter how much he struggles or begs, don't let him go," she added as they took hold of my arms and pinned my legs to the ground with their own.

"I'm not sure I feel very comfortable with this," I said out loud.

"It's not supposed to be comfortable. They're holding you down," Sylia replied, clearly entertained by my embarrassment.

Before I could protest further, Araya held her hands near my head and started chanting. The circle below me began to glow as if it was the sun. Before I knew it, the light that the circle produced began to wrap itself around me like a blanket. At first, there was a slight sting but nothing that couldn't be handled. Very quickly, the stinging turned to a stabbing pain. It was as if my whole body was being stabbed by hundreds of needles over and over. I started to let out small gasps of pain against my will.

The worst came when the dark magic started to get expelled. The darkness slowly began leaving my body through my invisible stab wounds before being eradicated by the blanket of light. My insides began to boil, and my body started violently convulsing. Thankfully, Kuhani and Pauline were still able to hold me down despite the gap in our strength stats. Eventually, the darkness began slowly spewing out of my mouth until it started shooting out of every orifice in my face.

With one last push from Araya, a large amount of darkness made its way out of my face, and a small pulsating heart-like ball of darkness shot out of my mouth. It hit the ground with a soft squish before bouncing a few times, leaving a small black puddle wherever it landed.

"What the hell is that?" Pauline shouted out in disgust.

"I've never heard of the darkness corrupting someone's organs. But...in theory, it's possible," Araya muttered deep in thought.

Panic slowly set in as I realized what she was implying.

"Calm yourself, Master. The priestess isn't entirely wrong, but in this case, she is. It seems Yami was attempting to slowly corrupt you. I never imagined that she'd sacrifice enough power to create an internal organ of darkness to create and pump dark energy throughout your body. She must have really taken a liking to you. Of course, she's always had a specialty when it comes to interfering with mortals," Foda explained.

After I caught my breath and calmed myself, I relayed Foda's words to the others.

"YAMI! As in THE mother spirit of darkness! Do you know how lucky you are to have an archpriest in your party? Not only did you survive absorbing all those magicules, but you also prevented her from corrupting you! Did God give you plot armor along with that glove?" Pauline shouted out.

"I like this girl. It's like having a second me here," Sylia said. "She is right, though. It was remarkable before, but knowing that you basically survived the power of a deity? It's almost unfathomable," she added.

"A deity? I figured that the gods were the only deities in this world," I said.

"How did you come to that conclusion? Gods are ancestral beings capable of creating or destroying the universe. Deities are powerful creatures that could potentially destroy the world," Sylia explained.

After her explanation, a sinking feeling came over me. "Huh… I really should be dead," I realized.

"Definitely. Either way, crisis averted. Hopefully she doesn't come back for you. Otherwise, we'll be in huge trouble. We can't worry about that now, though, because you four need to get down to the arena. Good luck. You don't have to win. Just…do your best. Anyone with a brain would be amazed at the display you've all made so far. Gray's girlfriend, you coming with me?" she asked as she started heading for the door.

Pauline looked around before awkwardly asking, "D-do you mean me?"

Sylia looked back toward her and said, "Who else could I possibly be talking to?"

As I picked up Foda, I interjected, "She's not my girlfriend, Sylia. How many times am I going to have to tell you that we're just friends?"

Sylia gave a raised eyebrow and replied, "You guys can lie to yourselves all you want, but it's painfully obvious that you two have some sort of feelings for each other. We can't have this argument now, though, are you coming or not?"

At this point, Pauline and I were both blushing and nervously looking around. "Y-yeah. G-good luck, e-everyone!" she squeaked as she ran and joined Sylia.

When the door closed, I embarrassedly said, "Please don't make fun of me. At least wait until we're back home."

Without missing a beat, Kuhani said, "Why would we make fun of you two? You two are so cute together!"

Araya smiled and added, "I assumed your date went well, but I didn't think it went that well! I'm so proud of you, Gray!"

I let out a sigh. "Thanks, guys. Just…let's not talk about this until we get home?" I said as I started to leave before Foda said, *"Hold on. Go take the heart of darkness. In theory, I should be able to absorb it to generate darkness magic faster."*

In a rush, I grabbed the ball of darkness. The pulsating from it really sold the fact that it was a heart. Hastily, I held it next to Foda. Once it got close enough to him, the heart disappeared, and Foda had a dark purple glow surround him. *"Magnificent,"* he uttered.

By the time we reached the gate, it was already time for us to head out into the arena for our fight. The announcer was apologizing to the crowd for the long wait, but my mind was focused on trying to comprehend everything that had been happening to me. *Usually, I'd just brush my near-death experiences off, but I was targeted by something that could destroy the world! I'm definitely going to have to get stronger if I want to avoid stuff like this.* Even while I was lost in my thoughts, I couldn't shake the presence of the three people in front of me.

Falkeen, the other-worlder of luck, equipped with his armor that made him look like a signature paladin. Violet, the absolute giant of a woman who was clad in full purple plate armor who wielded a large tower shield in one hand and a war hammer in the other. Lastly, there was Klaus, otherwise known as "salad bowl," the elf healer whose green bowl-cut hair netted him said nickname. *All those months ago… Was that not a normal dream?* I wondered as I stared at the group in front of me. *If it wasn't, I can use my knowledge of them to help us!*

"We need to damage the guy in the silver armor. Just enough to bring his health below 100 percent, then we can go after the elf," I muttered to everyone.

"Wouldn't it make more sense for us to just go after the elf right off the bat so that he couldn't heal?" Kuhano questioned.

"Normally, yeah, but Falkeen has a sword that can shoot out beams of light when he swings it at full health," I responded.

With the new information, Kuhano nodded to show that he understood.

"On this side, we have the Wondrous Woods who despite all odds have managed to make it all the way to the finals! Talk about a tough group of newbies! Speaking of tough, they have the man that summoned a dark spirit after countering a spell that causes instant death! Hopefully performing such a feat hasn't taken too much out of him!

Over here, we have the group that needs absolutely no introduction, but due to the terms in my contract, I have to introduce them! Here we have Falko, the group of Palladium-ranked adventurers that are so strong they were allowed to have a group without a fourth member! Legend says that their damage dealer, Falkeen, could go head to head with a dragon! Others say that the beautiful Violet could besiege an entire castle by herself! Even their healer is rumored to be able to cure plagues before they even happen! It's no surprise they got this far without breaking a sweat, but could this battle be the one to break that streak? Let's find out!" the announcer shouted as he began to count down.

As soon as the announcer reached one, the battle started, and three beams of light flew out of Falkeen's sword toward me. If it wasn't for my skill enhancing my perception and agility, I wouldn't have even been able to see them, much less dodge them.

Even though I avoided the attack, I took a heavy blow that sent me down to the ground before I could react. I quickly flipped myself over so I could see my enemy. "Huh? Wait… Do I know you from somewhere?" Falkeen asked, looming above me.

Using his hesitation to my advantage, I quickly got back up and made distance between us. "Yeah, you saved me a few months ago from that woman, Myrolda, or whatever. Thanks for that, by the way," I replied as I ripped a potion out of a pouch and chugged it. *Thank God for magically reinforced glass. Otherwise, all of these would've broken a long time ago,* I thought.

"Really? Maybe my memories are just hazy then. The energy you give off and your looks are completely different," he said as he dropped his guard. "I'm surprised that you've grown so much while remaining in the Wood rank. Most people I fight aren't able to dodge my attacks, especially ones that I've taken care to hide up until now," he said with a glare of suspicion.

"Lucky guess?" I innocently asked before I nocked and fired an arrow while thinking, *Fly into the back of his knee.* Usually, this wouldn't work, but with the short distance between us, the arrow flew fast and far. He barely dodged the arrow, allowing it to only scrape his face, leaving a small cut. Luckily, this was the perfect outcome for me. He kept his eyes on me as the arrow made a U-turn in the air before flying straight into his unarmored knee pit.

As he grunted in pain and kneeled down to rip the arrow out, I thought, *Just as I thought. There are gaps in his armor! I'm amazed that my gamble paid off there. If I'm able to keep this as a ranged battle, I should be able to have the advantage and maybe even beat him!*

I fired another arrow, which also barely skimmed his face, and then another one. After the third arrow, I realized something was wrong. The arrows were no longer flying toward the target I willed them to. "Wha—How are you doing that?" I asked in astonishment.

"Don't be surprised, boy, you managed to hit me. No one else in this tournament could do that. I'm merely acknowledging your skills and using my own. Forgive me for not going all out from the beginning," Falkeen humbly said. "Let's fight each other with everything we've got! Roll the dice!" he shouted out before he threw down a pair of ethereal dice and charged at me. As soon as they stopped rolling, his speed increased exponentially. I could barely keep up with his new speed, but it wasn't impossible as I focused only on him and nothing else.

First, a slash came from the left that I barely dodged, then a slash from the right that cut just above my eye, then a lunge that I luckily sidestepped. I could just barely see him beyond the blood blinding my right eye, but his moves were simple. He was relying only on his speed and strength to overpower me. If I could just keep dodging him, I could buy enough time for the others to take out the healer, Klaus. *We actually have a chance of winning this!* I gleefully thought.

"Guys, go for the elf. I can handle Falkeen for a little while longer," I thought out to everyone. When I didn't get a response, I made the mistake of looking away. Everyone else in my party was already out and considered dead. Based on where they were positioned, they had been instantly taken out of the fight. Instantly, my glee turned to despair, and in that small instance, Falkeen was able to slice right through my belly.

"Looks like my innards are being turned into out-tards," I joked as I held my stomach. I barely felt any pain thanks to the pain nullification field, but I knew that if this happened in real battle, I would be freaking out and definitely not joking.

"You're going out with a joke?" he asked as he plunged his sword into my chest to assure his victory.

"All my friends are dead. Maybe if I had something like a Phoenix Down, I'd give it a chance, but we're out of our league at this point. We're lucky that we even got this far. I'd rather happily go down and be proud of how far we've gotten than be upset that it ends here," I reasoned.

"I see. An odd mentality but respectable nonetheless. What you lack in stats you make up for in technique and spirit. If you were at a higher level, I think we could've actually lost. Hell, you even knew to target me instead of—"

"Instead of Salad Bowl over there, right?" I cut him off. "We'll get stronger. Next year, we'll beat you!" I added with a competitive smile.

Falkeen let out a chuckle. "Big words for a Wood. I'll hold you to it, though, kid. Hell, I'll even make it easier for you since I like you. I'll work something out with the Guildmaster to give your group exclusive rights to special quests from the areas I've helped. I can't do everything myself, so it would be nice to have some assistance. Plus, it'll get you all good experience points and dosh. It'll be great to be able to get some rest and finally have a challenge to look forward to!" he finished as he pulled his sword out of my chest. We finally lost our first battle in the arena.

The medics flooded the field, and within a few minutes, we were all back on our feet. "That was an absolute massacre!" Kuhani said cheerfully, holding out a peace sign with her fingers.

"I don't know if you're supposed to be happy about that," I said with a furrowed brow.

"I...I didn't even get to react before it was all over. I can't believe you were able to last fourteen seconds, Grayson!" Araya said heavily.

"Hah, yeah it was pretty unlucky. On the plus side, I think I just got us job security," I said before explaining what Falkeen said while we were fighting.

"You guys were able to have that long of a conversation in that short amount of time? Perception and agility combos are overpowered!" Kuhani complained as she puffed out her cheek.

With a laugh, Falkeen announced his presence. "Don't worry, as you level up, you'll find other combinations that are just as powerful or even more so. Having high perception and agility means nothing against an enemy with high fortitude. Even I couldn't take your friend out in one blow unless I got a critical hit by hitting a vital spot with my weapon."

"Oh...right," Kuhani uncomfortably said.

"I take it you've already told them about my offer, kid?" he asked me.

I gave him a nod. "So what do you guys say? It's a pretty decent deal, right? You'll technically be working for me too, so you'd get tons of benefits!" he persuaded.

"That definitely does sound great. What's the catch?" Pauline said from behind me, making me jump in surprise.

"Jesus, where the hell did you come from?" I asked in surprise as she walked up next to me.

"That doesn't matter right now, Grayson. What does matter is that this should be discussed with Miss Sylia as well as with the Guildmaster," she said, sounding as confident as she had when she was talking about God. She leaned over and whispered to me, "That was amazing, by the way, I didn't actually think you'd be able to hurt him, much less take out 8 percent of his health! I owe you one for keeping your promise."

Falkeen let out a groan. "Why do you have to be here, girl? If I needed a businesswoman, you know I would've called for you."

"I'm not here for you. I'm here because you're trying to take advantage of my...my... That doesn't matter! I'm here because you're trying to take advantage of new members of the guild!" she shouted out.

Her what? I wondered, hoping that Sylia didn't brainwash her.

"I wasn't trying to take advantage of them! Hell, I'll even take you up on your offer so I can prove that. There's a meeting going on at the guild tomorrow. We'll use the meeting room until it starts! How's noon sound?" he shouted in response.

"Sounds just dandy! Let's go, guys!" Pauline shouted to us all.

Without questioning it, everyone except for me started following her. I just looked at her in confusion until she yelled, "Grayson, come on! You're ruining our exit!"

When we got through the gate and started making our way through the hall to leave, she said, "Imagine gaining more luck and not maxing the stat out. It'd make him practically invincible. Couldn't be him, I guess."

Everyone gave her an odd look, except for me.

"What does that have to do with anything?" I asked.

"Nothing, just thinking out loud. Although, if he had just gone up more in luck, then maybe something would've made it so I couldn't have stopped you guys from taking his deal. Also, why would he say noon? He knows to say midday in this world. You two just refuse to not give subtle hints that you're not from here, huh?" she asked.

I let out a nervous chuckle. *I definitely can't deny the fact that I do that.*

When we reached the lobby, we were about to leave when the woman at the front desk stopped us to give us our reward for being finalists in the Winner's bracket. *I had completely forgotten that we got anything except for clout for reaching the finals,* I thought. The woman gave the four of us new identification tags that were made of iron instead of wood.

Does having a higher rank really mean anything if we aren't the proper level? At least it saves time, I guess, I thought to myself. After we gave her our wooden tags, we were allowed to leave.

"All right, you four, you better be at the guild's meeting room at midday. I-I'll see y-you guys then!" Pauline said as she blushed before randomly hugging me and running off without an explanation.

"Di-did what I think just happened happen?" I nervously asked as my heart pounded against my chest.

As if they were one in the same, Kuhani and Araya let out an embarrassing, "Awww!"

I looked to Kuhano for an actual response to my question.

"I don't usually think things are cute, but I have to agree with those two," he thought to me. The rest of the night, I felt like I was in daze as the short moment haunted me.

*****

The next day, I awoke with a feeling of fullness from our celebratory dinner the night before. After we found Sylia, she took us to a tavern to celebrate. It just so happened that the owner recognized us from our fights and was a fan. He gave us free drinks for the night and half off of whatever we ordered as thanks for netting him a large sum from gambling.

I glanced at the clock and noticed that it was almost time to leave for our meeting at the guild. I hastily gathered my things so I could leave and wake everyone up. When I opened my door, however, I was face-to-face with Kuhani. She had her arm up and was mid-knock when I grabbed her hand before she hit my face.

"G'morning. Guess we had the same idea about waking everyone up, huh?" I asked as I let go of her hand.

"Yeah. Actually, Lady Sylia asked me to wake you up so that we could leave. Remember to grab everything because we're going home after the meeting."

"Oh, man, I can't believe I almost forgot! Thanks for reminding me!" I said to her as I walked back in to grab Foda. Usually, I wouldn't have forgotten him, but I thought that it would be rude to bring him to a meeting.

"So…what's going on with you and Miss Pauline? You two insist that you aren't dating, but it seems like she's making an effort to get closer to us all. Seems to me like she wants to become friends with us to get closer to you!" Kuhani said as I grabbed Foda and we left.

"If you asked me a few days ago, I would just say that she wants to keep tabs on me because we're both other-worlders. But honestly, I'm not even sure now. Though, getting close to my friends and family in an attempt to get closer to me would be a good strategy if she does want to take that step," I responded as I walked with her toward the lobby.

"In other words, you two aren't getting together? At least, you aren't getting together yet?" she asked as a frown took over her face.

"I guess? I dunno, Kuhani, I'm super awkward when it comes to this stuff, so even though I like her, I'm not really sure how to get about something like this. We're going to see her soon anyway, so wouldn't it just be easier for you to ask her yourself? Y'know, girl talk it up and all that?"

At my words, Kuhani turned slightly red. "I can't just ask her that! I barely know her! To ask something so personal would be weird, rude even. It's weird, though, she's so cute, but something about her is scary too."

Before I could come up with a response, we were in the lobby with the rest of the group in front of us. When we walked up to them, Sylia held out her hand expectantly. Without thinking, I instantly took my room key out of my pocket and gave it to her. *Dear God, do I just know what she expects by her body language at this point! Actually, wait, what else would she be reaching out for. Wow, I really am an idiot,* I thought.

She looked at it for a second and then said, "That's everyone's. Get ready to leave after I turn these in, everyone." After she left, we all stood around awkwardly until I broke the silence.

"What do you mean by 'She's scary?'" I asked Kuhani.

"Well, she's really quiet and nice, but then she gets really serious about something. Like when we were going to accept Mr. Falkeen's proposal, she suddenly took over and was so confident. I'd love to be able to be like that," she answered with a chuckle.

"Oh, Miss Pauline?" Araya asked, to which we both nodded. "I like her, she's really nice and cute. Plus, she's not afraid to yell at Grayson when he does something dumb. She's perfect for you. I can't believe you two aren't dating!" she said as Sylia came toward us.

"All right, when you guys go to that meeting, I'm going to go to my own meeting. If I'm not at the guild hall when you all are done, then head on toward home. I'm sure Crice's been lonely since we haven't been there for a whole week. Obviously, take that deal, but try to squeeze out more than you think you can. If all else fails, leave negotiations to Pauline because she's got a good head on her shoulders."

"Who could you be meeting? Are you going to meet with your uncle?" I asked.

With an annoyed sigh and the roll of her eyes, she gave me a nod. "I don't know why he couldn't have just talked with me on one of the tournament days."

"Well, it's not like he could've just up and left during a match. Plus, he was probably being escorted out as soon as all the matches for the day concluded in case of assassins or something," I reasoned.

"Assassins? Lady Sylia, why would your uncle be targeted by assassins?" Kuhani cried out in distress.

I gave her a confused look. "Kuhani? How do you think we're legally living in an old military outpost? You can't just go and claim something like that unless you know someone," I said.

"So is he a commander or someone in the military?" she asked.

I was going to answer, but before I could, Sylia let out another sigh. "No, he's the king," she said dully.

As if everyone in the group had practiced it, they all let out a resounding, "THE KING!" Luckily, there weren't many people around because Sylia already looked like she was going to die from embarrassment.

"Can we please not make a big deal about it?" she said with a flushed face.

"How can we not! You basically just told us you're royalty!" Kuhani argued.

"I'm not royalty or anything close to it. Even if I was, I still wouldn't want anyone to make a big deal about it. Please just drop it, okay? I'm not asking as your group's overseer but as a friend," she said, seeming like she was on the verge of tears. I'd only seen Sylia like this once.

I expected her to be upset about it, but I had thought she would be leaning more toward angry upset than crying upset. Maybe it's a so angry that she's crying upset, though.

Seeing her like this, Kuhani instantly said, "O-okay. I'm sorry, I wasn't trying to be rude or anything!" She grabbed her in a hug.

I guess that Sylia's relation to the king just overwhelms her with thoughts of how messed up her life was because of her dad, I thought.

"Are you going to be okay going by yourself?" I asked out of genuine concern.

"I'll be fine. You don't need to use that tone with me," she said as she tried to escape from Kuhani. When she finally got out of Kuhani's grasp, she said, "You guys are going to be late if you don't leave now."

"Bu—" Kuhani started before Sylia cut her off.

"No buts. I already forgive you, so don't feel bad about it. Worst case, just let me pet you later!" she said with a large grin before disappearing.

I guess if she isn't here, Kuhani can't really argue, I thought.

Kuhani's ears drooped. "You may forgive me, but I still feel really bad," she muttered. "I don't want you to pet me either, though!" she added as she grabbed her tail in frustration.

"Kuhani? How about you think about what you can do while we head over to the guild because we kinda gotta go," I said, realizing just how pressed for time we were.

"Urm, right. Okay. Yeah, let's go," she replied.

Kuhani's tail was wagging like an excited dog the whole way to the guild. *I'm pretty sure that it's a bad thing when a cat wags its tail, right? What about a cat girl, though?* I wondered to myself as we were walking in the door to the guild hall.

"You guys made it! It's so late I almost thought you weren't coming. Come on, everyone's already upstairs in the meeting room," Pauline said as soon as we walked in.

"Why is everyone always in such a rush?" I wondered out loud as she led us upstairs.

"Because people have things to do, Grayson. If we had technology, then we'd be able to take things slower, but you don't see much of that here, do you?" Pauline asked as she led us to the first door on the left side of the hallway.

When she opened the door, we were greeted by a large room that looked more like it belonged to a large corporation instead of the run-down guild hall. Two large tables were pushed together to create a makeshift conference table. Each side could fit eight people as well as one person at either end. The chairs surrounding were nothing special. The seats were made up of four planks, and the backs were only two, one near the lower end and one at the top.

I guess the simplistic design was easier to get a lot of, huh? I thought. Looking around the table, the Guildmaster was sitting at the head of the table in front of a large window that let in a vast amount of sunlight. On the left side, three seats were taken up by Falkeen and his group. Three other seats were also being claimed by Pauline's group. We took our seats opposite of Falkeen and his group. To my surprise, Pauline took a seat next to me instead of with her party.

"Why are you guys here?" I politely asked as I looked toward Mia, Maya, and Noah. Noah was sleeping on the table with his head in his arms, but Mia shot a look of disgust at me.

"You think we want to be here? We're just here because this girl insisted that you needed her help," she said as she pointed toward Pauline.

"Come on, Mia, that's no way to talk about Polly!" Maya said as she slapped the back of her sister's head, sending her into the table and recoiling off of it. "We couldn't leave Polly behind, so this was the best option. Plus, I get to sate my curiosity about you," she added with a look that left me feeling uneasy.

"Any more questions, Mr. Grayson? Or may we start?" Falkeen said as he swirled a glass of wine in his hand. With a shake of the head from me, the meeting officially started.

"Mr. Falkeen and Miss Pauline here have given me a rundown of what this meeting is about. With that being said, I'm also going to hijack the meeting to kill two birds with one stone. Before we get started, will everyone who knows an other-worlder raise their hand?" the Guildmaster stated.

Instantly, everyone in Falkeen's group raised their hand. After exchanging glances and nods between each other, we followed their lead and raised our hands. The only one from Pauline's group was Pauline herself.

"I see. Would those who didn't raise their hand, please le—" the Guildmaster started before being cut off by Mia.

"Why are you raising your hand, girl? Who could YOU possibly know that's powerful enough to be from another world?" she said condescendingly to Pauline.

"I uhh… I know, uhh, I…" Pauline stammered.

They don't know! God da—She must have a reason to have never told them, though. I let out a soft sigh. *I'm gonna have to bail her out, aren't I?* I thought.

"She knows me. Pretty much everyone here already knows, so you don't have to try to keep my secret, Pauline," I said.

At my words, Mia let out a resounding sound of surprise.

While she was freaking out, Falkeen said, "You're… Wait, that make's so much sense." He put his elbows on the table and raised his hands to his head.

"I literally made a Final Fantasy reference to you! How did you not realize then?" I shouted out at him.

"I don't know, it just didn't click! When you've been here as long as me, you start to forget things like that."

"What do you mean? How long have you been here?" I asked.

"Hmm… If I had to take a guess, I'd say around six years? That sound about right to you, four-eyes?" he asked as he directed his attention to the Guildmaster.

"How many times must I tell you to refer to me as Guildmaster? But yes, six years is correct. That was when I officially became master of the guild. Amazing to think that it's been this long."

"S-six years! That makes my six months feel like nothing," I said.

"You've only been here for half a year? Jeez, kid, how did you adjust to this world so quickly? You didn't kill people in your past life or something like that, right?" Falkeen asked me.

"What? Of course I didn't kill people! To answer your question, though…I dunno. I guess that since I played a lot of video games, it's just easy for me to think of this world like one of those. I thought it would be that easy for every one of us. Was it hard for you?" I asked.

"Waking up from the dead in front of God and then getting placed down in a fantasy world with nothing but a skill that relied on my luck? Yeah, it was hard, kid. I was twenty-four at the time, and I was an idiot. I thought that everything would be an adventure that I had sought my whole life. I eagerly headed here and joined the guild before getting accepted into my first group. The next day, I was coming back to the guild alone. They all got slaughtered. It was just some slimes, and I convinced them that they were just low-level farm mobs. I barely escaped with my life as they absorbed my friends and dissolved them into nothing but bones," he explained before he downed his glass of wine.

"You know what the worst part about it was, kid? I didn't even feel remorse until I realized there's no resurrection spells or anything like that in this world. I rushed in headfirst and became responsible for the deaths of people that accepted me. Take this as a lesson to learn about this world so that you don't come to have the same regrets," he finished.

"Wow. I'm sorry, I didn't expect you to have a past like that," I said when he finished.

"I don't think any of us did nor do any of us care," Mia added. "How the hell is this girl important enough to have attracted the eye of an other-worlder? Explain that one to me," she directed at me.

"What the hell's the matter with you?" Maya angrily said with a dark expression. "Leave now, sister! You evidently don't wish to be here and you won't contribute anything but useless words! If you continue this behavior, I will have no choice but to tell father of the disrespect you show to not only Polly but to those who wield such an extreme power."

Something about the words Maya chose told me that she cared more about relations than her sister did. *So she's one of those types that only cares about networking, huh? Probably a useful skill she was taught due to being a noble,* I thought as Mia pushed herself up from her chair and slammed the door on her way out.

"Please forgive my sister. She's the type who speaks her mind and has been spoiled by our father. One could say that she's as rotten as they come! She's not one to blackmail or sell information for personal gain, though, so your secrets are safe," she assured me.

"Right," Falkeen grumbled. "Anyway, I don't expect any sympathy. Like I said, just take it as a lesson. Enough about my past, though, I'm sure we have a lot to discuss."

"First, we'll discuss your hiring contract and the terms. What has been suggested so far is for Mr. Grayson and his group to have exclusive rights to taking quests that stem from side effects of Mr. Falkeen's quests. For example, six months ago, Mr. Falkeen's group cleansed a Molten Giant from the tomb of fire. This quest resulted in the temple no longer having a source of fire magicules since SOMEONE destroyed the heart of the giant, which was a mature spirit supplying the temple with ample amounts of fire magic. In this case, Grayson and group would have had to figure out and supply a replacement for the fire spirit," the Guildmaster explained.

"That's a good start, but surely, cleaning up Falkeen's mess shouldn't be a reward. He gets to not worry about messing up just for these four to get some money and potentially get some experience? Only a couple of idiots would take this deal as it is," Pauline interjected.

"What would you propose then?" the Guildmaster asked.

"Two terms. The first, Grayson and his group can't take a quest that will likely bring them into danger until they are a higher level and can handle themsel—"

"Out of the question! Most of our quests are in high-level areas that are just dangerous to live in. Besides, I've gotten to see his skills for myself, they'll be fine. Plus, if they have exclusive rights, then other groups can't accept the quest, and they usually need to be completed quickly after being issued out. In other words, we can't wait for them to be at a higher level," Falkeen argued.

Most of the points that he brought up made sense, but Pauline didn't back down. "Don't interrupt me. I was getting to that. For the second term, I want the group to have the rights to use your licensed farming spots. This way, they'll level up much faster and can farm experience and drops in the downtime between your quests," she added.

Falkeen went deep into thought after Pauline finished.

"Mr. Falkeen, you can't actually be considering allowing these... newbies to use our farming spots! The amount of money that we spent to buy those lands would all be for naught if we just let another group use them!" Klaus complained.

"Klaus, be quiet," Falkeen said as he raised his hand in front of the elf. The light air that was usually around Falkeen was more than gone by this point, and things became even more serious than when he was talking about his past. "I will agree to let them use the farming spots we no longer use. They'll be allowed to keep any items they get, but any magical tomes they cannot use will be given to us. However, if we find out they are bringing other groups into those spots or selling those tomes off, they will lose the right to use the farms."

At the last addition, Pauline's poker face broke for a split second. *So she wanted to use the farming spots with us? Has she been using me this whole time just to get to this point?* I thought.

"Either take out that last part or add the first term I suggested. If you can't do one of those, then the deal's off," Pauline replied as she gently grabbed my hand.

SHE GAVE HIM AN ULTIMATUM! I screamed out in my mind out of surprise, both from her grabbing my hand and her new tactic.

"I see... How about we let the boy speak for himself? He's been awfully silent during these negotiations," Falkeen said as he directed his attention to me.

Nervously, I tightened my grip on Pauline's hand.

"I... uhh... Could I alter the terms?" I asked.

Falkeen let out a hearty laugh. "You can certainly try, of course. If it's too outlandish, I'll deny it. That being said, what'll it be, kid?"

"It's not a whole lot. But I want Pauline's group to also be able to use the farm spots on the condition that any drops they get that your group could benefit from you may claim ownership of. I'm also willing to chaperone their group so that you can be sure they aren't doing any unwanted things," I said. *This way, we all get something we want,* I thought. *Pauline gets access to the farming spots to boost her group's experience, I get to spend time with Pauline and people won't make a big deal about it, and Falkeen's group gains items and gold from a farm that would be lying dormant. Plus, Pauline's group has tons of money, so unless they get an ultra-rare drop, they could probably work out a deal to buy items from Falkeen,* I reasoned to myself as I awaited his response.

"I'm the other-worlder of luck. Any item drops they get will just clog my inventory, so take that out. Though, the passive income would be a bit of a mogul move, so keep that part in. This term seems to benefit everyone aside from you. Is this really what you want?" Falkeen asked suspiciously.

"I think I gain something out of this, so yeah, that's what I want," I responded as I stared him dead in the eyes.

"Hm... You look pretty serious. Honestly, that look scares me a bit. But I don't lose anything and I actually gain. I accept the term. Keep in mind, though, if you didn't have that other term as leverage, I wouldn't have accepted so readily. In future negotiations, try to offer something you know your opponent wants, just a tip. Let's go over the contract one more time so we can wrap this up, four-eyes," Falkeen said.

With a sigh, the Guildmaster started. "Mr. Grayson and his group will have exclusive rights to quests that come to existence due to Mr. Falkeen's incompetence. They will receive payment for the quest after completion has been confirmed. In addition, Mr. Grayson will have accessibility to Mr. Falkeen's monster farming lands that are currently not in use by Mr. Falkeen's group. Mr. Grayson may only share access to the lands with the group of Miss Pauline, the later of which must be accompanied by Mr. Grayson and must forfeit any money earned to Mr. Falkeen," he read off. "If these terms are acceptable, I ask that those three provide their mark on the line," he said as he set the contract down on the table.

I expected him to give us a pen to write our names, but when Falkeen pricked his finger and marked it with his blood, I knew that the pen wasn't coming. I let out a sigh and muttered, "Why couldn't we just write our names down?"

I let go of Pauline's hand before pricking my thumb with my dagger. *I really hope I don't light on fire because of this enchant*, I prayed. After I bled enough to lightly cover my thumb in blood, I pressed it against the parchment. Following my lead, Pauline bit her thumb and waited for the blood to coat her finger. "You can actually do that hard enough to break skin? You're insane," I complimented her. *Being able to bite down hard enough to make yourself bleed is actually crazy difficult. Color me impressed*, I thought as I resisted the urge to try it myself.

"That's not the only thing I can do with my mouth," she responded. I had to go over her words again to realize what she had just said. "I-I-I can tie a knot w-with a cherry stem!" she quickly added, clearly flustered after realizing what she had just said. Once she stuck her thumb down and all of our "marks" were on the paper, it burned up into flames, and a beam of purple energy shot into all three of our chests.

"All right. Now if any of you break the terms, the contract will be severed, and every one of you will be alerted. The contract magic will hopefully make sure you all keep your word. Now to move onto the next order of business. Everyone here is locked into a duty now, so it's best you all pay attention," the Guildmaster said before explaining everything about other-worlders and why they were brought to this planet.

Once he finished his explanation for the people who didn't know about other-worlders, he began the tale of the tower that suddenly showed up a few months ago. Of course, Pauline and I already knew, so we played invisible games of tic-tac-toe on each other's hands underneath the table. *I can't believe we're this childish or the fact that we've tied every single game*, I thought.

When the Guildmaster finished, Falkeen said, "So he finally made a move, huh? If he actually created that tower, anyone that doesn't have any understanding of the mythology surrounding him won't stand a chance."

I stopped forming an O on Pauline's hand and looked up. "What do you mean?" I asked.

"Were you big into Greek mythology as a kid?" he asked in turn.

"I mean…probably as much as anyone else. I don't know a whole lot about Ares, but over all, I feel like I know a good deal."

"Then think about what existed in those stories and what he could bring to existence! The man literally was the father of a dragon! If he created that tower, then he has the power to bring powerful monsters from the myths into it. If that's the case, then we NEED to know how to fight them," Falkeen explained.

"I see what you're saying… So having high levels isn't going to be enough. We'll need to find out what's in there and look back on myths to figure out their weaknesses."

"Precisely. You catch on quickly. I suppose it's a good thing your groups can go farm experience and join the rai—" He stopped himself as realization slowly set into his face. "YOU TWO KNEW ABOUT THIS, DIDN'T YOU?" he screamed out.

"Err… Kind of?" I nervously said.

While Falkeen was having still dazed from his realization, Maya asked, "I understand that the God the church worships is real and that this Ares is another god, but why would he want this world?"

Everyone turned their attention to her.

"That's a…good question. It was never really explained to us either, was it?" I asked Falkeen as I racked my brain for a possible reason.

"You can't attempt to make sense of a god's actions. No one can truly understand why gods do what they do. All we can do is deal with their actions as they come," Araya said suddenly. I had completely forgotten that my party was here since they had been so quiet.

"Wise words, Priestess. You could learn from her, kid," Falkeen said to me, seemingly already recovered. "That being said, there's no use thinking about why Ares would want this world. All we can do is prepare for when we're going to storm that tower. I imagine you told them to level so that they could join as part of the raiding party?" he directed to the Guildmaster.

"Perceptive of you," he said as he pushed up his glasses, which again caught the light behind him. "Indeed, I want them to reach a high enough level to join, and I want you to lead the party. You have the most connections to those that would be best for this type of job. Of course, everyone will be greatly compensated for the job, so that should help convince them to join. With you as the leader, I expect you to relay any information you have on the potential threats as well."

"Sheesh. You know that I'm not a fan of leadership. I'll do it since I owe you, but don't expect me to be the leader when we actually have to fight that SOB."

"Don't fret. Hopefully, Grayson will be ready by that point. If Ares moves faster than expected, though, I fear I'll have to call on you again," the Guildmaster said apologetically.

"The kid? You can't possibly mean to tell me that he's the God Killer! Four eyes? Why aren't you laughing?" Falkeen started asking.

When the Guildmaster didn't respond, he turned to me. "He's serious? You're the God Killer?" he asked.

I looked away but gave him a nod.

"What does he mean, Gray? What's this God Killer thing they're calling you?" Kuhani asked, sounding concerned.

"The God Killer is what it sounds like. With each level he increases, he gains an obscene amount of power. In other words, when he reaches a high enough level, he'll be able to rival the strength of the gods," Falkeen explained as if he was in a trance. "Now that I know that we've found him, he'll be ready. I'll make sure of it, four eyes. Man, this is insane. But we all have our roles now. Do you wanna get this little get together over with?" Falkeen asked.

"In a moment. Grayson, Kuhani, Kuhano, and Araya, please rise," the Guildmaster asked politely.

Without argument we stood up from our seats as asked. Kuhano probably should've stayed on his seat, though, since he disappeared beneath the table.

"With the contract complete and recognition from the country's current hero, I now bestow upon your group the title of 'The Hero's Assistants.' With this title displayed, no one will be able to deny your importance nor your power," he said as a bar of text appeared above each of us, stating our name as well as our title. Above my head was probably "Grayson, Hero's Assistant.'

"For the love of God, I told you not to call me a hero. Please turn those off before you leave and only enable them if it's absolutely necessary to show someone. The title system is so stupid too. Let me show you guys what to do," Falkeen said as if a wave of embarrassment came over him. He taught us how to disable the title before marking the farming spots we were allowed to access on our maps.

"Four eyes will give you the location of the other farms as you become a high enough level to actually make use of them. Take care, everyone, we're off!" he shouted when he left with his two group-mates. Violet gave the room a slight bow before leaving whereas Klaus shot glares at us before nodding his head.

With them gone, a previously unnoticed air of tension disappeared. I let out a quiet sigh of relief, and before I knew it, everyone was getting ready to leave. I at least wanted to talk to Pauline before we left, so I sat back down next to her. She was still sitting in her chair, seemingly stunned.

"You good, Pauline?" I asked as the rest of her group walked out the door.

She turned slightly toward me and said, "Yeah, I guess it just hit me how powerful you're going to be one day. Thanks, by the way."

I raised an eyebrow at her. "For what?" I asked.

"For making that deal and sacrificing your time to make it so I can level up too. I can't even imagine what you stand to gain from that," she explained.

I gave her a wry chuckle and quietly said, "I get to see you more."

Instantly, Pauline started stuttering, "W-w-what! Y-you wasted part of the deal for m-m-me?"

I gave her a smile and said, "I didn't waste anything. I just enjoy being with you, and this just seemed like a good excuse. Kinda pathetic now that I'm saying it out loud, though, eh?"

Pauline took a moment to compose herself before saying, "Y-you could've just asked me to g-get together. I would be l-lying though if I said I disliked your company. Here. Accept my friend request so we can talk and make plans to get together sometime. Not just for training either," she said as a box appeared in my vision—"Pauline [Redacted] wishes to be your friend" along with two buttons, one to accept and one to deny.

Obviously, I pressed the accept button. *I guess our family names don't exist in the system?*

"Great! Now we can talk to each other whenever we want," she said with a giddy smile.

As soon as it was revealed that I had accepted, Kuhani, Araya, and Maya let out another, "Aww!"

The two of us turned to our respective groups and both said together, "WOULD YOU PLEASE STOP THAT?" At the realization that we both had the same issue, we turned back to each other and laughed together.

"I should actually add you three too," Pauline said to the rest of my group as she started crazily moving her hands. "All right, I sent out the requests. I'll see you all later! If you want to talk, let me know. Be safe out there! Especially you, Grayson," she said, pointing at me with a smirk before leaving with Maya and Noah who was somehow walking while still sleeping. As they left, you could hear Maya telling her how cute we were as well as Pauline's attempts to get her to stop.

"Did any of you know that the system had a friend list?" I asked, to which everyone in the group shook their heads.

The Guildmaster let out a small chuckle. "It's hard to believe that you really are the God Killer. But the proof is undeniable. The fact that you've been able to connect with three other-worlders already is amazing. First the outcast Crice, then the hero Falkeen, and somehow, you've melted Pauline's icy heart? You really might just be the one to bring them all together, Grayson. I'll send your specialized quests via courier so you'll get them as soon as possible."

A few things he said bugged me. "How do you know about Crice? And what do you mean by Pauline's icy heart?" I asked.

"In relation to Crice, I have my sources. I'm glad you're the one who found him, though. Anyone else might've killed him on sight. For Miss Pauline, she was a bit of a problem before you came along. Absolutely no one could get close to her, much less have a relationship like you two do. You're a promising adventurer. I can't wait to see what you become. You might just get promoted from assistant to hero if you work hard enough," he said as he walked out the door with a laugh that seemed more nervous.

I feel like it started out as a joke, and then he realizes that if that happens, we're going to be screwed, I thought.

"I find that hard to believe that Pauline could be like that, but I digress. You guys ready to finally head home?" I asked everyone.

"Of course! I can't wait to take a bath!" Kuhani shouted gleefully as she sprinted toward the door.

"A bath does sound heavenly right now. However, I must admit I do miss Crice's cooking. Just the thought is making me salivate! Wait for me, sister!" Kuhano followed after projecting his thoughts.

"I don't think I've ever heard Kuhano look forward to something before," I said as I crossed my arms.

Araya giggled next to me before saying, "Everyone looks forward to going home. Let's go so they don't get too far ahead!" she said as she started running, mimicking them. She made it to the doorway before she tripped on her robes.

I helped her up and said, "You okay? How about we follow at a reasonable pace so that that doesn't happen again?" Part of me felt like I was a dad talking to my child.

She shot me a beaming smile and agreed. When we went down the stairs, we found the two siblings being congratulated on their performance at the tournament from the other patrons. Among them was Sylia who had a familiar looking giant with her.

"Uncle Horrad!" Araya exclaimed as she completely neglected our pact to go at a reasonable pace. She nearly tripped again but fell right into his arms.

"I heard you did good at tournament! That my girl!" he rumbled as he gently held Araya.

I smiled at the situations my party members found themselves in as I walked up next to Sylia.

"So I take it your meeting went well? I can't get a lick of information out of these two with how mobbed they are by people," she said with a defeated sigh.

"Yeah, it went great. In fact"—I enabled my title—"you could say it went assistantly. Assistingly? It was supposed to be like swimmingly, but with assistant in front of it, it just sounded dumb," I said with a large grin as I disabled my title.

Sylia gave me a hard blank stare before saying, "I don't think an idiot like you would be able to assist anyone."

"Har, har, funny. That aside, I imagine we're going to stay here a little longer? I was wondering if Araya was going to go see Horrad at some point," I said, not even thinking about Kuhani and Kuhano being trapped by their mob.

"If you guys are fine with it being dark when we head back, I don't care. Let's claim a table, though, so we can at least eat while we talk," Sylia said as she walked over to a table and sat down. Obviously, I followed her and took a seat next to her. I explained everything that happened with the discussion and our meeting.

"You like her enough to have made a term in the contract that benefits her? I can't say I'm not proud of you, though. If I was your age and liked someone, I probably wouldn't have done anything. She's a smart girl too, but something tells me she feels the same way. There's no doubt in my mind that you two will get together. Just make sure that you can protect her when that day comes, all right? You two are going to be in some seriously dangerous stuff. I don't want it to end in disaster," Sylia said.

As if they had a sixth sense, everyone in the group appeared at the table along with Horrad. "Were you talking about Gray and Miss Pauline?" Kuhani asked as she slid across a bench.

"Who this Miss Pauline?" Horrad asked Araya.

"She's a really nice girl that Gray's in love with," she quickly explained.

"I-I'm not in l-l-love with her! I just really c-care for her, enjoy b-being with her, and think about her a lot," I said, completely flustered.

"Me see. You all no joke," he stated. "No need be embarrassed, love good!" he added.

"Not you too, man. Why do we always have to somehow end up on this topic?" I cried out in desperation.

"Because it's fun to annoy you, simple as that," Kuhano thought out.

"No, it's because we need to convince you to pursue this so that you don't feel regret later!" Kuhani said.

"I just want you and Miss Pauline to be happy," Araya said.

I let out a sigh. "Thanks, guys. But let's just chill with this whole thing and focus on preparing for the raid, all right?" I said in an attempt to stop them from involving themselves in my love life.

"I actually have to agree with Gray here. As much as I enjoy tormenting him, you guy's need to focus on getting yourselves ready for that battle. A great way to start with that is to eat some food so you can build up your muscles!" Sylia said as she touched a piece of paper on the table. After she took her hand off of it, a bowl of some sort of stew appeared on the paper.

She just wanted to come with an excuse to start eating! Though I'm kinda glad she did that first because I had no idea that's how we're supposed to order food here.

"Order some food and eat your fill 'cause it's a long way home! Plus, you guys are going to be traveling a lot now, so this might be your last chance for a while to eat your fill!" she said.

At her words, everyone looked toward each other, and it became an absolute flurry of hands touching the paper and then grabbing whatever dish came out.

As I watched the three of them all fighting over what dishes were theirs and whose turn it was to order something next, I couldn't help but laugh. *We're all practically just kids and we're supposed to even-*

tually fight a god. If I wasn't living through this, I'd assume this was just a rip-off of some J-RPG! I thought. That was when I realized, "This is all just some story, isn't it?"

At my words, no one acknowledged what I said. In my vision, a menu pop-up appeared, stating, "Unlocked Passive Ability: Self Awareness."

Does this mean I was right? I've been in a story this whole time! You've gotta be freakin' kidd—I thought before my mind started to get fuzzy as I started getting assaulted with all types of information I couldn't make sense of.

"Master? What's going on? It's like your mind is becoming overloaded! It's as if you're…about to go onto a new plane of existence. Master? Focus on my voice. We can't suddenly have your brain get fried so soon after everyone's attempts to keep you alive!" I heard Foda shout in my mind. As I stared blankly forward, I couldn't even try to respond to Foda.

"I can feel your fear, Master, but trust in yourself. Our minds are linked, so I'll try to lessen the load on you, but you must focus on not dying here. If you do, then everything we've been working for ends!" Foda exclaimed as the fuzziness started to fade.

Is this because of you, Foda? I thought out, pain shooting through my brain as I did.

"Partially, Master. It seems that we're coming to the end of whatever this is. I never thought I'd get to witness the ascendance of one's mind in such a raw form," he said as my brain started to feel lighter. I came back to reality and started letting out heavy breaths.

"Gray? Are you all right? You're super pale," Sylia said as she looked at me and put her hand on my forehead. "You're burning up! Is this because of the dark energy? Araya get over here!" she shouted, causing the others in the party to stop their bickering and notice the situation.

"I'm…fine… Don't worry… Never felt better!" I lied before I passed out and slammed my head into the table.

About the Author

Thomas Karl is a twenty-one-year-old who is making his debut as an author. He's a NEET (Not in Education, Employment, or Training) who simply enjoys stories and playing video games. After a sarcastic comment from a friend, he started writing out of spite and soon found a love for being able to share a world that he created.